CRITICS SALUTE RAMSES

"A PLOT AS SINUOUS AS THE RIVER NILE, WITH CHARACTERS LYING LIKE CROCODILES IN THE SHALLOWS.... THIS BOOK MAKES ANCIENT EGYPT AS RELEVANT AND 3-D AS TODAY'S NEWS."
—J. Suzanne Frank, author of *Reflections in the Nile*

"Officially, Christian Jacq was born in Paris in 1947. In fact, his real birth took place in the time of the pharaohs, along the banks of the Nile, where the river carries eternal messages.... Who could ever tell that Christian Jacq, Ramses' official scribe, was not writing from memory."
—*Magazine Littéraire*

"With hundreds of thousands of readers, millions of copies in print, Christian Jacq's success has become unheard of in the world of books. This man is the pharaoh of publishing!"
—*Figaro Magazine*

"In 1235 B.C., Ramses II might have said: 'My life is as amazing as fiction!' It seems Christian Jacq heard him.... Christian Jacq draws a pleasure from writing that is contagious. His penmanship turns history into a great show, high-quality entertainment."
—*VSD*

"It's *Dallas* or *Dynasty* in Egypt, with a hero (Ramses), beautiful women, plenty of villains, new developments every two pages, brothers fighting for power, magic, enchantments, and historical glamour."
—*Libération*

"He's a pyramid-surfer. The pharaoh of publishing. His saga about Ramses II is a bookselling phenomenon!"
—*Le Parisien*

"Moves at a breakneck pace.... A lot of fun."
—*KLIATT*

RAMSES
Volume I: The Son of Light
Volume II: The Eternal Temple
Volume III: The Battle of Kadesh
Volume IV: The Lady of Abu Simbel

COMING SOON FROM WARNER BOOKS:

Volume V: Under the Western Acacia

RAMSES

VOLUME IV

THE LADY OF ABU SIMBEL

CHRISTIAN JACQ

Translated by Mary Feeney

WARNER BOOKS

A Time Warner Company

Originally published in French by Editions Robert Laffont, S.A. Paris, France.

Warner Books Edition
Copyright © 1996 by Editions Robert Laffont (Volume 4)
All rights reserved.

Warner Books, Inc., 1271 Avenue of the Americas, New York, NY 10020

Visit our Web site at
http://warnerbooks.com

 A Time Warner Company

Printed in the United States of America

First U.S. Printing: November 1998
10 9 8 7 6 5 4 3 2 1

Library of Congress Cataloging-in-Publication Data

Jacq, Christian.
    [Dame d'Abou Simbel. English]
    The lady of Abu Simbel / Christian Jacq.
        p.   cm. — (Ramses ; v. 4)
    ISBN 0-446-67359-5
    I. Title.   II. Series: Jacq, Christian. Ramsès. English ; v. 4.
    PQ2670.A2438D3513   1998
    843'.914—dc21   98-7948
                                                                CIP

Book design and composition by L&G McRee
Cover design and illustration by Marc Burkhardt

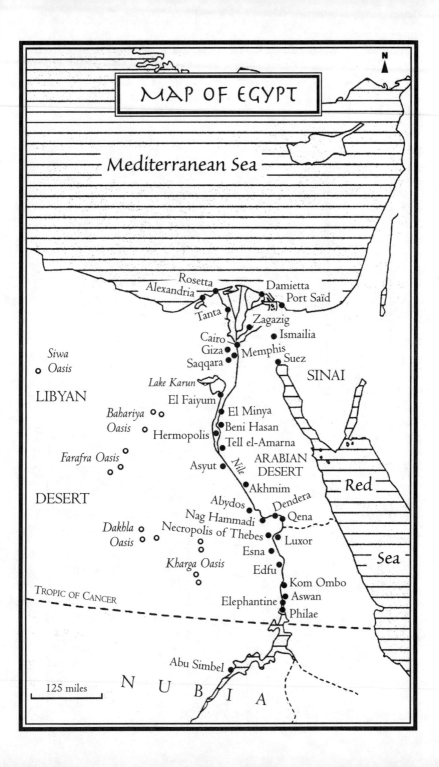

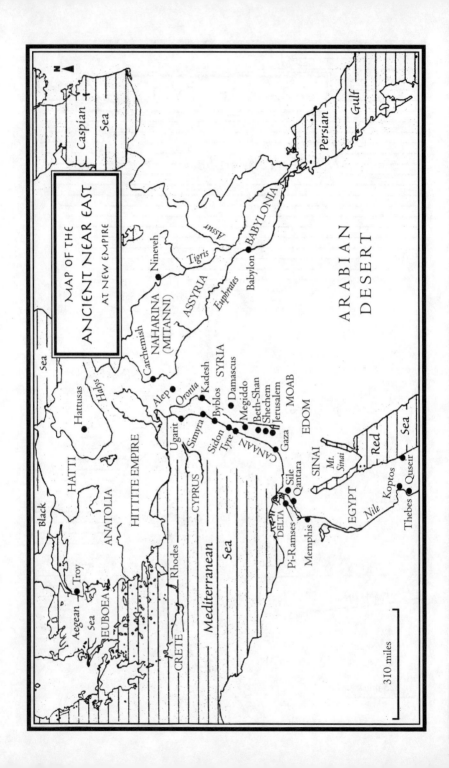

ONE

Fighter, Ramses' pet lion, let out a roar that froze both the Egyptians and the rebel foe in their tracks. The huge beast wore a fine gold collar, his award for valor in battle against the Hittites at Kadesh. He was twelve feet long and weighed more than six hundred pounds; a thick mane flared around his head, neck, shoulders, and upper chest. His tawny coat was sleek.

For leagues in every direction, Fighter's fury resounded. Clearly, his fury echoed that of Ramses, the young pharaoh whose victory at Kadesh had made him Ramses the Great.

Yet had he earned true greatness, when with all of his stature the Hittites continued to defy him?

The Egyptian army had proved disappointing in combat. The generals, cowardly or incompetent, had abandoned Ramses, leaving him to face the enemy single-handed, one man against a host of thousands, certain that victory was theirs. But the god Amon, concealed in the light, had heard the pharaoh's prayer and endowed his son with supernatural strength.

After five tumultuous years as Pharaoh, Ramses had believed the defeat at Kadesh would humble the Hittites for years to come and that the entire region would enter into an era of relative peace.

He had been sadly mistaken—he, the Mighty Bull, beloved of Ma'at, Lord of the Two Lands, Son of Light! Did he deserve his coronation names when sedition continued to brew in Canaan and southern Syria, Egypt's traditional protectorates? Now the Hittites not only refused to submit, but furthermore had launched a vast offensive. Their latest allies were the Bedouins, a people of pillaging murderers who cast a covetous eye on the rich Nile Delta.

The commander of Ramses' Ra division approached him.

"Your Majesty, the situation is more critical than expected. This is no ordinary rebellion. According to our scouts, all of Canaan is up in arms against us. Once we get over the first hurdle, another one will turn up, and then another . . ."

"And you're afraid we can't go the distance?"

"Our losses may be heavy, Your Majesty, and the men have no wish to die needlessly."

"Egypt's survival should be a good enough reason."

"I didn't mean to imply . . ."

"That's what you're thinking, though. You generals learned nothing from Kadesh. Why must I always be stuck with cowards who lose their lives in the process of trying to save them?"

"My obedience to you is beyond question, Your Majesty, like that of my fellow commanders. We were only trying to alert you."

"Has our intelligence network found information on Ahsha?"

"No, I'm sorry to say, Your Majesty."

Ahsha, the king's boyhood friend and newly appointed secretary of state, had been waylaid by the Prince of

Amurru.* Had Ahsha been tortured? Was he still alive? Would his captors use the diplomat as a valuable pawn?

As soon as he learned the news in a coded message from Ahsha, Ramses had mobilized his troops, still reeling from Kadesh. To rescue Ahsha, they would have to travel through territory once again hostile to Egypt. The local rulers had flouted their oaths of allegiance and sold themselves to the Hittites in exchange for precious metal and hollow promises. Who wouldn't dream of invading the land of the pharaohs and exploiting its reputedly inexhaustible riches?

Ramses the Great had ambitious projects to oversee in Egypt—the Ramesseum (his mortuary Temple of Millions of Years at Thebes); additions to the temples at Karnak, Luxor, and Abydos; his final resting place in the Valley of the Kings; and now Abu Simbel, the poem in stone he planned as a gift to his beloved wife, Nefertari. Yet here he stood on a hilltop overlooking the first fortress within the borders of Canaan, observing the enemy position.

"Your Majesty, if I may say . . ."

"Out with it, General."

"Your show of force is most impressive. I'm convinced that Emperor Muwattali has already gotten the message and will free Ahsha any day."

Muwattali, the Hittite emperor, was a ruthless and cunning ruler, well aware that sheer force was the basis of his power. Kadesh had shattered the unprecedented Near Eastern coalition he had put together, but Muwattali would never stop trying to conquer Egypt, even if it meant

*Modern-day Lebanon.

resorting to deals with the Bedouins and third-party rebels.

Only Muwattali's death—or Ramses'—would put an end to the conflict, and the future of the entire region hinged on it. If Egypt fell, a Hittite military dictatorship would clamp down on the Two Lands—the Twin Kingdoms of upper and lower Egypt—destroying a civilization that had lasted more than a thousand years, since the days of the first pharaoh, Menes.

Ramses' thoughts strayed to Moses, another close friend from his school days. Wanted for murder, the Hebrew had fled the country. Could he be hiding somewhere in this desert? While serving as chief builder of Pi-Ramses, the new capital Ramses founded in the Delta, Moses had become a leader to his people. Some claimed he'd formed a rebel faction, but Ramses refused to believe that Moses could ever become his enemy.

"Your Majesty, are you listening?"

He looked the general in the eye. A typical officer, well fed, battle-shy, and intent on preserving his rank. The man reminded him of the person he hated most in the world: Shaanar, his older brother. The traitor had allied himself with the Hittites in the hope of seizing the throne of Egypt. While being transferred from the main Memphis prison to a desert penal colony, Shaanar had escaped in a blinding sandstorm. Ramses believed that his brother was still alive and up to no good.

"Prepare your troops for combat, General."

The commander sheepishly took his leave.

Ramses wished he could be spending the day in a garden with Nefertari, his son, and their daughter. He much preferred the simple pleasures, far from the clash of arms. Yet only he could save his country from the thundering, bloodthirsty hordes poised to pull down the temples and destroy law and order. The stakes were higher than his personal fate. He had no right to consider his own comfort, to think of his family. He must keep Egypt safe from harm, even if it cost him his life.

Ramses studied the fort blocking the route that led into the heart of Canaan. The tall walls sloped on both sides, protecting a sizable garrison. In the battlements, archers waited. The ditches were filled with pottery shards to cut the feet of soldiers advancing to erect the ladders.

A sea breeze cooled the Egyptian troops, who were huddled between two sun-drenched hills. The pace of their march had been grueling, with brief rest stops in makeshift camps. Only the well-paid mercenaries were ready and willing to do battle. The young recruits, already exhausted and homesick, were afraid of losing their lives in gruesome combat. Everyone hoped that Pharaoh would settle for shoring up the northeastern border rather than heading into a full-fledged campaign that might prove disastrous.

Not long before, the governor of Gaza (the capital of Canaan) had hosted a splendid banquet for the Egyptian high command, swearing never again to side with the cruel and barbaric Hittites. At the time, his obvious hypocrisy had turned Ramses' stomach. Today, his betrayal hardly surprised the pharaoh; at twenty-eight, Ramses knew all too well what lurked in the hearts of men.

The lion again began to roar, growing restless.

Fighter had changed since the day Ramses had found him as a cub in the Nubian grasslands, hovering near death from a cobra bite. A bond had been forged between them on the spot. Luckily Setau had been along on that journey. Another friend of Ramses' since their school days, Setau had gone on to become a snake charmer and a healer. His remedies and the lion cub's remarkable constitution had allowed Fighter to survive and grow into a magnificent specimen, a bodyguard any king would envy.

Ramses stroked Fighter's mane. The beast remained edgy.

Now Setau came heading up the hill, dressed in his working costume of antelope skins. The tunic's multiple pockets were stuffed with powders, pills, and vials. The man was of average height, stocky and square-jawed, dark and stubbly. His passion for snakes and scorpions had only increased in adulthood. The venom he harvested became strong medicine. With his stunning Nubian wife, Lotus, he now directed the palace laboratories.

Ramses had once more asked the pair to head the army's medical service. They had taken part in all the king's military campaigns, not out of any love for war, but to help the wounded and collect a few snakes in the bargain. The soldiers were delighted to have the lovely Lotus along, and Setau wanted to be close at hand in case anything happened to his friend Ramses.

"Morale isn't what it should be," Setau reported.

"The generals want to turn back," admitted Ramses.

"Considering how your commanders behaved at Kadesh, is that any wonder? The decision will be yours alone, as usual."

"I'm not alone, Setau. I have the sun and the wind to counsel me, the spirit of my lion and the voice of the earth. They never lie. The trick is to understand what they're telling me."

"There's no better war council."

"Have you consulted your snakes?"

"Of course I have. They know all the secrets. This time they were straightforward: don't turn back. What's making Fighter so nervous?"

"That oak grove over there to the left, about halfway to the fort."

Chewing on a reed stem, Setau looked where the king was pointing.

"I don't like the look of it, either. An ambush, like Kadesh?"

"That one worked so well that the Hittites may have decided to try it again. When we attack, we'll be brought up short, while the archers mow us down from the battlements."

Menna, Ramses' chariot driver and shield bearer, bowed to the king.

"Your chariot is ready, Your Majesty."

The king stopped to pat his two horses, Victory in Thebes and the Goddess Mut Is Satisfied. Besides Fighter, they were the only ones who stayed by his side at Kadesh when the battle seemed all but lost.

Ramses took the reins, to the incredulous stares of his driver, the generals, and the crack chariot regiment.

"Your Majesty," stammered Menna, "you're not going to . . ."

"Let's swing to the left of the fort," ordered the king, "and bear down on that oak grove."

"Wait, Your Majesty! You're forgetting your coat of mail!"

Waving a corselet covered with small metal disks, the driver ran helplessly behind the chariot. Ramses was heading straight for the enemy, alone.

TWO

Tall in his speeding chariot, Ramses the Great looked more like a god than a man. On his broad, high forehead he wore a tight-fitting blue crown. Beneath full, arched brows, his eyes darted like a falcon's. His nose was long and hooked, his ears round and delicate, his chin strong, lips full. Ramses was the image of power and strength.

At his approach, the Bedouins emerged from their hiding place in the oak grove, some drawing bows, others brandishing spears.

In a flashback to Kadesh, the king was a whirlwind, covering long distances faster than a jackal. Like a sharp-horned bull on a rampage, he felled the first line of attackers, piercing the rebels with arrow after arrow.

The head of the Bedouin commando somehow made it through the monarch's furious charge. On one knee, he was poised to toss a long dagger straight at Ramses' back.

Horror-stricken, the few remaining Bedouins saw Fighter spring into the air. Despite his size, he seemed to fly like a bird. Claws bared, he pounced on the chief, crunching the man's skull between his fangs.

The sight was so horrifying that many of the enemy warriors threw down their arms and ran for their lives. Fighter was already mangling two other Bedouins who had come to their commander's rescue.

The Egyptian charioteers, followed by foot soldiers in the hundreds, were close behind Ramses. They quickly dispatched the last pockets of resistance.

Fighter sat calmly by, licking his bloody paws and gazing fondly at his master. Detecting the gratitude in Ramses' eyes, he purred contentedly and settled near the right wheel of the chariot, still on alert.

"A resounding victory, Your Majesty!" declared the Ra division general.

"We've just averted a disaster. Why didn't any of our scouts realize that an enemy squadron was lying in ambush?"

"We didn't have them check the oak grove. It looked too small to be of any consequence."

"Take a lesson from my lion, General."

"Shall I convene the war council to discuss the attack on the fort?"

"We'll attack at once."

The Pharaoh's tone of voice told Fighter that his rest was over. Ramses stroked the hindquarters of his two horses, who looked at each other for the strength to go on.

"Your Majesty, here you are, please!"

Winded, the driver Menna caught up with them, waving the shiny breastplate. Ramses donned the coat of mail without too much damage to his long-sleeved linen gown. On each wrist he wore a gold and lapis lazuli bracelet with the heads of a pair of wild ducks entwined in the center, symbolizing the royal couple. Like migrating birds, they would fly toward the great beyond. Would he see Nefertari again before the great journey began?

Victory in Thebes and the Goddess Mut Is Satisfied

pranced impatiently in their headdresses of blue-tipped red plumes and matching caparisons, eager to ride into battle.

The foot soldiers tried to revive their courage with a chant composed on the triumphant march home from Kadesh: "Ramses' arm is strong, his heart is valiant. He is a peerless archer, a wall protecting his soldiers, a flame burning his enemies."

A jittery Menna filled the king's twin quivers with arrows.

"Have you checked those?" asked Ramses.

"Yes, Majesty. They're light and sturdy. The enemy archers won't have a chance against you."

"You know that flattery is a deadly sin, don't you, Menna?"

"Yes, but I'm so afraid! Without you, these barbarians would have exterminated us."

"Make sure my horses' feed is ready. They'll be hungry when we get back."

As soon as the Egyptian chariots approached the fort, the Canaanite archers and their Bedouin allies fired off several volleys. The arrows fell short of the horses. Some of them whinnied, a few of them reared, but the king's calm advance kept his handpicked unit from giving way to panic.

"Bend your longbows," he commanded, "and wait for my signal."

The arms factory in Pi-Ramses had produced a number of acacia-wood bows with bowstrings of beef sinew. The carefully calculated curve allowed the arrows to fire in a long, high arc, overreaching any battlements.

"Fire!" shouted Ramses resoundingly, his voice releasing the men's pent-up energy.

Most of the arrows hit the mark. With a shaft through the head, eye, or neck, the enemy archers fell like flies, dead or seriously wounded. Their replacements fared no better.

Assured that his foot soldiers were not about to perish under enemy fire, Ramses signaled the order to storm the fort's wooden gates. Soon the men were hacking them down with their battle-axes. The Egyptian chariots drew closer and Pharaoh's archers fired with ever more deadly accuracy, eliminating any potential for resistance. The jagged shards in the ditches had no deterrent effect, since, contrary to his usual practice, Ramses would use no ladders on this occasion.

The Canaanites resisted with all their might, but before long the gates gave way. The ensuing melee was appallingly violent. Pharaoh's infantry clambered over enemy corpses and swept like a tidal wave through the fort's interior.

The rebels gradually lost ground. They fell in heaps, their long scarves and tasseled robes spattered with blood.

Egyptian swords cut through headgear, shattered bone, slashed flanks and shoulders, hacked tendons, dug into entrails.

Soon silence hung heavy on the vanquished fort. Women begged their assailants to spare the survivors huddled in the courtyard.

Ramses' chariot made its entry into the recaptured citadel.

"Who's in charge here?" inquired the king.

A man of about fifty, his left arm missing, emerged from the sorry huddle of defeated troops.

"I'm the senior soldier . . . all my superiors are dead. I beg Pharaoh's indulgence."

"What forgiveness can be granted to those who break their word?"

"At least kill us quickly, Lord of the Two Lands."

"Here's what I've decided, Canaanite wretch. Your province's trees will be cut down, and the wood shipped to Egypt. All prisoners—men, women, and children—will be sent in convoys to the Delta to serve in public works projects. Canaan's livestock and horses will become our property. Any remaining troops will be drafted into my army and fight henceforth under my command."

The losers groveled before him, happy to escape with their lives.

Setau was relatively pleased. The number of seriously wounded was on the low side, and he had on hand enough fresh meat and honey poultices to stop their bleeding. With her quick, sure touch, Lotus approximated the edges of the wounds with cross-shaped adhesive strips. Her smile was an effective analgesic. Stretcher bearers were bringing casualties in to the field hospital, where they were treated with unguents, pomades, and potions before being shipped home to Egypt.

Ramses addressed these men who had suffered bodily harm in defense of their country. Then he convened the high command, revealing his intention to continue north through Canaan, recapturing each and every fort under joint Hittite-Bedouin control.

The pharaoh's enthusiasm was contagious. The climate of fear lifted, and there was rejoicing over the day and night of rest accorded the men. Ramses himself was dining with Setau and Lotus.

"How far north do you expect to go?" asked the healer.

"All the way through Syria, at least."

"To Kadesh?"

"We'll see."

"If the expedition lasts too long," Lotus remarked, "we'll run out of medical supplies."

"The Hittites reacted swiftly; we have to be even more decisive."

"Will this war ever come to an end?"

"Yes, Lotus, the day we totally defeat the enemy."

"This is no time for politics," grumbled Setau. "Come, darling. Let's spend some time in bed before we go hunting snakes tonight. I have a feeling they're waiting for us out there."

Ramses celebrated the rites of dawn in the little chapel erected in the center of the camp, near his tent. A modest shrine compared to the temples of Pi-Ramses, yet the Son of Light's fervor was unabated. His father Amon would never reveal his true nature to mere mortals. Never would he take on a concrete form. Still, the invisible was ever present and felt by all.

When the sovereign emerged from the chapel, he noticed a soldier leading a balky oryx. Strange-looking soldier, he mused, with his long hair, striped tunic, goatee, and shifty eyes. And what was this wild beast doing in camp, so close to the royal tent?

He had no time for further speculation. The Bedouin released the oryx to charge at Ramses, its sharp horns pointed at the unarmed sovereign's midsection.

Appearing from nowhere, Fighter lit into the oryx's side, sinking his claws into the beast's neck. It collapsed beneath the lion, killed instantly.

Rooted to the spot, the Bedouin pulled a knife from his tunic, but never managed to use it. He felt a sharp pain in his back, followed immediately by an icy fog that blinded him and sent his weapon clattering. He fell forward, a lance protruding from between his shoulder blades.

Calm and smiling, Lotus had displayed surprising skill in handling the lance. The lovely Nubian seemed quite unruffled by the experience.

"Thank you, Lotus."

Setau emerged from his tent. So did a number of soldiers, watching the lion devour its prey and inspecting the Bedouin's body. Horrified, Ramses' shield bearer, Menna, threw himself at the Pharaoh's feet.

"I'm so sorry, Your Majesty! I promise to find the sentries who let this criminal into our camp and punish them severely."

"Call the trumpeters, Menna. Have them sound the call for departure."

THREE

More and more irritated, mostly with himself, Ahsha spent his days looking out at the sea from the second-story window of the Amurru palace where he was being held prisoner. How could he, the head of Egyptian espionage, have fallen into this pathetic trap?

The only son of a rich and noble family, a brilliant alumnus of the Royal Academy in Memphis, Ahsha was refined and elegant. He loved women; the attraction was mutual. Always immaculately turned out, he had a long, thin face, slender limbs, lively, intelligent eyes, and a spellbinding voice. But behind the trappings of society lay a man of action and a seasoned diplomat, an expert linguist with an intimate knowledge of Egypt's protectorates and the Hittite empire.

Ahsha's daring espionage mission during the recent hostilities had played a pivotal role in Ramses' victory at Kadesh. In recompense, Ramses had appointed his friend as the new secretary of state.

Although the unexpected defeat seemed to have checked Hittite expansion for the present, Ahsha had decided to head straight back to Amurru, where the Lebanese coast hugged the Mediterranean, east of Mount Hermon and the trade center of Damascus. His intent was to use the province as a base of military operations, training local troops as elite commandos. Their presence would check any potential Hittite advance toward Palestine and the Delta borderlands.

When he entered the port of Beirut in a ship laden with gifts for Amurru's corrupt ruler, Prince Benteshina, little did Ahsha suspect that the welcoming committee would include Hattusili, the brother of the Hittite emperor—for Hatti had already bought back the Prince of Amurru.

Ahsha had made a thorough study of Hattusili. Small and unimposing, but intelligent and devious, the man was a tough opponent. He had forced his prisoner to write an official dispatch to Ramses, hoping to lure the Pharaoh into a trap. Fortunately, Ahsha had managed to insert a coded warning.

How would Ramses react? The national interest dictated that he should abandon all thought of his friend and hurry north to counter the Hittite threat. Knowing the Pharaoh, Ahsha was convinced he would respond in kind to enemy aggression, no matter the risk. Still, the head of Egyptian diplomacy would represent an excellent bargaining chip, and to Benteshina, Ahsha figured, he was worth his weight in gold. It was a slim hope, but he clung to it.

Captivity grated on his nerves. Ever since adolescence, Ahsha had been a mover and a shaker. This forced passivity was unbearable. One way or another, he had to act. Perhaps Ramses believed that his friend was dead. Perhaps he was outfitting his troops with new arms before launching a full-scale offensive.

The more Ahsha pondered, the more clearly he saw that his only chance was to make a break for it.

A servant brought him the usual copious breakfast. He could hardly complain about palace hospitality. Ahsha was enjoying a steak when he heard his host's heavy tread approaching.

"And how is our distinguished Egyptian guest?" Benteshina asked jovially. A portly fifty, the prince still sported a luxuriant black mustache.

"Honored by your visit," replied Ahsha.

"I've been meaning to drink a toast to your new appointment."

"Why isn't Hattusili with you?"

"Our distinguished Hittite visitor has business elsewhere."

"Amurru is certainly a popular spot. When will I see Hattusili again?"

"I have no idea."

"So your country is back in the Hittite fold?"

"Times change, my dear Ahsha."

"You don't fear the wrath of Ramses?"

"Pharaoh can't possibly penetrate my domain."

"Does that mean the Hittites bought Canaan, too?"

"Don't ask for specifics . . . I'm sure you're aware that I need to barter your precious existence for all it's worth. I hope that nothing untoward happens to you in the process, but . . ."

With a malicious smile, Benteshina informed Ahsha that he would have to be eliminated if there were any suggestion he might report what he'd seen and heard in Amurru.

"Are you sure you're siding with the winner, Benteshina?"

"But of course, my dear Ahsha! Though to tell the truth, the Hittites didn't leave us much choice. Then there's been talk of all the problems Ramses is facing. I hear that a possible coup, a military defeat, or a combination of the two may result in his death and his replacement with a more, shall we say, *compliant* ruler."

"You don't understand Egypt, Benteshina, and you're certainly underestimating Ramses."

"I stand by my judgment. Kadesh was only a temporary setback. Muwattali will win in the end."

"A risky bet."

"Fond as I am of wine, women, and gold, I'm no gambler. The Hittites have war in their blood. You Egyptians don't."

Benteshina slowly rubbed his hands together. "If you'd like to avoid any unpleasantness when we exchange you, my dear Ahsha, I strongly suggest you reconsider your allegiance. Suppose you fed false information to Ramses . . . you'd be well rewarded, once he's out of the way."

"You're asking me, the head of Egyptian diplomacy, to betray my country?"

"Doesn't everything depend on circumstances? I'd sworn allegiance to your pharaoh too . . ."

"I find it hard to think when I'm so lonely."

"Are you saying you need a woman?"

"A refined and cultured woman, very understanding . . ."

Benteshina emptied his goblet and wiped his moist lips with the back of his right hand.

"To help you reflect on your situation, I'm prepared to make any sacrifice."

Night had fallen. Two oil lamps cast their dim light over Ahsha's chamber as he lay on his bed, dressed only in a short kilt.

The thought wouldn't let him alone: Hattusili had left Amurru. Yet his departure did not coincide with any southward expansion into the protectorates of Palestine and Phoenicia. If the Hittite initiative was as far-reaching as Benteshina hinted, why would Hattusili abandon his Lebanese command post? Muwattali's brother would hardly dare venture farther south on his own. Therefore, he had probably returned to his own country, but why?

"My lord . . ."

A hesitant voice interrupted Ahsha's musings. He sat up and saw, in the semi-darkness, a young woman dressed in a short tunic, barefoot, with flyaway hair.

"Prince Benteshina sent me. He told me to . . . he wants . . ."

"Come sit beside me."

The woman reluctantly obeyed. She looked about twenty and was blond and shapely, very appealing. Ahsha put an arm around her shoulder.

"Are you married?"

"Yes, My Lord, but the prince promised my husband would never hear of this."

"What does he do for a living?"

"He's a customs inspector."

"Do you work, too?"

"I sort dispatches at the central post office."

Ahsha slipped the blonde's dress off one shoulder, nuzzled her neck, and pushed her down on the bed.

"Do you see dispatches from Canaan?"

"Yes, but I'm not supposed to discuss them."

"Are there a lot of Hittite soldiers here in the capital?"

"I'm can't talk about that, either."

"Do you love your husband?"

"Oh, yes, My Lord."

"Does the thought of making love with me disgust you?"

She turned away.

"Answer my questions and I won't even touch you."

The blonde gazed hopefully at the Egyptian captive. "Do I have your word?"

"By all the gods of Amurru."

"All right," she said. "There aren't too many Hittites around yet; a few dozen trainers are working with our soldiers."

"Has Hattusili left Amurru?"

"Yes, My Lord."

"Where did he go?"

"I don't know."

"What's the situation in Canaan?"

"Uncertain."

"Isn't the province under Hittite control?"

"There are different rumors. Some claim that Pharaoh has taken back Gaza, the capital of Canaan, and the governor was killed in battle."

The news instantly breathed new life into Ahsha. Not only had Ramses found the red flag, he had acted on Ahsha's coded message. His counterattack would stop the Hittites in time. That was why Hattusili had headed north—to warn the emperor.

"Sorry, sweetheart," the diplomat said, reaching for the girl.

"You're going to keep your promise, aren't you?"

"Yes, but I have to take certain precautions."

Ahsha bound and gagged his companion. He needed a few hours' head start. Spying the cloak she had dropped in his doorway, he hit on a plan to get out of the palace. He donned the garment, pulled up the hood, and crept down the stairs.

On the main floor, a banquet was in progress.

Some of the guests lay passed out on the floor. Others were feverishly entwined. Ahsha stepped over naked bodies.

"Where do you think you're going?" a voice said thickly.

Ahsha had nowhere to run. Several armed guards were posted at the palace gates.

"Already done with that Egyptian? Come here, my lovely."

A few paces ahead of him lay freedom.

Benteshina's sticky hand pulled back the hood of his cloak. "Nice try, Ahsha," said the prince.

FOUR

Pi-Ramses, the Pharaoh's new capital in the Delta, was dubbed "the Turquoise City" for the shiny blue tiles that adorned the fronts of its buildings. In the streets of Pi-Ramses, sightseers goggled at the temples, the royal palace, the artificial lakes, the harbor. They admired the orchards, canals full of fish, noble villas with flower gardens and shady pathways. They sampled apples, pomegranates, olives, and figs, sipped fine wines, and learned the local anthem: "What joy to be in Pi-Ramses, where the poor man lives like a king, in the shade of acacias and sycamores, in the glint of turquoise and gold, where the cool breeze wafts and the birds love to sport in the marshlands."

But Ahmeni, the king's private secretary, old school friend, and unfailing servant, didn't feel like singing. Like many in Pi-Ramses, he felt that something was missing when Ramses was gone.

Gone, and in danger.

Refusing to heed any reasonable counsel, brushing aside any urge to temporize, Ramses had marched north to reclaim Canaan and Syria, staking his troops and his life on an uncertain outcome.

Ahmeni's official title was sandal-bearer to the Pharaoh. He was short, slight, pale and balding, small-boned and frail, with long, slender hands that drew exquisite hiero-glyphs. His origins were humble, yet an invisible bond connected him to Ramses. In keeping with the ancient expression, he was "The King's Eyes and Ears," remaining in the background, his staff of twenty handling the daily business of government. He was a tireless worker, sleeping little and staying thin as a rail no matter how much he ate. Ahmeni rarely left his office. The centerpiece of his desk was the gilded scribe's kit that Ramses had given him long ago. Whenever he felt his energy flagging, he had only to touch the lotus-shaped box to find the impetus to plow through another pile of documents that would have daunted any other scribe. He allowed no one else to clean his office, where papyrus scrolls were carefully arranged in earthenware stands and leather pigeonholes.

"A military courier to see you," announced one of his assistants.

"Show him in."

The exhausted-looking soldier was covered with dust.

"I bring a message from Pharaoh."

"Show it to me."

Ahmeni identified Ramses' seal. Despite his weak lungs, he took off for the palace at a run.

Queen Nefertari had been conferring with the vizier, the chief steward, the scribe in charge of the royal accounts, a priestly delegate, the Keeper of Secrets, the superior of the House of Life, a chief judge, the head of the Treasury, the director of the granaries, and various other high officials in search of precise directives. None of them wished to make a move without the approval of the Great Royal Wife, who was governing in her husband's absence. Fortunately, Ahmeni was there to guide her, and Tuya, her mother-in-law, was always available with sound advice.

Indescribably beautiful, with lustrous black hair, blue-green eyes, and the luminous face of a goddess, Nefertari shouldered the lonely burden of power. As a girl, she had trained as a temple musician and was fond of studying the ancient texts. A cloistered life had been all she aspired to—until Ramses' love transformed her from a shy maiden into a queen, unswerving in her devotion to duty.

Simply running her own household demanded a great deal of work. The queen's household was a thousand-year-old institution encompassing a boarding school for outstanding young women, both native and foreign-born. Girls were also trained in the arts and crafts. There were skilled weavers, as well as workshops that turned out jewelry, mirrors, vases, fans, sandals, and religious objects. Nefertari's staff included priestesses, scribes, stewards of the queen's estates, workers and peasants. She made an effort to become acquainted with the key people from each sector. Her aim in life was to avoid error and injustice.

These were difficult days, with Ramses risking his life to keep Egypt safe from a Hittite invasion. She knew she must try harder than ever to hold the country on course, no matter how great an effort it required.

"Ahmeni!" she greeted the panting secretary. "Is there news?"

"Yes, Your Majesty. A messenger just brought this scroll from the front."

The queen had not moved into Ramses' office, which remained empty, waiting for his return. Her headquarters was a vast room adorned with light blue tiling. It looked out on the garden where Watcher, the king's old dog, slept at the foot of an acacia tree.

Nefertari broke the seal on the dispatch and read the cursive text, signed by Ramses himself.

No smile lit the queen's grave face.

"He's trying to reassure me," she said flatly.

"Has nothing been accomplished?"

"Oh, yes. Canaan is back in our hands. The turncoat governor was killed."

"I'd call that a victory!" said Ahmeni with enthusiasm.

"The king is continuing north."

"Why are you so sad?"

"Because he'll go back to Kadesh, no matter how great the risk. First he'll try to free Ahsha, putting his life on the line for his friend. What if his luck runs out?"

"His magic never will."

"How would Egypt survive without him?"

"First of all, Your Majesty, you are the Great Royal Wife, and you know perfectly well how to run the country. Besides, Ramses will come back. I'm sure of it."

In the hallway, the sound of hurrying footsteps drew nearer. When the knock came at the door, Ahmeni answered.

A midwife burst in, all aflutter. "Your Majesty . . . the Lady Iset is in labor. She's asking for you."

Iset the Fair had saucy green eyes, a small nose and delicate mouth—an inordinately attractive face, under normal circumstances. Even in pain, her charm was undiminished, and it was possible to see why she had been the love of

Ramses' youth. Iset often dreamed of a rustic hut at the edge of a wheat field outside of Memphis and the long-ago nights of that first summer she had shared with her handsome prince.

Then Ramses met Nefertari, and Nefertari became the queen of his heart. Iset, being neither jealous nor ambitious by nature, had stepped aside. It was plain that neither she nor anyone else could rival Nefertari; Iset the Fair accepted the role of secondary wife. Though his power frightened her, nothing could change the love that Iset felt for Ramses.

In a long-ago moment of weakness, she had almost let Shaanar talk her into backing one of his plots, but in the end her loyal heart won out. Her true claim to glory had been bearing Ramses' firstborn son, the exceptionally gifted Kha.

Nefertari, meanwhile, had lost her first daughter, then nearly died giving birth to her second, Meritamon. Knowing she could have no more children, she had insisted that Ramses let his secondary wife give him another son, many more if possible. At first he agreed, reuniting with a joyful Iset, but soon he came up with the idea of selecting "royal children" from all levels of society, bringing a hundred-odd talented boys and girls to the palace for their education. Their number would symbolize the royal pair's fertility and eliminate any question of succession should Ramses outlive the children of his body.

Still, the reunion with Iset had produced the desired effect, and she was thrilled. She had done the traditional test, mixing her urine with wheat and barley. The barley had sprouted; she would have a boy.

Now Nefertari found her friend squatting, supported by four midwives, known as "The Gentle Ones" or "The Firm-Fingered Women." The ritual words had been chanted to banish evil spirits from the birth chamber. Incense and potions helped ease the pain of childbirth.

Iset felt the small life inside her preparing to leave the peaceful waters where it had been growing for the past nine months.

The tender touch of a hand and the scent of lilies and jasmine made Iset the Fair feel she had entered a heavenly garden where all pain would cease. Turning her head to one side, she saw that Nefertari was standing in for one of the midwives. She held a damp cloth to Iset's forehead.

"Your Majesty . . . I was afraid you wouldn't have time for me."

"You called me, so here I am."

"Have you had news of the king?"

"Good news, Iset. Ramses has taken Canaan and will soon have the other provinces back in hand. The Hittites are going to be sorry."

"When is he coming home?"

"I'm sure he'll be eager to see his child."

"Our child . . . will you welcome it?"

"I'll love this child as much as my own daughter, or your son Kha."

"I was so afraid you might . . ."

"We're in this together, Iset. Now on with the battle."

Suddenly the pain grew more intense, and as Iset cried out, the lead midwife sprang into action.

Laboring, Iset wished she could escape from the fire tearing through her belly. She wished she could fall into the deepest sleep, stop struggling, and dream of Ramses . . . but Nefertari was right. She must fight her way through this great mystery that had claimed her body.

Nefertari caught the baby, cradling it as a midwife cut the cord. For a moment, Iset swooned.

"Is it a boy?" she asked at last.

"Yes, it is. A fine, big boy, Iset."

FIVE

Kha, the son of Ramses and Iset the Fair, was copying the maxims of Ptah-hotep onto blank papyrus. Centuries earlier, the sage had distilled the wisdom of his hundred and ten years into these writings. Though Kha himself was only ten, he rarely indulged in child's play and spent his time studying, despite gentle reprimands from Nedjem, the agriculture secretary who supervised his education. Nedjem would have liked him to be more well-rounded, yet the boy's intellectual capacities were astounding. Kha learned quickly, retained everything, and already wrote like an experienced scribe.

Nearby, pretty little Meritamon, the daughter of Ramses and Nefertari, was playing the harp. At the age of six, she displayed a remarkable gift for music as well as a genuine sense of style. As he wrote his hieroglyphs, Kha like to hear his sister pluck melodies and sing old ballads. She was the breathtaking image of her mother. Watcher, the king's old dog, sighed happily, resting his head on her feet.

When the queen came into the garden, Kha dropped his brush and Meritamon stopped playing. The two excited youngsters ran to greet her.

Nefertari kissed them.

"Everything went well, and Iset has a baby boy."

"You and my father have probably picked out a name for him."

"So you think we think of everything?"

"Yes, because you're the king and queen."

"Your little brother will be called Merenptah, 'Beloved of the Ptah,' the god of the creative urge and patron of architects."

Dolora, Ramses' sister, was a tall and perpetually weary brunette, always doctoring her oily complexion with unguents. After an idle youth, she had found inspiration in Ofir, the Libyan sorcerer. He had converted her to the heretic king Akhenaton's radical belief in a single god. Admittedly, Ofir had been forced to commit murder in order to safeguard his freedom. Still, Dolora supported him and had vowed to help his cause, no matter what it cost her.

On the advice of the sorcerer, who had remained in Egypt but had gone underground, Dolora had returned to the palace and lied her way back into Ramses' good graces. The sorcerer had kidnapped her, she claimed. He had used her to cover his own escape from the country. Dolora loudly proclaimed her relief at escaping the worst and being back with her family.

Had Ramses believed her story? On his orders, Dolora was required to remain at court in Pi-Ramses—exactly as she had hoped. Before long she would be funneling information to Ofir. Unfortunately, with Ramses gone to wage war in the northern protectorates, she had not been able to make further headway with the king.

Dolora spared no effort to win over Nefertari, knowing how much influence she had with her husband. As soon as the queen left the council chamber where she had been meeting with canal superintendents, Dolora approached her, bowing low.

"Your Majesty, may I help you see to Iset?"

"What exactly do you have in mind, Dolora?"

"Supervising her staff, purifying her room each day, using soap made from the bark and fruit of the desert date to wash the mother and infant, cleansing every object in her household with a mixture of ashes and soda . . . and I've put together a cosmetic kit for Iset with pots of rouge, flasks of flower essences, kohl and applicators. She needs to stay beautiful, doesn't she?"

"She'll appreciate you thoughtfulness."

"If she lets me, I'll do her makeup myself."

Nefertari and Dolora walked a short way down a corridor with murals of lilies, cornflowers, and mandrake.

"I hear the baby is splendid."

"Merenptah will be a strong and healthy man."

"Yesterday I wanted to spend time with Kha and Meritamon, but I wasn't allowed to. It pained me deeply, Your Majesty."

"Those are Ramses' orders, and mine as well, Dolora."

"How much longer will everyone mistrust me?"

"Is it any wonder? Your escapade with that sorcerer, your ties to Shaanar . . ."

"Haven't I had my share of unhappiness, Your Majesty? My husband was killed by Moses, that cursed Ofir tried to brainwash me, Shaanar always treated me with the utmost contempt. And everyone blames me! A quiet life is all I aspire to now. It would mean so much to me if only my family were closer. I admit that I've made mistakes, serious mistakes, but will I always be branded a criminal?"

"You plotted against Pharaoh, didn't you, Dolora?"

The gangly woman knelt before the queen. "I was the slave of evil men," she pleaded, "and I was prone to their influence. That's all over now. I wish to live on my own, at the palace, as Ramses has ordained. I want to forget the past. Will I ever be pardoned?"

Nefertari was shaken. "Go care for Iset, Dolora. Make her beautiful again."

Meba, the chief assistant to the secretary of state, arrived to see Ahmeni. A career diplomat, scion of a rich diplomatic family, Meba was by nature haughty and condescending. He was proud of belonging to a superior class of people, people with wealth and power. He disdained lesser mortals. It had come as a shock when Shaanar, the king's older brother, had summarily replaced him as secretary of state some years earlier. Shunted aside, he began to believe he would never regain center stage, until the day a Hittite agent recruited him.

Treason? Everything happened so quickly that Meba never thought of it that way. He plunged into double-dealing, making the most of his connections. Before long he was back at the State Department, apparently delighted to be working in a lesser capacity. Ahsha's former boss now posed as his faithful second in command. Sharp as he was, even the new young secretary of state had been fooled by Meba's act. He was flattered to have an experienced assistant who had once been Shaanar's right-hand man.

Since Ofir, the head of the Hittite intelligence network in Egypt, had gone underground, Meba had been waiting for orders that never came. He welcomed the silence, using the interval to consolidate his contacts at the department and in high society. He also took care to spread his message: he'd been the victim of grave injustice; Ahsha was brilliant, but perhaps too intellectual to make a good director. Meba was so occupied that he began to forget he'd sold out to the Hittites.

Munching on a dried fig, Ahmeni was composing a letter of remonstrance to the granary superintendents and reading an appeal from a provincial chief concerning a shortage of firewood.

"What's going on, Meba?"

The diplomat detested the crude little scribe. "Perhaps you're too busy to meet with me?" he inquired urbanely.

"I can spare a moment, if you keep it brief."

"While Ramses is gone, I presume you're the one in charge?"

"If you have any cause for unhappiness, request an audience with the queen. Her Majesty personally reviews all my decisions."

"Let's not play games. The queen will only send me back to you."

"What seems to be the matter?"

"The lack of clear directives. My secretary has been detained abroad, the king is away at war, and my department is racked by doubt and uncertainty."

"Wait until Ramses and Ahsha come back."

"And what if . . ."

"If they don't come back?"

"A dreadful prospect, but mustn't it be faced?"

"I don't believe so."

"You're sure of yourself."

"I am."

"I'll wait, then."

"It's your best course of action, Meba."

Serramanna had led a remarkable life. Born in Sardinia, he grew to be a giant and was a notorious pirate captain when his path crossed Ramses'. The prince spared his life, and the pirate became the head of the royal bodyguard. Just prior to the battle of Kadesh, Ahmeni had suspected the Sard of treason and threw him in jail. Soon realizing his error, the scribe worked hard to clear Serramanna's name and make amends.

The Sard would rather be battling beside the king, bashing and hacking away at Hittites. But Pharaoh had ordered him to remain behind and provide security for the royal family. Serramanna threw himself into the role with all the gusto he had once displayed commandeering rich merchant vessels in the Mediterranean.

In the giant's eyes, Ramses was the most formidable warlord he'd ever met, and Nefertari the most beautiful, most inaccessible woman. The royal couple was such a daily source of wonder that serving them had become his life. Well-compensated, enjoying the pleasures of the table as well as the splendid examples of womanhood Egypt had to offer, he was perfectly willing to sacrifice his life for the good of this magical realm.

There was one cloud on the horizon, however. His hunter's instinct wouldn't let him rest. Something told him that Dolora's reappearance at court posed a threat to Ramses and Nefertari. He saw the king's sister as unstable and dishonest. Although he couldn't prove it, Serramanna sensed that she was still in league with her mysterious sorcerer.

The Sard had been investigating the identity of the blond woman whose body had been found in the abandoned villa where he had finally tracked the sorcerer—a villa belonging to Ramses' treacherous brother, Shaanar.

Now Shaanar had gone missing in the desert and Dolora had only the flimsiest of explanations to offer regarding the murdered woman. He was ready to concede that the blonde had merely been the sorcerer's medium, but Dolora's claim that she knew nothing more about the woman was preposterous. She was hiding something, playing the victim to cover up important facts. But since Dolora had wormed her way back into Nefertari's good graces, Serramanna needed more than premonitions to build a case against her.

A successful pirate is a stubborn man. The sea will be empty for days on end before any prey appears. Presuming, of course, that he'd picked the right area to sweep. That was why he'd put out feelers in Memphis as well as Pi-Ramses, sending his sleuths through the city with an accurate sketch of the blond victim.

Someone, somewhere, was bound to talk.

SIX

Halfway between Memphis and Thebes stood the ruins of the City of the Horizon of Aton, once the proud capital of the heretic pharaoh Akhenaton. Now, some hundred years later, the palaces, mansions, workshops, and craftsmen's dwellings all lay empty. The temples were silent, the streets deserted. Markets and alleyways bustled with life no longer. Akhenaton and Nefertiti's ghostly chariot rolled down a sand-swept avenue.

On this desolate site in the vast Nile floodplain, nestled against a backdrop of cliffs, Akhenaton had raised a city to the solar orb he worshiped as the One True God.

Not a soul ever visited the place. After the discredited pharaoh's death, the population had returned to Thebes, taking everything of worth, emptying the temples and archives. Here and there were pieces of pottery, or a half-finished bust of Nefertiti in some sculptor's workshop.

Over the years, the buildings had begun to deteriorate. Whitewash chipped off, plaster crumbled. The hastily constructed capital did not fare well in torrential rains and sandstorms. The stone slabs Akhenaton had erected to mark the borders of his god's sacred territory were now barely legible. Time would erase the hieroglyphs, reducing the royal mystic's mad undertaking to nothing.

Tombs for the regime's high officials had been dug in the cliffs, but no mummy lay in rest there. The burial chambers had been cleaned out along with the rest of the city. No one dared set foot in the defiled tombs, for it was said that spirits roamed them, waiting to pounce on curious visitors.

No one, that is, except Ramses' brother, Shaanar, and the sorcerer Ofir, who had set up housekeeping in the tomb of the high priest of Aton. The antechamber, with its rows of columns, was comfortable enough. The images of temples and palaces on the walls testified to the heretic capital's lost glory. The stone carver had immortalized Akhenaton and Nefertiti worshiping the solar orb. Its long rays ended in hands that gave life to the royal couple.

Shaanar's beady dark eyes often strayed to the carvings that depicted Akhenaton as the sun king. The fugitive prince was thirty-five, moon-faced, with a short, heavy frame, and allergic to the sun. The carvings reminded him of his nemesis, Ramses, the Son of Light.

Ramses, the tyrant he had tried to overthrow with the help of the Hittites. Ramses, who had exiled him to a desert penal colony. Ramses, who had planned to drag him through the courts and see him condemned to death.

As Shaanar was being transferred from the main Memphis jail to the desert outpost, a sudden sandstorm had allowed him to escape. The hatred he felt toward his brother and his thirst for revenge had given him the strength to survive in the desert. He had instinctively headed for the one place he knew would be safe—the heretic king's abandoned city.

His partner in crime, Ofir, the onetime head of Hittite espionage in Egypt, was there to meet him. The Libyan sorcerer had an imposing appearance with his hawklike face, prominent cheekbones, thin lips, strong chin. This was the man who would make Shaanar his brother's successor.

Fuming, the prince picked up a stone and hurled it at a carving of Akhenaton, smashing the pharaoh's crown.

"Damn him! Damn all the pharaohs and their godforsaken country!"

For Shaanar's dream had been shattered. Not long ago he had pictured himself at the head of a vast empire stretching from Anatolia to Nubia; now he was an outcast in his own country. Ramses should never have survived Kadesh. Shaanar would have seized the throne, collaborated with the Hittite victors, then thrown off their yoke to become the sole master of the whole Near East. Ramses should have been the ruin of Egypt, Shaanar its savior. Should have been . . .

Shaanar turned to face Ofir, seated in the depths of the tomb.

"Where did we go wrong?" he asked.

"Our luck will change."

"But when, Ofir?"

"Magic may be an exact science, yet it can never exclude the unpredictable."

"The unpredictable turned out to be Ramses himself!"

"Your brother is endowed with rare and fascinating powers."

"Fascinating? He's nothing but a despot. Could you be falling under his spell, Ofir?"

"I need to learn all I can about him if we're to win in the end. After all, this is a man who summoned the power of Amon to help turn the tide at Kadesh."

"Do you really believe that ridiculous story?"

"There's more to this world than meets the eye, Shaanar. Secret forces are at work, secret forces that lay the warp of reality."

Shaanar slammed his fist into the wall where Aton's orb figured.

"Look where your fine speeches have gotten us! Shut up in a tomb, alone and powerless! We'll die here like wretches!"

"That's not entirely accurate, since the followers of Aton are feeding and protecting us."

"Your little flock is a bunch of deluded idiots!"

"I quite agree, but they're certainly useful."

"Do you think you can whip them into an army?"

Ofir made no reply, but traced strange geometric figures in the dust.

"Ramses defeated the Hittites," Shaanar pressed on. "Your intelligence network is in shambles. I haven't one supporter left in Egypt. What are our alternatives besides living here like outlaws?"

"Magic will provide us with alternatives."

Shaanar winced. "Your magic couldn't kill Nefertari. You didn't come close to disabling Ramses."

"You're being unfair," the sorcerer said evenly. "Thanks to me, the queen's health will never be the same."

"Iset the Fair will produce another son for Ramses. I hear he plans to adopt a herd of children. Our attempts on his family have hardly troubled him."

"They'll wear him down eventually."

"Didn't you ever learn that a pharaoh's powers are renewed after the thirtieth year of his reign?"

"We're not at that point yet, Shaanar. The Hittites haven't given up the battle."

"I thought the coalition they formed fell apart at Kadesh."

"Emperor Muwattali is a master strategist. He's wily enough to know when to take a step backward. The new alliance he's put together will come as a nasty shock to Ramses."

"I'm tired of pipe dreams, Ofir."

From a distance came the sound of pounding hooves. Shaanar grabbed hold of a sword.

"This isn't when your followers usually bring our food," he said as he hurried toward the entrance to the tomb, overlooking the plain and the ghost town.

"Two horsemen."

"Headed this way?"

"They're at the edge of town now, and yes, coming toward the cliffs! We'd better get out of here and find another hiding place."

"Let's not rush; there are only two of them." Ofir stood up. "This may be the sign I've been waiting for, Shaanar. Take a good look."

Shaanar recognized the lay deacon of Ofir's congregation. When it dawned on him who the other man was, he could barely speak.

"Meba? What's Meba doing here?"

"You know he's my second in command."

Shaanar lay down his sword.

"No one in the king's entourage suspects him," continued the sorcerer. "It's time you two put aside your differences."

Shaanar made no reply. He felt nothing but contempt for Meba, whose only ambition was to protect his personal fortune and his position in society. When the old diplomat had revealed his identity as a Hittite agent, Shaanar had doubted the sincerity of his commitment.

The two men dismounted where the path forked toward the high priest of Aton's tomb. The deacon stayed back with the horses, while his distinguished visitor advanced toward the hideout.

A shudder went through Shaanar. What if Meba, reinstated in the government, had betrayed them? What if the police were on his heels? Still, no one else appeared on the horizon.

On edge, the diplomat dispensed with the usual greeting.

"I've taken a great risk in coming here. What on earth could have made you request such a meeting?"

Ofir's reply was stinging. "You answer to me, Meba. You'll go wherever I tell you. Now report."

Shaanar was taken aback. Here, underground, the sorcerer was still directing his network.

"The news isn't good, I'm afraid. The emperor's latest initiative fell short of the mark. Ramses launched a vigorous counteroffensive; he's already recaptured Canaan."

"Is he pressing on to Kadesh?"

"I haven't been able to find that out."

"You ought to, Meba. Work on improving your sources. Have the Bedouins kept up their end of the bargain?"

"The rebellion seems quite widespread. But you realize that I can't ask too many questions without arousing Ahmeni's suspicions."

"You do work at the State Department, don't you?"

"Caution dictates . . ."

"Do you ever chance upon Ramses' son?"

"Little Kha? Occasionally, but why would . . ."

"I need to lay my hands on an object he's especially fond of, Meba, and I need it right away."

SEVEN

Moses, along with his wife and son, had left the land of Midian, south of Edom and east of the Gulf of Aqaba, where he had taken refuge some time ago. Now he had decided to return to Egypt, against his father-in-law's advice. Since Moses was wanted for murder, the old man argued, it would be folly to turn himself in to Pharaoh's police. He'd surely be imprisoned and sentenced to death.

But no amount of reasoning could change Moses' mind. God had spoken to him on the mountain. God had ordered him to lead his Hebrew brethren out of Egypt. They must be free to practice their faith in a land that belonged to them. The odds were overwhelmingly against them, but the new prophet had no doubt that he would succeed.

His wife, Zipporah, had also tried to dissuade him, to no avail.

So the small family group set out on their way to the Delta. Moses kept a slow and steady pace with the aid of a knobby walking stick. Zipporah soon found that he always knew which way to turn.

When a cloud of sand announced the approach of horsemen, Zipporah gathered her son in her arms and huddled close to Moses. Tall, bearded, broad-shouldered, he had the build of an athlete.

"We need to hide," she begged.

"It wouldn't do any good."

"If it's Bedouins, they'll kill us. If it's Egyptians, they'll arrest you."

"Don't fret so."

Moses waited, unflinching. And as he waited he thought of his days at the royal academy in Memphis, where he had been indoctrinated in the ageless wisdom of the Egyptians and also formed a close friendship with Prince Ramses, the future pharaoh. After graduation, an administrative post at the harem at Merur had given him considerable responsibility for a man of his age. Eventually, after serving as superintendent of various building projects, he had overseen the construction of Pi-Ramses, the pharaoh's new capital in the Delta. The appointment was an honor, making Moses one of the most influential men in Egypt.

Yet his was a tortured soul. Ever since he could remember, a fire had consumed him. Only after the miracle of the burning bush did the pain disappear. At last, Moses had discovered his mission in life.

The horsemen, when they arrived, did prove to be Bedouins. In the lead rode Amos, bald and bearded, and the tall, thin Keni—the two tribal chiefs who had lured Ramses into an ambush at Kadesh. Their men formed a ring around Moses.

"Who are you?" barked Amos.

"My name is Moses. This is my wife and son."

"Moses . . . could you be the famous friend of Ramses? The one who was wanted for murder and fled to the desert?"

"I am he."

Amos jumped down from his horse and slapped the Hebrew on the back.

"Then we're in the same camp! We want to overthrow Ramses, too."

"I still consider the King of Egypt my brother," Moses said evenly.

"You can't be serious, when he's put a price on your head! We Bedouins and you Hebrews should band together with other desert nomads. We'll join forces with the Hittites to vanquish Ramses once and for all. The Pharaoh's strength has become a legend, my friend. Come ride with us. We'll raid the Egyptian battalions pushing their way into Syria."

"Sorry. I'm going south."

"South?" Keni said warily. "What's in that direction?"

"Egypt. I'm heading to Pi-Ramses."

The two Bedouins exchanged an astonished glance.

"Are you putting us on?" questioned Amos.

"I'm stating facts."

"But you'll be arrested and put to death!"

"Yahweh will protect me. I need to lead my people out of Egypt."

"Have you lost your mind, man?"

"That's the mission Yahweh has given me."

Now Keni slipped off of his horse. "Stay where you are, Moses."

The tribal chieftains moved out of earshot, where they could talk.

"He's a madman," Keni insisted. "The desert has that effect sometimes."

"I think you're wrong."

"Just look at his eyes."

"I did, Keni. The man is sane. What's more, he's clever and determined."

"Wandering in the desert with a wife and small child—you call that clever?"

"Yes, Keni. A brilliant disguise. Who'd pay him the least attention? But Moses still has followers in Egypt, and he's planning to lead a Hebrew rebellion."

"It will never work. Pharaoh's police will be all over him."

"Yes, but if we help him, he could be of use to us."

"What do you mean, Amos?"

"We can help him across the border and later supply the Hebrews with arms. They'll probably be exterminated, but they'll stir things up in Pi-Ramses."

Moses inhaled the Delta air deeply. This land still enchanted him, though by rights he should hate it. How could he feel any enmity toward the lush green fields, the graceful palm groves? He felt like a young man again, the Pharaoh of Egypt's close friend and associate, who had dreamed of spending his whole life at Ramses' side, serving him, helping him transmit the ideal of truth and justice that had nurtured the dynasties through the ages.

Now that ideal was a thing of a past. Henceforth Yahweh alone would guide Moses' footsteps.

Thanks to Keni and Amos, the Hebrew crossed into Egypt in darkness, along with his wife and son, evading the border patrol as it roamed between two outposts. Zipporah, while terrified, offered no objection and voiced no criticism. Moses was her husband. She had vowed to obey him and would follow wherever he led.

With the sunrise and the resurrection of nature, Moses felt his hopes revive. Here he would fight the good fight, no matter what forces aligned against him. Ramses must be made to understand that the Hebrews demanded their liberty with the desire to form a nation, according to divine will.

The family stopped in villages where they were welcomed with the customary hospitality offered to strangers. Moses' speech showed clearly that he was of Egyptian stock, which didn't hurt matters. Slowly but surely, the Hebrew, his wife, and his son reached the outskirts of the capital.

"I built a good part of this city," Moses revealed to Zipporah.

"It's so big, so beautiful! Are we going to live here?"

"For a while."

"Where will we stay?"

"Yahweh will provide."

They made their way through the bustling maze of craftsmen's shops. Zipporah, accustomed to the seclusion of her desert oasis, felt confused. On every side there were shouts and cries. Carpenters, tailors, and sandal makers were hard at work. Donkeys threaded slowly through the narrow streets, laden with earthenware vessels containing meat, dried fish, or cheese.

Straight ahead lay the homes of the Hebrew brickmakers.

Nothing had changed. Moses recognized every house, heard familiar chants, and experienced a surge of memory in which rebellion mingled with youthful enthusiasm. As he lingered in a little square with a central well, an old brickmaker hobbled up to take a good look at him.

"I've seen you before, haven't I? But wait, it can't be! Don't tell me you're Moses, the famous Moses?"

"I am, old man."

"You're supposed to be dead!"

"Oh? They forgot to tell me," Moses said with a smile.

"When you were around, they treated us brickmakers better. Now anyone who falls behind has to go fetch his own straw. You'd never have stood for it. Imagine, having to haul your own straw! And we fight tooth and nail for the smallest pay raise."

"Do you have a house, at least?"

"I'd like bigger lodgings, but my request is tied up in paperwork. Back then, you would have helped me."

"I'll help you now."

The brickmaker's eyes narrowed. "Aren't you still wanted for murder?"

"Yes."

"You killed Ramses' sister's husband, or so they say."

"He was a blackmailer and a bully," Moses objected. "I never intended to hurt him. We had an argument and it got out of control."

"So you did kill him. But I understand, I do!"

"Would you take me and my family in for the night, old man?"

"Follow me," he replied.

As soon as Moses, his wife, and child were asleep, the old brickmaker left his bed and crept through the darkened room toward the door to the street, opening it ever so carefully. It gave a loud creak, and the brickmaker froze. Once he was certain that Moses had not awakened, he slipped across the doorstep.

The price on his guest's head was a big one. He'd go straight to the police. But he had barely set foot outside when a powerful hand flattened his back against a wall.

"Where do you think you're going, scum?"

"I needed a breath of air, that's all."

"You're planning to turn Moses in, am I right?"

"No, no, of course not!"

"I ought to strangle you."

"Let him go," ordered Moses, appearing in the doorway. "He's a Hebrew, the same as you and me. And who are you, coming to my aid in the night?"

"My name is Aaron."

The man was no longer young, but vigorous, with a rich, deep voice.

"How did you find out that I was staying here?"

"Don't you know that we were all watching you? Everyone knows you in these parts. The council of elders would like to meet with you, Moses."

EIGHT

Benteshina, the Prince of Amurru, was having a wonderful dream. A young noblewoman, Egyptian-born and naked as the day she was born, smelling of myrrh, was working her way up his legs like a clinging vine.

Suddenly she paused and began to rock like a sinking boat. Benteshina gripped her neck for dear life.

"Your Highness, wake up! Wake up!"

Opening his eyes, the prince discovered he was in the act of strangling his majordomo. The first light of dawn filtered into the bedroom.

"Why are you disturbing me so early?"

"Get up, I beg of you, and look out the window."

Reluctantly, Benteshina followed his servant's suggestion. His flabby bulk he moved slowly.

Not a hint of mist on the sea: the day would turn out to be beautiful.

"What is there to see?"

"Look at the entrance to the harbor, Your Highness."

Benteshina rubbed his eyes. Three Egyptian warships stood there, forming a blockade.

"The overland routes?"

"They're closed off, too. A huge Egyptian army has us surrounded! The city is under siege, My Lord."

"What shape is Ahsha in?" asked Benteshina.

The majordomo hung his head. "On your orders, they threw him in the dungeon."

"Bring him to me."

Ramses always fed his horses himself. Victory in Thebes and the Goddess Mut Is Satisfied, as the two superb mounts were called, were inseparable in peacetime as well as in battle. Both the mare and the stallion welcomed the king's caresses and would whinny proudly whenever he praised their courage. They were not in the least afraid of

Fighter, the Nubian lion, their stalwart companion in facing down thousands of Hittite soldiers.

The Ra division general bowed to the king.

"Your Majesty, our troops have been deployed as you ordered. Not one inhabitant can escape from Beirut. We're ready to attack."

"Intercept all the caravans that were heading into the city."

"Shall we plan on a siege?"

"Possibly. If Ahsha is still alive, we'll free him."

"That is our hope, Your Majesty, but can the life of just one man be worth it?"

"The life of just one man is sometimes very precious, General."

Ramses spent the remainder of the morning with the horses and his lion. Their calmness seemed like a favorable omen, and indeed, before the sun had reached its highest point, the aide-de-camp arrived with the message the king had been expecting.

"The Prince of Amurru requests an audience, Your Majesty."

Dressed in an ample robe of multicolored silk that concealed his paunch, wearing his favorite scent, attar of roses, Benteshina appeared relaxed and smiling.

"Hail, Son of Light! Hail . . ."

"I have no use for a traitor's flattery."

The Prince of Amurru remained unruffled. "Our meeting is intended to be constructive, Your Majesty."

"Selling out to the Hittites was a bad choice, Benteshina."

"There's still one point in my favor: I have Ahsha."

"Do you think the fact that he's in one of your dungeons will keep me from razing this city?"

"I'm certain of it. Aren't you known the world over for your sense of friendship? Besides, a pharaoh's disloyalty would offend your gods . . ."

"Is Ahsha still alive?"

"He is."

"I'll require proof."

"Your erstwhile secretary of state will make an appearance on top of the main palace tower, Your Majesty. Ahsha may be a bit worse for the wear after his stint in the dungeon, I admit. He hasn't been there long, though, only since an escape attempt."

"What are you asking in exchange for his freedom?"

"I want your pardon. When I release your friend to you, you'll forgive this slight transgression on my part. You'll issue a decree stipulating that your trust in me is unwavering. It's a great deal to ask, I know, but I need to maintain my position and my modest fortune. And of course, if you give in to the misguided notion of holding me prisoner, your friend will be executed."

There was a long silence before Ramses replied. "I need to think," he said calmly.

Benteshina had only one fear: that Ramses would put statecraft ahead of friendship. The Pharaoh's hesitation made him tremble.

"I need time to convince my generals," explained the king. "Do you think it's easy to give up a victory and pardon a criminal?"

Benteshina felt better. "Isn't 'criminal' an overstatement, Your Majesty? Regional alliances are a political balancing act. Since I'm trying to make amends, can't we forget the past? Egypt represents my future, and I promise to prove my loyalty. If I may, Your Majesty . . ."

"What now?"

"The people of Beirut would prefer to avoid a blockade. My subjects and I are used to a certain standard of living, which depends on the regular delivery of food and trade goods. You wouldn't want your friend Ahsha to starve, now would you?"

Ramses rose. The meeting had come to an end.

"Your Majesty, if I may . . . How long do you think you might need to decide?"

"A few days."

"I'm sure we'll be able to reach an agreement that will be to our mutual advantage."

Ramses sat meditating by the sea, his lion curled at his feet. Waves broke in front of him as dolphins leaped playfully in the distance. The wind blew hard from the south.

Setau sat down at the king's right hand.

"I've never cared for the sea," he remarked. "Not enough snakes in it. You can't even see to the other side."

"Benteshina is blackmailing me, Setau."

"And you can't decide between Ahsha and Egypt."

"Can you blame me?"

"I'd only blame you if your choice was easy. But I know which way you have to go, and I can't say I like it."

"Do you have a plan?"

"Why else would I interrupt the Lord of the Two Lands when he's deep in thought?"

"Make sure it's not dangerous for Ahsha."

"That's more than I can promise."
"Is there any chance that your plan will work?"
"A slight one."

Benteshina's majordomo did his best to satisfy his master's incessant requests. The Prince of Amurru drank heavily and demanded the finest of vintages. The palace wine cellars were regularly restocked, but it was hard to keep up with the ruler's constant entertaining. Thus the majordomo kept an eye out for his shipments.

When the Egyptian troops surrounded Beirut, he had been expecting a caravan with a hundred amphorae of Delta Red. The prince would settle for nothing less.

To the majordomo's delight, he saw a procession of wagons laden with wine jars pull into the palace courtyard. The blockade had been lifted at last! Benteshina must have struck a bargain with Ramses!

The majordomo rushed in front of the lead wagon and shouted his instructions to the driver: part of the shipment should go to the main cellars, part to a storeroom adjacent to the kitchens, the rest to a storage area near the banquet room.

The unloading began, to the sound of singing and laughter.

"Shall we have a sample?" the majordomo asked the lead driver. "Just for quality's sake, of course."

"Good idea."

The two men ducked into the wine cellar. The majordomo bent over a jar, already tasting its delicious contents. As he was caressing the rounded vessel, a violent blow to the back of the head knocked him cold.

The lead driver, an officer in Ramses' army, freed Setau and the other members of the commando from the jars. Armed with light, hollow-backed hatchets with solid lacing around three grips on the handle, they dispatched the Lebanese guards, who were unprepared for an inside attack.

As a few members of the strike force opened the main gate to the city, letting the Ra division infantry storm through, Setau headed straight for Benteshina's private quarters in the palace. When two guards attempted to bar the snake charmer's entry, he pulled a pair of squirming and angry vipers from a sack.

At the sight of the reptiles Setau was brandishing, Benteshina began to tremble.

"Let Ahsha go, or you're a dead man."

Benteshina didn't wait to be asked twice. Heaving like a winded ox, he led the way to the room where Ahsha was held prisoner.

At the sight of his friend, alive and well, Setau momentarily forgot himself. One hand fell open. The viper struck Benteshina like lightning.

NINE

Heading gracefully toward fifty, slender, with a fine, straight nose, almond eyes that were huge and sharp, and a determined chin, Queen Mother Tuya remained the guardian of tradition and the conscience of the Kingdom of Egypt. Supervising a sizable staff, she advised without giving orders, yet insisted on respect for the values that had made Egypt's monarchy great and lasting, forging a link between the visible world and the invisible one.

Official inscriptions styled her "The God's Mother, Who Bore Ramses, the Powerful Bull." In truth, Tuya saw herself as Seti's widow. Together they had built a strong and serene country that their son must keep happy and prosperous. Ramses had his father's energy and faith in his mission. Nothing mattered more to him than his people's well-being.

To save Egypt from an invasion, Ramses had been forced to wage war on the Hittites. Tuya had approved of her son's decision, for compromising with evil led only to disaster. Combating it was the only acceptable option.

But the conflict wore on, and Ramses took ever-greater risks. Tuya prayed that Seti's soul, in its new incarnation as a star, would protect his successor. In her right hand, she held a mirror with a papyrus-stalk handle. The hieroglyph for the plant signified blooming health. When such a mirror was placed in a tomb, it assured eternal youth for the occupant's soul. Tuya pointed the polished bronze disk toward the sky and asked her mirror the secret of the future.

"May I have a word?"

The Queen Mother turned around slowly. "Nefertari..."

The Great Royal Wife, in her long white dress with a red sash, was as lovely as the paintings of goddesses on the walls of eternal dwellings in the Valleys of the Kings and Queens.

"My dear, I sense that you bring me good news."

"Ramses has freed Ahsha and recaptured the province of Amurru. Beirut is back under Egyptian control."

The two women embraced.

"When will he be back?"

"I don't know," confessed Nefertari.

As they entered into conversation, Tuya sat down at her vanity table, massaging her face with a pomade made from honey, red natron, alabaster powder, donkey's milk, and fenugreek seed. This treatment smoothed wrinkles, firmed the skin, and brightened the complexion.

"Something's worrying you, Nefertari."

"I'm afraid that Ramses may still be pushing northward."

"Toward Kadesh, you mean?"

"Toward another trap that the Hittite emperor has laid for him. Letting him retake our protectorates with relative ease may well be part of Muwattali's plan."

The tribal elders were meeting in Aaron's spacious mudbrick home. They had sworn all of the Hebrews to silence about Moses' return to Egypt; the Pharaoh's police must be kept in the dark.

Moses was still popular. Many Hebrews hoped that he would once again help the brickmakers hold up their heads. Yet the elders' elected chairman, Libni, had his reservations.

"What brings you back here, Moses?" the old man asked gruffly.

"I saw a burning bush on the mountaintop—a bush that burned without being consumed by the fire."

"It was just your imagination."

"No, a sign from God."

"Have you lost your mind, man?"

"God called to me from that bush and He spoke to me."

A murmur swept through the assembly.

"What did He say?"

"God has heard the cries and moans of the children of Israel in their bondage."

"Come now, Moses. We're paid for the work we do here. It's not as if we were prisoners of war."

"The Hebrew people are not free to follow their conscience."

"Of course we are! You're not making sense."

"Yahweh told me: 'Once you've led the people out of Egypt, you will come to worship me on this mountain.'"

The elders clucked in consternation. "Out of Egypt!" one of them exclaimed. "What does that mean?"

"God has seen His people's misery in Egypt. He wishes to free us and lead us to a land of plenty."

It was more than Libni could take. "You've been away too long, Moses. The Hebrews have lived in this country for generations. You yourself were born here. Egypt has become our home."

"I've spent the last few years in Midian, working as a

shepherd. I married and had a son. I thought I'd settle in the desert, but God had other plans for me."

"You were hiding from the law."

"I killed an Egyptian, it's true, but only because he attacked a Hebrew."

"We can't blame Moses for what he did," one of the elders chimed in. "Now it's our turn to protect him."

The rest of the council voiced their assent.

"If you desire to live among us," declared Libni, "we agree to hide you. But you must give up this crazy plan of yours."

"I'll win you over, one at a time if I have to. It's the will of God."

"We have no intention of leaving Egypt," the youngest member of the council said firmly. "We have our houses and gardens. There's just been an increase in incentive pay for brickmakers. No one goes hungry here. Why would we want to go anywhere else?"

"Because I'm bound to lead you to the Promised Land."

"You're not our elected leader," protested Libni. "You can't tell us what to do."

"You'll end up doing as God commands."

"Are you challenging my authority?"

"I didn't mean to offend you, Libni, but I have no right to hide my intentions. What man could be vain enough to believe his will is stronger than the will of God?"

"If you're really His messenger, you'll have to prove it."

"There'll be plenty of proof. Don't worry."

Prone on a nest of cushions, Ahsha was letting the lovely Lotus work out the knots in his muscles. Slender as she was, her skilled hands were amazingly strong.

"How does your back feel now?"

"Better, but farther down the pain is still unbearable."

"You'll have to live with it!" thundered Setau, ducking into Ahsha's tent.

"Your wife is divine."

"I'm glad you remember she's mine."

"Setau! You can't be thinking . . ."

"Diplomats are all liars, and you're up there with the best of them. Get up now. Ramses is expecting us."

Ahsha turned to Lotus. "Can you help me?"

Setau yanked his friend upright. "You're good as new. No more massages, friend!"

The snake charmer handed the diplomat a kilt and shirt. "Now hurry. You know how the king hates to be kept waiting."

After naming a replacement for the Prince of Amurru (an Egyptian-educated Lebanese who might prove more loyal than Benteshina), Ramses had proceeded with a series of appointments throughout Phoenicia and Palestine. He was determined that the princes, mayors, and heads of villages should be natives and that each of them would swear an oath to uphold the alliance with Egypt. If they broke their word, the Egyptian army would react immediately. To this end, Ahsha had instituted a system of observation and reporting which he hoped would bring better results. The military presence would be de-emphasized and the network of informants well compensated. The head of Egyptian diplomacy believed in the virtues of espionage.

On a low table, Ramses had spread out a map of the region. His troops' efforts were paying off. Canaan, Amurru, and southern Syria once again formed a vast buffer zone between Egypt and Hatti.

It was Ramses' second victory over the Hittites. One more decision faced him, a decision vital to the future of the Twin Kingdoms.

Setau and Ahsha, somewhat more disheveled than usual, finally made their appearance in the spacious tent where the council of generals and officers had convened.

"Have all the enemy fortresses been dismantled?"

"Yes, Your Majesty," the Ra division general advised. "The last one, at Shalom, fell yesterday."

"*Shalom* means *peace*," Ahsha informed them. "That's the goal we've finally achieved here."

"Should we continue north," asked the king, "to take Kadesh and deal a fatal blow to the Hittites?"

"Speaking for your officers, that would be our preference," the general declared. "We'd like to top off our victory by flattening the barbarians."

"It will never work," assessed Ahsha. "Just as before, the Hittites have backed away from our advance. Their troops are intact and as they head north they're laying traps that could take a serious toll on our forces."

"With Ramses leading us, we can't lose!" said the general fervently.

"You don't know the territory," countered Ahsha. "The Hittites will have the advantage in the high plateaus, the gorges and forests of Anatolia. Even at Kadesh, our men would die by the thousands, and there's no guarantee we could take the fortress."

"Diplomats always preach caution. This time we're ready!"

"This meeting is dismissed," ordered Ramses. "You'll learn my decision at dawn tomorrow."

TEN

Thanks to Aaron's hospitality, Moses spent several untroubled weeks among the brickmakers. His wife and son were free to explore the bustling Egyptian capital. Once they felt at home in the Hebrew community, they branched out to mingle among the Delta natives, Middle Easterners, Palestinians, Nubians, and other members of Pi-Ramses' diverse population.

Moses, however, lived like a recluse, appearing in public only before the council of elders. He repeatedly asked to address them, airing the same unpopular views and incredible claims as the first time.

"Is your soul still tormented?" Aaron inquired.

"Not since I saw the burning bush."

"No one here believes that you talked with Yahweh."

"When a man knows his mission in life, he's no longer assailed by doubt. I see the path before me, Aaron."

"But you're the only one on it, Moses!"

"It only looks that way. In the end, the elders will see the light."

"The Hebrews have a good life here in Pi-Ramses. How will you feed them in the desert?"

"God will provide."

"You're a born leader, Moses, but you're on the wrong track. Change your name and the way you look, forget your outlandish plans, and reclaim your place among your people. You'll live to a ripe old age and be honored as a patriarch."

"That's not what fate has in store for me, Aaron."

"You're the master of your fate, are you not?"

"Not any longer."

"Why waste your life when prosperity is within your reach?"

Someone then pounded on the door to Aaron's house.

"Open up, police!"

Moses smiled.

"You see, Aaron, it's not up to me."

"Make a run for it!"

"There isn't another way out."

"I'll cover for you."

"No, Aaron."

Moses got up and answered the door himself, to find Serramanna gaping at him.

"So it wasn't a lie after all. You're back!" said the hulking Sard.

"Would you care to come in for a bite to eat?"

"A Hebrew turned you in, Moses. A brickmaker who was afraid that having you back in town might mean he'd lose his job. Come with me. I'm taking you to prison."

"Moses deserves to stand trial," Aaron intervened.

"He will."

"Unless you get rid of him before he appears in court."

Serramanna grabbed Aaron by the collar of his tunic.

"Are you calling me a murderer?"

"You have no right to manhandle me!"

Sobered, the Sard let go. "Of course not. But do you have the right to insult me?"

"If Moses is arrested, he'll be executed."

"The law applies to everyone, even Hebrews."

"Run, Moses! Go back to the desert," Aaron pleaded.

"You know I'm not going back without you."

"They'll never release you from prison."

"God will help me."

"Let's get going," said Serramanna impatiently. "Don't make me tie up your hands."

Hunched in a corner of his cell, Moses watched the sunlight darting between the bars. It sparkled through the thousands of suspended dust particles. It fell on the dirt floor trodden smooth by countless prisoners.

And Moses was filled with the light of the burning bush, the energy of Yahweh's sacred mountain. His past, his wife and his child, were no longer of consequence. All that counted from now on was the exodus, the Hebrew people's departure for the Promised Land.

A crazy notion for a man locked up in the main jail in Pi-Ramses, a man who would soon be sentenced to death for premeditated murder, or at the very least to a life of forced labor in a remote penal colony. Despite his trust in Yahweh, Moses felt the occasional glimmer of doubt. How would God go about freeing him and allow him to accomplish his mission?

The Hebrew was dozing off when the sound of distant shouting roused him. The noise grew louder by the minute until it was deafening. The entire city seemed to be in an uproar.

Ramses the Great had returned.

He wasn't expected for several months, but here he was, as big as life in his chariot behind Victory in Thebes and the Goddess Mut Is Satisfied, festooned in their blue-tipped red plumes. To the right of the chariot loped Fighter, the Nubian lion, watching the curious herd of onlookers strain forward. Ramses was resplendent in his blue headdress, the golden cobra of the uraeus on his forehead, clad in vestments with blue-green wings to place him under the protection of Isis, the falcon goddess.

The infantry sang with one voice the song that was already a tradition: "Ramses' arm is strong, his heart is valiant. He is a peerless archer, a wall protecting his soldiers, a flame burning his enemies." He was the chosen son of the divine light. He was the falcon of soaring victories.

Generals, cavalry and infantry officers, army scribes, and rank-and-file soldiers had all donned parade dress to march behind the standard-bearers. As the crowds cheered, the men dreamed of leave and spending their combat pay. The best part of military life was returning home, especially in triumph.

Usually the gardeners decked the main avenue out with flowers, all the way to the temple of Ptah, the god of creation through the Word, and Sekhmet, the terrifying lion goddess with the power to cure or kill. This time they had been caught unawares. The palace chefs sprang into action, grilling geese, sides of beef, slabs of pork, heaping baskets with dried fish, fresh fruits and vegetables. Jars of beer and wine were hustled out of the cellars. Bakers made cakes as fast as they could. Noblemen shook out their finest garments; servant girls perfumed their mistresses' hair.

At the end of the line marched several hundred prisoners from Canaan, Palestine, Syria, and other eastern lands. Some had their hands trussed behind their backs. Others walked unfettered, women and children at their sides. Their meager possessions had been bundled on the backs of donkeys. All would be registered and assigned to work on temple estates or construction sites. After serving the term of their captivity, they could either become full members of Egyptian society or else return to their own country.

Was this a lasting peace or simply a truce? Had Pharaoh finally crushed the Hittites, or was he only back to regroup his forces? The least informed had the most to say on the subject: the gossip ran that Muwattali was dead, Kadesh had fallen, the Hittite capital was in ruins. No one could wait for the awards ceremony when Ramses and Nefertari would dispense gifts of gold from their window of appearance.

To everyone's surprise, Ramses drove straight by the palace and headed for the temple of Sekhmet. Only he had noticed the cloud that appeared in the sky, growing rapidly larger and darker. The horses were nervous, the lion growled.

A storm was brewing.

The atmosphere of joy was replaced with fear. If Sekhmet unleashed the wrath of the heavens, wasn't that a sign that war still loomed and Ramses must once again march off to battle?

The soldiers stopped singing.

All present were keenly aware that Pharaoh was engaged in a new combat. He must appease Sekhmet and keep her from raining plagues and suffering on Egypt.

Ramses dismounted, patted his horses and his lion on the head, then prayed at the entrance to the temple. The cloud had broken into ten clouds, a hundred clouds. The darkening sky was beginning to blot out the sun.

Shaking off the fatigue of the journey, forgetting the prospect of celebrations, the monarch steeled himself for an encounter with the terrible goddess. Only he was able to quell her anger.

Ramses pushed open the huge gilded doors and entered the sanctuary, where he laid down his crown of blue. Then he slowly made his way between the columns of the first hall, went through the door to the inner sanctum, then made for the *naos,* the holiest part of the temple.

That was when he saw her, aglow in the semi-darkness.

Her long white robe shone like the sun. The scent of her ritual wig was enchanting. Her noble stance was the equal of any temple carving.

Nefertari's voice rose, smooth as honey. She said the words of worship and appeasement that had been used since the dawn of civilization to turn the awful Sekhmet into her more benign incarnation. Ramses raised his hands, palms upward, toward the statue of the lion-headed woman, and read the magic words on the temple walls.

When the litany was finished, the queen, who had worked her own magic, presented the king with the red crown of lower Egypt, the white crown of upper Egypt, and the scepter of power.

In his twin crowns, the scepter in his right hand, Ramses

bowed to acknowledge the positive energy now present within the statue.

When the royal couple emerged from the temple of Sekhmet, sunlight was flooding the Turquoise City. The storm had blown over.

ELEVEN

As soon as the awards ceremony was finished and all the Gold of Valor handed out, Ramses went to visit Homer, the Greek bard who had decided to end his days in Egypt, composing his epics in peace. His comfortable villa near the royal palace was set in a garden, the centerpiece of which was a lemon tree. The old poet feasted his near-blind eyes on it and spent many hours there stroking his long white beard and fashioning verses. Ramses found him, as usual, smoking sage leaves tamped into a pipe bowl made out of an oversize snail shell, and drinking wine flavored with anise and coriander.

The poet rose and leaned on a gnarled walking stick.

"Don't get up, Homer."

"When the Pharaoh of Egypt isn't given a proper greeting, it will be the end of civilization."

The two men settled into garden chairs.

"Does this passage of mine mean anything to you, Your Majesty? *Fight boldly or hold yourself back, the result is similar. The same honor goes to the coward as to the valiant. Is it for naught that my heart has braved so many dangers? Is it for naught that I have risked my life in so many battles?*'"

"No, Homer, it doesn't."

"Then you've come home a victor again."

"The Hittites have been pushed back within their traditional boundaries. Egypt won't be invaded."

"Let's celebrate, Your Majesty. I've just gotten in some remarkable wine."

Homer's cook brought out a narrow-necked Cretan wine jar, pouring out a thin stream of a special vintage mixed with sea water (bottled on the night of the summer solstice, with the wind from the north) and aged for three years.

"My account of the battle of Kadesh is finished," Homer revealed. "Your secretary, Ahmeni, took it down for me and gave the text to the stone carvers."

"It will be written on the temple walls to proclaim the victory of order over chaos."

"Alas, Your Majesty, it's a never-ending battle, with chaos always trying to win the upper hand."

"That's why pharaonic rule was instituted. It's the main support of the law of Ma'at."

"Then by all means do everything in your power to keep it going. I intend to live a long time yet in your fair land."

Hector, Homer's black and white cat, jumped in the poet's lap and bared its claws against his tunic. "As far as your Pi-Ramses is from the Hittite capital, is it far enough to stay out of harm's way?"

"As long as the breath of life is within me, I intend to make sure of that."

"Yes, but how many times will you have to go to war?"

Outside Homer's dwelling, Ramses found Ahmeni waiting for him. Thinner and paler than usual, his hair ever sparser, the king's private secretary looked fragile to the point of breaking. A forgotten reed brush was tucked behind his ear.

"I have an urgent matter to discuss with you, Your Majesty."

"A problem you couldn't solve while I was away?"

"Nothing like that."

"May I have a few minutes with my family first?"

"Protocol dictates a certain number of ceremonies and audiences beforehand. I won't insist on that, but something important has come up." He lowered his voice to a whisper. *"He's back."*

"Do you mean . . ."

"Yes, Moses."

"Here in Pi-Ramses?"

"You can't fault Serramanna for arresting him. Leaving Moses at liberty would have been a miscarriage of justice."

"You've put him in prison?"

"We had to."

"Bring him to me immediately."

"Impossible, Your Majesty. Pharaoh must not intervene in a criminal case, even when a friend is involved."

"We have proof of his innocence!"

"It's indispensable to follow the normal procedures. Unless Pharaoh serves as the prime respecter of Ma'at and of justice, the country will fall apart."

"You're a true friend, Ahmeni."

Young Kha was copying out a famous text that prospective scribes had memorized for generations:

> *The learned scribes of the early days have made heirs for themselves from the works that they have composed. The writing palette is their loving son. Their books are their pyramids, the reed pen their child, the stone covered with hieroglyphs their wife. Monuments disappear, sand buries plaques with proclamations, but the wise words that they have written will preserve the name of scribes forever. Be a scribe, and carve this thought into your heart: a book is more useful than the most solid wall. It will serve as your temple when you have perished. Your book will keep your name on the lips of men. It will prove more solid than a well-built house.*

Kha was not in complete agreement with the author of these maxims. Writing did, of course, survive through the generations, but so did tombs and temples that were the work of master builders. The author of this passage had exaggerated the importance of his profession. Kha vowed that he would become both a scribe and a builder, so as not to limit his horizons.

Since the day when his father had forced him to confront death in the guise of a cobra, Ramses' eldest son had matured a great deal, leaving childish games behind for good. What fun was a wooden horse on wheels compared to the fascinating mathematical problem he had found in the wonderful papyrus that Nefertari had given him? The scribe Ahmes likened the circle to a square with one side representing ⅚ of its diameter, yielding the geometric value of 3.14. As soon as he was able, Kha planned to study how Egypt's great monuments were engineered and learn the secrets of the great builders.

"May I interrupt Your Highness's thoughts for a moment?" came the voice of Meba, the undersecretary of state.

The boy did not look up.

"If you must."

For some time, the old diplomat had been paying regular calls on the prince. Kha disliked the man's haughtiness and worldly ways, yet appreciated his culture and knowledge of literature.

"Still at work, Your Highness?"

"What better pastime could there be?"

"A serious comment from one so young! But I can't say I disagree with you. As a scribe and prince of the blood, you'll be issuing orders to dozens of servants. Your hands will never touch a pick or plow. You'll be exempt from manual labor—no heavy lifting for you! You'll live in a splendid mansion with a stable full of beautiful horses. You'll have fresh garments to wear every day, made of the finest linen. A comfortable sedan chair will take you around, and your father will dote on you."

"Plenty of lazy upper-class scribes do live that way, Meba. But I want to be able to read scholarly texts, help write prayers for special occasions, and be allowed to carry offerings in processions."

"Modest ambitions for a prince, young man."

"I wouldn't say so, Meba. I'll have to work awfully hard."

"Shouldn't Ramses' eldest son be aiming for a somewhat more prominent role in the government?"

"Hieroglyphs are my guide. Have they ever lied?"

Meba was unnerved by the twelve-year-old's answers. It was like having a conversation with an experienced scribe, self-possessed and immune to flattery.

"There's more to life than work and discipline."

"It's the life I aspire to, Meba. Is there anything wrong with that?"

"No, nothing at all."

"You have an important job yourself, Meba. Does it leave you much time to enjoy yourself?"

The diplomat avoided Kha's direct gaze.

"I am quite busy, since Egypt's international policy requires a certain expertise."

"Isn't my father the one who makes the decisions?"

"Certainly, but my staff and I do all we can to facilitate the process."

"I'd like to know exactly what you do."

"It's quite complex, I'm not sure whether . . ."

"I'll make every effort to understand."

Meritamon pranced in, much to the diplomat's relief. "Are you playing with my big brother?" she inquired.

"No, I came to bring him a present."

Kha looked up, his interest piqued. "What is it, Meba?"

"A case for your brushes, Your Highness."

Meba produced a pretty gilded box in the shape of a column. Inside were a dozen reed brushes of various sizes.

"Oh, thank you!" exclaimed the prince, setting the well-worn brush he'd been using down on a stool.

"Can I see?" asked Meritamon.

"Yes, but be careful," Kha said gravely.

"Can I write with one of them?"

"If you pay close attention and try not to make mistakes."

Kha gave his sister a scrap of used papyrus and a new

brush. She dipped the tip in the ink under the prince's watchful eye, then slowly began forming hieroglyphs.

Caught up in the task, the two youngsters forgot all about Meba. It was precisely the moment he'd been waiting for.

He palmed Kha's old brush and stole out of the room.

TWELVE

All night, Iset had dreamed of her first summer with Ramses, the wild nights spent in a reed hut on the edge of Memphis. They had met in secret, without a thought for the future, living for the moment in a blur of desire.

Iset had never had any wish to become Queen of Egypt. The responsibility would crush her. Only Nefertari was equal to the role. But how could she forget Ramses, or the love that still burned in her heart for him? When he was off waging war, she worried terribly. Her spirits drooped, she neglected her appearance, wore any old garments, went without sandals or makeup.

As soon as he came back, the clouds lifted. And Iset's newfound beauty would have moved the most jaded seducer if he happened upon her, anxious and trembling, in the hall leading from Ramses' office to his private quarters. When the Pharaoh emerged she would speak to him. No, no, she wouldn't dare.

If she began getting on Ramses' nerves, he'd send her away from the capital. Her punishment would be to never see him. Could there be anything worse?

When the king appeared in the hallway, Iset felt weak in the knees. It was impossible to run away. She couldn't take her eyes off Ramses, his godlike power and presence.

"What are you doing there, Iset?"

"I wanted to ask . . . have you seen our new son yet?"

"The nursemaid showed him off to me. A beautiful baby, our Merenptah."

"I'll love him as much as Kha."

"I know you will."

"Only let me be the plot of land that you garden, the pond where you bathe . . . Do you wish to have other sons, Ramses?"

"I've provided for that. I'm already choosing my royal children."

"Ask of me what you will . . . I belong to you, body and soul."

"You're wrong, Iset. Long ago you taught me that no human being can belong to another."

"But I'm yours, and you hold me in your hands like a fledgling fallen from the nest. Without your warmth to protect me, I can't survive."

"I love Nefertari, Iset."

"Nefertari is a queen; I'm only a woman. Couldn't you love me with a different kind of love?"

"With her, I'm building a world. Only the Great Royal Wife can share in this secret."

"Will you let me stay here in the palace?"

Iset's voice had grown very faint, for her future hung on Ramses' answer.

"You'll stay here to bring up Kha, Merenptah, and my daughter, Meritamon."

The Cretan was one of Serramanna's mercenaries. His current assignment was investigating settlements near Akhenaton's abandoned capital in middle Egypt. Like his boss, he was a former pirate who enjoyed the standard of living Egypt offered. While he missed the sea, navigating the Nile in quick little boats was some consolation. He liked to try to outwit the river. Even an experienced sailor was bound to respect the current, the sandbanks lurking just beneath the surface, and the herds of angry hippos on the banks.

The Cretan had shown the portrait of the murdered blond woman to hundreds of villagers, without success. To tell the truth, he was only going through the motions, since the girl was most probably from Pi-Ramses or Memphis. Serramanna had sent his men into every province, searching for some essential new piece of evidence. But luck hadn't smiled on the Cretan. All he found was a peaceful region where life was in tune with the seasons. He wouldn't be the one to earn the handsome bonus the Sard was offering. Still, he made sure to be thorough, especially since that meant spending long hours asking question in wayside taverns. Two or three more days of this and he'd head back to Pi-Ramses, empty-handed but grateful for the free vacation.

From his strategic table, the Cretan observed the barmaid serving beer. She laughed and flirted openly with the customers. He decided to take a chance.

"I like your looks," he said, grabbing the sleeve of her tunic.

"And who would you be?"

"A real man."

"That's what they all say!" she countered with a saucy laugh.

"I can prove it."

"I can imagine how."

"I'll bet you can't."

"Men are all talk."

"Some are all action."

The barmaid ran a finger over her lips. "Be careful what you say. I might take you up on it, and I have a big appetite."

"I have a big one, too."

"That's what you think."

"Would you like me to show you?"

"What kind of girl do you think I am?"

"I think you're pretty. You don't mind a man who's forward."

"Where are you from?" she asked, her voice growing husky.

"The island of Crete."

"And what kind of man are you?"

"I give as good as I get."

They arranged to meet in a barn in the middle of the night. Dispensing with the preliminaries, they coupled hungrily, tiring only after several rounds. Afterward they lay contentedly side by side in the straw.

"You remind me of someone," said the Cretan. "Your face makes me think of a girl I've been trying to find."

"What girl?"

He showed her the picture of the blond victim.

"I've seen her before," said the barmaid.

"Does she live around here?"

"She was staying in the little village on the edge of the ghost town, out near the desert. I used to see her in the marketplace—but that was months ago."

"What's her name?"

"I don't know. I never spoke to her."

"Did she live by herself?"

"No, there was a much older man hanging around her, some kind of sorcerer who still believed in the heretic pharaoh's lies. Everyone left him alone."

Unlike most of the neighboring villages, this one looked shabby. Run-down houses, flaking plaster, peeling paint, overgrown gardens . . . who'd want to live here? The Cretan wandered down the main street strewn with waste that goats were eating.

A wooden shutter banged.

A little girl took off down the street, clutching a rag doll. When she stumbled, the Cretan caught her by the wrist.

"Where does the magician live?"

The child struggled.

"Answer or I'll take your doll."

She pointed toward a squat dwelling with wooden bars on the windows and its door closed. Releasing the girl, the Cretan ran toward the dilapidated house and broke down the door with his shoulder.

It was dark inside the one square room with a dirt floor. On a palm-frond bed, an old man lay dying.

"Police," the Cretan announced. "Don't worry, I won't hurt you."

"What do you want?" the man groaned.

"Tell me who this young woman is," he said, displaying the portrait.

"Lita . . . my little Lita. She thought she was descended from Akhenaton. The man took her away."

"What man?"

"A stranger . . . a foreign sorcerer who stole Lita's soul."

"What's his name?"

"He's come back here. He's hiding out in the tombs. In the tombs, I'm sure of it," the old man said feebly.

His head rolled to one side. He was still breathing, but he could no longer talk.

The Cretan was afraid.

The dark mouths of the abandoned tombs looked like the jaws of hell. To take refuge here, you'd have to be something of a demon yourself. The old man could have been lying, but the Cretan felt it was his duty to check out the lead. With a little luck, he'd lay his hands on Lita's murderer, haul him back to Pi-Ramses, and collect the bonus.

Despite this welcome prospect, the mercenary felt uneasy. He'd rather fight in the open air, clobber a bunch of pirates out on deck . . . these tombs gave him the creeps, but he pressed forward.

After climbing up a steep slope, he entered the first of the burial places. It had a fairly high ceiling and wall paintings that paid tribute to Akhenaton and his wife, Nefertiti. He slowly made his way to the very back, finding neither a mummy nor any trace of human presence. No demons jumped out at him.

Relieved, the Cretan explored a second tomb, as disappointing as the first. The porous rock was crumbling; the carvings would never withstand the centuries. Bats flapped around him, their sleep disturbed.

The old man in the village must have been delirious. Still, Serramanna's deputy took care to visit two or three more large tombs before he left the abandoned site.

Everything here was good and dead.

He followed the path along the cliff overlooking the plain where the City of the Horizon of Aton had stood. His last stop was the tomb of Merire, high priest of Aton. The carvings were meticulous. The Cretan admired one of the royal couple lit by the rays of the solar orb.

At his back came the faint sound of footsteps.

Before the Cretan had time to turn around, the sorcerer Ofir had slit his throat.

THIRTEEN

Meba had squeezed his eyes shut. When he opened them again, the Cretan's dead body lay on the ground.

"You shouldn't have, Ofir, you shouldn't have . . ."

"Stop whining, Meba."

"But you've just killed a man!"

"And you're an accessory to murder."

Ofir's expression was so menacing that the diplomat backed deeper into the tomb. He wanted to flee those incredibly cruel eyes pursuing him into the shadows.

"I know who this snoop is," announced Shaanar. "One of Serramanna's henchmen."

"A paid investigator," mused Ofir. "The Sard must be trying to find out who Lita was. The fact that his sleuth made it this far means he's launched an intensive effort."

"We're no longer safe even in this wretched place," concluded Shaanar.

"Let's not be alarmist. This is one detective that will never talk."

"Even so, he found us. Serramanna will do the same."

"Only one person could have told him where we're hiding: Lita's guardian, the old fool the villagers consider their wise man. He's on his deathbed, but he still managed to betray us. I'll take care of him as soon as it's dark out."

Meba felt obliged to protest. "You're not going to commit another murder!"

"Come out here where I can see you," snarled Ofir.

Meba stalled.

"Hurry up."

The diplomat came forward, a nervous tic deforming his mouth.

"Don't touch me, Ofir!"

"You're our ally and my subordinate. Don't forget that."

"Of course not, but these murders . . ."

"This isn't your comfortable office at the State Department. You belong to a spy network with the mission of undermining Ramses, if not overthrowing him, and allowing the Hittites to take over Egypt. Do you think diplomatic posturing will get us there? One day it will be your turn to eliminate someone who threatens your security."

"I'm a government official and I . . ."

"You're an accomplice in the murder of this detective, Meba, whether you like it or not."

The diplomat's gaze once again fell on the Cretan's lifeless body.

"I never thought it would come to this."

"Now you know where we stand."

"As you were saying before we were so rudely interrupted, Meba," Shaanar reminded him, "you have something to report?"

"Why else would I risk coming to this godforsaken place? I came to say that my mission is accomplished, of course."

The sorcerer's voice was silken. "Nice work, friend. We're proud of you."

"I keep my promises. Don't forget yours."

"The future government won't overlook your talents. Now show us your treasure, Meba."

The diplomat exhibited Kha's reed brush. "The prince used it to write with."

"Excellent," approved Ofir. "Really excellent."

"What do you plan to do with it?"

"We can use this personal possession to capture Kha's energy and turn it against him."

"He's only a child!"

"Kha is Ramses' eldest son."

"No, Ofir, not a child . . ."

"You've chosen sides, Meba. There's no turning back." The sorcerer held out his hand.

"Give me the brush, Meba."

The diplomat's reluctance amused Shaanar. He hated the

craven fool so much that he was quite prepared to strangle him with his own hands.

Meba slowly relinquished the brush.

"Is it really necessary to involve such a young boy?"

"Go back to Pi-Ramses," ordered Ofir. "And don't come back here again."

"Will you be staying long?"

"Long enough to work my spell."

"What then?"

"Don't be too curious, Meba. I'll be in touch with you."

"My position in the capital may become untenable."

"Keep your head and everything will be fine."

"What should I be doing?"

"Carry on as usual. My instructions will arrive when the time comes."

The diplomat made as if to leave the tomb, then turned around.

"Think it over, Ofir. Ramses won't stand for anyone laying a hand on his son."

"Be on your way, Meba."

From the tomb's entrance, Ofir and Shaanar watched their associate head down the path and mount his horse, concealed behind the ruins of a mansion.

"He's losing his nerve," Shaanar observed. "Old Meba is like a rat caught in a trap. Why not get rid of him right away?"

"As long as Meba is in an official position, he's useful to us."

"What if he decides to reveal our whereabouts?"

"Do you suppose I haven't thought of that?"

Since Ramses' return, Nefertari had spent almost no time alone with her husband. Ahmeni, the vizier, the cabinet members and high priests had besieged the king's office, and the queen herself was continuing to respond to requests from scribes, workshop foremen, tax collectors, and other officials involved with the running of her household.

She often regretted not following her girlhood dream of becoming a temple musician. She could have lived quietly, removed from the distractions of everyday life. But the Queen of Egypt had no right to such a refuge, and must fulfill her duties regardless of fatigue and the stress of responsibility.

With Tuya's constant support, Nefertari had learned the art of governing. During the seven years of his reign, Ramses had spent many months abroad and on the battle-field. The young queen had needed to draw on unsuspected emotional reserves to bear the weight of the crown, to continue celebrating the rituals that maintained the indispensable link between god and man.

Having virtually no time to think of herself did not displease Nefertari. There were not enough hours in the day; that was as it should be. The one drawback was that she was often apart from Kha and Meritamon, losing the precious chance to watch them grow up. Although Kha and Merenptah were Iset the Fair's sons and not her own, she loved them as much as her daughter, Meritamon. Ramses had done right in asking Iset to supervise the three children's upbringing. The two women were neither rivals nor friends. Unable to bear more children, Nefertari had pleaded with her husband to again be intimate with Iset the Fair, who could provide him with heirs. But once Iset was pregnant, he'd decided not to continue their relationship, planning instead to adopt an unlimited number of royal children to symbolize the royal couple's fertility.

The love the queen shared with Ramses went far beyond the physical and its pleasures. She loved him for what he was, what he stood for. They were two halves of the same being. Their souls were united even when they were apart.

Nefertari wearily put herself in her servants' capable hands for a manicure and pedicure. After a long working day, it was a pleasure to tend to her personal grooming. She must always appear perfectly serene, no matter what cares weighed upon her.

The crowning moment was her evening shower. Two servants poured warm scented water over the queen's naked body. Then she stretched out on a bed of heated tiles for a long massage with a pomade of incense, turpentine, and lemon oil to relax her muscles for a good night's sleep.

Nefertari contemplated the glitches for which she was responsible, the errors she had committed, her pointless fits of temper. She sought the proper response in each situation, for right actions strengthened the law of Ma'at in Egypt and kept chaos at bay.

Suddenly the hands on her back changed their rhythm, becoming bolder.

"Ramses . . ."

"You don't mind if I take over, do you?"

"I need to think."

She turned very slowly to meet his adoring gaze.

"I thought that you had some evening meeting with Ahmeni and the granary administrators from all over the country."

"No, darling. Tonight belongs to us."

She undid the waistband of Ramses' kilt.

"What's your secret, Nefertari? Sometimes I start to think that your beauty is not of this world."

"Is our love?"

They embraced on the steaming tiles. Their scents mingled, their lips met, and off they rode on a wave of desire.

Ramses wrapped Nefertari in a long shawl. Spread out, it bore the wings of the goddess Isis, constantly moving, producing the breath of life.

"It's amazing!"

"I commissioned it from the weavers' workshop in Sais. I don't want you ever to be cold again."

She clung to the king.

"I pray that from now on we'll never part."

FOURTEEN

Lit by three tall, barred windows, Ramses' office was stark, in the style of his father, Seti's: bare white walls; one large table; a straight-backed armchair for the king and straw-seated chairs for visitors; a cabinet for papyri containing magical texts protecting the royal person; a map of the Near East; and a statue of the late Pharaoh, his eternal gaze watching over his son at work.

Near his writing tools the king kept two forked acacia branches tightly bound at one end with linen string. The divining rod Seti had passed on to him had already proved useful on a number of occasions.

"When is Moses' trial?" the monarch inquired of Ahmeni.

"In a couple of weeks."

The frail-looking scribe had, as usual, arrived carrying his weight in documents. Weak as his back might be, he insisted on personally transporting confidential files.

"Has Moses been informed?"

"Of course."

"And what was his reaction?"

"He seems serene."

"Have you told him that we can prove it was self-defense?"

"I hinted that his case wasn't hopeless."

"Why not come right out with it?"

"Because no one can predict the outcome of a trial, not even you."

"But he has a legitimate defense!"

"Moses killed a man, Ramses. What's more, that man was your sister Dolora's husband."

"I'll personally testify what I thought of the wretch."

"No, Your Majesty. As Ma'at's representative on earth, Pharaoh must remain impartial and exert no influence over any judicial proceeding."

"Do you think I don't know that?"

"Would I be your friend if I didn't help you restrain your nature?"

"You have a hard job, Ahmeni."

"And I'm hardheaded enough to do it."

"Moses returned to Egypt of his own free will. That must be a point in his favor."

"Yes, but it doesn't excuse what he's done."

"Must you argue against him?"

"Moses is my friend, too. I plan to present our case in his defense. But will it convince the vizier and the judges?"

"Moses was always popular with his peers in the government. They'll understand the circumstances that led him to kill Sary."

"Let's hope so, Your Majesty."

Though he'd spent a pleasant night with two very willing and able female companions, Serramanna was in a foul mood. He dismissed the pair of them before breakfast, "the rinsing of the mouth," as the Egyptians called it.

It nagged at him that the mysterious murder victim still hadn't been identified, despite his best efforts.

The Sard had believed that his investigators, armed with the blond woman's portrait, would quickly turn up new leads. But no one seemed to have seen her about in Pi-Ramses, Memphis, or Thebes. There was only one possible conclusion: she had been kept in strict seclusion.

He was sure that one person knew a great deal more than she told: Dolora, Ramses' sister. Unfortunately, Serramanna was limited in the techniques he could use to interrogate her. The penitent Dolora had ingratiated herself with the royal family again, at least to some extent.

Exasperated, the Sard consulted the reports his men had submitted upon their return to the capital. Investigations in Elephantine, El-Kab, Edfu, towns in the Delta—nothing. One detail caught his attention, however, as he checked the reports against the list of assignments. There was nothing from the Cretan he'd sent to middle Egypt. Yet the man was an old pirate like himself, money-hungry and well aware of the penalty for not completing a job.

Without shaving, he threw on his clothes and ran to see Ahmeni. The twenty-odd members of the scribe's staff hadn't shown up yet, but Ramses' private secretary and sandal-bearer was already hard at work after a meal of barley porridge, figs, and dried fish. No matter how much he ate, Ahmeni stayed thin as a reed.

"A problem, Serramanna?"

"A missing report."

"What's so unusual about that?"

"It's one of my mercenaries, a Cretan. A stickler for completing his assignments."

"Where did you send this Cretan?"

"To middle Egypt, let's see, the province of El-Bersha. Specifically, the area around Akhenaton's abandoned capital."

"The middle of nowhere, in other words."

"Yes. You've taught me how to be thorough."

Ahmeni smiled. The two men hadn't begun as friends, but since their reconciliation they had developed a genuine appreciation for each other.

"Perhaps something held him up."

"The Cretan should have made it back here a week ago or more."

"Frankly, it doesn't seem like anything major."

"My instincts tell me it's serious."

"Why talk to me about it? You have the authority to follow up on the matter."

"Because nothing adds up, Ahmeni."

"Go on."

"The vanishing sorcerer, Shaanar's missing corpse, the blond girl nobody can identify . . . I tell you, I'm worried."

"Ramses is Pharaoh and well in control of the situation."

"We're not at peace, as far as I know. The Hittites still want to conquer Egypt."

"So you think the Hittite spy network is still operating in some form?"

"To me it feels like the calm before the storm. And my intuition rarely fails me."

"What are you suggesting?"

"I'm leaving for Akhenaton's ghost town. Take care of the Pharaoh while I'm gone."

Dolora, Ramses' older sister, was assailed by doubts. The tall brunette had returned to a life of aristocratic ease, an endless round of parties and palace obligations. She exchanged small talk with shallow society matrons while a flock of pathetic ladies' men, young and old, bored her silly with their attentions.

Since her conversion to the belief in Aton as the sole True God, Dolora was obsessed. She wanted to spread the truth throughout Egypt, banishing false idols and their misguided worshipers. Here in Pi-Ramses, everyone she met seemed to be blindly content with the status quo.

Her chambermaid, a dark young woman with merry eyes, changed the bed and swept the room.

"Not feeling well, Your Highness?"

"It isn't easy being a princess."

"Nice clothes, beautiful gardens, plenty of handsome men . . . I might trade places with you."

"Are you unhappy with your life?"

"Oh, no! I have a good husband, two healthy children,

and we make a decent living. We've almost finished building our new house."

Dolora asked what she always wanted to, but rarely dared.

"What about God? Is that something you think about?"

"God is everywhere, Your Highness. It's enough to worship our deities and contemplate nature."

Dolora let the subject drop. Ofir was right: their religion would have to be imposed by force. It was no good waiting for the people to convert on their own. Once they were properly indoctrinated, they would renounce their erroneous beliefs.

"Your Highness . . . have you heard the latest?"

The chambermaid's sparkling eyes showed that she was simply bursting to talk. Dolora sensed a chance to pick up some interesting gossip.

"They say you plan to remarry and all the noblemen are fighting for your hand."

"Don't believe everything you hear."

"That's too bad. You've been grieving long enough. I don't think it's right for a woman like you to be alone."

"I'm happy just as I am."

"You seem so sad sometimes. I guess it's normal. You must think about your poor husband. It's awful that he was murdered. Do you ever wonder what happened to him in the Judgment Hall of the Dead? With all due respect, Your Highness, I hear that he wasn't exactly blameless."

"I'm afraid you're right," she sighed.

"Then why not get on with your life?"

"I have no wish to remarry."

"Well, better days ahead, Your Highness. Especially if your husband's murderer is convicted!"

"What are you talking about?"

"Moses is going on trial soon."

"Moses—I thought he was still a fugitive!"

"It's supposed to be a secret, but my husband is friends with the warden of the main prison. They have the Hebrew locked up there. They'll ask for the death penalty!"

"Is he allowed to have visitors?"

"No, they're keeping him in solitary because the charges against him are so serious. You'll surely be asked to testify. Then you can get revenge!"

Moses, back in Egypt! Moses, who worshiped the One True God! It had to be a sign, Dolora thought. A sign from heaven.

FIFTEEN

The trial was held in the main courtroom, with the vizier presiding as Ma'at's representative. Dressed in a starched and heavy robe, his only ornament was a heart, the symbol of human conscience, to be weighed on the scales in the Judgment Hall of the Dead.

Before the hearing, the vizier had met Ramses in the temple of Ptah to renew the Pharaoh's oath to uphold justice. Refraining from mentioning any particulars, the king had confirmed his commitment to an impartial legal process.

The courtroom was full. This was one trial no member of the court would want to miss.

A few Hebrew elders were among the spectators. Opinion was sharply divided. Some remained convinced of Moses' guilt, while others believed he would be exonerated. They were all acquainted with the defendant's strong personality; no one doubted that he had known what he was doing.

The vizier opened the hearing with an invocation to Ma'at, the divine law that would outlive the human race. Forty-two strips of leather were lined up on the courtroom floor, a reminder that the verdict would be valid in all of Egypt's forty-two provinces.

Two soldiers accompanied Moses into the courtroom. All eyes were riveted on the Hebrew. His face was weathered and bearded, his stature impressive. Ramses' former chief of construction appeared surprisingly calm. The guards showed him to a seat that faced the vizier.

On either side of the attorney general sat the fourteen-member jury, including a surveyor, a priestess of the goddess Sekhmet, a doctor, a carpenter, a housewife and mother, a farmworker, a Treasury scribe, a noblewoman, a builder, a woman weaver, the general of the Ra division, a stone carver, a scribe attached to the granaries, and a sailor.

"Is your name Moses?" the judge began.

"It is."

"Do you have cause to disqualify any member of this jury? Look at them and take time to think."

"I trust in your country's justice."

"Isn't it your country, too?"

"I was born here, but I'm a Hebrew."

"You're an Egyptian citizen, and will be tried as such."

"Would the proceedings and the verdict be different if I were a foreigner?"

"Of course not."

"What does it matter, then?"

"That's for the court to decide. Are you ashamed of being Egyptian?"

"That's for the court to decide, as you just said."

"You stand accused of killing a foreman named Sary, then fleeing the law. Do you acknowledge these facts?"

"I do, but they require an explanation."

"That's the point of this trial. Do you consider the charges against you to be incorrect?"

"No."

"You will therefore understand that in keeping with the law I must seek the death penalty in this case."

A murmur ran through the crowd. Moses was stone-faced, as if these dreadful words had nothing to do with him.

"Given the grave nature of the accusations," the vizier continued, "I am placing no limits on the length of this trial. The defendant will have all the time he needs to present his side of the case. I demand absolute silence and will suspend proceedings if there is the least disorder in the court. The offenders will be held in contempt and liable for heavy penalties."

The judge then turned to face Moses.

"At the time of the incident, what was your occupation?"

"I was a government official, in charge of construction at Pi-Ramses. One of my duties was supervising the Hebrew brickmakers."

"By all accounts, your performance was exemplary. You were a personal friend of the Pharaoh's, were you not?"

"Yes, I was."

"You graduated from the royal academy in Memphis, were appointed junior administrator with the harem at Merur, served as supply officer and surveyor in the late Pharaoh Seti's army, directed his renovations at Luxor, then went on to supervise the construction of Pi-Ramses. In short, you were a rising star. The victim, Sary, was exactly the opposite. He had been Ramses' private tutor, rose to become director of the royal academy, but later emerged from exile to become a construction foreman, working with the Hebrew brickmakers. Were you informed of the reasons for his demotion?"

"I had my opinion."

"Please state it for the record."

"Sary was an evil man, ambitious and greedy. It was Fate that struck him through my hand."

Ahmeni requested the floor. "The defense can show evidence that Sary repeatedly plotted against the king. Because he was married to the princess Dolora, Ramses declined to press charges."

A number of the influential spectators appeared surprised.

"Let the princess Dolora appear before this court," ordered the vizier.

The lanky brunette came meekly forward.

"Do you agree with the statements made by Moses and Ahmeni?"

Dolora hung her head.

"If anything, they're much too moderate. My husband had become a monster. Once he understood his academic career was finished, he was a broken man. He took his frustrations out on his subordinates. In the end, he was consumed with hatred for the brickmakers he supervised. His cruel mistreatment of the Hebrew workers amounted to persecution. If Moses hadn't killed him, someone else would have."

The vizier looked intrigued. "Are you sure you're not exaggerating?"

"I swear I'm not! My husband was making my life a living hell!"

"Are you saying you're glad he died?"

Dolora slumped even more. "I was, well, relieved, and ashamed of feeling that way. But how could I miss a man who'd become so cruel?"

"Any further information that pertains to the case?"

"No, Your Honor." Dolora returned to her place among the nobles.

"Does anyone wish to testify in Sary's defense or challenge his widow's testimony?"

The courtroom was silent. The scribe who was serving as court reporter took notes in a sure and rapid hand.

"Give your version of the events in question," the vizier instructed Moses.

"It was a sort of accident. Although my relations with Sary were strained, I never intended to kill him."

"Why the strained relations?"

"Because I'd found out that the man was an extortionist who abused the Hebrew brickmakers in his work gang. I was defending one of them against Sary when I accidentally killed him, only to save my own life."

"You therefore claim that you acted in self-defense?"

"It's the truth."

"Why did you flee the scene?"

"Because I panicked."

"A strange reaction for a man who's innocent."

"Killing a man is a profoundly shocking experience. In the aftermath, you're confused. You feel like you might be drunk. Then you realize what you've done and the only thing you want to do is get away. Away from yourself, from the horrible act you've committed. You want to forget, to be forgotten. That is why I hid in the desert."

"Once you were more rational, you should have returned to Egypt and surrendered to the proper authorities."

"I took a wife and we had a son. Egypt faded into the distance."

"Why did you come back?"

"I have a mission to accomplish."

"What mission?"

"For the moment, that's my secret. It has no bearing on the trial, I promise. In time all will be revealed."

Moses' responses irritated the vizier.

"Your version of the facts is hardly convincing. I can't say your conduct pleads in your favor. Your explanations are unsupported. I believe you murdered Sary with premeditation because he was an enemy of your people. Your motive is understandable, but the fact remains that it was a capital crime. On your recent return to Pi-Ramses, you continued to live in hiding, which is tantamount to an admission of guilt. A man with nothing on his conscience would never behave that way."

Ahmeni decided it was time to step in.

"I have proof of Moses' innocence."

The magistrate frowned. "It had better be admissible, I warn you."

"The Hebrew brickmaker involved in the incident was named Abner. Sary was extorting money from him. Abner complained to Moses, and Sary was planning to get revenge. Moses broke in on their fight. An accidental blow killed Sary. There was no premeditation; it was self-defense. Abner was there as a witness. He later gave a deposition in accordance with the law, which I now submit to the court."

Ahmeni handed the document to the vizier.

The magistrate checked the judge's seal on the papyrus, then broke it, noted the date, and perused the text.

Moses took care not to show his emotion, but exchanged a meaningful glance with Ahmeni.

"This document is authentic and admitted as evidence."

The trial was over. The charges would be dismissed. Surely the jury would vote for acquittal.

"Before the jury deliberates," the vizier announced, "I'd like to call one last witness."

Ahmeni's brows knitted.

"I request that the brickmaker Abner appear before me," the judge intoned, "and provide confirmation of the facts in person."

SIXTEEN

Ramses vented his anger. Ahmeni listened.

"Indisputable evidence, a legal deposition sworn and sealed—and Moses is still in prison!"

"The vizier is only being thorough," said Ahmeni in his secretary's voice.

"What more does he need?"

"He wants to question Abner for himself."

There was no way around it. A judge had every right to call a witness. Ramses sighed.

"Have they issued the subpoena?"

"Yes, and that's the hitch."

"Why?"

"Abner seems to have disappeared. The elders say that no one's seen him for months."

"They're lying! They want to hurt Moses' case."

"Could be. But what can we do?"

"Let Serramanna look for him."

"We'll have to wait. Serramanna is following up on an investigation near Akhenaton's old capital in middle Egypt. He's a man with a mission. He won't rest until he learns the identity of that murdered girl, the one involved with the sorcerer. And frankly, he's convinced that the Hittite spy network was never disabled."

Ramses felt the anger drain out of him.

"What do you think, Ahmeni?"

"Shaanar is dead, his co-conspirators have scattered or given up. But Serramanna trusts his instincts."

"Perhaps he should, Ahmeni. Instinct is an unfiltered form of intelligence, beyond the reasoning we use to mislead or reassure ourselves. My father honed his instincts until they became intuition—and intuition is a form of genius."

"Seti was a king, not a pirate."

"Serramanna is versed in the ways of darkness. It sounds like he's onto something. Get in touch with him as soon as you can and have him come back to Pi-Ramses."

"I'll send a courier at once."

"And please communicate my request to the vizier: I want to meet with Moses."

"But he's in prison!"

"He's had the chance to stand trial and state his case. My seeing him won't influence the outcome."

Strong winds buffeted the plain where Akhenaton's capital, the City of the Horizon of Aton, had been hastily built and now lay in sorry ruin. As Serramanna walked down an abandoned street, the side of a building crumbled. Though no stranger to peril, the Sard felt his spine tingle. Dangerous shadows lurked in these empty houses and palace halls. Before questioning the villagers, he had wanted to get a feel for the place, confront its ghosts, assess the cruel legacy of its misguided religion.

As evening drew near, Serramanna went to the neighboring village in search of food and a few hours' needed rest. The place seemed deserted; not a donkey, goose, or dog was about. Doors and shutters gaped open. Even so, he kept his short sword unsheathed. It would have been smarter not to come here alone, but he would rely on his experience and strength.

On the dirt floor of one tumbledown house huddled a grief-stricken old woman, her head on her knees.

"Go ahead and kill me," she said with a sob. "I've nothing left to steal."

"Don't worry. I'm with Pharaoh's security force."

"Go away, stranger. This village is dead, my husband is gone, and I'm only waiting my turn."

"Who was your husband?"

"A good man who he spent his life helping others, and then they accused him of practicing magic! The sorcerer killed him, that was all the thanks he got."

Serramanna sat down next to the widow. Her dress was grimy, her hair matted.

"Can you describe this sorcerer?"

"What does it matter?"

"He may be wanted for another murder."

The widow looked up in astonishment. "Are you serious?"

"Do I look like the type to fool around?"

"But it's too late. My husband is already dead."

"I can't bring him back to life; that's in the hands of the gods. But I *can* take care of the sorcerer."

"He's a tall man, tall and lean, with a hawk face and cold eyes."

"What's his name?"

"Ofir."

"An Egyptian?"

"No, Libyan."

"How do you know all this?"

"For months he used to come here and talk with our adopted daughter, Lita. The poor girl . . . she had visions, spells you might say. She got the idea she was descended from Akhenaton. My husband and I tried to talk sense to her, but she would only listen to the sorcerer. One night she disappeared and we never saw her again."

Serramanna showed the old woman the drawing of the mysterious murder victim.

"Is this her?"

"Yes, my daughter, my little blond Lita. Is she . . ."

The Sard didn't like to hide the truth. He gave a silent nod.

"When is the last time you saw this Ofir?"

"A few days ago, when he came to see my husband on his sickbed. I know he gave him something that killed him off. I know Ofir!"

"Is he living somewhere nearby?"

"He's hiding in the old tombs up on the cliffs. They're

full of demons. Cut Ofir's throat, Officer. Trample his body and burn it!"

"You should get away from here, Mother. It's not good to live with ghosts."

Serramanna left the hut and jumped onto his horse, spurring him into a fast gallop in the direction of the tombs. Day began to break.

Abandoning his mount at the foot of the slope, the Sard hit the ground running, sword in hand; he wouldn't have surprise on his side, but he wanted to be ready to strike a sudden blow. He chose the largest entrance to the tombs and snuck inside.

Throughout the tombs, he found only emptiness. The only inhabitants of these deserted sepulchres were the people carved on the walls, the last survivors of a bygone reign.

Meritamon, Ramses and Nefertari's daughter, was playing the harp for her parents with a skill that astonished the monarch. Seated on folding chairs at the edge of a pool dotted with blue lotus blossoms, Pharaoh and the Great Royal Wife, hand in hand, were blissfully happy. Not only was their eight-year-old daughter a prodigy, her music also conveyed a depth of feeling unusual for her age. Fighter, the enormous Nubian lion, and Watcher, the old yellow dog curled between his front paws, also seemed to be under the spell of Meritamon's tune.

The final notes softly faded, leaving a tender silence in their wake.

The king kissed his daughter.

"Did you like it?"

"You're a gifted musician, but you'll still have to work very hard."

"Mother promised me that I can study at the temple of Hathor. It's a wonderful school."

"If that's your wish, it will certainly be granted."

The girl's beauty was as dazzling as her mother's, with the same luminous gaze.

"If I become a temple musician, will you come to see me?"

"Do you think I could live without your playing?"

A glum-looking Kha approached them.

"You look upset," the queen remarked.

"I'm missing something. It must have been stolen."

"Are you sure?"

"I put my writing things away every night. One of my reed brushes has disappeared. It was old, but I still liked to use it."

"You couldn't have misplaced it?"

"No, I looked everywhere."

Ramses took his son by the shoulders. "You're making a grave accusation."

"I know better than to speak lightly. That's why I thought hard before I mentioned it."

"Do you suspect someone in particular?"

"Not for the moment, but I'll try and figure it out. I really liked that brush."

"You have others."

"True, but none exactly like that one."

The lion lifted his head. The dog perked up his ears. Someone was coming.

Dolora approached nonchalantly. She wore an elaborate wig with long braids and a green dress that flattered her sallow complexion.

"Your Majesty wishes to see me?"

"Your behavior at Moses' trial was commendable," Ramses declared.

"I only told the truth."

"Describing your husband so unsparingly took some courage."

"There's no lying in front of Ma'at, not to mention the vizier."

"Your testimony strengthened Moses' case."

"I was pleased to do my duty."

The palace cellar master arrived with some of the year's new wine, and the conversation turned toward the details of the children's education.

When she left the garden, Dolora was certain she had regained the king's trust. Where before their relations had been superficially cordial, with flashes of suspicion showing through, now there was genuine warmth.

Dolora dismissed her sedan chair. She wanted to stroll through the streets on her way home.

In the guise of a humble water bearer, much thinner and with a full beard and mustache, Shaanar was unrecognizable.

"Convinced now, my darling sister?" he said, dipping a drink for her.

"Your plan was excellent."

"Our brother is blinded by friendship. Since you came to Moses' aid, Ramses is sure you're on his side."

"Now that I have him fooled, what's our plan?"

"Keep your ears open. The slightest bit of information

may be precious. When I need to contact you, I'll come in this disguise."

SEVENTEEN

Ramses and Ahmeni had listened attentively to Serramanna's story. Contrasting with the tension that filled Ramses' office, gentle sunlight flooded the room. As the hot months drew to a close, Egypt wore soft and shimmering gold.

"Ofir, a Libyan sorcerer," repeated Ahmeni, "and Lita, a delusional girl he manipulated . . . are they really anything to worry about? The sorcerer fled the law, has no support within the country, and has probably crossed the border by now."

"You underestimate the seriousness of the situation," argued Ramses. "Are you forgetting where he was hiding—the City of the Horizon of Aton, the heretic pharaoh's old capital?"

"It's been a ghost town for ages."

"But Akhenaton's ideas are still around, stirring up trouble. This Ofir is probably using them to build a network of sympathizers."

"A network . . . are you suggesting that Ofir is a Hittite spy?"

"I'm sure of it."

"But the Hittites have no use for Aton and the concept of a single god!"

"The Hebrews do," interjected Serramanna.

Ahmeni had been afraid he'd say that. The Sard was as undiplomatic as ever, blurting out whatever was on his mind.

"We know that Moses was contacted by someone posing as an architect," the bodyguard continued. "His description matches the sorcerer's exactly. Isn't that enough to convince you?"

"Now, wait a minute," said Ahmeni.

"Go ahead," ordered Ramses.

"I may not know much about religion," the Sard went on, "but I do know that the Hebrews worship a single god. Do I have to remind you, Majesty, that I suspect Moses of treason?"

"Moses is our friend!" protested Ahmeni. "Even if he did meet with this Ofir, does that mean he's been plotting against Ramses? The man must have contacted all kinds of important personalities."

"Why ignore the obvious?" asked the Sard.

The Pharaoh rose and looked out his office window. In the distance was the lush Delta countryside, the inherent sweetness of life in Egypt.

"Serramanna is right," Ramses said decisively. "The Hittites have launched a two-pronged offensive, attacking us from within and without. We won the day at Kadesh, ran them out of our protectorates, and dismantled their spy ring. But where has it all gotten us? The Hittite army is still a force to be reckoned with, and Ofir is still at large. A man like that, who casually resorts to murder, will never stop trying to harm us. But Moses can't be involved with the sorcerer; he's simply incapable of such duplicity. I say Serramanna is right, except when it comes to Moses."

"I hope that's the case, Your Majesty."

"I have a new assignment for you, Serramanna."

"Don't worry. I'll find Ofir."

"First I want you to find me the Hebrew brickmaker called Abner."

Nefertari wanted to celebrate her birthday at the royal estate in the heart of the Delta, now run by Nedjem, the agriculture secretary. Mild-mannered, a true nature lover, he showed the royal couple a new kind of plow specially adapted to the thick, rich Delta soil, personally demonstrating how it turned the earth to the proper depth without undue harm.

The workers on the estate were clearly overjoyed. Having the king and queen in their midst was a gift from the gods, a blessing on the year to come. The harvest would be bountiful, the orchards bursting with fruit. The livestock would multiply.

Yet Nefertari sensed that Ramses was only going through the motions. At the end of a copious meal, she was able to have a private word with him.

"I can tell that something's bothering you. Is it Moses?"

"I'm worried about what will happen to him, I admit."

"Has Abner been found yet?"

"No, and if he doesn't reconfirm his deposition, I doubt that the vizier will move for acquittal."

"Serramanna won't let you down. What else is on your mind? I'm sure there's something more."

"The law of the pharaohs requires me to protect Egypt from interior threats as well as enemies outside our borders, and I'm afraid I've failed."

"You've taken the Hittites in hand, so are you saying there's a threat from within?"

"We still have to struggle against the forces of darkness. I feel them advancing, portraying themselves in a false light."

"Strange that you should say so, but somehow it's not surprising. Yesterday evening, when I led the evening prayers at the temple of Sekhmet, the eyes of the statue shone with an eerie light. I said the liturgy to appease the lion goddess. It worked in the temple confines, but can we keep evil at bay in the outside world?"

"The heretic pharaoh's ideas were never completely stamped out, Nefertari."

"Didn't Akhenaton himself set limits on the worship of Aton?"

"Yes, but he unleashed forces that he could no longer control. And Ofir, a Libyan sorcerer and Hittite minion, awoke the demons slumbering in the abandoned capital."

Nefertari said nothing for a moment. Her eyes remained closed. Freeing herself from the transitory present, her thoughts flew toward the invisible world, searching for some glimmer of truth in the murky future. Her discipline as a priestess had developed the queen's second sight, a direct contact with the creative matrix of life. At times, her intuition was able to lift the veil and see to the core.

Somewhat uneasily, Ramses awaited the Great Royal Wife's verdict.

"A dreadful clash," she said when she opened her eyes again. "Ofir's invisible host will be no less deadly than the Hittite army."

"Since you confirm my fears, we need to take action at once. We'll tap the energy in the most important temples, letting the gods and goddesses weave a protective web to fling over Egypt. I could never do it without your help."

Nefertari embraced Ramses with infinite tenderness. "Do you even need to ask?"

"We'll be undertaking a long voyage and facing a great many dangers."

"Would our love have meaning if we didn't make a gift of it to Egypt? We offer our lives in exchange for the life she gives us."

Young peasant girls, bare-breasted, wearing reed head-dresses and grass skirts, performed a fertility dance and tossed cloth balls to ward off evil spirits.

"I wish we had their skill," whispered Nefertari.

"Something's worrying you, too, my darling."

"It's Kha."

"Has he done something wrong?"

"No, but that brush of his has been stolen. Remember when my favorite old shawl disappeared? I'm sure that the missing sorcerer, Ofir, used it to cast a spell on me. He was trying to wreck my health and undermine our union. Before that, I almost died in childbirth and nearly lost Meritamon. Setau saved me that time. I'm afraid this sorcerer is planning a new attack, this time against a child, your eldest son."

"Has Kha been sick?"

"Dr. Pariamaku has just examined him and found nothing out of the ordinary."

"That doesn't satisfy me. Get hold of Setau and have him construct a magic wall around Kha. Starting today, he should alert us the moment he notices anything. Have you warned Iset?"

"Of course."

"We have to find out who took the brush and whether the thief belongs to the palace staff. Serramanna can question them one by one."

"I'm afraid, Ramses. Afraid for Kha."

"Let's put our own fear aside; it could harm the boy. Black magic preys on the slightest weakness."

Equipped with a scribe's palate and brushes, Kha arrived at Setau and Lotus's laboratory. The Nubian beauty was milking cobra venom that her husband would turn into a remedy for digestive problems.

"Are you my magic teacher?" asked the boy.

"Your only teacher will be magic itself. Still afraid of snakes, son?"

"Oh, yes!"

"Good for you—only imbeciles have no fear of reptiles. Snakes were in this world before us. They're full of knowledge that we need. They're everywhere, above the ground and under it."

"Since you and my father took me to face the cobra, I know that I won't die a terrible death."

"You still need protection, though, it would seem."

"Someone stole one of my brushes, and a sorcerer might be trying to use it against me. The queen told me so."

Kha's poise and maturity amazed Setau.

"Snakes cast a spell on us," the expert explained. "At the same time, they can show us how to break spells. That's why I'm going to have you start taking a daily dose of a potion made from onion paste, snake blood, and stinging nettles. In two weeks or so, I'll add copper filings, red ochre, alum,

and lead oxide. Then Lotus will give you a remedy she in-
vented."

Kha made a face. "It must not taste very good."

"We'll have you wash it down with a little wine," grinned
the snake charmer.

"I've never tasted wine."

"One more way we'll be furthering your education."

"Wine troubles the mind and keeps the scribe from
having a steady hand."

"And too much water is no fun at all. To know what fine
wine is, you have to start tasting early."

"Will wine keep me safe from black magic?"

Setau toyed with a pot of greenish paste.

"A passive subject has no hope of resisting black magic.
Only an intensive effort can help you fight off invisible
attacks."

"I'm ready," said Kha.

EIGHTEEN

For six solid days it had rained on Hattusa, the capital of
the Hittite empire, built on the central Anatolian plain
where arid steppes alternated with gorges and ravines.

Stooped and weary, with a barrel chest, short legs, and

darting dark eyes, Emperor Muwattali felt the cold keenly. He sat by the fire, wearing his woolen cap and long red and black coat even inside the palace.

Despite the defeat at Kadesh and the failure of his counteroffensive, Muwattali still felt safe in his mountain stronghold. There was a lower town and an upper town topped with a citadel where the imperial palace stood. Gigantic fortifications carved into the cliff made Hattusa an impregnable fortress.

Yet the proud and invincible city now echoed with criticism of the emperor. For the first time, his acute sense of strategy had not led his army to victory.

On the miles of ramparts, bristling with turrets and battlements, soldiers kept watch day and night as everyone wondered whether tomorrow Muwattali would continue to preside over the empire's fortunes. Until recently, the man they dubbed "Great Chief" had successfully checked any challenges to his position, but now doubt was creeping in.

Two men coveted the throne: the emperor's son, Uri-Teshoop, who had the support of the military elite, and Hattusili, Muwattali's brother, a clever diplomat who had organized a powerful coalition against Egypt. With the aid of costly gifts, Muwattali was attempting to hold this coalition together.

The emperor had just spent a delightful afternoon with a lovely, amusing, and cultured young woman who had made him forget his cares. He wished he could devote his life to memorizing love poems, as she did, and forget about military posturing. But that was only a dream, and a Hittite emperor had neither the time nor the right to dream.

Muwattali rubbed his hands over the fire. He was still having trouble deciding: should he eliminate his brother, his son, or both? A few years earlier, he would have had to act quickly and brutally. A number of plotters, as well as a number of rulers, had succumbed to poison, the method of choice at the Hittite court. Now, however, the rivalry between the two men might better serve his purposes. Hattusili and Uri-Teshoop seemed to cancel each other out, allowing him to appear as an indispensable mediator.

Another factor, unfortunately, also entered into his decision. His government was on shaky ground. The repeated military defeats, the expense of war, the disruption of international trade, all threatened the existence of the vast Hittite empire.

Muwattali had prayed at the Storm God's temple, the showpiece among all twenty-one of the lower town's shrines. Like every celebrant, he had broken three loaves and poured wine on a block of stone, intoning, "May it last forever." This time the emperor meant his country. His worst nightmare was seeing it conquered by Egypt and betrayed by its allies. How much longer would he be able to gaze out from his citadel at the terraced cliffs studded with mansions, or down to the monumental gates to his capital?

The chamberlain notified the emperor that his guest had arrived, passing through a number of checkpoints on the way to the imperial palace, which was surrounded by reservoirs, stables, an armory, and a guard post.

Muwattali liked to receive his guests in a cold and forbidding pillared hall decorated with arms to commemorate various military victories.

He would recognize Uri-Teshoop's heavy martial tread anywhere. Tall, muscular, robust, with flowing locks and a reddish fleece covering his body, he had established himself as a fearsome warrior always ready for combat.

"How are you these days, my son?"

"Not well, Father."

"You look to me in excellent form."

"Have you called me here to discuss my health?" snapped Uri-Teshoop.

"Remember who you're talking to," Muwattali said sternly.

Uri-Teshoop deflated. "Forgive me. My nerves are on edge."

"What has you so riled?"

"I was the commander of a victorious army, and now I'm reduced to serving as Hattusili's underling, when he lost the day at Kadesh! Isn't that a waste of what I have to offer my country?"

"Without Hattusili, the coalition would never have been formed."

"What good did it do us? If you'd let me have my way, I would have beaten Ramses!"

"You keep making the same mistake, son. Why dwell on the past?"

"Get rid of Hattusili and put me back in charge where I belong."

"Hattusili is my brother. Our allies respect him, and the merchants listen to him. Without their cooperation, the war effort doesn't exist."

"Then what do you propose I do?"

"We must all overcome our differences and unite to save Hatti."

"Save Hatti? I didn't know it was in danger."

"We haven't gotten the better of Egypt yet, and all around us alliances are shifting. Our situation could change more quickly than I once supposed."

"Then who has time for talk? I was born to fight, Father, not to waste time in intrigues that end up diminishing Hatti's stature."

"Don't be too hasty, son. If we're to regain our supremacy, we must first address our internal divisions. The first step, as I see it, is your immediate reconciliation with Hattusili."

Uri-Teshoop slammed a fist into one of the pillars holding up the mantel. "Never! Don't make me grovel to that worthless coward!"

"Healing our differences can only make us stronger."

"Lock your brother and his wife up in a temple and let me march on Egypt. That's what will make us stronger!"

"Do you refuse any form of reconciliation?"

"I do."

"Is that your final word?"

"Get rid of Hattusili and I'll pledge you my support— mine and the army's."

"Should a son set conditions on the love he bears his father?"

"You're more than a father. You're the Emperor of Hatti. All our decisions should be in the country's best interest. You know I'm right. In time you'll come around to my way of thinking."

The emperor looked haggard. "Perhaps I will. I need to think it over."

Leaving the audience chamber, Uri-Teshoop felt certain he had convinced his father. Soon the aging emperor would have no choice but to grant his son full decision-making powers, eventually yielding the throne to him.

Wearing a red robe, a golden necklace, silver bracelets, and leather sandals, Hattusili's wife, Puduhepa, was burning incense in the crypt beneath the temple of Ishtar. At this late hour, the citadel was plunged in silence.

Two men were descending the staircase. Hattusili, short like his brother and wearing a headband and a heavy multicolored cloak, with a silver cuff on his right elbow, walked in front of the emperor.

"It's so cold down here," said Muwattali, clutching his woolen mantle tighter around his shoulders.

"It's not very comfortable," admitted Hattusili, "but it's the once place that we can be sure is completely private."

"Would you like to sit down, Your Majesty?" inquired Puduhepa.

"This stone ledge is fine. Despite my brother's long journey, he looks less fatigued than I am. What do you have to report, Hattusili?"

"I'm concerned about the state of our coalition. Certain of our allies appear ready to back out on us. They're increasingly greedy in their demands, but I've managed to satisfy them so far. I'm afraid the coalition has become extremely expensive. However, that's not the worst of it."

"Say what you mean."

"The Assyrians have begun to pose a threat."

"Since when do the Assyrians amount to anything?"

"They've followed our example. Apparently they believe our recent defeats and internal conflicts have weakened us and that they should strike us when we're down."

"We'd trounce them in a matter of days!"

"I'm not so sure. And would it be a good idea to divide our army when Ramses is preparing to attack Kadesh?"

"Is that a fact?"

"According to our spies, Ramses is planning a new offensive. This time the Canaanites and Bedouins won't stand in his way. He'll head straight for Hatti, and we shouldn't have half our forces off battling Assyrians."

"Then what's our best course, in your opinion?"

"We need to heal our internal rifts. That has to come first. The conflict between your son and me has gone on too long and done us no good. I'm prepared to meet with him and acquaint him with my view of the situation. We're at a turning point. If we can't come together now, we'll never last."

"Uri-Teshoop won't hear of it. He's demanding that I put him back in command of our troops."

"To go head-to-head with the Egyptians and risk a final defeat!"

"As he sees it, a frontal attack is our best defense."

"You're the emperor. You'll have to choose between the two of us. If you opt for you son's course of action, I'll concede."

Muwattali walked a bit to warm himself.

"There's only one reasonable solution," the handsome Puduhepa calmly announced. "As emperor, you are the guardian of Hatti's greatness. The fact that Hattusili is your brother and Uri-Teshoop your son is of no importance compared to the safety of our people. You know perfectly well that Uri-Teshoop's warmongering can only lead to disaster."

"Then what is your reasonable solution?"

"Since no one can convince a madman, Uri-Teshoop has to be eliminated. And since both you and Hattusili should remain above suspicion, I'll see to it myself."

NINETEEN

Moses stood up in his cell.

"You, here?"

"The prosecution gave me permission to see you."

"Does Pharaoh need permission to visit his prisons?"

"In your case, yes, since you're being tried for murder. But first of all you're my friend."

"So you haven't rejected me."

"Would I abandon a friend in need?"

Ramses and Moses met in a long embrace.

"Man of little faith," chided the king, "why did you run away?"

"Sheer panic, at first. At least that was what I thought. Later, in Midian, I began to see things differently. It wasn't an escape; it was a call."

Moses' cell was clean and well ventilated, with a dirt floor. The king sat down on a three-legged stool, facing his Hebrew friend.

"And where did this call come from?"

"The god of Abraham, Isaac, and Jacob. A call from Yahweh."

"Yahweh is the name of a mountain in the Sinai desert. I'm not surprised to hear it used for a god. After all, the

Peak of the West, in Thebes, is the home of the goddess of silence."

"Yahweh is the One God. He's everywhere, not only in the desert."

"How did you spend your exile, Moses?"

"I met God on that mountaintop. He appeared to me as a burning bush and told me His name: 'I Am.' "

"Why limit himself to a single aspect of reality? Atum, the creator, is both 'He Who Is' and 'He Who Is Not.' "

"Yahweh has given me a mission, Ramses, a sacred mission that may not be to your liking. I have to deliver the Hebrew people from Egypt and lead them to a Holy Land."

"Have you really heard the voice of God?"

"It was clear and deep as your own voice."

"The desert is full of mirages."

"You can't make me doubt what I saw and heard for myself. God has determined my mission; I plan to fulfill it."

"When you say the Hebrews, do you mean all of them?"

"The whole Hebrew people will be freed from bondage in Egypt."

"But you're already free to come and go as you please."

"I demand official recognition of my people's faith and permission to begin an exodus."

"The first thing is getting you out of prison. That's why there's a search on for Abner. His testimony will give you an instant acquittal."

"Abner may have left the country."

"You have my word: no effort will be spared to bring him before the court."

"My friendship for you is unchanged, Ramses, and when I learned of your war against the Hittites, I hoped you'd win. But you're the Pharaoh, and I'm the future leader of the Hebrews. If you won't grant my request, I'll become your most implacable foe."

"Can't friends always find some common ground?"

"Our friendship is less important than my mission. Even if it tears my heart in two, I must obey the voice of Yahweh."

"We'll have time to talk it over. Now let's concentrate on getting you acquitted."

"I don't mind being in prison. The solitude helps me prepare for ordeals to come."

"A heavy sentence could be the first one you're facing."

"Yahweh will protect me."

"I hope so, Moses. Now think: is there anything else in your past that might help your case?"

"I told the truth and the truth will out."

"You're not giving me much help."

"When you're Pharaoh's friend, why worry about injustice? I know you won't rest unless justice rules."

"Did you ever meet a man named Ofir?"

"I don't recall."

"He would have been posing as an architect. Did he contact you in Pi-Ramses while you were in charge of construction? He could have been preaching Akhenaton's banned religion."

"Yes, now that you mention it."

"Did he propose anything specific?"

"No, but he seemed sensitive to the Hebrew people's distress."

"Distress? Isn't that an exaggeration?"

"You're an Egyptian. You can't understand."

"All right. But let me warn you that Ofir is a Hittite agent who was heading a spy ring here in Egypt. He's also a murderer. Any collusion with him could bring a charge of high treason against you."

"Anyone willing to help my people deserves my thanks."

"How can you hate the land where you were born?"

"My life as a child and young man, our school days in Memphis, the years I spent helping you build your vision . . . all of that is gone and forgotten, Ramses. I love only one land: the Promised Land where God will lead my people."

Nedjem, the secretary of agriculture, was flustered. Usually friendly and cheerful, today he had snapped at his secretary for no reason. Unable to concentrate on his work, he left his office and headed for Setau and Lotus's laboratory.

Lovely Lotus was bent over a thrashing redheaded viper.

"Move that copper bowl," she ordered Nedjem.

"I don't know if . . ."

"Hurry up."

Nedjem reluctantly retrieved the bowl, which contained a thick brownish liquid.

"Don't spill a drop, it's very corrosive."

Nedjem trembled. "Where can I put it down?"

"On the shelf there."

Lotus slid the viper into a basket and fastened the lid.

"What can I do for you, Nedjem?"

"You and Setau . . ."

"Is someone asking for Setau?" came the snake charmer's gruff voice.

Disturbing vapors escaped from vials of various sizes. On the shelves sat pots and strainers, gourds and tubing, philters and potions.

"What I came to say . . ." A coughing fit prevented Nedjem from continuing.

"Well, go ahead and say it!"

Unkempt, abrupt, and square-shouldered, barely visible in the smoke-filled section of the laboratory where he was working, Setau was decanting diluted venom.

"It's about young Kha."

"What's the matter with him?"

"Well, you've . . . Kha has . . . What I'm trying to say is that up to now I've seen to his education. He loves to read and write, displays an exceptional maturity for his age, the knowledge he already has would be the envy of many scribes, and yet he goes on probing the secrets of heaven and earth, he wants . . ."

"I know all that, Nedjem, and I'm a busy man. Get to the point."

"You . . . you're not an easy man, Setau."

"Life isn't easy. When you spend your time around snakes, you quickly learn to dispense with trifles."

"This isn't a trifle!" Nedjem said, hurt to the quick.

"Then will you finally say what you want to say?"

"All right. I'll just be direct. Why are you leading Kha astray?"

"You barge into my laboratory, Nedjem, disturb my work, and on top of it you insult me! You may be one of Ramses' top officials, but I'm about ready to punch you in the nose."

Nedjem backed away, bumping into Lotus.

"Forgive me . . . It's not that . . . but the boy . . ."

"You think Kha's too young to be learning magic?" the Nubian beauty asked with a winning smile.

"Yes, that's it," said Nedjem, brightening.

"Your reservations do you justice, but your fears are unfounded."

"But for a child so young to deal with such an ancient body of knowledge, and one so dangerous . . ."

"Pharaoh has ordered us to protect his son. If we're to do that, Kha must be involved."

"Protect him? But from what?"

"Do you like beef stew?" asked Lotus.

"I . . . yes, of course."

"It's one of my specialties. Would you stay for lunch?"

"Oh no, I'd be imposing . . ."

"Stay," urged Setau. "Kha is no fragile little thing. He's Ramses' eldest child. Someone is trying to attack him, to weaken the royal family and the country as a whole. We'll build a magic wall around young Kha to repel the evil influences working against him. It's a job that demands precision. The work will be hard and the outcome uncertain. Lotus and I need all the help we can get, Nedjem."

TWENTY

In the Hebrew quarter, beams were laid across the rooftops and reeds woven through them to shelter the narrow streets from the sun. Housewives conversed on their doorsteps. When the water bearer came by, they paused to take a drink, then resumed their endless discussions. Neighborhood craftsmen chimed in when they took a break;

brickmakers on their way home from work stopped to have a word.

The trial was everyone's favorite subject. Some of the locals believed that Moses would be sentenced to death; others thought he'd get off with a few years in prison. A few extremists favored an outright rebellion, but the majority was fatalistic. How could they stand a chance against Pharaoh's army and police force? Besides, Moses would only be getting what he deserved. He *had* killed a man, after all. An eye for an eye would be fair, people thought, no matter how much they liked and respected Moses. He'd championed the rights of the brickmakers and won them better working conditions. Many hoped to see him become a master builder once more and continue to look out for their interests.

Aaron shared in the reigning pessimism. He knew that Moses' fate was in the hands of Yahweh, but Egyptian justice had never been soft on crime. If Abner had agreed to testify, the charges would have been dismissed by now. But the brickmaker had refused, retracting his original story. Furthermore, he planned to remain in seclusion until the trial was over. Since Aaron had no leverage to use on Abner, he could hardly ask the man's tribal elder to force his appearance in court.

About this time Aaron noticed a beggar crouched in a nook in the shady street. The man nibbled pieces of bread passersby threw down to him, a hood concealing his face. When he first spotted the beggar, Aaron tried to ignore him. The second day, he gave him some food. On the third day, he sat down beside him.

"Have you no family?" Aaron inquired.

"Not anymore."

"Never married?"

"My wife is dead and my children are gone."

"How did you end up this way?"

"I was a grain merchant, I had a nice house, a good life . . . until I was unfaithful to my wife."

"God punished you for your sin, then."

"He did, but a man was the real cause of my downfall. He found out about the affair, blackmailed me, drove me to ruin, and destroyed my marriage. My wife died of a broken heart."

"What kind of monster would act that way?"

"A monster who's still at large, spreading his poison. I'm not the only one who's been hurt by him."

"What's his name?"

"I'm ashamed to tell you."

"Why?"

"Because he's a Hebrew, like you and me."

"My name is Aaron and I have some standing in the community. It's wrong of you not to speak out, for a black sheep like the man you describe can contaminate the whole flock."

"What does it matter now? I'm alone and desperate."

"I sympathize, but you still need to think of your brethren."

"His name is Abner," the beggar rasped.

Now Aaron had a legitimate complaint to use against Abner. That very evening, he called a meeting of the council of elders and other tribal leaders where he recounted the onetime grain merchant's sad story.

"I remember hearing," one of the elders admitted, "that

Abner demanded a cut from the brickmakers, but no one would speak against him. We couldn't act on hearsay. It's easy to understand why Abner would resist being called as a witness. He's a prominent man, and his reputation could suffer serious damage."

"But Moses is in prison and only Abner can save him!"

The elders were in a bind. After a conference, one of the tribal chiefs stood to deliver a summary.

"Let's be frank. Moses has committed murder and focused unwelcome attention on our community. It's not unjust that he should be punished. Furthermore, he only returned from exile to stir up trouble with his wild ideas. Our best course would be to not intervene further."

"Coward!" Aaron lashed out. "You're all cowards! You'll cover for a wretch like Abner because he's one of your own, but you'll let Moses hang. Moses, who fought for the good of all Hebrews! The wrath of Yahweh on all your miserable heads!"

The dean of the elders, a retired brickmaker, now spoke forcefully. "I agree with Aaron. We've behaved contemptibly."

"We're only protecting Abner," one of the tribal leaders protested. "We have no right exposing him to possible charges when there's no solid evidence against him."

Aaron banged his walking stick furiously. "Let me guess," he said, dripping sarcasm. "Has he been giving you a percentage?"

"How dare you!"

"Let's bring Abner face to face with the beggarman."

"Fair enough," the elder declared.

Abner's hiding place was a two-story house in the heart of the brickmakers' quarter. He could afford it. As long as the trial was in session, he stuffed himself with cakes and slept the days away.

When the counsel of elders and tribal leaders had ordered him to answer the beggar's charges, he'd laughed out loud. First of all, it would be a broken man's word against his. Then he would counterattack, accuse the Hebrew community of letting the man live in misery, which was against Egyptian law. If by some extraordinary chance things turned against him, Abner could have his hirelings conveniently dispose of the worm.

The meeting took place on the ground floor of his house, in the main room with comfortable pillows on low seats. Present were the dean of the elders, a tribal leader chosen by his peers, and Aaron, who walked in supporting the beggar, so stooped he could barely walk.

"Is this the miserable wretch who's been spreading lies about me?" Abner began in a mocking tone. "He doesn't even look like he can talk. The best thing would be to give him a decent meal and send him to finish his days on some farm in the Delta."

Aaron helped the beggar to a seat.

"We can waive these proceedings," the dean of the elders announced, "if you agree to testify on Moses' behalf and confirm the facts as they appear in your sworn deposition."

"Moses is a dangerous outsider, while I've given many of our brethren their start in life. Why should I risk my neck for an agitator?"

"Out of concern for the truth," Aaron said firmly.

"The truth can vary so much . . . and would the truth be enough to set Moses free? He did kill a man, after all. We have nothing to gain by getting mixed up in this mess."

"Moses saved your life. You should save his."

"It all happened so long ago, my memory is unclear. Isn't it better to look toward the future? Just having my deposition will work in Moses' favor. Since there's a reasonable doubt, he won't get the death penalty."

"Only life in prison," Aaron said acidly.

"Moses should have controlled himself and not killed Sary."

Exasperated, Aaron again slammed down his walking stick. "This man is a scoundrel. He's cheated his fellow Hebrews and he'll keep on cheating."

"Don't lose your head," Abner said soothingly. "I'm a generous man. I've agreed to provide for your needs. I believe in showing respect for my elders."

If the two other members of the delegation hadn't been there, Aaron would gladly have bashed in Abner's skull.

"Let's leave it at that, my friends," said Abner, "and seal our agreement with the meal I'm prepared to offer you."

"Are you forgetting the beggar, Abner?"

"Oh, him! What does he have to say for himself?"

Aaron gently addressed the broken man. "Speak up. Don't be afraid."

The beggar still sat hunched over. Abner chortled.

"So much for your confrontation! Let's be done with him. My servants will take him to the kitchen for a bite to eat."

Aaron was mortified. "Please talk," he asked the beggar.

Slowly, the man straightened up, rising to a stupendous height. He pulled back the hood to reveal his face.

Dumbstruck, Abner mouthed the name of this unexpected and fearsome guest.

"Serramanna . . ."

"You're under arrest," said the Sard, flashing his pirate's leer.

As Abner's hearing got under way, Serramanna was torn. Part of him, the part that wanted to keep the treacherous Moses safe in jail, regretted ever having caught Abner. Another part was proud of a job well done. It was proof of Ramses' exceptional powers that an old pirate willingly did his bidding, even while mistrusting the man he was helping set free. The Pharaoh's confidence in Moses was misplaced, but who could criticize a great king for being such a loyal friend?

The whole city of Pi-Ramses was waiting for the judge to hand down his verdict, once the jury finished deliberating. The trial had only served to increase Moses' standing within the Hebrew community. The common folk as well as the vast majority of the brickmakers were now on his side. He was the champion of the downtrodden.

Serramanna's final hope was that Moses would be sent into exile, eliminating the threat to the harmony that the royal couple maintained with such care.

When Ahmeni emerged from the courtroom, the Sard went to meet him. The scribe's pale face was glowing.

"Moses has been acquitted."

TWENTY-ONE

The court was assembled in the audience chamber of the royal palace in Pi-Ramses. A monumental staircase adorned with figures of slain enemies led up to it. No one knew why Pharaoh had called this special session of his cabinet and top government officials, but everyone was expecting an important announcement.

Passing through the monumental door where Ramses' coronation names stood out in their cartouches, blue letters on a white background, Ahmeni was obviously discontented. The king hadn't breathed a word of this to him. A glance at a grim-looking Ahsha suggested that the diplomat had no inkling either.

The room was so crowded that it was impossible to admire the decor of faience painted to represent lush gardens and teeming fishponds. People were pressed between the columns, and against the wall a fantasy world was painted in shades of pale green and deep red, light blue, sunny yellow, and off-white. But, in these tense moments, who could notice the scenes of waterfowl sporting in papyrus marshes? They were all too nervous to enjoy their surroundings.

Nevertheless, Setau's gaze did linger on the portrait of a young woman meditating in front of a hollyhock hedge.

She looked exactly like the queen. A frieze of lotus blossoms, poppies, daisies, and cornflowers enclosed her peaceable kingdom.

Cabinet officers, department heads, royal scribes, ritualists, keepers of secrets, priests and priestesses, noblewomen and other important personages fell silent when Ramses and Nefertari took their seats on the throne. The monarch radiated strength from every pore. His personal presence was without equal. Wearing the twin crown that symbolized his rule over upper and lower Egypt, in a white robe and golden kilt, Ramses held the scepter called "magic" in his right hand. It was a shepherd's crook that helped gather his flock on the invisible plane and maintain cohesion in the visible world.

If Ramses was power, Nefertari was grace. Every member of the audience perceived the deep love that bound them and gave them an aura of eternity.

The chief celebrant recited a hymn to Amon, singing of the hidden god's presence within every form of life. Then Ramses spoke.

"I wish to communicate a certain number of decisions in order to dispel rumors, and to outline the policies I plan to implement in the immediate future. These choices stem from long discussions with the Great Royal Wife."

Several royal scribes prepared to take down the monarch's pronouncements, which would instantly have the force of law.

"I will reinforce the northeastern border of Egypt, build new fortresses, consolidate the old walls, double the size of the garrisons and increase their pay. The King's Wall must become unbreachable, protecting the Delta from any potential invasion. Gangs of stonemasons and brickmakers will leave starting tomorrow to undertake the necessary work."

An elderly noble requested the floor.

"Your Majesty, will the King's Wall be enough to stop the Hittite horde?"

"Not in and of itself. It's merely the final element in our defense system. Thanks to our army's recent campaign, which halted the Hittite counteroffensive, we've retaken all our protectorates. Now Canaan, Amurru, and southern Syria stand between us and the Hittite invaders."

"But haven't the rulers of those provinces betrayed us in the past?"

"They often have, I agree. That's why I'm putting Ahsha in charge of administrative and military affairs in the buffer zone. He'll be entrusted with maintaining our supremacy, overseeing the local leaders, establishing a reliable information network, and training a special force that will check any Hittite attack."

Ahsha remained unruffled, though all eyes were on him— some admiring, others envious. The secretary of state was becoming more important than ever in Ramses' government.

"I've also decided to embark on a long journey with the queen," continued Ramses. "During my absence, Ahmeni will be my administrative delegate, consulting daily with the Queen Mother. The courier service will keep us in touch; no decrees will be enacted without my approval."

The court was stunned. Ahmeni's role behind the scenes was no secret, but why would the king and queen be going away at such a crucial juncture?

The chief of protocol broke the silence, posing the question on everyone's mind.

"Your Majesty . . . may we know the purpose of your journey?"

"To reinforce Egypt's spiritual foundation. The queen and I will go first to Thebes, where we'll see how my Eternal

Temple is coming along. Then we'll proceed to the Deep South."

"Do you mean Nubia?"

"I do."

"Forgive me, Your Majesty, but is this long trip necessary?"

"Not only that—it is indispensable."

The assembly understood that the Pharaoh would say no more, leaving everyone to speculate on the secret reasons behind this surprising decision.

Watcher, the king's yellow-gold dog, licked the Queen Mother's hand while the lion, Fighter, dozed at her feet.

"These two faithful companions wanted to pay their respects," Ramses told her.

Tuya was arranging flowers for an offering to the goddess Sekhmet. How grand the Queen Mother was in her long, gold-trimmed linen dress, a short cape covering her shoulders, the striped ends of her red sash reaching almost to the floor! How noble she was, with her piercing eyes, her spare and fine-boned face! She was a powerful woman, demanding and intractable.

"What do you think of my decisions, Mother?"

"Nefertari had spoken to me about them at length, and I'm afraid I may even have inspired them to some extent. The only effective means of securing our northeast border is to rule our protectorates with a firm hand and ward off a Hittite invasion. That was your father's policy. It should be yours as well. Nine years' reign, my son . . . how are you able to bear the weight?"

"I haven't had much time to consider it."

"That's just as well. Steady as you go, my son. Do you feel that the crew of your ship is with you?"

"My close associates are few and steadfast, and that's how I intend to keep things."

"Ahmeni is a remarkable person," commented Tuya. "His vision may not be broad, but he possesses two very rare qualities: honesty and loyalty."

"Do you have as much good to say about Ahsha?"

"He also has one exceptional virtue: courage, a particular brand of courage based on his powers of penetration. You could find no one more capable to handle matters for you in the problematic north."

"I rely on Setau as well. Do you think I should?"

"He detests social conventions. He's completely open and aboveboard. Everyone could use a friend like your snake charmer."

"My other close friend was Moses . . ."

"I know how much the two of you have in common."

"But you don't approve of him."

"No, Ramses. His Hebrew faith has set the two of you on a collision course. No matter what the circumstances, your country must always come before personal considerations."

"Moses hasn't caused any trouble yet."

"If he does become a political agitator, the law of Ma'at must serve as your only guide. It may prove to be a rough ride, even for you, Ramses."

Tuya straightened a lily stem. The bouquet looked larger than life.

"Will you agree to govern the Two Lands in my absence?"

"Do you leave me any choice? I tell you, I'm beginning to feel my age."

Ramses smiled. "You hide it well."

"You're too full of strength to imagine what age can feel like. Now will you tell me the real reason for this long trip?"

"The love of Egypt and Nefertari. I want to stoke the temples' hidden fires, make them produce more energy."

"Then the Hittites aren't the only enemies we face?"

"There's a Libyan sorcerer, Ofir, who's using the forces of darkness against us. I may be overestimating his ability to harm us, but I can't ignore the risk. Nefertari has already suffered too much from his spells."

"The gods have favored you, my son. Could there be any greater blessing than such a splendid wife?"

"No, and I'd be a fool not to show my gratitude. I've thought of a way to make her light shine through the ages, to show that the royal couple is Egypt's intangible support."

"Good. Your reign will achieve true greatness. Nefertari is the magic without which no act of yours will last. Though war and suffering may never end, as long as the royal couple rules as one, there will be harmony on this earth. Make your union the cornerstone of your reign, for your love is the greatest gift you can give your people."

The floral arrangement was finished. The goddess would be satisfied.

"Do you ever miss Shaanar, Mother?"

A wistful look crossed Tuya's face. "How could a mother forget her son?"

"He isn't your son anymore."

"You're the king and I should listen to you. Will you forgive me my weakness?"

Ramses held Tuya tenderly to him.

"Depriving Shaanar of a proper burial," she pointed out, "is a terrible punishment from the gods."

"I faced death at Kadesh. Shaanar met his in the desert. Perhaps it purified his soul."

"And what if he's still alive?"

"The thought has occurred to me, too. If he's lurking somewhere, still intent on harming me, will you still call him your son?"

"You are Egypt, Ramses, and I will stand in the way of anyone trying to hurt you."

TWENTY-TWO

Ramses prayed before the statue of Thoth in the lobby of the Ministry of Foreign Affairs, laying a bunch of lilies on the altar. The patron of writing—hieroglyphs were "the words of the gods"—was represented as a great stone baboon, his gaze lifted to the heavens.

Pharaoh's visit was a singular honor. Ahsha welcomed the monarch, bowing low. When Ramses embraced his friend, the young cabinet officer's subordinates felt privileged to be working for a man on such intimate terms with the king.

The two men retreated to Ahsha's well-appointed office: it was filled with roses from Syria, arrangements of daffodils and marigolds, acacia chests, chairs with lotus-blossom carvings, colorful cushions, bronze-footed ornamental stands. The walls were decorated with scenes of a waterfowl hunt in the marshes.

"Much fancier than my office," noted Ramses. "All this place needs is Shaanar's collection of vases."

"Don't remind me! I sold them off and put the proceeds in the department treasury."

Smartly dressed and wearing a lightweight, scented wig, his small mustache neatly trimmed, Ahsha looked like he was on his way to a dinner party.

"When I'm able to spend a few peaceful weeks in Egypt," he admitted, "I tend to enjoy myself. But never fear, I haven't forgotten Your Majesty's mission."

That was Ahsha: cynical, something of a dandy, a ladies' man, and at the same time a veteran statesman, an expert in foreign affairs, a perceptive and daring adventurer.

"What do you think of my new initiative?"

"I applaud the measures you're taking, Your Majesty."

"Do you consider them . . . adequate?"

"Only one thing is missing—which I suspect is the reason for this unannounced visit. Let me guess: could it be Kadesh?"

"Of course you're right, or you wouldn't be my secretary of state and head of intelligence."

"Do you still want to take the fortress?"

"We won an important battle at Kadesh, but the Hittite stronghold still sits there, a thorn in our side."

Frowning, Ahsha poured some wine, a lovely shade of red, into two silver goblets with handles fashioned like gazelles.

"I knew that Kadesh would never let you rest. Yes, the fortress is still a sore spot—and still a threat."

"That's why I see it as permanently endangering our protectorate in southern Syria. Any Hittite attack will be launched from Kadesh."

"Sound reasoning, it would appear," Ahsha said evenly.

"But you don't agree we should take it."

"If you had a nice middle-aged career diplomat ensconced in this office, he'd bow and scrape to you and say something like 'Ramses the Great, mighty king, great soldier, go forth and conquer Kadesh!' And the man would be a blooming idiot."

"Why let Kadesh stand?"

"Because you've shown the Hittites that they're not invincible. Their army is still powerful, of course, but you've made them doubt it. Muwattali promised his country an easy invasion and a stunning victory. Now he's forced to explain away a retreat. Plus he has problems at home: the power struggle between his son, Uri-Teshoop, and his brother, Hattusili."

"Who's the probable winner?"

"I'd say it's even, at this point."

"You think that Muwattali's days are numbered?"

"I do, since murder is a common complaint in the Hittite ruling class. A warrior nation can't have a leader who loses in combat."

"Then wouldn't this be the perfect time to go after Kadesh?"

"Yes, if our principal concern was to undermine the Hittite empire."

Ramses appreciated his friend Ahsha's insight and irreverent outlook, but even he was taken aback at this remark.

"I thought that was the major goal of our foreign policy."

"I'm not so sure anymore."

"How can you be serious?"

"When a decision translates into life or death for thousands of human beings, I'm not inclined to joke."

"You mean you've discovered information that will radically change my outlook?"

"Just a hunch, based on a few intelligence reports I ran across. Have you ever heard of the Assyrians?"

"A warrior people, like the Hittites."

"Yes, and under the sway of the Hittites until just recently. But when Hattusili formed his regional coalition, he bought Assyrian neutrality in exchange for a great deal of precious metal. They turned the windfall into armaments. Now the military has the upper hand in the country, and Assyria is poised to become the next great power in the region, more ambitious and more destructive than Hatti."

Ramses thought for a moment. "Are you saying that Assyria is about to take control of Hatti?"

"Not yet, but they're bound to sooner or later."

"Why doesn't Muwattali nip the problem in the bud?"

"Because he's having trouble holding on to the throne and he's keeping a watchful eye on Kadesh. He still sees us as his country's main enemy."

"Don't his rivals?"

"His son, Uri-Teshoop, is like a blind man. His only thought is of overrunning Egypt and slaughtering as much of the population as possible. Hattusili is broader minded, though, and he must be aware of the threat looming on his doorstep."

"You've done more than merely analyze the situation, I'm sure. What's your plan of action, Ahsha?"

"I'm afraid it won't appeal to you. It goes against your way of thinking."

"Tell me anyway."

"All right. Our best plan would be to make the Hittites

believe we're preparing to march on Kadesh. Rumors, classic disinformation, feeding them false documents, troop maneuvers in southern Syria, and so on . . . I'll handle that part."

"Nothing I object to yet."

"The next part is a bit trickier. Once we have them convinced, I'll go under cover to Hatti."

"Under cover?"

"A secret mission, with broad negotiating powers."

"But what do you want to negotiate?"

"A peace treaty, Your Majesty."

"Peace . . . with the Hittites?"

"It's the best way to keep Assyria from becoming a monster much more dangerous than Hatti."

"The Hittites will never sign a treaty!"

"With your full support, I believe it's feasible."

"If anyone but you were proposing this, I'd suspect him of treason."

Ahsha smiled. "I thought you might . . . but I put my faith in the great Ramses' foresight."

"The sages teach that flattery has no place in friendship."

"I'm not addressing you as a friend, but as Pharaoh. Clearly the short-term solution would be to seize the moment and attack the Hittites while we have a real chance of winning. But with Assyria emerging on the international scene, we need to modify our strategy."

"You admitted yourself that it's only a hunch, Ahsha."

"It's my job to try to predict the future. Sometimes intuition is the best indicator."

"I can't let you run such a terrible risk again."

"It worked the last time."

"You must really love those Hittite prisons."

"I can think of better places for a vacation, but someone has to volunteer for this job."

"You'll be hard to replace."

"I plan to make it home, Ramses. And in the long run I'd be bored as a provincial administrator. Wine, women, and song go only so far, you know. I'll need a new adventure to keep my wits sharp. I can exploit the Hittites' weaknesses and get them to sign the treaty. At least let me try."

"Your plan is sheer madness. You know that, don't you?"

"I love a challenge."

"You can't really believe that I'll consent to it."

"I do, because you're not some doddering old monarch who can no longer change the world. I await my orders."

"I'm heading south, perhaps for months, and you'll be going back north."

"Since you're taking care of spiritual matters, leave the Hittites to me."

TWENTY-THREE

The royal sons were fifteen to twenty-five years old. They wore their heads shaved except for a sidelock above the right ear, and were decked out in earrings, wide gold collars, and tucked kilts. Each proudly clutched a staff topped with an ostrich plume.

Chosen for their physical and mental vigor, the young men were to serve as Ramses' representatives in the various

army battalions. On the battlefield, their task was to restore
the troops' failing energy—for the king had not forgotten
his army's lackluster performance against the Hittite coalition at Kadesh.

The royal sons would now be serving in the administration of the buffer zone, following strict orders from Ahsha.

Already widespread was the legend of Ramses the Great
as a tireless progenitor and prolific father, who had sired a
hundred children as proof of his divine potency. It was a
fabulous legend, one that sculptors would translate into
stone and scribes would perpetuate with relish.

In the shade of his lemon tree, Homer was grooming his
long white beard. Hector, the black and white cat, had
grown plump. He purred when Ramses petted him.

"Excuse my saying so, Majesty, but you seem perturbed."

"Let's say, well, preoccupied."

"Bad news?"

"No, but I'm about to leave on a voyage that may be
fraught with peril."

The Greek poet stuffed more sage leaves into the snail-
shell bowl of his pipe. "Ramses the Great . . . that's what
the people call you now. Listen to this new verse of mine:
'The magnificent gifts of the gods are not negligible. Only the gods can give
them, for no one can acquire them on his own.'"

"What makes you so fatalistic?"

"It comes with age, Your Majesty. I've completed my *Iliad*
and *Odyssey,* and I've just put the finishing touches on my
account of your victory at Kadesh. All that's left for me now
is smoking my pipe, drinking my special wine, and having
my olive oil massages."

"Don't you want to reread your epics?"

"Only mediocre authors like to gaze in the mirror of their words. Tell me, Majesty, why this long journey?"

"My father told me not to neglect the temple at Abydos. I haven't followed his orders, and now I need to make up for lost time."

"There's more to it than that."

"My father's definition of a pharaoh was 'The one who makes his people happy.' And how is that done? By following Ma'at and pleasing the gods, so that they shower their blessings on humankind."

"I sense the queen's hand in this."

"With her, and for her, I want to build a monument that will produce the luminous energy we so dearly need, while protecting Egypt and Nubia from harm."

"Have you chosen the site?"

"In the heart of Nubia, Hathor has left her imprint on a place called Abu Simbel. A place where Lady of the Stars has imprinted the secret of her love in the stone. That love is the gift I want to give Nefertari, that she may become forever the Lady of Abu Simbel."

Hairy and bearded, the cook hunkered in front of his brazier, fanning the flames beneath the trussed goose he had skewered through the mouth. Once the bird's feathers were singed, he would pluck it, clean it, cut off the head, feet, and wing tips, then turn it slowly on the spit.

A noble lady called out to him.

"Is all your poultry spoken for?"

"Almost all."

"If I order a whole goose, can you have it ready this evening?"

"Well, it won't be easy . . ."

Dolora, Ramses' sister, tugged at the left shoulder strap of her dress, which tended to slip. Then she set a pot of honey at the cook's grimy feet.

"Your disguise is perfect, Shaanar. If you hadn't told me exactly where to look, I never would have recognized you."

"Have you learned something important?"

"I think so," his tall, dark sister told him. "I've come from the king and queen's audience."

"Come back in two hours. Your goose will be ready. I'll close up shop and you'll follow me. I'll take you to Ofir."

At the edge of the warehouse district, the streets of cooks' and butchers' shops grew quiet only after dark. A few heavily laden shop boys headed toward the mansions where they would deliver succulent meats for the night's banqueting.

Shaanar headed down an empty side street, stopped in front of a low blue door, and gave four slow knocks. As soon as the door opened, he motioned Dolora to follow. The lanky brunette steeled herself and ducked into a low-ceilinged room crammed with baskets. Shaanar lifted a trap door and led his sister down a wooden stairway to the cellar.

At the sight of Ofir, Dolora threw herself at his feet and kissed the hem of his robe.

"I was so afraid I'd never see you again!"

"I promised you I'd come back. My time of meditation in Akhenaton's lost capital has confirmed my faith in the One God who will one day rule over this country."

Dolora fixed her ecstatic gaze on the hawk-faced sorcerer. He fascinated her—Ofir, the prophet of the true faith. Yes, one day his strength would guide the people. One day soon he would overthrow Ramses.

"Your help is very precious to us," said Ofir in his deep and soothing voice. "Without you, how could we fight against this unbelieving and hated tyrant?"

"Ramses has dropped his guard; I think he even trusts me now, because my testimony helped his friend Moses."

"What are the king's current plans?"

"He's sending the Royal Sons to oversee the northern protectorates, under Ahsha's orders."

"That scum!" bellowed Shaanar. "He played me for a fool and then betrayed me! I'll get Ahsha someday, I'll trample him . . ."

"Let's stick to business," Ofir cut in. "Dolora has more to tell us."

The princess was delighted with her newfound importance. "The king and queen are leaving on a long journey."

"What's their destination?"

"Upper Egypt and Nubia."

"Do you know why they're going?"

"Ramses wants to make an extraordinary gift to the queen. A temple, it seems."

"Is that the only reason for their journey?"

"Pharaoh wants to spark Egypt's divine forces, focus their energy, and weave a protective web that will cover his kingdom."

Shaanar snickered. "Has our darling brother gone mad?"

"No," protested Dolora. "He realizes that mysterious foes are at work against him. There's nothing he can do but appeal to the gods and assemble an invisible host to aid him in his fight."

"He's crazy," Shaanar said, "crazier by the day. An invisible army? Ridiculous!"

The wayward prince was silenced by an icy glance.

"Ramses has recognized the danger," said the sorcerer.

"You can't really believe . . ." his voice trailed off. A terrifying aura of violence surrounded Ofir. For a second, Shaanar no longer doubted the Libyan's occult powers.

"What about the child Kha? Who's protecting him in their absence?" Ofir asked Dolora.

"Setau, the snake charmer. He's tutoring Kha in magic and doing all he can to build a magic wall around the boy."

"Snakes embody the earth's magic," Ofir acknowledged. "Anyone who's been around them knows that. Thanks to the brush Meba stole from Kha, I'll still be able to penetrate his defenses. But it will take me longer than I'd planned."

Dolora's heart sank at the thought that Kha must suffer in this surreptitious power struggle, yet she bowed to the sorcerer's logic. An attack on his son would weaken Ramses, deplete his *ka*—his spiritual essence—and perhaps lead him to abdicate. However cruel the means, Dolora believed the end was worth it.

"It's time for us to go," Ofir announced.

Dolora clutched at his robe. "When will I see you again?"

"Shaanar and I are going to leave the capital for a time. We can't stay for long in any one place. You'll be the first to hear when we come back. In the meantime, keep on gathering information."

"And I'll keep the faith," she said fervently.

"Is there anything more important?" murmured Ofir with a knowing smile.

TWENTY-FOUR

To celebrate Moses' acquittal, the Hebrew brickmakers threw a huge party in their modest neighborhood. Feasting on triangular flatbread, pigeon pie, stuffed quail, stewed figs, strong wine and cool beer, they sang well into the night, raising cheers to Moses, their hero.

Weary of the hubbub, the guest of honor left as soon as his newfound supporters were too drunk to notice his absence. Moses felt the need to be alone and consider the struggles to come. Persuading Ramses to release the entire Hebrew population from Egypt would be no easy task. Yet he must accomplish his mission from Yahweh, no matter what the cost. If need be, he would move mountains.

As Moses sat on the edge of the communal grinding stone, two men approached him. Bedouins, they were—bald, bearded Amos and stringy Keni.

"What are you two doing here?"

"Joining in the festivities," declared Amos. "Truly a special occasion, isn't it?"

"You're no Hebrews."

"We can be your allies."

"I don't need you."

"You may be overestimating your people's strength. Unarmed, you'll never fulfill your dream, my friend."

"I'll use my own weapons."

"If the Hebrews join forces with the Bedouins," said Keni, "they'll make a real army."

"And what would this army do?"

"Fight the Egyptians and win!"

"A dangerous notion," said Moses, frowning.

"Who are you to criticize? Leading your people out of Egypt, defying Ramses, putting yourself above this country's laws . . . your ideas are just as dangerous, I'd say."

"Who told you about my plans?"

"Every brickmaker knows what you're up to! They even say that you'll raise the standard of Yahweh, the warrior god, and seize control of the kingdom."

"Then their imagination is running away with them."

A wicked gleam showed in Keni's shrewd eyes. "The fact remains that you plan to lead a Hebrew uprising against the Egyptian government."

"Get away from me, both of you."

"You're making a mistake, Moses," insisted Amos. "Your people will have to fight, and they lack experience. We could help you train them."

"Go now and leave me to my thoughts."

"As you wish . . . but we'll be seeing you."

Ambling along on their donkeys like simple peasants, and furnished with traveling papers signed by Meba, the two Bedouins stopped to rest in a field south of Pi-Ramses. They were just beginning their meal of onions, fresh bread, and dried fish, when two other men joined them.

"How did your talk with Moses go?" inquired Ofir.

"He's a stubborn character," Amos admitted.

"Try threats," insisted Shaanar.

"It wouldn't work. Let him go ahead with his crackpot plans. Sooner or later he'll realize he needs us."

"Have the Hebrews accepted him?"

"The acquittal made him a people's hero, and the brickmakers believe he'll defend their rights as he did before."

"What do they think of his exodus?"

"It's very controversial, but there are a few firebrands in the younger generation who dream of independence."

"Encourage them," said Shaanar. "The more trouble they stir up, the greater the challenge to Ramses. If he suppresses the movement, it will make him unpopular."

Amos and Keni were the two surviving members of what had once been a thriving Hittite spy ring in Egypt. Working outside the commercial loop, they had escaped detection by Serramanna. They still had useful contacts in the Delta.

Ofir, Shaanar, Amos, and Keni formed a virtual war council, meeting to launch a fresh offensive against Ramses.

"Where are the Hittite troops?" asked Ofir.

"Bedouin spotters tell us they're holding their position around Kadesh," Keni answered. "The garrison has been reinforced in preparation for an Egyptian attack."

"I know my brother," Shaanar said acidly. "He'll strike while the iron is hot."

At the battle of Kadesh, Amos and Keni had lured Ramses into an ambush, letting themselves be captured and pretending to crack under pressure, then feeding him false information. By rights the Pharaoh never should have left Kadesh alive. The Bedouins were still smarting from the defeat.

"What are the orders from Hatti?" the sorcerer inquired of Keni.

"Use every possible means to destabilize Ramses."

Ofir knew only too well what this vague directive signified. On one hand, Egypt had regained control of the buffer states, and the Hittites did not feel up to winning them back; on the other, the emperor's son and brother were locked in a desperate struggle to wrest the power from Muwattali, who was hanging on by a thread.

The defeat at Kadesh, the failed counteroffensive in Canaan and Syria, and the protectorates' capitulation to Egyptian rule seemed to prove that the Hittite empire was on the wane and riddled with divisions. But this sad reality would not keep Ofir from pursuing his mission. Once Ramses toppled, Hatti would blaze anew.

"Keni, Amos," Ofir commanded, "I want you to continue infiltrating the Hebrews. Your agents should profess their belief in Yahweh and encourage the brickmakers to follow Moses. Dolora, the king's elder sister, will serve as our palace informant. I plan to work on Kha, break through the magic wall around him."

"I'll handle Ahsha," muttered Shaanar.

"You'll be wasting your time," snapped Ofir.

"I want to kill him with my own hands. Then I'll go after my brother!"

"What if you started with him instead?"

The sorcerer's suggestion ignited Shaanar's smoldering hatred for the tyrant who had cheated him out of his rightful place on the throne.

"I'm going back to Pi-Ramses to coordinate our efforts," announced Ofir. "You head south, Shaanar."

The renegade prince scratched his beard. "You mean I'm to try to disrupt Ramses' journey?"

"I expect more of you."

"What's my assignment?"

Ofir was forced to unveil Muwattali's strategy. "When the Hittites invade the Delta, the Nubians will flood across the southern border and attack Elephantine. Ramses won't be able to put out so many fires at once."

"What kind of manpower will I have?"

"A squadron of well-trained warriors is waiting for you near the City of the Horizon of Aton, along with Nubian tribal chiefs we've been plying with bribes for the last several months. Ramses has no idea that he's sailing up the Nile straight into the trap we've set for him. You're to make certain he doesn't come back alive."

A smile spread across Shaanar's face. "I don't believe in God, singular or plural, but I'm beginning to trust my luck again. Why didn't you tell me about this sooner?"

"I had my orders," Ofir informed him.

"And today you're ignoring them?"

"I trust you, Shaanar. Now you know the scope of my mission in Egypt."

Livid, Shaanar pulled some grass, threw it into the wind, stood up, and took a few steps. Finally, he was being given the power to act on his own, without the sorcerer's direct control. Ofir relied too heavily on the occult; he, Shaanar, would adopt a less complicated and more brutal strategy.

He was already bursting with ideas. He would find a way to cut short Ramses' southern journey. Nothing else mattered now.

Ramses . . . Ramses the Great, whose unprecedented success tormented his brother. Shaanar had no illusions about his own shortcomings, but he did have one quality that had remained intact through all his reversals of fortune: his dogged persistence. Ramses might be a formidable adversary, but Shaanar's ever-increasing hatred was a match for his brother's power. His hatred would give him the strength to waylay the Lord of the Two Lands.

For a moment, steeped in the peace of the countryside, Shaanar wavered.

What blame could he pin on his brother? Since he first took the throne, Seti's successor had given his all to his country, his people. He had sheltered them from adversity, shown uncommon valor in war, guaranteed prosperity and justice.

What could Shaanar find to blame him for, except being Ramses the Great?

TWENTY-FIVE

Assembling his advisory body of select representatives from the military and merchant classes, Emperor Muwattali recalled the words of his predecessors: "In our day, murder has become commonplace among the royal family; the queen was assassinated, along with the king's son. We therefore deem it necessary to decree that no one may draw sword or dagger against a member of the royal family, nor kill them in any other way, and that there be cooperation in choosing a successor to the ruling monarch."

While stressing that his succession was not an issue, the

emperor said he was gratified that murder was no longer prevalent, reasserting his trust in Hattusili, his brother, and Uri-Teshoop, his son. He renewed the latter's command as head of the imperial army and put his brother in charge of stimulating the economy and maintaining strong ties with Hatti's foreign allies. In other words, he stripped Hattusili of any military powers and made Uri-Teshoop untouchable.

Uri-Teshoop's triumphant smile and Hattusili's downcast expression left no doubt as to whom Muwattali had chosen as his successor, without mentioning names.

Weary and stooped, muffled in his black and red woolen cloak, the emperor made no further comment on his decisions. He withdrew, surrounded by his bodyguard.

Mad with rage, Puduhepa stomped on the silver earrings her husband, Hattusili, had given her the evening before.

"Your brother the emperor blindsided you this time," railed the handsome priestess. "He's treating you like dirt!"

"Muwattali has always been a secretive man. And he's left me important duties."

"Without the army, you're only Uri-Teshoop's puppet."

"I still have connections among the generals and the fortress commanders along the frontier."

"But your nephew is already the acknowledged master of the capital!"

"Uri-Teshoop frightens the moderates."

"How much will we have to offer to keep them on our side?" asked Puduhepa.

"The merchants will help us."

"I don't understand what's come over the emperor. He

seemed to disapprove of his son. He went along with my plan to get rid of him."

"Muwattali never acts on impulse," Hattusili reminded her. "He must have heard rumblings from the military, and he's trying to calm them down by putting Uri-Teshoop back in charge."

"It doesn't make sense! Why set him up to seize power?"

Hattusili thought for quite a while before answering.

"I wonder if the emperor isn't trying to send us a subtle message. Uri-Teshoop is becoming Hatti's strongman. Therefore, he'll no longer take us seriously. Isn't this the very best time to attack him? I'm convinced that it's Muwattali's way of telling you to hurry. It's time to strike, and strike quickly."

"I was hoping that one day soon Uri-Teshoop would come to have his omens read at the temple of Ishtar. With his new appointment, he'll need it done right away. The new head of the Hittite army needs to know his future, and only a look at a vulture's entrails can tell it. I'll handle the consultation myself. Once he's dead, I'll explain that the wrath of the gods killed Uri-Teshoop."

Heavily laden with tin, fabrics, and foodstuffs, the donkeys made their plodding way into the Hittite capital. The lead men drove them to a counting house where a merchant checked invoices, issued bills, signed contracts, and threatened creditors.

The principal representative of the merchant class, an obese sexagenarian, strode through the commercial district, keeping a watchful eye on business transactions. He was quick to intervene in any dispute. When Hattusili crossed his path, the professional smile left his face. Wearing a headband and a crude multicolored garment, the emperor's brother appeared more nervous than usual.

"The news is bad," confessed the merchant.

"Problems with your suppliers?"

"No, much worse than that: Uri-Teshoop."

"But the emperor left me in charge of the economic sector!"

"Uri-Teshoop doesn't seem to notice."

"What kind of trouble is he causing?"

"The emperor's son has decided to impose a new tax on each commercial transaction, to go toward his soldiers' pay."

"I'll lodge a strong protest."

"It won't do any good."

Hattusili was lost in a storm. For the first time, the emperor had failed to take him into his confidence and he was hearing important news secondhand.

"I'll ask the emperor to repeal this tax."

"He'll refuse," predicted the merchant. "Uri-Teshoop wants to rebuild the military by crushing the merchant class and appropriating our riches."

"I'll oppose it."

"May the gods help you, Hattusili."

For more than three hours, Hattusili was made to wait in a small, cold palace antechamber. Usually he was shown directly in to see his brother; today two members of Muwattali's personal bodyguard had blocked his way and a chamberlain had noted his request for an audience without promising anything.

Night was falling when Hattusili finally spoke to one of the guards. "Tell the chamberlain I can't wait much longer."

The soldier hesitated, shot a glance at his comrade, then ducked out of the room. The remaining guard seemed ready to use his lance if Hattusili tried to force his way inside.

The chamberlain reappeared with six grim-looking soldiers. The emperor's brother thought they might arrest him and throw him in prison forever.

"What are you here for?" inquired the chamberlain.

"To see the emperor."

"Didn't I tell you that he's not receiving visitors today? It's useless to wait any longer."

Hattusili withdrew. The guards stayed in place.

As he was leaving the palace, he ran into Uri-Teshoop. More forceful than ever, the commander-in-chief of the Hittite army looked right through his uncle.

From atop the palace, Emperor Muwattali surveyed his capital, Hattusa. The fortified city sat on an enormous rock formation in the midst of arid steppes. It had been built to attest to a nation's invincible strength. At the very sight of it, any invader would turn tail. No one could ever take control of its battlements, no one could reach the gates of the imperial citadel that towered over the temples.

No one but Ramses.

Since this last pharaoh had assumed the throne of Egypt, he had sent shock waves through Muwattali's stronghold and dealt severe blows to his empire. At times, the hideous possibility of defeat even crossed his mind. He'd avoided a total disaster at Kadesh, but would his luck hold?

Ramses was young, a conquering hero, a favorite of the gods. He would never relent until the Hittite threat to Egypt was eliminated.

He, Muwattali, the chief of a warrior people, must devise another strategy.

The chamberlain announced Uri-Teshoop.

"Show him in."

The prince's martial tread shook the flagstones.

"May the Storm God watch over you, Father! The army will soon be ready to regain lost ground."

"Haven't you just imposed a new tax that angers the merchants?"

"They're cowards and leeches! A percentage of their profits will help build up our army."

"You're encroaching on the territory I entrusted to Hattusili."

"What do I care about Hattusili? Didn't you just refuse to see him?"

"I don't have to justify my decisions."

"You've chosen me as your successor, Father, as well you should have. The army is gratified and the people feel more secure. Rely on me to reassert our strength and slaughter the Egyptians."

"I appreciate your valiance, Uri-Teshoop, but you still have much to learn. Hatti's foreign policy can't be reduced to a perpetual conflict with Egypt."

"There are only two kinds of men: the victors and the vanquished. The Hittites have always been victors. I plan to keep it that way."

"Plan to obey my orders."

"When will we attack?"

"I have other priorities, my son."

"Why delay a conflict so crucial to the empire?"

"Because we must negotiate with Ramses."

"The Hittites negotiate with an enemy? Your mind must be going, Father."

"I forbid you to take that tone with me!" Muwattali said testily. "Kneel to your emperor and apologize."

Uri-Teshoop remained immobile, arms crossed.

"Do as I say, or . . ."

Panting, his lips twisted into a grimace, eyes glazed, Muwattali clutched his chest and collapsed on the flagstone floor.

"My heart . . . my heart feels like a stone . . . call for the doctor."

"I demand full powers. From here on in, I'll be the one who issues the army's orders."

"The doctor, quickly!"

"Give up the throne."

"I'm your father. You're just going to let me . . . die?"

"Give up the throne."

"I will. You have . . . you have my word."

TWENTY-SIX

The council of tribal chiefs listened attentively to Moses. The acquittal had increased his popularity to such an extent that the man now known as "The Prophet" could not be ignored.

"God protected you," Libni opened gruffly. "Give Him praise and spend the remainder of your existence in prayer."

"You know my true intentions."

"Don't press your luck, Moses."

"God has ordered me to lead the Hebrew people out of Egypt, and I'll obey Him."

Aaron pounded the floor with his staff.

"Moses is right. We must win our independence. When we have our own homeland, we'll be happy and prosperous. Let's all leave Egypt together and fulfill the will of Yahweh!"

"Why expose our people to such peril?" Libni said vehemently. "The army will massacre the insurgents, the police will arrest all sympathizers!"

"First we must banish fear," recommended Moses. "Our faith will give us the strength to overcome Pharaoh and avoid his wrath."

"Why can't we be content with serving Yahweh here, in the land where we were born?"

"God spoke to me on the mountain," Moses reminded

them. "It's God who has traced your course. Refusing to follow would be the end of us."

Kha was fascinated. Setau was telling him about the energy that circulates in the universe and animates all living things, from a grain of sand to a star. A concentrated form of that energy, he said, was found in statues of the gods. Ramses' eldest son, inside the temples where Setau gained him admittance, could never get his fill of contemplating their bodies of stone.

The child was awestruck. A priest had purified his hands and feet, dressed him in a white kilt, then made him cleanse his mouth with natron. From the moment he set foot inside the fragrant and silent world of the temple, Kha had perceived the presence of a strange force, the "magic" that linked the elements of life and on which Pharaoh drew so that he might nurture his people.

Setau showed the young prince around the laboratory attached to the temple of Amon. The walls were covered with inscriptions revealing the secret formulas for unguents used in religious ceremonies and ingredients that preserved the sacred eye of Horus, keeping its light alive in the world.

Kha read the texts avidly, memorizing as many of the hieroglyphs as he could. He would have liked to spend time in each of the temples they visited, studying the inscriptions in detail. These life-bearing symbols were what transmitted the wisdom of the ages.

"This is where true magic is revealed," Setau told the boy. "It's the weapon God has given man to ward off evil and triumph over fate."

"But how can we change our destiny?"

"We can't, but if we become fully aware of it, we can rise above it. If you can bring magic into your everyday life, you'll be in touch with the force that tells you the secrets of heaven and earth, of day and night, of the mountains and rivers. You'll understand the language of birds and fish, you'll wake at dawn with the sun at your side, and you'll see divine power skimming the waters."

"Will you teach me how?"

"Perhaps, if you try hard, if you fight hard against vanity and laziness."

"I'll fight with all my might!"

"Your father and I are heading for the Deep South. We'll be gone for several months."

Kha's face fell. "I wish you could stay and teach me magic."

"Turn your disappointment into an opportunity. You're to come here each day and immerse yourself in the sacred symbols that live on in stone. That way you'll be protected from any outside attack. For additional security, I'm going to equip you with an amulet and a protective inscription."

Setau lifted the lid of a gilded wooden box and produced an amulet in the shape of a papyrus plant, which symbolized vigor and growth. He hung it on a cord and looped it around Kha's neck. Then he unrolled a slim strip of cloth and with fresh ink drew an eye, healthy and intact. As soon as the ink was dry, he twisted the strip around the boy's left wrist.

"Take care with both of these things," he advised solemnly. "They'll prevent negative influences from getting into your blood. The magnetizing priests have imbued them with fluid that will build up your immunity."

"Are snakes the ones who hold the secret formulas?"

"They know more than we do about life and death, the two sides of reality. Understanding their message is the basis of all knowledge."

"I'd like to be your apprentice and make medicines with you."

"You're meant to be a ruler, not a healer."

"I don't want to be king! What I like is hieroglyphs and secret lore. A pharaoh has to meet with a lot of people and solve all kinds of problems. I prefer peace and quiet."

"Life doesn't always turn out the way we want it to."

"It should, when we have magic!"

Moses was lunching with Aaron and two tribal chiefs intrigued by the idea of an exodus.

A knock came at the door. When Aaron opened it, Serramanna came barging in.

"Is Moses here?"

The two tribal chiefs moved to shield the prophet.

"Come with me, Moses."

"Where are you taking him?"

"That doesn't concern you. Don't make me use force."

Moses stepped forward. "I'm coming, Serramanna."

The Sard had the Hebrew get in his chariot. Escorted by two other police vehicles, they drove briskly to the edge of town, through the fields, and out toward the desert.

Serramanna pulled up at the foot of a little rise that overlooked a stretch of sand and gravel.

"Go up to the top, Moses," he ordered. It was an easy climb. Seated on a windblown boulder, Ramses was waiting.

"I like the desert as much as you do, Moses. Don't you remember our adventures in the Sinai?"

The prophet sat down next to the Pharaoh and they looked off in the same direction.

"What god is this haunting you, Moses?"

"The One God, the True God."

"Your Egyptian education should have opened your mind to the multiple facets of the divine."

"Don't try to take me back to the past. My people have a future, but only outside of Egypt. Let the Hebrews go into the desert, three days' distance, where we can make sacrifices to Yahweh."

"You know quite well that it's out of the question. Such an excursion would require significant military protection. In the current circumstances, we can't rule out the possibility of a Bedouin raid. An unarmed population could sustain a great number of casualties."

"Yahweh will protect us."

"The Hebrews are my subjects, Moses. I'm responsible for their safety."

"Subjects? We're your prisoners."

"The Hebrews are free to come and go as they please, in and out of Egypt, providing they obey the law. Your demand is unrealistic in time of war. Furthermore, many of your people would refuse to follow."

"I'll guide my people to the Promised Land."

"And where is that?"

"Yahweh will reveal it to us."

"Are the Hebrews unhappy in Egypt?"

"That doesn't matter. All that counts is the will of God."

"Why are you so inflexible? In Pi-Ramses, we have places of worship where foreign gods are welcome. The Hebrews can live their faith as they wish."

"That isn't enough for us. Yahweh can no longer suffer the presence of false gods."

"Aren't you missing the point, Moses? Through the ages our country has honored the divine as a single principle with multiple manifestations. When Akhenaton tried to make Aton supersede all other forms of the sacred, he was in error."

"His doctrine is being revived, in a purified form."

"Belief in a unique and exclusive god would prevent religious exchanges with neighboring countries and tarnish the hope of peace among people on earth."

"Yahweh is the protector and refuge of the just."

"Are you forgetting Amon? He banishes evil, hears the prayers of all loving hearts, hastens to help those in need. Amon is the healer who gives the blind man back his sight. Nothing escapes him, for he is both one and many."

"The Hebrews worship Yahweh, not Amon, and Yahweh alone will guide their destiny."

"A rigid doctrine leads to death, Moses."

"My decision is made and I'll hold firm. It's the will of God."

"Isn't it vain to believe you're His chosen one?"

"Your opinion means nothing to me."

"Then nothing remains of our friendship?"

"The Hebrews have chosen me as their leader. You, Ramses, are the head of the country holding us prisoner. My mission must take precedence over our friendship and my respect for you."

"If you persist, you'll be flouting the law of Ma'at."

"What do I care?"

"Do you think you're above the guiding principle of the universe, which existed before humanity and will live long after our own extinction?"

"The only law the Hebrews respect is the law of Yahweh. Will you grant us your permission to go in the desert and sacrifice in His name?"

"No, Moses; as long as we're at war with the Hittites, it would be against the national interest. Nothing must compromise our defenses."

"If you continue to refuse, Yaweh will guide my arm to make me work wonders that will be the despair of your country."

Ramses stood up.

"You seem to have all the answers, my friend. Add this to your list: I'll never cave in to threats."

TWENTY-SEVEN

The caravan was trudging through a wasteland. The Egyptian delegation, composed of thirty men on horseback, scribes and military men, and a hundred donkeys laden with gifts, progressed between cliff walls carved with giant figures of Hittite warriors marching southward, toward Egypt. Ahsha deciphered the inscription: *The Storm God traces the warriors' route and leads them to victory.*

The head of Egyptian diplomacy had already been forced to lecture his little troop several times. Their harsh and unfamiliar surroundings made the men jittery—the massifs and mountain passes, the unknown forces lurking in the forests. Although not particularly at ease himself, Ahsha pressed on, relieved not to encounter any of the marauders that roamed the region.

The delegation exited the canyon, hugged a river, passed more boulders carved with menacing soldiers, then emerged onto a windswept plain. In the distance was a promontory topped with a fortress, the empire's enormous and menacing border post.

The donkeys balked; their driver tried every trick he knew to keep them moving toward the sinister fortress.

In the battlements, archers prepared to fire.

Ahsha ordered his men to dismount and lay their arms on the ground.

Brandishing a boldly striped standard, the herald took a few steps toward the entry to the stronghold.

An arrow shattered the flagstaff. A second whizzed to the ground at his feet. A third grazed his shoulder. Wincing in pain, he retreated.

The Egyptian soldiers grabbed their weapons.

"No," cried Ahsha, "put them down!"

"We're not going to let them slaughter us!" an officer protested.

"This behavior is unusual. The Hittites would never be so easily provoked, so much on the defensive, unless something was seriously wrong within the country. But what? I won't know until I talk with the commander of the fortress."

"After a welcome like this, you can't be thinking . . ."

"Take ten men and ride hard to our fallback position. The provincial troops should be put on high alert, as if a Hittite attack were imminent. Send couriers to inform

Pharaoh of the situation so that our northeastern defensive line is combat-ready. As soon as possible, I'll fill in the details for him."

Thankful to be dispatched toward less hostile territory, the officer acted immediately on his orders. He selected his escort, packed up the wounded herald, and led the squadron off at a gallop.

The men remaining with Ahsha felt their hearts sink. Yet their chief calmly took a sheet of papyrus and wrote a note in Hittite, giving his name and titles. After he attached the document to an arrowhead, an archer sent it flying to the door of the fortress.

"Now we'll see," he told the delegation. "Either they'll talk or they'll come after us."

"But we're official envoys of the Egyptian government!"

"If the Hittites are exterminating diplomats who've come to open talks, that will tell us that the war has entered a new phase. A crucial piece of intelligence, wouldn't you say?"

The scribe gulped. "Couldn't we just retreat?"

"It would be unworthy. We represent His Majesty's government."

Unconvinced by this lofty argument, the scribe and his colleagues quaked with fear.

The gates to the fortress parted, giving passage to three Hittite horsemen.

A helmeted officer wearing thick armor snatched up the message and read it. Then he ordered his men to surround the Egyptians.

"Follow us," he commanded.

The interior of the fortress was just as grim as the exterior. Cold stone, chilly halls, an armory, bunk rooms, foot soldiers drilling . . . Ahsha felt claustrophobic, but spoke reassuringly to his group, aware that they already felt like prisoners.

After a brief wait, the helmeted officer reappeared.

"Which one of you is the ambassador Ahsha?"

He stepped forward.

"The commander wishes to see you."

Ahsha was shown into a square room with a fireplace for heat. Near the hearth stood a short, slight man draped in a thick woolen mantle.

"Welcome to Hatti. I was hoping we'd meet again, Ahsha."

"May I say that I'm surprised to find you here, Hattusili?"

"And may I ask why Pharaoh's sending such a high-ranking emissary?"

"Bearing gifts for the emperor."

"Rather unconventional, considering we're at war."

"Must the conflict between our two countries be everlasting?"

Hattusili's face registered shock. "What are you suggesting?"

"That I'd like to meet with the emperor to tell him Ramses' intentions."

Hattusili warmed his hands.

"It will be difficult . . . very difficult."

"Do you mean impossible?"

"Go back to Egypt, Ahsha . . . No, I can't let you go . . ."

In light of his host's confusion, Ahsha decided to spring the news on him.

"I've come to make a peace proposal to Muwattali."

Hattusili wheeled around. "Is this a trap? Or some kind of joke?"

"Pharaoh is convinced that it's the best option for Egypt as well as Hatti."

"Ramses wants peace? I can't believe it!"

"It's my job to convince you otherwise and conduct the negotiations."

"Give up, Ahsha."

"Why?"

Hattusili sized up the diplomat. Was he sincere? But at this point, what was there to lose by telling him the truth?

"The emperor has been taken ill. He can no longer speak or move, and he's unable to govern."

"Who's running the government, then?"

"His son, Uri-Teshoop, supreme commander of the armed forces."

"He didn't leave you in charge?"

"Only of the economic sector and the foreign service."

"Then you're the man that I've come to see."

"I'm nobody, Ahsha. My own brother slammed the door in my face. As soon as I learned Muwattali had been stricken, I took refuge here; the garrison commander is a friend."

"Will Uri-Teshoop proclaim himself emperor?"

"As soon as Muwattali dies."

"Why give up so easily, Hattusili?"

"I have nothing left to fight with."

"Is the whole army under Uri-Teshoop's sway?"

"Some of the officers fear his hard-line tendencies, but they'd never dare speak out."

"I'm ready to go to your capital and lay out my peace proposal."

"Peace? Uri-Teshoop doesn't know the meaning of the word. It will never work."

"Where is your lovely wife, by the way?"

"Puduhepa stayed on in the capital."

"Was that wise?"

Hattusili again turned toward the hearth.

"Puduhepa has a plan to check Uri-Teshoop's rise."

The proud and noble Puduhepa had been meditating in the temple of Ishtar for three days. When the soothsayer deposited the carcass of a freshly killed vulture on one of the altars, she knew her time had come.

Draped in a long garnet robe, a silver diadem in her hair, Puduhepa clutched the handle of the dagger she would sink into Uri-Teshoop's back when he bent to look at the vulture's entrails, as the soothsayer would certainly suggest.

The handsome priestess had dreamed of a peace that could never be, a balance of power within Hatti and a truce with Egypt; but Uri-Teshoop's very existence reduced such aims to nothingness.

She alone could prevent this demon from wreaking havoc. She alone could help transfer power to her husband, Hattusili, who would set the empire to rights again.

Uri-Teshoop entered the sanctuary. Puduhepa was hidden behind a massive column near the altar.

The emperor's son had not come alone, she noted with annoyance. Puduhepa knew that she should give up and slip out of the temple unseen. But when would another such opportunity come her way? Uri-Teshoop's security would only grow tighter. If she moved swiftly enough, she could dispatch her husband's rival, most likely falling prey herself to his bodyguards.

Shirking this sacrifice would be dastardly. She must think about her country's future, not her own existence.

The soothsayer slashed the vulture's belly. A terrible stench filled the air. Plunging his hands into the entrails, he spread them out on the altar.

Uri-Teshoop approached, leaving a gap between himself and his bodyguards. Puduhepa gripped the dagger handle even tighter and prepared to strike. She must pounce like a wildcat, concentrating all her energy in one deadly blow.

A sudden cry from the soothsayer stopped her in her tracks. Uri-Teshoop backed away.

"Your Highness, it's horrible!"

"What do you see in these entrails?"

"You must defer all your plans. At this time the outlook is unfavorable."

Uri-Teshoop's impulse was to slit the priest's throat. Even if he did, the members of his entourage who were present would broadcast the news of the unfavorable reading. In Hatti, no one ignored a soothsayer's predictions.

"How long must I wait?"

"Until the omens change, Your Highness."

His blood rising, Uri-Teshoop stormed out of the temple.

TWENTY-EIGHT

The Egyptian court was rife with conflicting rumors about the royal couple's departure for the south. Some claimed it was imminent, others that it had been postponed indefinitely, given the unstable situation in the protectorates. Some even thought that the king, despite having sent his royal sons to head the regiments, would be forced to march off to war again.

Light flooded Ramses' office as he stood in prayer before his father's statue. On the broad table sat dispatches from Canaan and southern Syria. Watcher, the yellow-gold dog, slept curled in his master's armchair.

Ahmeni burst into the office. "A message from Ahsha!"

"Can you authenticate it?"

"The handwriting is his, and he inserted my name in code."

"How was it sent?"

"One of the couriers brought it direct from Hatti. He says that it never left his hands."

Ramses read Ahsha's letter detailing the extent of the Hittite empire's internal troubles. He understood why the earlier dispatches had persuaded his friend to put the forts along the northeastern border on high alert.

"The Hittites are in no shape to attack us, Ahmeni. The queen and I can leave."

Outfitted with his amulet and his magic wristband, Kha was copying a mathematical formula that showed how to calculate the ideal angle for hoisting stones up a building under construction, surrounded by earthworks. His sister, Meritamon, grew more skilled each day at her harp. She loved to play with their little brother, Merenptah, whose first attempts at walking were closely monitored by Iset the Fair and Fighter. The enormous Nubian lion liked to gaze through half-closed eyes as the human cub toddled around.

Fighter's head snapped to attention when Serramanna appeared at the garden gate. Interpreting the Sard's intentions as peaceful, the lion gave a small roar and settled back into his sphinx-like pose.

"I'd like to speak with Kha," Serramanna said to Iset the Fair.

"Has he done something wrong?" she asked, haltingly.

"No, of course not. But he may be able to help with my investigation."

"Wait here. As soon as he's worked out his problem, I'll send him over."

Serramanna had made progress.

He knew that a Libyan sorcerer named Ofir was responsible for murdering Lita, his sadly deluded protégée. As the leading proponent of Akhenaton's heresy, he had used religion as a cover for his role as a Hittite spy, as well as to spread sedition. These were no longer theories; they were facts gleaned from a peddler nabbed by Serramanna's men when he showed up at Ofir's former Memphis residence (a house deeded to Shaanar). The peddler was only a small-time Hittite agent, to be sure, working on call for the Syrian merchant Raia. He never heard that Raia had fled to Hatti and the underground network had been dismantled. Fearing rough treatment, he was more than willing to talk, and with his cooperation Serramanna tied up a number of loose ends.

But Ofir still eluded him, and Serramanna was not at all convinced that Shaanar had died in the desert. Had the two of them taken off for Hatti together? Experience had taught the Sard that evildoers never gave up and their imagination was limitless.

Kha approached the giant and looked straight up at him.

"You're tall. You must be awfully strong."

"Will you answer some questions for me?"

"Are you good at math?"

"I know how to count my men and the arms I issue them."

"Do you know how to build a temple or a pyramid?"

"Pharaoh gave me another job: catching criminals."

"What I like is writing and reading hieroglyphs."

"That's just what I wanted to talk to you about—the brush you're missing."

"It was my favorite one. I really miss it."

"You must have given this some thought, then. I'm sure you can help me figure out who's guilty."

"I have an idea, but I'm not sure. An accusation of theft is not something to be made lightly."

The boy's maturity astounded the Sard. If there really was a clue, Kha would never have overlooked it.

"Have you noticed anyone around you behaving strangely?"

"For a few weeks, I seemed to have a new friend."

"And who was that?"

"Old Meba, the diplomat. He showed a sudden interest in my work. Then, just as suddenly, he was gone."

A broad grin lit the hulking Sardinian's weather-beaten face.

"Thank you, Prince Kha."

In Pi-Ramses, as in Egypt's other cities, the Feast of Flowers was a day of public celebration. As the nation's chief priestess, Nefertari never forgot that from the First Dynasty forward the government had relied on a cycle of feast days cementing the marriage of heaven and earth. The royal couple's continuation of the tradition involved the population as a whole in the life of the gods.

On temple altars as well as doorsteps, floral arrangements vied for attention. Here were huge bouquets, palm fronds, bunches of roses; there were lotuses, cornflowers, mandrakes with their stems.

Dancing with round or square tambourines, waving acacia branches, wearing garlands of cornflowers and poppies, women in the service of Hathor roamed through the city's main streets, crushing thousands of petals beneath their feet.

Ramses' sister, Dolora, had positioned herself near the queen, whose beauty dazzled everyone lucky enough to catch sight of her. Nefertari remembered her girlhood dream of a cloistered life. How could she have conceived of a Great Royal Wife's obligations, which seemed to weigh more heavily each day?

The procession surged toward the temple of Amon, where it was greeted with rousing cheers.

"Has your departure date been settled, Your Majesty?" inquired Dolora.

"Our ship will cast off tomorrow morning," Nefertari answered her.

"The court is uneasy. There's talk that your absence will last several months."

"It's possible."

"Will you really go as far as Nubia?"

"That's what Pharaoh has decided."

"Egypt needs you so badly!"

"Nubia is part of our kingdom, Dolora."

"It can be dangerous down there . . ."

"This won't be a pleasure cruise."

"I'm sure it's a pressing matter, to keep you away from the capital so long?"

Nefertari smiled dreamily. "It's love, Dolora. Only love."

"I don't understand, Your Majesty."

"I was thinking out loud," the queen said, still distant.

"I'd like so much to help out . . . how can I be of use to you during your absence?"

"Give Iset a hand, if she wants one; my only regret is missing out on the children's upbringing."

"May the gods watch over them, and their mother as well."

As soon as the feast was over, Dolora would pass the information she had gathered on to Ofir. In leaving the capital for an extended period, Ramses and Nefertari were making a mistake that their enemies would put to good use.

Accompanied by his sandal-bearer, Meba set out for a leisurely boat ride on Pi-Ramses' yachting basin. The diplomat felt the need to reflect, gazing out on the tranquil waters.

Caught up in a whirlwind, Meba was no longer quite himself. His highest aim had been a life of luxury, along with the distinction of high public office, requiring the occasional intrigue to shore up his position. Now he was heading a Hittite spy ring, working toward the destruction of Egypt . . . No, he had never wished it.

But Meba was afraid. Afraid of Ofir, his icy stare, his simmering violence. There was no way out. Meba's future depended on Ramses' fall.

The sandal-bearer hailed a boatman dozing on the shore. Serramanna came between them.

"May I be of help, Your Excellency?"

The old diplomat flinched. "I don't believe so."

"Oh, I'd love a chance to get out on the water. Won't you let me row you?"

The Sard's sheer bulk was daunting. "As you wish."

With a push from Serramanna, the boat was quickly under way.

"It's so lovely here. It's too bad that you and I have so little time to enjoy it."

"Why do you want to see me?"

"Don't worry, I have no intention of interrogating you."

"Why would you?"

"I simply need your advice on a delicate point."

"I'm not sure I can help you."

"Have you heard of the strange case involving Prince Kha? It seems his favorite brush has been stolen."

Meba avoided making eye contact.

"Stolen? Are you sure?"

"The prince has no doubt about it."

"But Kha is only a child."

"I wonder whether you might know who the thief could be."

"The very idea! Row me back to shore at once, please."

Serramanna flashed a carnivorous grin.

"Yes, sir. And thank you for a most educational outing."

TWENTY-NINE

In the prow of the royal flagship, Ramses clasped Nefertari tenderly. The royal couple was celebrating an intensely happy moment, communing with the spirit of the river, the great giver of life, the celestial stream emptying out of the heavens to form Egypt's lifeblood.

The water level was high, and the sailing fast, thanks to a brisk tailwind. The captain remained on constant alert, for the current was full of dangerous eddies. One false move could result in a shipwreck.

Each day, Nefertari was more of a wonder. Her beauty married grace with queenly authority, miraculously combining a radiant personality with a flawless physique. This long journey south would be the expression of Ramses' love for she whose serene presence was the light of Egypt and its pharaoh. His life with Nefertari had taught Ramses why the sages had advised that a royal couple should rule over the nation as one.

After nine years on the throne, Ramses and Nefertari were enriched by all they had been through together, and still as much in love as the moment when they first realized they were bound together for life and death.

Her hair in the breeze, wearing a simple white dress, Nefertari was admiring the marvelous scenery of middle Egypt; palm groves, fields along the riverbanks, white villages perched on hilltops were a heavenly sight, like what the just would see in the next world. The royal couple had striven to build such a heaven on earth.

"Aren't you afraid that our absence . . ."

"I've spent the greater part of my reign in the north. The time has come for me to concentrate on the south. Egypt can never survive unless the two lands are united. And this war against Hatti has made me spend too much time away from you."

"The war isn't over."

"The Near East is in a period of upheaval. If there's a chance for peace, shouldn't we take it?"

"So this is what's behind Ahsha's secret mission," said Nefertari.

"Yes. The risks he's running are huge. But I know he's the man for the job."

"You and I are together, through joy or suffering, hope or fear. May the magic we seek on this journey protect our friend Ahsha!"

Setau's footsteps echoed on the bridge.

"Excuse me for interrupting," he began.

"Go ahead, Setau."

"I wish I could have stayed close to Kha. The boy will

make a tremendous magician. As far as his safety goes, don't worry; he's well protected. No one will break through the wall of magic I built around him."

"Won't you and Lotus be glad to see Nubia again?" asked Nefertari.

"Yes, it has the world's finest snakes. But I really came to tell you that the captain's worried about what he reads in the currents. He thinks we may run into trouble and plans to head for shore once we pass that grassy island."

The Nile meandered, ran past a sheer wall where vultures nested, then flowed away from the cliffs. Soon a long semicircle of mountains stretched before them.

Nefertari's hand flew to her throat.

"What's the matter?" Ramses asked anxiously.

"A catch in my throat . . . it's nothing."

A violent blow rocked the ship. Nearby was the whoosh of a whirlpool.

On the shore stood the crumbling buildings of Akhenaton's ghostly capital.

"Take the queen into our cabin," Ramses ordered Setau, "and keep an eye on her."

Some of the sailors began to panic. One of them fell off the mainmast as he tried to haul in a sail, striking the captain. With the captain too dazed to issue clear orders, confusion ensued.

"Silence!" Ramses thundered. "Every man to his post. I'll tell you what to do next."

Within a few minutes, the danger was evident. The rest of the flotilla, riding on a countercurrent and unable to comprehend why the royal vessel was bucking wildly, was abruptly cut off and unable to lend any aid.

When the flagship's course was righted, the king saw the reason for their trouble—but no way around it.

In the middle of the river was a huge whirlpool. The landing at the City of the Horizon of Aton, which should have been easy to pass, was dammed with rafts. On the rafts sat charcoal burners. The king could either sacrifice his ship to the river or have it catch on fire if he rammed the blockade.

Who would have laid such a trap near the abandoned city? Ramses knew what had so upset Nefertari; with her second sight, she had sensed the danger.

The king had only moments left to think. This time, his lion could do nothing to help him.

"Ship ahoy!" yelled the lookout.

Tossing aside the goose drumstick he was gnawing, Shaanar lunged for his bow and sword. The mighty prince and sybarite had hardened into a warrior.

"Is Pharaoh's boat cut off from the others?"

"Just as you planned it, My Lord. The escort is at some distance."

The mercenary was salivating. The handful of men Ofir had recruited for this ambush would be richly compensated, to hear Shaanar tell it. His fiery speeches had whipped them into a killing frenzy.

Yet no hired killer would dare touch Ramses, for fear of being thunderstruck. Ever since Kadesh, the tale of his supernatural powers had been circulating. Shaanar simply shrugged and promised to finish off the tyrant himself.

"Half of you head for the rafts; the rest come with me."

So Ramses was about to die near the City of the Horizon of Aton, as if Akhenaton's heresy would finally win out over Amon and the other divinities that the King of Egypt worshiped. Taking Nefertari hostage, Shaanar would have no trouble convincing his dead brother's escort to accept him as their new king. Ramses' demise would open a gaping breach into which Shaanar would leap without delay.

Several mercenaries jumped off the landing onto the rafts and were preparing to launch flaming arrows toward the royal flagship while their fellow recruits attacked it from the rear, under Shaanar's command.

There was no way that they could lose.

"All oarsmen to starboard!" cried Ramses.

A first flaming arrow struck the wooden wall of the cabin amidships. Lotus, alert and nimble, snuffed out the fire with some sackcloth.

Ramses climbed on the cabin roof, drew his bowstring, took aim at one of the attackers, held his breath, and fired. The arrow pierced the mercenary's throat. His comrades crouched behind the coal fires to take cover from the monarch's deadly shots. Their own arrows, fired at random, disappeared in the churning waters around the ship.

The ship had changed tack so suddenly following Ramses' shouted orders that it bucked like a wild horse and veered sideways, pounded by the raging river on the port side. There was a chance they could make it to shore if they weren't sucked into the whirlpool or overtaken by Shaanar's men in their more easily maneuvered boats. Shaanar himself had already picked off two men on the poop deck. Arrows through their chests, they splashed into the river.

Setau ran to the prow, gingerly carrying a clay egg. Covered with inscriptions, this talisman was a replica of the "egg of the world" preserved in the inner sanctum of the great temple of Thoth at Hermopolis. Only state magicians like Setau were authorized to use such a powerful and highly charged tool.

Setau was not at all pleased. He had planned to use the talisman in Nubia, if some unexpected threat to the royal couple arose. He hated to part with it, but there was no other way to deal with this wretched whirlpool.

The snake charmer lobbed the sacred egg into the swirling waters. They bubbled, as if coming to a boil. A spout formed and a wave crashed over the rafts, putting out some of the fires and killing two mercenaries.

The flagship was safe now from fire and shipwreck, but the situation on deck was deteriorating. Shaanar's men had thrown grappling hooks and were climbing up the rigging. Their chief unleashed arrow after arrow, holding the Egyptian sailors at bay.

Two flaming arrows hit the mainsail, starting another fire that Lotus again extinguished. Although he was exposed to enemy fire, Ramses held his position and continued to pick off the mercenaries. Alerted by shouts from the rear of the ship, he wheeled to find a pirate with his ax poised over an unarmed sailor's head.

Pharaoh's gaze briefly met the wild eyes of the enemy leader, a bearded, frantic man who was aiming straight for him. The monarch dodged the arrow with the slightest of movements to the left; it only grazed his cheek. His frustrated attacker ordered the remaining mercenaries to retreat.

A falling spark caught Lotus's dress on fire. She plunged into the river, only to be sucked into the dying whirlpool. She waved a struggling arm, calling for help.

Ramses dove into the river after her.

Emerging from the cabin amidships, Nefertari saw her husband disappear into the Nile.

THIRTY

The minutes flew by.

The flagship and its escort had anchored in now-calm waters near the abandoned landing. Three or four mercenaries had managed to escape, but Nefertari and Setau did not give them a thought. Like Fighter's, their eyes were trained on the spot where Ramses and Lotus had gone under.

The queen had burnt incense to Hathor, the goddess of navigation. With a quiet dignity that won the sailors' hearts, Nefertari awaited the search party's report. Some men were dragging the river, others were beating the towpaths, the better to comb the high grass along the banks. No doubt the current had already swept the king and the Nubian beauty far away.

Setau stayed close to the queen.

"Pharaoh will come back," she murmured.

"Your Majesty . . . the river can be unforgiving."

"He's fine, and he's saved Lotus."

"You think . . ."

"Ramses' work is unfinished. A pharaoh with so much left to do can't possibly die."

Setau saw that there was no disputing the queen's touching conviction. But how would she react when she was forced to accept the inevitable? The magician set aside his own grief to share Nefertari's. He was already imagining the grim return to Pi-Ramses and the announcement of Ramses' death.

Shaanar and his companions waited until they had covered a good distance, with the help of a strong northward current, before pausing to rest. They sank their boat and waded into the verdant countryside, where they would swap amethysts for donkeys.

"Where are we going?" demanded a Cretan henchman.

"You there, go to Pi-Ramses and debrief Ofir."

"I hope he won't shoot the messenger."

"We have nothing to be ashamed of."

"Ofir doesn't like to lose."

"He knows the odds against us; he knows that I'm doing all I can. And you have two valuable pieces of information to give him. First, I saw Setau on board the royal flagship. That means Kha is no longer under his wing. Second, I'm going to Nubia, as we agreed. I'll kill Ramses there."

"I'd rather go with you," said the mercenary. "My comrade would make a better messenger. I'm good at fighting and tracking game."

"All right."

Shaanar was not in the least discouraged. The brief and

bloody clash had turned him into a full-fledged war chief, releasing years of pent-up rage. With a handful of men and a bit of imagination, he had taken the mighty Ramses by surprise. In fact, he had almost triumphed!

The next time, he would do more than come close.

Silence reigned over the royal flotilla. No one dared engage in conversation for fear of disturbing the queen. As evening drew near, she still stood in meditation in the flag-ship's prow.

Setau also kept the silence, letting her cling to the last shred of hope. Once the sun went down, Nefertari would have to face the unspeakable facts.

"I knew it," she said so softly it startled Setau.

"Your Majesty . . ."

"Ramses is over there, on the roof of the white palace."

"Your Majesty, it's getting darker, and . . ."

"Take a good look."

Setau squinted at the spot where Nefertari pointed. "You're seeing things."

"I'm not," she said firmly. "Let's move closer."

Setau reluctantly relayed the queen's command. The flag-ship raised anchor and sailed toward the City of the Horizon of Aton, already fading in the dusk.

The snake charmer looked once more toward the roof of the white palace that had once been home to Akhenaton and Nefertiti. Suddenly, he saw what looked like the standing figure of a man. He rubbed his eyes and looked again. It was no illusion.

"Ramses is alive," Nefertari repeated.

"Full speed ahead!" yelled Setau.

And Ramses' silhouette drew nearer, larger by the minute, in the sun's last rays.

Setau was fuming.

"Why couldn't the Lord of the Two Lands simply signal for help? That would be no disgrace!"

"I had other things to do," answered the king. "Lotus and I swam underwater, but she lost consciousness, and I thought she'd drowned. We came ashore at the far end of the ghost town. I magnetized Lotus until she came back to life. Then we walked through the town looking for the highest point, where you'd be more likely to spot us. I knew Nefertari was following our every step. She'd look in the right direction."

Quietly radiant, the queen discreetly displayed her emotion by clinging to Ramses' arm as he stroked his lion.

"I thought the egg had failed to save you," muttered Setau. "If you'd died, it would have compromised my career as a magician."

"How is Lotus?" inquired the queen.

"I gave her a sedative. After a good night's sleep, she'll forget this unfortunate incident."

A steward poured cool white wine into goblets for them.

"About time," Setau commented archly. "I was beginning to think we'd left civilization behind."

"During the fighting," Ramses questioned him, "did you get a good look at the enemy leader?"

"They all looked pretty fierce to me. I didn't even notice there was a leader."

"He was bearded, angry and wild-eyed . . . and for a second, I felt sure that it was Shaanar."

"Shaanar was lost in a sandstorm on his way to jail. Even scorpions die eventually."

"What if he didn't die?"

"If so, his only thought would be to stay out of sight. He'd hardly be roaming the country with a band of mercenaries."

"This attack was planned, and it nearly succeeded."

"Could hatred turn a prince into a warrior chief who'd ambush his own brother and assault the sacred person of Pharaoh?"

"If it was Shaanar, we already know the answer."

Setau glowered. "If that villain really is alive, we'll have to be careful. The fury of the desert demons is in his blood."

"This was no chance encounter," said Ramses. "Call together the stone carvers from the surrounding towns."

Some came from Hermopolis, the city of Thoth, others from Assiut, the city of Anubis. Several dozen stone carvers set up a tent city and within hours of their arrival set to work. The speech Ramses gave them was brief and to the point; he placed them under the supervision of two master builders.

In front of the ghostly city's abandoned palace, Pharaoh had handed down his orders. The City of the Horizon of Aton must vanish from the earth. One of Ramses' predecessors, Horemheb, had dismantled some of its temples, using the stones to fill in his monumental gates at Karnak.

Ramses, however, planned to raze the palaces, houses, workshops, riverfront, and other structures. Only then would his work be done. Stone and mud brick would be recycled. The tombs, which harbored no mummies, would be left intact.

The royal flagship lay at anchor until the buildings had been leveled. Only the foundations were left, and soon the sands would drift over them, reducing the wayward capital to nothingness, no longer a gathering place for negative forces.

The salvaged building materials were loaded onto barges. They would be distributed to neighboring towns according to need. The demolition workers were offered meat, oil, beer, and clothing as incentives.

Ramses and Nefertari visited the royal palace one last time before it was razed. The painted tiling would be reused in the royal palace at Hermopolis.

"Akhenaton was wrong," commented Ramses. "The religion he preached was narrow and intolerant. He betrayed the very spirit of Egypt. Unfortunately, I think that Moses is headed down the same road."

"Akhenaton and Nefertiti were a strong couple," Nefertari reminded him. "They respected our laws and were wise enough to acknowledge that their ideas were an experiment. At least they confined the cult of Aton to this remote spot."

"But the poison spread beyond it . . . and I'm not certain that razing this place will clear away the dark shadows. But at least we'll be giving it back to the mountains and desert, and no rebel group will use it as a base again."

When the last stonemason left the leveled city, shrouded forever in silence and neglect, Ramses gave the order to set sail for Abydos.

THIRTY-ONE

Approaching Abydos, Ramses felt a lump in his throat. It had been too long between visits, knowing how much his father had loved the great temple, the importance he had placed on completing his shrine to Osiris. Yes, the Hittite wars and national security had claimed Ramses' time and energy of late, but would any excuse matter to the god of resurrection when they met in the Judgment Hall of the Dead?

Setau had pictured a large turnout of "pure priests" with shaved heads, scented and dressed in spotless white, along with peasants bearing offerings, and priestesses playing the lute and lyre. Instead, the temple landing was deserted.

"Something's not right," he declared. "Let's stay on board."

"What are you afraid of?" asked Ramses.

"Suppose that some other band of marauders has taken over the temple and is waiting to spring a new trap for you."

"Here, on the sacred ground of Abydos?"

"There's no use taking risks. Let's continue south and send in the army."

"And admit that a single iota of my kingdom is off limits to me? Never—especially not Abydos!"

Ramses' anger raged like one of Set's thunderstorms. Not even Nefertari attempted to quell it.

The flotilla landed. Pharaoh took personal command of a unit of chariots hastily assembled from parts stored in the holds of the ships.

The avenue leading from the landing stage to the temple complex was also deserted, as if the holy city had been abandoned. Before the monumental gateway, bearing the mark of stonemasons, tools lay neatly in chests. Wooden sledges laden with blocks of Aswan granite sat idle beneath the tamarisks.

Puzzled, Ramses made his way to the palace adjoining the temple. On the steps leading to the main doorway, an old man was spreading goat cheese on slices of bread. The charioteers' sudden appearance made him lose his appetite. Panic-stricken, he abandoned his meal and tried to run, but was intercepted by a foot soldier who brought him before the king.

"Who are you?" inquired Ramses.

The old man's voice trembled. "One of the palace washermen."

"Why aren't you at work?"

"There's, uh, nothing to do, since everyone's gone. Well, almost everyone . . . a few priests, the ones my age, are still around the sacred lake."

Despite an energetic effort on Ramses' part, early in his reign, the temple remained unfinished. Breaching the monumental gateway, the king and a handful of soldiers walked through the administrative enclave, made up of offices, workshops, a butcher shop, bakery, and brewery—all unstaffed. Their pace quickened as they approached the resident priests' quarters.

Seated on a stone bench, hands resting on the knob of his acacia-wood cane, an old man with a shaved skull attempted to rise and greet the king.

"Spare yourself the trouble, servant of god."

"You are Pharaoh . . . I've heard so much about the Son of Light whose power shines like the sun! My eyes are weak, but there's no mistaking you . . . How lucky I am to see you before I die. At the age of ninety-two, the gods have given me great joy."

"What's going on here at Abydos, old man?"

"Oh, it's the half of the month when the staff is all requisitioned."

"On whose orders?"

"The mayor of the next town over . . . He decided there were too many people working here and that repairing canals made more sense than saying prayers."

The mayor was a jolly fellow with plump cheeks and thick lips. Since his paunch made it hard for him to walk far, he usually got about in a sedan chair. But it was a chariot that now took him to Abydos at a very fair clip.

Wheezing, the mayor prostrated himself before the king, who was seated on a gilded wooden throne with lion-claw feet.

"Forgive me, Your Majesty, I wasn't forewarned of your arrival! If I'd known, I would have provided a reception worthy of you, I would have . . ."

"Are you responsible for requisitioning personnel from Abydos?"

"Yes, but . . ."

"Have you forgotten that it's strictly against the law?"

"No, Your Majesty, but I thought that the temple staff

was underemployed and might be put to good use serving the province."

"You took them away from duties assigned by my father and upheld by me."

"Still, I thought . . ."

"You've committed a very grave infraction, the punishment for which has been set down in a decree: a hundred lashes, the nose and ears cut off."

The mayor blanched and stammered.

"It can't be true, Your Majesty. That's inhuman!"

"You knew what you were doing, and you were aware of the punishment. There's not even any need of a trial."

Aware that a judge would hand down an identical sentence, if not something harsher, the mayor began to plead and sob.

"I admit that I did wrong, but it wasn't for my personal benefit! With the help of the temple staff, the dikes were repaired in record time and the canals thoroughly dredged."

"In that case, I'll offer you the choice of another sentence: you and your municipal staff can serve as construction workers at the temple until its completion."

Each priest and priestess accomplished his or her ritual task, ensuring that the temple of Osiris was like the horizon, illuminating all that gazed upon it. Ramses had dedicated a golden statue of his father; he and Nefertari also made a ceremonial offering to Ma'at. The gods felt at home in the temple, with its electrum-plated Cedar of Lebanon doors, silver floors, granite trim, and brightly painted bas-reliefs. On the altars were flowers, flasks of perfume, and food for the unseen hosts.

There were stockpiles of gold, silver, royal linen, oils for special occasions, wine, honey, myrrh, and unguents. The stables housed fat oxen, healthy cows and calves; the storerooms were bursting with top-quality grain. As a hieroglyphic inscription proclaimed: *Pharaoh multiplies all species for the gods.*

In a speech to the province's notables, gathered in the palace audience chamber at Abydos, Ramses decreed that the boats, fields, land, livestock, donkeys, and all other property of the temple could not be removed from the premises on any account. As for the wardens, bird-catchers, fishermen, farmers, beekeepers, gardeners, vintners, hunters, and other workers on the temple estates, they were to remain in service to Osiris and never to be requisitioned for work in any other domain.

Anyone found in violation of the royal decree would be subject to corporal punishment, stripped of all functions, and sentenced to several years' hard labor.

At Ramses' urging, the construction work moved rapidly ahead. The chapels glowed with continual services. Evil was banished. The temple once again basked in the law of Ma'at.

It was a happy time for Nefertari. Her stay in Abydos was her girlhood dream come true, giving her the unhoped-for chance to live in close contact with the gods, steep herself in their beauty, and glean their secrets as she celebrated the daily rites.

As the time came to close the doors of the *naos*—the inner sanctum—for the night, Ramses was nowhere near. The queen went to look for him and found him in the long corridor where the list of kings was inscribed, going back to the First Dynasty. Through the power of hieroglyphs, their names would live forever in human memory. The name of Ramses the Great would follow his father's.

"How can I live up to their example?" the king wondered aloud. "Prevarication, cowardice, falsehood . . . what pharaoh will ever succeed in cleansing them from the hearts of men?"

"No pharaoh ever will," replied Nefertari. "But all of them fought the good fight, and some won battles even though the war was lost in advance."

"If even the holy ground of Abydos is infringed upon, is it even worthwhile handing down my decrees?"

"It's not like you to be so discouraged."

"That's why I've come to consult my ancestors."

"They can only have given you one piece of advice: go on, learn the uses of adversity, let it make you stronger."

"I wish we could stay in this temple, Nefertari. There's a peace here that I can never find in the outside world."

"It's my duty to warn you against the temptation, no matter how completely I agree."

Ramses took his queen in his arms.

"Without you, nothing I do would have meaning. In two weeks' time, the Mysteries of Osiris will be celebrated. We'll take part in them, and I have a proposition for you. The decision will be entirely yours."

Wielding clubs and uttering hoarse cries, a band of rascals attacked the head of the procession. Wearing the mask of the jackal god, the Abydos priest serving as "trailblazer" fended off his attackers with ritual curses. The enactment would keep evil forces away from the bark of Osiris.

The initiates lent a hand to the trailblazer, pushing aside the enemies of light. The procession resumed its way toward the "Island of the First Morning," where Ramses, in the role of Osiris slain by his brother Set, lay on a bed with a lion-head carving. The waters of the Nile surrounded the primeval mound to which the sister goddesses Isis and Nephtys would make their way over a footbridge.

The island was deep inside a colossal building formed of ten monolithic pillars supporting a ceiling worthy of the old-time pyramid builders. The secret sanctuary of Osiris culminated in a long, narrow transverse chamber; here rested the god's sarcophagus.

Nefertari played the role of Isis, the bride of Osiris, while Iset the Fair was Nephtys, whose name means "Queen of the Temple." She assisted Isis in the rites that would bring Osiris back from the dead.

Nefertari had accepted Ramses' proposal, approving of Iset's participation in the pageant.

The two women knelt, Nefertari at the head of the bed, Iset the Fair at the foot of it. A ewer of fresh water in the right hand, a round loaf of bread in the left, they recited the long and moving litanies that would pump new life into the form lying still on the bed.

Their voices rose in a single melody, under the protection of the sky goddess whose vast body, spangled with stars and decans, was depicted above the bed of resurrection.

At the end of a long night, Ramses-Osiris awoke. And he pronounced the words that every pharaoh before him had said in this identical pageant: "May I be granted light in the sky, creative power on earth, a true voice in the great beyond, and the ability to travel to the head of the stars. May I grasp the front rope of the bark of the night and the back rope of the bark of the day."

THIRTY-TWO

Uri-Teshoop was in a rage.

Consulting with another soothsayer in the temple of the Storm God had done no good: the same dire predictions, the same advice not to launch an offensive. The majority of the soldiers were so superstitious that Uri-Teshoop could not afford to disregard the omens. And none of the oracles could tell him when the outlook might change.

Although the palace doctors were unable to improve Muwattali's condition, the emperor refused to die. To tell the truth, Uri-Teshoop was glad that old man lingered; no one could accuse him of killing his father. The medical staff confirmed that the emperor had suffered a heart attack and warmly approved of his son's daily visits. Uri-Teshoop criticized Hattusili for staying away, as if unconcerned for his brother's health.

When he happened upon the haughty Puduhepa, Uri-Teshoop could not let the opportunity pass.

"Is your husband in hiding?"

"Hattusili is on a mission at the emperor's request."

"My father didn't mention it to me."

"According to the doctors, Muwattali has lost the power of speech."

"You don't seem terribly upset about his condition."

"And you won't let anyone see him—anyone except you."

"Muwattali needs rest."

"We hope he'll soon be back in full command of his faculties."

"Of course you do, but suppose he remains incapacitated . . . There will have to be a decision."

"With Hattusili away, it's quite impossible."

"Have him come back to the palace."

"Is that a suggestion or an order?"

"However you want to take it, Puduhepa."

Puduhepa had left the capital at night, with a very limited retinue, checking several times to make sure that Uri-Teshoop had not had her followed.

At the sight of the sinister fortress where Hattusili had taken refuge, she shivered. By now the garrison might have taken her husband prisoner as a peace offering to the commander-in-chief. In that case, her existence, like Hattusili's, would come to a brutal end behind those gray walls.

Puduhepa did not want to die. She felt able to serve her

country, ready to live through a great many more scorching summers, hike the wild trails of Anatolia again and again, and see Hattusili reign over Hatti. If there was a chance, however slim, of overcoming Uri-Teshoop, she was prepared to grasp at it.

The way she was greeted at the fortress reassured the priestess. She was immediately escorted to the central tower, where the commander had his private quarters.

Hattusili ran to meet her. They embraced.

"Puduhepa, at last! You managed to escape . . ."

"Uri-Teshoop has already taken over the capital."

"We're safe here. All the men in the garrison hate him. Too many soldiers have suffered abuse at his hands."

Puduhepa noted the presence of a man seated by the fire.

"Who is that?" she asked under her breath.

"Ahsha, Pharaoh's secretary of state and special envoy."

"Ahsha, here!"

"He may be our only chance."

"But what does he have to offer?"

"Peace."

Hattusili now witnessed an extraordinary phenomenon. His wife's dark brown eyes grew lighter, as if glowing from within.

"Peace with Egypt," she repeated in amazement. "We know it can never be!"

"Shouldn't we use this unexpected ally to further our interests?"

Puduhepa untwined herself from Hattusili and approached Ahsha. The diplomat rose to greet the lovely visitor.

"Forgive me, Ahsha. I should have spoken to you sooner."

"I wouldn't have wanted to interrupt your reunion."

"You're putting yourself at considerable risk by staying here."

"I was planning to head for the capital, but your husband persuaded me to wait until you arrived."

"You've heard about the emperor's illness."

"I'll still try to talk to him."

"No use, he's dying. The empire already belongs to Uri-Teshoop."

"I've come in search of peace, and I won't leave without it."

"Are you forgetting that Uri-Teshoop's goal in life is the destruction of Egypt? I disapprove of his obsession, yet I must concede that war is what has always held our empire together."

"Have you considered the very real danger you're facing?"

"You mean the Egyptian army out in full force, with Ramses at its head?"

"Don't discount another possibility: the unchecked rise of Assyrian power."

Hattusili and Puduhepa could barely suppress their astonishment. Ahsha's information network must be far more efficient than they had supposed.

"Assyria will attack you eventually, and Hatti won't know which way to turn, warring on two different fronts. And the notion that the Hittite army can destroy Egypt is unrealistic. We've learned from our past mistakes and reinforced defenses in our protectorates. Working your way past them will be difficult, and the delay will give the main force time to mount a swift counterattack. On top of that, you've already learned the hard way that Amon takes care of Ramses and helps him fight with the strength of a thousand men."

"So you've come to announce the downfall of the Hittite empire?" Puduhepa asked sharply.

"No, my lady, for Egypt has nothing to gain by it. There's no enemy like an old enemy, don't you agree? Despite his reputation to the contrary, Ramses is a peace-loving pharaoh, and the Great Royal Wife supports him in this course of action."

"What does Queen Mother Tuya think?"

"She shares my views, namely that Assyria is bound to pose a threat, first to the Hittites and before long to Egypt."

"An alliance against Assyria . . . is that what you're really proposing?"

"A peace agreement and an alliance to protect both our nations from invasion. The next emperor of Hatti will have to make a decision with far-reaching consequences."

"Uri-Teshoop will never stop trying to vanquish Ramses!"

"What would Hattusili decide?"

"My husband and I no longer have any power."

"Give me your answer," Ahsha insisted.

"We'd agree to begin negotiations," declared Hattusili. "But what's the point?"

"Only the unattainable amuses me," the Egyptian said with a smile. "Today, the two of you may be nothing, yet I'm betting on you to brighten my country's prospects. If Hattusili becomes emperor, our discussion will mean a great deal."

"That's only a dream," Puduhepa objected.

"It's fight or flight for you now," Ahsha said coolly.

The priestess's proud eyes blazed. "We'll never run."

"Then you and Hattusili need to win or buy the trust of as many officers as you can. The fortress commanders will take your side, since Uri-Teshoop disdains them and blocks their promotion, claiming that they play only a defensive role. Almost all the merchant class prefers you; get them to spread it around that the Hittite economy can't survive another war and that conflict with Egypt will only bring hardship and ruin. Undermine Uri-Teshoop and keep digging away at him until your nephew looks like a troublemaker, unable to lead the nation."

"It won't happen overnight."

"If you don't try, there will never be peace in our time."

"Meanwhile, what do you plan to do?" Puduhepa inquired of Ahsha.

"It may be a bit risky, but I'm going to make overtures to Uri-Teshoop."

Ahsha contemplated the ramparts of Hattusa and fantasized what the Hittite capital might look like brightly painted, with fluttering banners and gorgeous young women dancing on the battlements. This lovely vision faded, however, as he faced the oppressive reality of the stronghold clinging to the mountainside.

Only two of his countrymen, a groom and a sandal-bearer, accompanied the secretary of state. The rest of the delegation had returned to Egypt. When Ahsha displayed his official seal at the lower town's first guard post, the sentry was speechless.

"Please inform the emperor of my presence."

"But . . . you're Egyptian!"

"Special ambassador. Could you please hurry?"

Nonplussed, the sentry kept Ahsha under close surveillance, dispatching one of his men to the palace.

Ahsha was not overly surprised to see an infantry unit arrive a short time later. The men stepped smartly, holding their lances, commanded by a brute whose only form of thought was blindly carrying out his orders.

"The commander-in-chief wishes to see the ambassador," the soldier announced.

Ahsha greeted Uri-Teshoop, reciting his official titles.

"Ramses' most trusted adviser, here in Hattusa . . . what a surprise!"

"I see that you've been promoted, Your Highness. Please accept my congratulations."

"Egypt will have to watch its step now."

"We've certainly taken note of valor in war. I've been careful to strengthen the defenses in our protectorates."

"I'll crush them anyway."

"They're prepared to resist, no matter how overwhelming the attack."

"So much for small talk, Mr. Ambassador. What are you really here for?"

"I've heard that Emperor Muwattali is ill."

"You'll have to settle for rumors. Our leader's health is a state secret."

"The Lord of Hatti is our enemy, but we respect his greatness. That's why I've come."

"State your purpose, Ahsha."

"I have medicine with me that can cure your father."

THIRTY-THREE

At seven years of age, the boy was acting on the proverb drilled into him by his father, who had learned it from his own father: "Give a man a fish and he'll eat for a day; teach a man to fish and he'll eat for a lifetime."

His stomach growled as he beat the water with a stick to drive his catch toward the tall papyrus stalks where his equally hungry friend lay in wait with the net.

Suddenly, the lad saw them.

A fleet was sailing in from the north. The flagship bore a golden sphinx on its prow. Yes, it had to be Pharaoh's ship!

Forgetting both fish and net, the budding fishermen dove into the Nile and swam toward the bank in order to alert the village. This would mean several days of feasting.

The immense hall of columns in the temple of Karnak looked magnificent: the twelve soaring columns in the central nave manifested the power of creation arising from the primordial ocean.

It was here that Nebu, the high priest of Amon, walking with the aid of his fine gold-plated cane, came to greet the royal couple. Despite his rheumatism, he managed a bow. Ramses helped him to his feet.

"I'm happy to see you, Your Majesty, and delighted to set eyes on your beautiful queen."

"Are you becoming a perfect courtier, Nebu?"

"No hope of that, Your Majesty. I'll continue to speak my mind, as I just have."

"How is your health?"

"The older I get, the more my joints ache, but the temple doctors have prescribed a willow extract that seems to help. I confess that I haven't much time to dwell on my problems . . . you've given me so much responsibility!"

"And it would appear that I have good reason to be satisfied with my choice."

Nebu was in charge of eighty thousand men, nearly a million head of livestock, a hundred-odd barges, fifty busy construction sites, a huge amount of arable land, gardens, woodlands, orchards, and vineyards—such was the world of Karnak, the rich domain of Amon.

"The most difficult part, Your Majesty, is coordinating the efforts of the scribes on the estates, in the granaries, the ones in the accounting department, and all the rest of them . . . without close supervision, the infighting would quickly get out of hand."

"You've become quite the diplomat, Nebu."

"I know of only two virtues: to obey and to serve. Everything else is nonsense. And at my age, I have no time for nonsense."

Ramses and Nefertari admired, one by one, the hundred and thirty-four columns engraved with the names of the deities to whom Pharaoh made offerings in scene after scene. The tall stone stalks eternally linked the floor (symbolizing the primordial swamp) with the blue-painted ceiling sparkling with stars.

As Seti had wished, this vast hypostyle hall would forever attest to the glory of the hidden god, at the same time revealing his mysteries.

"Will you be stopping long in Thebes?" asked Nebu.

"To lead Egypt toward peace," answered Ramses, "I must satisfy the gods by providing residences fit for them, and by completing my eternal dwelling, as well as Nefertari's. The spark of life in our hearts is something the gods may take back at any time; we must be prepared to appear before them, so that the people of Egypt do not suffer by our death."

Ramses summoned the divine force slumbering within Karnak's *naos* and saluted its presence: "Hail to thee, giver of life, who brings forth gods and men, creator of my country and of distant lands, who makes the blooming prairies and the flood waters. All creation is full of thy perfection."

Karnak was awakening.

Daylight replaced the glow of oil lamps. Celebrants filled purification vessels with water from the sacred lake, replaced the cones of incense releasing their scent through the chapels, decked the altars with flowers, fruit, vegetables, and fresh bread. Processions gathered to distribute the offerings, all in the name of Ma'at. She alone could renew the diverse forms of life. She alone invigorated the world with the fresh scent of dew as the sun rose.

With Nefertari at his side, Ramses walked down the avenue of sphinxes leading toward the temple of Luxor.

At the monumental gate, a man stood waiting for the royal couple. A square-jawed, solid man, a former Inspector of the royal stables. He had also been Ramses' instructor in boot camp.

"Bakhen made me fight him," the king told his wife. "I still remember how proud I was not to be beaten."

After giving up the military life, the rugged young man had changed markedly. Ramses eventually named him Fourth Prophet of Amon, moving Bakhen to tears, and seeing the Pharaoh again today moved him beyond words. Since he preferred to let his work speak for him, he gave the royal couple a tour of Luxor's impressive facade, which was flanked by two slender obelisks and several colossal statues of Ramses. The handsome sandstone was covered with scenes that told the tale of the battle of Kadesh and the King of Egypt's victory.

"Your Majesty," Bakhen declared fervently, "the building is completed!"

"But the work must go on."

"I'm ready."

The royal couple and Bakhen entered the forecourt just past the pylon, where statues of Ramses stood between the columns, fostering his *ka*, the immortal energy that kept him fit to reign.

"The stonemasons and sculptors have done fine work, Bakhen, but I cannot grant them any leave. I must even confess I'm about to take them on a difficult, if not dangerous, mission."

"May I ask what it is, Your Majesty?"

"Erecting several places of worship in Nubia, including a great temple. Bring the workmen together and poll them; I'll only take volunteers."

The Ramesseum was to be the mortuary temple where Ramses the Great's soul would be glorified forever—his Eternal Temple. Built according to the king's own plans, this Temple of Millions of Years had become a grandiose monument, the largest on the West Bank of Thebes. Granite, sandstone, and basalt had been used to raise pylons, courtyards, and chapels. Several gilded bronze gates marked off the various sections of the complex, walled all around with mud bricks.

Shaanar had crept into an empty storeroom at nightfall. The weapon he concealed was one that Ofir hoped would be decisive. Now Ramses' brother was waiting for total darkness before venturing into the sacred space.

At length he sneaked down one wall of the palace under construction and made his way across a courtyard. He stopped short at the entrance to a chapel commemorating Seti.

Seti, his father . . .

But a father who had betrayed him, choosing Ramses as Pharaoh! A father who had thrown him aside, putting a tyrant before him . . .

Once he completed this sinister errand, Shaanar would no longer be Seti's son. But what did it matter? Contrary to what the priestly initiates pretended, no one got past the obstacle of death. Nothingness had claimed Seti, as it would soon claim Ramses. Life had only one meaning:

grabbing all the power you could, by every possible means, and wielding it without constraint, shoving aside the weak and useless.

And to think that thousands of imbeciles already thought that Ramses was a god! When Shaanar toppled their idol, he would clear the way for a new regime. Outdated practices would be banned as he governed according to the only two policies worth pursuing: territorial conquest and economic development.

Once he was firmly on the throne, Shaanar would raze the Ramesseum and destroy every image of his brother. Even in its unfinished state, the Eternal Temple was producing energy that even Shaanar found difficult to resist. Hieroglyphs, carvings, and paintings were living proof of Ramses' power. The very stone was steeped in it.

No, he told himself, it was only the darkness that made it seem that way. Shaanar shook off his growing reluctance. He carefully executed Ofir's instructions, then silently left the temple complex.

Yes, it was taking shape; it was growing strong, this Eternal Temple. It was the keystone of Ramses' reign, and he paid homage to it. Henceforth it would be here that he came to draw on the force that nourished his every thought and deed.

As at Karnak and Luxor, the architects, stonemasons, sculptors, painters, and draftsmen had worked wonders. The sanctuary, several chapels and side-chapels, and a small columned hall were now completed, along with the shrine to Seti. The rest of the sacred domain was under construction, not to mention the brick storerooms, the library, and the priests' quarters.

Planted in Year Two of Ramses' reign, the Ramesseum's acacia tree had also grown amazingly fast. The lacy foliage was already providing welcome shade. Nefertari stroked the young tree's trunk.

The king and queen swept through the main courtyard. Awestruck, the stoneworkers laid down their mallets and chisels to watch them.

After conferring with their foremen, Ramses quizzed each of the men about the problems encountered. The king had not forgotten the thrilling weeks he spent in Gebel el-Silsila as an adolescent; he had once even hoped to make a career of stonework. To these men he promised a special bonus: wine and top-quality clothing.

The royal couple continued on their way to Seti's memorial chapel. Suddenly Nefertari froze, clutching at her heart.

"Danger . . . it's very near."

"Here, in this temple?" Ramses asked in amazement.

The moment passed. Then the king and queen approached the chapel where prayers for Seti's soul would be offered for all eternity.

"Don't touch the door, Ramses. The danger is there, behind it. Let me open it."

Nefertari nudged the gilded wooden door.

On the threshold lay a carnelian eye, smashed into several fragments. By Seti's statue at the back of the chapel was a red ball made from the hair of desert animals.

Invested with the power of Isis, the great magician-goddess, the queen put the eye back together. If the king's foot had touched the shattered and desecrated object, he would have been instantly paralyzed. Then Nefertari bundled the red ball in the hem of her dress, not letting it touch her fingers, and carried it outside where it could be burned.

The evil eye, the couple agreed. That was what some dark villain had dared to use in an attempt to sever the link between Seti and Ramses, reducing the Lord of the Two Lands to a simple despot, without benefit of his predecessor's supernatural counsel.

Who but Shaanar, thought Ramses, could be so depraved? Who but Shaanar and his sorcerer accomplice? Who else would be so determined to destroy what his own grudging heart could never hold?

THIRTY-FOUR

Moses hesitated.

He had to accomplish his mission from Yahweh, but now he was stymied. There was no way around the fact that Ramses would never capitulate. Moses knew the King of Egypt well enough to realize that when he said he considered the Hebrews an integral part of his country's society, he meant it. And he would act on it.

Yet the concept of an exodus was gaining ground; day by day, resistance to the prophet's cause weakened. Many thought that Moses' special relationship with Ramses would make it easier to win his approval. One by one, the tribal chieftains had come around. The last time the elders met, there was no opposition when Aaron presented Moses as the leader of the Hebrew people, united in faith and purpose.

Now that the rifts were healed, the prophet had only one more enemy to overcome: Ramses the Great.

Aaron interrupted Moses' meditation.

"A brickmaker is asking to see you."

"Take care of him, will you?"

"He won't talk to anyone but you."

"What about?"

"Promises he says you made him in the past. He has faith in you."

"Show him in."

With a white band securing the short black wig that covered the forehead but left the ears exposed, Moses' caller had a deep tan, a short beard, and a ragged mustache. He looked more or less like any other Hebrew brickmaker.

Yet something about him set off an alarm. Moses had seen this man before.

"What do you want from me?"

"We used to share the same ideals."

"Ofir!"

"Yes, Moses, it's me."

"You've changed."

"I'm a wanted man."

"With good reason, I've heard. Is it true you're a Hittite spy?"

"I won't deny I worked for the Hittites, but my network has been destroyed and they no longer pose such a threat to Egypt."

"Then you lied to me. You were only using me to get at Ramses!"

"No, Moses. We both believe in a single all-powerful God. Now that I've worked with the Hebrews, I'm convinced it can only be Yahweh."

"You fooled me once. Why should I believe you this time?"

"Even if you doubt my sincerity, I'll serve your cause. It's the only one worthy of being served. I seek no personal reward, mind you—only salvation."

Moses was confused. "Have you renounced your belief in Aton?"

"I realize now that Aton was only a glimpse of the True God. Now that I've seen the light, I've put the past behind me."

"What happened to that young woman you were hoping to bring to power?"

"She was brutally murdered, and I was deeply upset by it. The Egyptian police accused me of a horrible crime I didn't commit. I took the tragedy as a sign. Today you're the only man who can stand up to Ramses. That's why I'll support you for all I'm worth."

"What do you want, Ofir?"

"To help you spread the belief in Yahweh, nothing more."

"Do you know that Yahweh intends my people to make an exodus?"

"It's a grandiose vision, and I approve. If it entails the fall of Ramses and the arrival of the true faith in Egypt, I'll be overjoyed."

"But once you're a spy, aren't you always a spy?"

"I no longer have any contact with the Hittites, and they're in the throes of a power struggle. That part of my life is over. You represent the future, Moses; you're my hope."

"How do you think you can help me?"

"Fighting Ramses won't be easy. My experience with the occult could be useful."

"My people simply want to leave Egypt, not rebel against Ramses."

"What's the difference, Moses? You're challenging Ramses, however you look at it. He'll reply in kind."

In his heart of hearts, the Hebrew had to admit that Ofir spoke the truth.

"I need time to think."

"I leave it up to you, Moses. But let me offer one bit of advice. Don't try anything while Ramses is gone on his journey. You may be able to negotiate with him, but his lackeys, Ahmeni and Serramanna—not to mention his mother—will prove much less indulgent toward your people. To maintain public order, they'll call for a bloody repression. Let's make use of the royal couple's absence to solidify our cause, convince the fainthearted, and gird ourselves for the inevitable conflict."

Ofir's determination impressed Moses. While not convinced he should enlist the sorcerer, there was no denying the soundness of his advice.

The Theban chief of police insisted that his men had spared no effort in tracking Shaanar and his potential accomplices. Ramses had given them a description of the assailant who had fired arrows at him during their skirmish on the river, but so far the investigation had been fruitless.

"He's left Thebes," asserted Nefertari.

"You think he's alive, as I do."

"I sense a dangerous presence, a dark force . . . is it Shaanar, is it the sorcerer, or even one of their henchmen?"

"It's Shaanar," Ramses said flatly. "He tried to sever the link between me and Seti, depriving me of my father's protection."

"The evil eye he left will have no effect. The fire eliminated its magic. With a special resin glue, we were able to repair the carnelian eye they stole from the temple of Set in Pi-Ramses."

"He used the hair of desert animals to make the red eye. Those animals are creatures of Set. Shaanar was trying to turn Set's terrible energy against me."

"He misjudged your connection to Set."

"Even so, I'll never stop watching my back. The moment you look the other way, Set's fire can turn against you."

"When are we heading south?"

"As soon as we've had a look at our death."

The royal pair drove out toward the southern edge of the hills around Thebes, to the vale called the "Place of Rebirth" or "Place of Lotuses." This Valley of the Queens would be the final resting place of Tuya, Ramses' mother, and Nefertari, the Great Royal Wife. Their tombs had been dug in the shelter of the peak, the home of the goddess of silence. Over this parched landscape reigned Hathor, the smiling sky goddess, who made the stars shine, made glad the hearts of her faithful.

And Hathor was the goddess Nefertari found on the walls of her tomb, infusing the Great Royal Wife with the energy of resurrection. In these paintings the queen was forever young, wearing a golden vulture headdress in her role as divine mother. The artists had managed to capture Nefertari, the "sweet of love," in tableaux of incredible perfection.

"Does this dwelling suit you, Nefertari?"

"So many splendors . . . I don't deserve it."

"It's one of a kind, like you. Your love is the breath of life, and you shall reign forever in the hearts of both gods and men."

Here were green-faced Osiris, dressed in white; Ra the radiant, crowned with an enormous golden orb; Khepri, the scarab-headed god of metamorphosis; and Ma'at, the universal law, a dainty young woman whose only emblem was an ostrich feather, light as the truth. The divine powers were gathered here to regenerate Nefertari throughout time and beyond time. Soon, on the columns still standing blank, a scribe from the House of Life would record the "Book of Coming Forth by Day" and the "Book of Doors," whose sacred formulas would serve as the queen's guide through the next world.

Here was no death—only mystery, smiling.

Nefertari spent several days becoming acquainted with the gods that would be her companions for eternity. She grew comfortable with next stage of her existence as she plumbed the silence of her tomb. Deep in the earth, it felt like heaven.

When Nefertari felt ready to leave the "Place of Lotuses," Ramses took her to the "Great Place," the Valley of the Kings, where pharaohs had been laid to rest since the beginning of the Eighteenth Dynasty. The king and queen spent hours in the tombs of Ramses' grandfather and namesake, as well as that of Seti. Each painting was a masterpiece. Column by column, Nefertari read the "Book of the Hidden Chamber," revealing how the dying sun comes back to life, the model for Pharaoh's resurrection.

Moved beyond words, she explored Ramses the Great's eternal dwelling. The painters were still mixing finely ground pigments in small pots, bringing the walls to life with symbolic scenes that would preserve the monarch beyond the grave. With the addition of water and acacia gum, the colored powders allowed for extraordinary precision.

The golden chamber with its eight pillars was near completion. Here the sarcophagus would lie. Death could call for Ramses at any time; he was prepared.

The king conferred with the architect.

"I want a corridor," he ordered, "like the ones you see in some of my ancestors' tombs. Cut through the rock and leave the walls rough. It will speak of the ultimate secret, which no human spirit can penetrate."

Nefertari and Ramses felt they had crossed a threshold. Awareness of their death was now an integral component of their love—death as awakening, not as doom.

THIRTY-FIVE

Serramanna was playing a waiting game.

Meba had left his house more than an hour earlier to attend a banquet given by Queen Mother Tuya. She carefully fostered good feelings among the court while the king and queen were off on their journey. In regular contact with Ramses by courier, Tuya was satisfied with Ahmeni's meticulous work and Serramanna's iron discipline. Both helped keep things on an even keel. Even the Hebrew troubles seemed to be calming down.

Yet the former pirate trusted his instincts, and they told him that this was only the calm before the storm. So far Moses had done nothing more than meet with the Hebrew leadership, but he had emerged as their uncontested chief. Furthermore, Egyptian officials, knowing how loyal the Pharaoh was to his friends, tended to look indulgently on Moses. Sooner or later, they thought, he'd come back into the government fold, leaving his troublesome notions behind.

Serramanna worried about Moses in the abstract, and Meba in the concrete. The Sard was sure the old diplomat was the one who'd pinched Kha's paintbrush, but what was his motive? The former pirate hated diplomats in general and Meba in particular. He was too slick, too accommodating—a born liar, in Serramanna's book.

What if Kha's brush was hidden somewhere in Meba's house? Serramanna could hold him on suspicion of theft, and the aristocrat would be forced to explain himself in court.

Meba's gardener was heading off to bed. The rest of the domestics were snug in their quarters. The Sard scaled the rear of the house and climbed to the balcony. On cat's feet, he opened the trapdoor leading to the attic. From there he had easy access to the living quarters.

Good. He had time for a thorough search.

"Nothing," declared the Sard, unkempt and fuming.

"The search was illegal anyway," Ahmeni reminded him.

"If I'd found the evidence, I could have put Meba out of commission."

"Why target him?"

"Because he's dangerous."

"Meba, dangerous? He's completely invested in his career. That keeps him out of trouble."

The Sard was gobbling down dried fish dipped in a spicy sauce.

"Maybe you're right," he said with his mouth full, "but I have a hunch that he's up to no good. I feel like putting him under surveillance. He's bound to slip up before long."

"All right . . . but watch your step!"

"Moses ought to be under surveillance, too."

"But he's Ramses' old school friend, and mine as well."

"The Hebrew is a flagrant agitator! You're Pharaoh's servant, and Moses will revolt against Ramses."

"He won't go that far."

"Don't bet on it. I used to see his type in my pirate crews. A troublemaker, I tell you—but you and Pharaoh won't listen."

"We know Moses. That's why we don't take such a dim view of him."

"One day you'll be sorry you wouldn't face facts."

"Go get some rest and be careful not to offend the Hebrews. Our role is to maintain order, not fan the flames of revolt."

Ahsha was housed in the citadel, offered simple but wholesome food, mediocre wine, and the professional attentions of a pretty blonde recommended by the thoughtful chamberlain. Utterly shameless, she was eager to learn for herself whether Egyptians deserved their reputation as great lovers. Ahsha was a willing subject, active or passive according to her whims, but ready for anything.

Was there any better way to pass the time? Uri-Teshoop was stunned by Ahsha's sudden appearance, yet flattered to be playing host to Pharaoh's secretary of state. This must mean that Ramses already recognized Muwattali's son as the future emperor of Hatti.

Uri-Teshoop burst into Ahsha's room, interrupting a flurry of kisses from his blond companion.

"I'll come back later," said the prince.

"No, stay," Ahsha countered. "The young lady certainly understands that business comes before pleasure."

The stunning Hittite courtesan took her leave. Ahsha threw on a well-cut tunic.

"How is the emperor doing?" he asked Uri-Teshoop.

"His condition is stable."

"I'm repeating my offer: please let me treat him."

"Why come to the aid of your own worst enemy?"

"It's a delicate question."

"I need an answer, and right away," Uri-Teshoop said curtly.

"Diplomats aren't in the habit of giving away all their secrets. Can't we just say it's a humanitarian mission and leave it at that?"

"No."

Ahsha frowned. "Well . . . Ramses has come to regard Muwattali with respect, even a certain admiration. His illness is a cause for concern."

"Don't make me laugh."

"I surmise," Ahsha said cautiously, "that you wouldn't care to be accused of murdering your own father."

Despite his rising anger, Uri-Teshoop did not protest. Ahsha pressed his advantage.

"Everything that goes on in Hattusa involves us. We know that the army wants the transfer of power to go smoothly, with the emperor designating his own successor. That's why I want to help him recover his health, using the resources of Egyptian medicine."

Uri-Teshoop could never subscribe to the demand. If Muwattali regained the power of speech, he'd have his son thrown in prison and hand the empire over to Hattusili.

"How is it that you're so well informed on the subject?" he asked Ahsha.

"I'm not at liberty . . ."

"Answer me."

"Sorry, I simply can't say."

"This isn't Egypt, Ahsha. You're on my home turf."

"As an ambassador on an official mission, what have I to fear?"

"I'm a soldier, not a diplomat. And we're at war."

"Shall I take that as a threat?"

"I'm not a patient man, Ahsha. You'd better talk."

"I suppose you'd try torture."

"I wouldn't hesitate."

Trembling, Ahsha wrapped himself in a woolen blanket. "If I talk, will you spare me?"

"We'll remain good friends."

Ahsha lowered his gaze. "I have to confess that my real mission was to propose a truce to the emperor."

"How long a truce?" Uri-Teshoop asked in amazement.

"As long as possible."

Uri-Teshoop could hardly contain himself. So Pharaoh's army really was on its knees! As soon as the confounded omens allowed it, the new master of Hatti would rush to attack the Delta.

"And then . . ." Ahsha said haltingly.

"What, then?"

"We know that the emperor has had a hard time deciding whether to name you or Hattusili as his successor."

"Who tells you these things?"

"Would you grant us this truce if you had the power?"

Why not rely on deception? thought Uri-Teshoop. It was what his father had always done.

"As I said, I'm a soldier, but I wouldn't rule out the possibility of a truce as long as it wouldn't weaken Hatti's position."

Ahsha relaxed.

"I told Ramses that you were a statesman, and I was right. If you wish, we can reach a peace agreement."

"We'll see. But you still haven't told me what I want to know. Where do you get your information?"

"From officers who secretly side with Hattusili, although they pretend they're supporting you."

The revelation hit Uri-Teshoop like a thunderbolt.

"Hattusili will never agree to a peace treaty," Ahsha continued, "or even a truce. His only goal is putting together another coalition, as he did at Kadesh, and crushing our troops."

"I want names, Ahsha."

"Shall we join forces against Hattusili?"

Uri-Teshoop suddenly felt his muscles tense, as they did when combat approached. Using an Egyptian to get rid of his rival was an unexpected twist of fate, an opportunity he couldn't pass up.

"Help me eliminate those traitors, Ahsha, and you'll have your truce. Maybe more."

Ahsha named names. Each one he gave was like a stab wound. The list included some of Uri-Teshoop's staunchest supporters, even commanding officers who'd fought alongside him, claiming they already considered him emperor-to-be.

Livid, Uri-Teshoop lumbered toward the door.

"Just one more thing," Ahsha said suavely. "Could you please send my lady friend back in?"

THIRTY-SIX

Hiking the Aswan granite quarries with Bakhen, Ramses could picture his father selecting stone for obelisks and statues. At seventeen, he had had the good fortune to discover this magical place with Seti as the Pharaoh hunted for veins of perfect granite. Today it was he, Ramses, who led the search and relied on the same ability.

He used Seti's old divining rod, allowing the earth's secret currents to pass through his hands. The world of men was only an outgrowth from the primordial ocean of energy, to which it would return when the gods created a new cycle of life. The earth's core, like the sky, was rife with metamorphosis; a perceptive mind could be trained to catch its echoes.

Outwardly, the quarry was lifeless, a closed and forbidding world, unbearably hot for most of the year. Yet it generously yielded its peerless granite, the material that made Egypt's tombs and temples endure.

Ramses suddenly came to a halt.

"Dig here," he ordered Bakhen. "You'll find a monolith you can make into a colossal statue for the Ramesseum. Have you talked to your workmen?"

"They all volunteered to go to Nubia. I had to restrict the number. Your Majesty, I don't like asking for favors, but . . ."

"Go ahead, Bakhen."

"May I go along on the expedition?"

"I have a good reason for turning you down: your appointment as Third Prophet of Amon at Karnak requires your presence in Thebes."

"I wasn't expecting a promotion," said Bakhen, flushing.

"I know, but your superior Nebu and I have decided that you're ready for more responsibility. You'll assist the high priest, make sure the estates continue to prosper, and oversee construction of my Eternal Temple. Thanks to you, Nebu's load will be lightened."

Hand over heart, Bakhen swore to discharge the duties of his new position.

The inundation was substantial, yet not so high as to damage the dikes, canals, and cropland. The water level made the journey easier for the royal couple, their escort, and the quarrymen. The churning rapids of the First Cataract gave way to eddies and whirlpools that made the going dangerous. There were sudden dropoffs and huge waves that might tip any boat incorrectly laden. The sailors took a wealth of precautions to sweep a channel through which the royal fleet could pass.

Ordinarily mellow and indifferent to human agitation, Fighter seemed on edge. The enormous lion was eager to be back in his native Nubia. Ramses calmed him, stroking the beast's thick mane.

Two men asked to come aboard and requested an audience with the king. The first, a scribe in charge of Nilometer recording, presented his report.

"Your Majesty, the water level has reached twenty-one cubits, three and one-third palms."

"Sounds excellent."

"Quite satisfactory, Your Majesty. This year will see no irrigation problems in your kingdom."

The other visitor was the chief of police from Elephantine. The news he brought was much less reassuring.

"Your Majesty, there's been a sighting of someone who corresponds to the description you broadcast. He went through a customs checkpoint."

"Why wasn't the man stopped?"

"The officer in charge was away, and no one wanted to take the responsibility, especially since the man's papers were in order."

Ramses held his anger in check.

"What else?"

"The suspect chartered a clipper heading south. He claimed to be a traveling merchant."

"What was his cargo?"

"Jars of dried beef for the forts near the Second Cataract."

"When did this happen?"

"A week ago."

"Circulate his description to all the fort commanders and say that they should arrest him on sight."

Relieved to escape without a reprimand, the policeman hurried off to do as told.

"Shaanar is heading us off in Nubia," Nefertari concluded. "Do you think it's wise to pursue our journey?"

"What do we have to fear from a fugitive?"

"Who knows what he may do? His hatred has reached the point of madness."

"I won't let Shaanar keep us from reaching our destination. There's no denying his intent to harm us, Nefertari, but it doesn't frighten me. One day we'll meet face to face. My brother will bow to his sovereign and take his punishment from the gods."

The king and queen embraced. This moment of communion only strengthened Ramses' determination.

A wary Setau was jumping from boat to boat, checking them stem to stern, examining the cargo, tightening the ropes, testing the sails, pounding on the rudders. Sailing was not his favorite pastime, and he had no faith in over-confident sailors. Fortunately the river authorities had made sure there was a broad channel, clear of reefs, navigable even at flood stage. Yet the snake charmer would not feel truly safe until he set foot on dry land for good.

Back in his cabin on the royal flagship, Setau inventoried his supplies. Jars with philters, vials, and assorted flasks filled with solid and liquid remedies, baskets for various sizes of snakes, grinders, mortars and pestles, bronze razors, small sacks of lead oxide and copper filings, pots of honey, gourds . . . practically nothing was missing.

Humming an old Nubian tune, Lotus was folding kilts and tunics, tucking them into wooden chests. In the rising heat she was naked; her feline movements intrigued Setau.

"The ships seem to be in good shape," he said as he caught her by the waist.

"Did you check them out thoroughly?"

"You know how thorough I am."

"Go have another look at the masts. I need to finish the packing."

"It can wait."

"I like things in their place."

Setau's loincloth fell to the cabin floor. "Then wouldn't you have a place for this?"

Lotus yielded to her husband's logic, as well as his knowing hands.

"You're taking advantage of me just when I'm almost home in Nubia."

"What better way is there to celebrate than making love?"

As the convoy of ships continued southward, the crowds grew thicker. A few bold urchins, using reeds for flotation, began to follow the fleet as far as the channel. On everyone's mind was the fact that the royal couple would offer the people a banquet, and the beer would flow like water.

The vessels built for the journey to Nubia were real floating palaces, both solid and comfortable. Equipped with a single center mast and a huge sail attached with a tangle of ropes, they had twin rudders, one each on the port and starboard sides. The cabins were spacious and well appointed, with strategic openings for ventilation.

Once past the cataract, the fleet picked up speed again.

Nefertari had been planning to invite Setau and Lotus for a drink in her cabin, but the sighs and laughter behind their door dissuaded her from knocking. Amused, the queen leaned her elbows on the prow beside Fighter, who was busily sniffing the Nubian air.

The Great Royal Wife thanked the gods for giving her so much happiness, a feeling she must in turn shower on her people. She had begun her career as a shy, quiet lute player, destined to serve in obscurity. Now she led a prodigious existence at Ramses' side.

With each new dawn her love for him grew with the serene power of a magic link that nothing and no one could ever shatter. If Ramses had been a farmer or stoneworker, Nefertari would have loved him just as ardently. But fate had assigned them a special role, precluding selfish thoughts of their personal feelings. They must constantly focus on the civilization that was their legacy and that they must pass intact to their own successors.

THIRTY-SEVEN

In places it flowed straight, direct and proud. In others it curved lazily, hugging a village that rang with childish laughter. This was the Nile of the Deep South, majestic as its celestial counterpart. Between parched hills and granite islands, it created a slim band of greenery, studded with dum palms. Cranes, ibises, flamingos, and pelicans hovered above the royal fleet as it confronted the absolutes of blue sky and desert.

When the king went ashore, the natives came to dance around the royal tent. Ramses conferred with the tribal chiefs. Setau and Lotus registered their complaints and requests. Evenings were spent around the fire, in praise of the great river, the inundation, and the name of Ramses the Great, guardian of Egypt and of Nubia.

Nefertari became aware that the Pharaoh was a god in the making; since the victory at Kadesh, the story of the battle had been repeated throughout the land, even in the most remote villages. Seeing Nefertari and Ramses in person was considered a gift from the gods. Amon's spirit had strengthened Ramses' sword arm, it was said, and Hathor projected her love through Nefertari.

The north wind died down, slowing their progress. Ramses and Nefertari enjoyed the pace, spending most of their time on the bridge in the shade of a parasol. Fighter was back in his usual mellow mood, dozing nearby.

The golden sand and the purity of the desert seemed like echoes from the other world. The closer the royal fleet drew to Hathor's domain, a forgotten region where the goddess fashioned a miraculous stone, the more Nefertari felt they were on the brink of a major accomplishment, a link to the origin of all things.

The nights were delicious.

In the royal couple's cabin stood Ramses' favorite bed, the mattress made of twisted skeins of hemp attached to the mortise-and-tenon frame. Twin straps kept it flexible. The frame was reinforced for strength. The bedstead was decorated with papyrus flowers, bachelor's button, and mandrake twining around the papyrus stalks and lotus blossoms that represented the north and the south of Egypt. Even in his sleep, Pharaoh united the Two Lands.

The nights were delicious, for in the heat of the Nubian summer Ramses' love was as vast as the starry sky.

Thanks to the small fortune in silver Ofir had furnished, Shaanar was able to hire about fifty Nubian fishermen, eager to better their lot even if it meant taking part in a wild and dangerous escapade. Most of them viewed the Egyptian as a rich thrill seeker. If he wanted to support their families for the next several years, who were they to complain?

Shaanar disliked Nubia. He suffered in the heat, sweating through the day. Yet even though he was forced to drink huge amounts of water and eat bad food, he was where he wanted to be. His latest strategy was sure to be the end of Ramses.

This country, however hateful, would furnish him with a cohort of ruthless killers that Ramses' soldiers would be unable to repel. The Nubians were difficult to discipline, perhaps, but fearless in battle.

He settled down to wait for Ramses' flagship.

The Viceroy of Nubia whiled away the days in his comfortable palace at Buhen near the Second Cataract. Several fortresses in the vicinity kept him safe from any Nubian aggression. In the past, tribal chiefs had rebelled, attempting to invade Egypt; the government therefore decided to reinforce the frontier with impressive strongholds whose regularly rotated garrisons earned top pay.

Also known by the title "Royal Son of Kush" (after a Nubian province), the viceroy had one overriding preoccupation: the mining of gold and its transport to Thebes, Memphis, and Pi-Ramses. Goldsmiths there worked the precious metal, "the flesh of the gods," on monumental doors, temple walls, and statues; Pharaoh used it to underwrite his diplomatic relations with several countries, buying their cooperation.

The viceroy's post was sought after, for although it required long absences from the homeland, it meant the chance to govern a huge stretch of territory with the support of an established military presence, including many native soldiers among its ranks. The present viceroy, fearing no unrest, was able to indulge his taste for fine food, music, and poetry. His wife, after giving him four children, was fiercely jealous, curtailing his enjoyment of Nubia's tantalizing young women. A divorce would be too costly, since his wife would be granted a generous settlement as well as maintenance.

The viceroy loathed any threat to his tranquil existence. Now this dispatch announcing the arrival of the royal couple, not even specifying the purpose of their visit or when they'd arrive in Buhen! And another dispatch calling for the arrest of Shaanar, Ramses' older brother, long given up for dead and drastically changed in appearance. The viceroy hesitated to send a boat out to meet the monarch. Since Pharaoh was in no danger on the river, it would make more sense to concentrate on drawing up guest lists of the welcoming banquets.

The commander of the Buhen fortress made his daily report to the viceroy.

"No trace of the suspect in the region, but there is one strange thing."

"I don't like things that are strange, Commander."

"You don't want to hear it?"

"If I must."

"Some local fishermen left their village for two days," the officer revealed. "When they got home, they started drinking and brawling. One of them died in a fight. In his hut I found a small silver ingot."

"That would be worth a fortune!"

"Yes, but we can't find out where it came from. I think someone paid these fishermen to hijack army supply shipments."

If the viceroy pursued the investigation and it led nowhere, Pharaoh would accuse him of being inefficient. The best course was to do nothing, in hope that His Majesty would never hear of the matter.

The wind was so feeble that the sailors spent their time sleeping or playing dice. They were grateful for the easy pace, the pleasure-filled layovers, and the chance to meet the welcoming Nubian beauties.

The captain hated to see his crew so unoccupied. He was organizing a cleaning detail when a violent collision shook the boat, knocking several sailors onto the deck.

"We've hit a rock!"

In the prow of the royal flagship, Ramses heard the crash. All the other ships immediately trimmed their sails and halted in the middle of the relatively narrow stream.

Lotus was the first to realize what had happened.

The muddy river was dotted with gray boulders, but a closer look revealed round eyes and minuscule ears poking above the surface.

"Hippos," she said to Ramses.

She nimbly climbed to the top of the mast and confirmed that the fleet was trapped. Back on the bridge, she made no attempt to hide the truth.

"I've never seen so many of them, Your Majesty! We can't move backward or forward. It's strange . . . you'd swear they'd been herded together here."

Pharaoh recognized the danger. Adult hippopotami weighed more than three tons and were equipped with fearsome tusks that could crack a ship's hull. This group seemed particularly irascible, though they floated with lordly ease and swam with surprising grace. Their huge jaws gaped menacingly at the slightest provocation.

"If the dominant males have decided to fight for the females," Lotus explained, "nothing will stand in their way.

They'll sink our boats. We could all end up mauled or drowned."

Dozens of ears wiggled, half-closed eyes blinked, nostrils bobbed above the surface, maws gaped, and sinister grunts scared off the egrets perching in nearby acacias. The males' huge bodies were crisscrossed with scars from earlier combat.

The sight of the horrible yellow tusks paralyzed the sailors. They quickly picked out the hefty males heading groups of twenty increasingly agitated hippos. If the herd rushed the fleet, their jaws would crush the rudders, making it impossible to steer; then they would ram the hulls until the boats sank. Jumping ship was an option only for those willing to swim through a pack of raging monsters.

"We'll spear them," suggested Setau.

"Not with this many," Ramses answered. "We'd only kill a few and make the rest of them even angrier."

"We can't just stand by and do nothing!"

"Is that what I did at Kadesh? My father Amon rules the winds; let us be still and listen for his voice."

Ramses and Nefertari raised their hands in offering, palms turned heavenward.

At his master's right, Fighter the lion stood firm, gazing into the distance.

The order was relayed from ship to ship until the entire fleet was silent.

Several of the hippos slowly lowered their jaws and gradually submerged their fragile hides, leaving only the tips of their nostrils and ears above water. Their eyelids appeared to droop.

For a few endless minutes, nothing moved.

Then Lotus felt a northerly breeze on her cheek—the breath of life. The royal flagship carefully advanced, and the

rest of the fleet soon followed, passing the suddenly paci-
fied hippos without incident.

From atop the dum palm where he had planned to watch
the fleet being shipwrecked, Shaanar witnessed Ramses'
latest miracle. A miracle? No, a stroke of luck, a soothing
breeze blowing out of nowhere in the middle of a heat wave!

Seething, Shaanar squeezed a handful of sun-ripened
dates to a pulp.

THIRTY-EIGHT

During the hot months, the Hebrew brickmakers were
laid off from their jobs. Some used the time to stay
home and rest, while others sought landscaping work on the
great estates. It looked like a remarkable year for the
orchards; Pi-Ramses' famous apples would figure promi-
nently on banquet tables.

Girls dozed in vine-covered wooden cabanas or took
dips in the artificial lake where young men swam in front of
them, showing off. Old people sought out shady nooks.
Everyone was talking about Ramses' latest exploit, subduing
a huge herd of frenzied hippos. The local song celebrating
the joys of life in the capital was in the air. Even the Hebrew
brickmakers hummed it as they worked.

Plans for an exodus seemed to be at a standstill. Yet when Ahmeni saw Moses walking into his office, he feared that the summer quiet was soon to end.

"Don't you ever rest, Ahmeni?"

"There's too much to do. When Ramses is gone, it's even worse. The king can make a decision in seconds. I need to mull things over."

"What will happen if you ever get married?"

"Don't even mention it! A wife would interfere too much with my work and keep me from serving Pharaoh as I should."

"Pharaoh, our friend."

"Is he still your friend, Moses?"

"Aren't you sure?"

"Your attitude makes me wonder."

"The Hebrew cause is just."

"Exodus makes no sense to me."

"If your people were enslaved, wouldn't you want to free them?"

"Enslaved, Moses? Everyone in Egypt is free, including you."

"What we need is freedom to worship Yahweh, the One True God."

"I'm an administrator, not a theologian."

"Would you agree to tell me when Ramses is coming back?"

"He hasn't told me."

"If he did, would you tell me?"

Ahmeni fiddled with a writing tablet. "I don't approve of your plans, Moses. As your friend, I ought to warn you that Serramanna considers you dangerous. Don't make trouble unless you're prepared to suffer the consequences."

"With Yahweh's help, I have nothing to fear."

"Be careful with Serramanna, though. If you disturb the peace, he'll come down hard on you."

"Wouldn't you try to stop him, Ahmeni?"

"Egypt is my religion. If you betray your country, I'll have no more to do with you."

"I'm afraid we have nothing in common anymore."

"Whose fault is that, Moses?"

Leaving Ahmeni's office, Moses brooded. Ofir was right: he should wait for Ramses' return and attempt to convince him, hoping that words alone would change his mind.

Ofir's new workshop was in the maze of Hebrew dwellings. He had already cast some experimental spells with young Prince Kha's paintbrush, though without success. The brush remained inert, giving off no vibrations, as if it had never touched a human hand.

The magical protection surrounding Kha was so effective that the Libyan sorcerer was worried. Did he have what he needed to break through the wall? Only one man could help him, and that was Meba.

Yet the Meba he found on his doorstep was far from a haughty and confident diplomat. Trembling, wrapped in a hooded cape that concealed his face, Meba seemed more like a fugitive.

"It's already dark out," observed Ofir.

"I still could have been spotted. Coming here is dangerous for me. I don't think we should meet this way."

"We have to meet face to face."

Meba regretted ever joining forces with the Hittite spy, but how could he work himself free?

"Why did you send for me, Ofir?"

"To tell you that change is sweeping over the Hittite empire."

"What does that mean for us?"

"Good news. And what news have you brought me?"

"Ahsha has been careful. Only Ahmeni is allowed to review his dispatches and summarize them for Ramses. They're sent in a code I'm not familiar with, and showing too much interest would raise suspicions."

"I need to know what's in those messages."

"But the risks . . ."

Ofir's icy stare told Meba it was better not to make further excuses.

"I'll do my best."

"Are you certain that the brush you stole really belonged to young Kha?"

"Beyond a doubt."

"And you're sure that Setau was the one who built the magic wall around Ramses' son?"

"I'm sure."

"Setau has left for Nubia with Ramses, but his shield is proving stronger than I would have expected. What exactly did he use?"

"Talismans, I think. But I can't get near Kha anymore."

"Why not?"

"Serramanna suspects that I stole the brush. One false move and he'll throw me in prison."

"Keep your head, Meba. Justice is more than a word here in Egypt. The Sard has no proof, so you're safe from him."

"I'm sure that Kha suspects me, too."

"Does he confide in anyone?"

The diplomat thought for a moment. "His guardian, Nedjem, probably."

"Then question Nedjem about the talismans."

"It's extremely dangerous."

"You're an agent of the Hittite empire, Meba."

The old diplomat shifted his eyes. "I promise I'll do my best."

Serramanna slapped the pretty Libyan hard on the bottom. What she lacked in skill, she'd made up in enthusiasm. She had breasts that his hands wouldn't soon forget and thighs no red-blooded man could ignore for long. Serramanna, for one, had paid her charms proper attention.

"Let's do it again," she whispered.

"Not now. I have work to do!"

The girl backed away. Serramanna jumped on his horse and galloped to the post where his men stood watch. Most shifts were spent playing dice or the popular game of snake as they discussed promotions and bonuses. With the royal couple away on their journey, Serramanna had put his guardsmen on double duty as added protection for the Queen Mother and other members of the royal family.

All was silent inside the guard post.

"Have you lost your voices?" inquired Serramanna, sensing trouble.

The post sergeant rose, shoulders slumping.

"We followed your orders, Chief."

"And?"

"We followed orders, but the lookout in the Hebrew quarter had no luck. He didn't catch sight of Meba."

"That means he was sleeping on the job!"

"It could mean that, Chief."

"And you call that following orders?"

"It was so hot today . . ."

"I ask you to tail a suspect, stick to him like glue, especially if he heads for the Hebrew quarter—and you lose him on me!"

"It won't happen again, Chief."

"One more mistake like this and I'll send you all back to where you came from, the Greek islands or wherever!"

Serramanna stormed out of the guard post. His instincts told him that Meba was mixed up with the Hebrew insurrectionists and planning somehow to further Moses' cause. And plenty of other officials, just as stupid, had no inkling how dangerous this new prophet was.

Ofir closed the door to his workshop behind him. His two visitors, Amos and Keni, did not need to know what he was working on. Like him, the two Bedouins had adopted the dress of Hebrew brickmakers and let their whiskers grow.

These two men and their network of desert nomads were his link with Hattusa, the Hittite capital. He paid dearly for the service, hoping they wouldn't double-cross him.

"Emperor Muwattali is still alive," revealed Amos. "His son Uri-Teshoop is supposed to succeed him."

"Any plans for a new offensive?"

"Not for the time being."

"Have you found any arms for us?"

"We have, but getting them here is a problem. We'll have to break it down into smaller shipments so that the authorities won't smell trouble. It will take a while, but we have to move cautiously. Has Moses agreed to the plan?"

"He will. Meanwhile, let's find volunteers to store the weapons in their cellars. There's no lack of partisans ready to fight."

"We'll make a list of the most reliable ones."

"When will the shipments start?" asked Ofir.

"As early as next month."

THIRTY-NINE

The officer in charge of security for the Hittite capital was among Uri-Teshoop's staunchest supporters. Like many other military men, he couldn't wait for Emperor Muwattali to die so that Uri-Teshoop could take over and finally overrun Egypt.

After personally checking to see that his men were stationed at strategic points throughout the city, the officer headed back to the barracks for a well-earned rest. In the morning he'd drill the slackers and send a few of them to the stockade. It was important to maintain discipline.

Hattusa was a grim place, with its fortifications and gray walls. One day soon the Hittite army would be celebrating in the lush Egyptian countryside, basking in glory on the banks of the Nile.

The officer sat down on his bed, took off his boots, and rubbed his feet with inexpensive nettle ointment. He was just on the brink of sleep when his door flew open.

Two soldiers, swords drawn, glared at him.

"What do you two think you're doing? Get out!"

"You're worse than a vulture, betraying our leader, Uri-Teshoop!"

"What are you talking about?"

"Here's your reward!"

Grunting like butchers at a slaughter, the two enlisted men rammed their swords into the culprit's stomach.

A pale sun rose. After a sleepless night, Uri-Teshoop needed sustenance. He was breakfasting on milk and goat cheese when his two henchmen were finally shown in.

"Mission accomplished," one of them reported.

"Any problems?"

"It went without a hitch. We surprised every one of them."

"Lay a bonfire at the Lion Gate and dump the cadavers there. Tomorrow morning I'll light the pyre myself. It will be a lesson to anyone who thinks of betraying me."

Thanks to the list of names supplied by Ahsha, the purge had been swift and brutal. Hattusili had no more informers in his nephew's inner circle.

Next the supreme commander paid a visit to his father. Two male nurses had propped the emperor in a chair on his palace balcony overlooking the upper town.

Muwattali stared into space, gripping the armrests.

"Can you talk to me, Father?"

The slack mouth opened, but no sound issued from it. Uri-Teshoop was relieved.

"Don't worry about the empire. I'm taking good care of it. Hattusili is hiding in the country. He's completely out of the picture, and I never even had to touch him. The coward can rot in oblivion."

Hatred glinted in Muwattali's eyes.

"You have no right to resent me, Father. Either power is given to you, or else you take it, don't you agree?"

Uri-Teshoop unsheathed his dagger.

"Aren't you tired of suffering, Father? A great emperor cares only for ruling his country. In your present state, that's hardly a possibility. Give me a sign and I'll put an end to your suffering."

Uri-Teshoop drew closer to Muwattali. The emperor's eyelids did not even flicker.

"Tell me to do it, Father. Give me your approval. Give me the power that's mine by right."

With all his might, Muwattali stared his son down.

Uri-Teshoop raised his arm, ready to strike.

"Surrender, in the name of all the gods!"

The emperor squeezed the cushioned armrest until it burst like a ripe fruit. Stunned, his son dropped the dagger, which clattered to the floor.

Within the sanctuary of Yazilikaya, on a hillside northeast of the Hittite capital, the priests were cleansing the Storm God's statue to keep his power dwelling among them.

Next they celebrated the rites intended to banish chaos and keep evil locked underground. They pounded nails into a piglet, seven each of iron, bronze, and copper, then burnt it to banish dark forces at work against Hatti.

Once the ceremony was over, the celebrants filed past a frieze of the twelve gods, paused at a stone table, and took a drink of strong spirits to chase away negative thoughts. Finally, they went down a stairway carved into the rock, entering a chapel hollowed deep in the hillside.

A priest and priestess left the procession and entered an underground chamber lit by oil lamps. Hattusili and Puduhepa pulled back the hoods that concealed their faces.

"It feels good to steal a moment of peace," she confessed.

"We're safe here," agreed Hattusili. "None of Uri-Teshoop's soldiers would dare set foot in this sacred place. Just to be careful, I've posted lookouts around the temple. Now tell me about your travels."

"It all went much better than I hoped. Many of the officers are much less enthusiastic about Uri-Teshoop than we supposed, and definitely attracted to the idea of making a fortune without sacrificing their lives. Some of them are also aware of the threat Assyria poses and stress the need to strengthen our defenses rather than rushing into another war with Egypt."

His wife's words were sweet as nectar to Hattusili.

"Is this a dream, Puduhepa, or are you really bringing us some hope?"

"It was amazing how people opened up at the sight of Ahsha's gold. I found a number of high-ranking officers who think Uri-Teshoop is arrogant, cruel, and vain, and hate him for it. They no longer believe in his boastful speeches or his ability to vanquish Ramses; they can't forgive his treatment of the emperor. He may not have assassinated his father yet, but he openly wishes him dead. If we maneuver correctly, Uri-Teshoop's reign will be short."

"My brother is dying and I can do nothing to help him . . ."

"Do you want to attempt a coup?"

"That would be a mistake, Puduhepa. Muwattali's fate is sealed."

The handsome priestess considered her husband with admiration.

"Do you have the courage to sacrifice your feelings to rule over Hatti?"

"If I must. But my feelings for you can never change."

"We'll fight together, Hattusili. We'll fight to win. Tell me what happened with the merchants."

"They haven't lost faith in me. In fact, because of Uri-Teshoop's blunders, they support me more strongly than ever. They're convinced that he'll bankrupt the empire. And we have strong support in the provinces, though not in the capital."

"Ahsha's gold will change that. I'll go to Hattusa and start working on the upper echelons of the military."

"If you fall into Uri-Teshoop's clutches . . ."

"We have friends in Hattusa. They'll hide me, and I'll arrange secret meetings, never in the same place twice."

"It's too dangerous, Puduhepa."

"We won't let up on Uri-Teshoop or waste a single hour."

The blond Hittite girl was slowly licking her way up Ahsha's back. Although half asleep, he eventually stirred, turned over, and embraced his partner, her breasts tingling with pleasure. He was growing inventive when Uri-Teshoop burst into the room.

"Is sex all you think about, Ahsha?"

"My stay here has proved quite educational."

Uri-Teshoop grabbed the blonde by the hair and tossed her out of the room while Ahsha made himself presentable.

"I'm in a good mood today," announced the prince. His muscles did seem to bulge more than ever. With his long hair and fleecy red chest, the emperor's son was every inch the warrior.

"I've gotten rid of all my enemies," declared Uri-Teshoop. "There's only one traitor left. The army is under my thumb."

Uri-Teshoop had thought hard before he ordered the purge. If Ahsha was telling the truth, the housecleaning was essential. If he was lying, it was still a way to eliminate potential rivals. All things considered, he couldn't go wrong with the Egyptian's idea.

"Do you still refuse to let me treat your father?"

"His condition is incurable, Ahsha. There's no use trying drugs that won't improve matters and might make him more uncomfortable."

"Since he's in no state to govern, will the empire remain without a leader?"

Uri-Teshoop flashed a triumphant smile. "The military will soon declare me emperor."

"Then you'll sign the peace pact?"

"Didn't I say so?"

"You gave your word."

"There's one major stumbling block: Hattusili."

"I thought he no longer had any influence."

"As long as he's alive, he'll be a thorn in my side. With

the merchants behind him, he can interfere with supplying
my army."

"Can't you intercept him?"

"Hattusili is slippery as an eel."

"It's awkward," Ahsha admitted, "but there is a solution."

Uri-Teshoop's eyes blazed. "Tell me."

"Lay a trap for him."

"You'll help me catch him?"

"Call it my inaugural gift to Hatti's next emperor."

FORTY

Using her psychic gifts, Nefertari confirmed Ramses'
premonitions. The incident with the frenzied hippos
had been no chance encounter. Trappers and fishermen had
herded the beasts together.

"Shaanar . . . Shaanar is behind this," Ramses told her.
"He'll never give up trying to destroy us. It's all he lives for.
Can you agree to continue south with me, Nefertari?"

"Pharaoh must carry out his plan."

The Nile and the Nubian scenery blocked out the
thought of Shaanar and his hatred. At each stop, Lotus and
Setau captured fine cobras, including one with black and
red stripes on its head. The venom harvest would be plen-

tiful. Lotus was more fetching than ever, the palm wine flowed, and the warm nights made the voyage seem like a honeymoon cruise.

As the dawn's clear light revived the green of the palm trees and gold of the hills, Nefertari savored the joy of the day's rebirth, hailed by the song of countless birds. Every morning, dressed in a traditional white dress with shoulder straps, she worshiped the gods of the sky, the earth, the world between. She thanked them for giving life to the people of Egypt.

Stranded on a sandbank was a small trading ship.

The royal flagship pulled up beside it. There were no signs of life on the abandoned craft.

Ramses, Setau, and two sailors took a rowboat to examine the wreck more closely. Nefertari tried to dissuade the king, but he was convinced that the boat must be Shaanar's and wanted to search for clues.

The bridge yielded nothing.

"The hold," said a sailor. "The door is stuck."

With Setau's help, he broke the wooden latch.

But why would a boat run aground where the river was easy to navigate? Why abandon ship without even taking the time to unload the cargo?

The sailor disappeared into the hold.

A horrible scream tore through the blue morning. Setau jumped back. Even he, who fearlessly handled the deadliest reptiles, froze in his tracks.

Several crocodiles had entered the boat through a gaping hole. The sailor disappeared legs first into their jaws. His screams had already stopped.

Ramses wanted to try to save the man. Setau held him back.

"You'll be next. There's nothing we can do for him."

A new trap, cruel as the last one. Shaanar had based his plan on his brother's notorious fearlessness.

Fuming, the king headed back to the rowboat with Setau and the other sailor, hopping off the wrecked hull and onto the sandbank.

In their path was a crocodile, monstrously large and staring at them, jaws parted, ready to spring. Huge as he was, they knew he could move like lightning. In hieroglyphs, after all, the crocodile stood for danger that struck without warning.

Setau looked around. They were hemmed in by crocodiles, their fangs showing. Some of the reptiles even seemed to be smiling at the thought of such a delicious breakfast.

From the flagship, no one could see their predicament. In a while the crew would wonder what was taking them so long, but it would be too late.

"I don't want to die this way," muttered Setau.

Ramses slowly pulled out his dagger. He wouldn't give in without a fight. When the beast attacked, he'd slip underneath it and try to slash its throat. It would be a desperate struggle and Shaanar would come out the winner, hiding behind the scenes.

The giant crocodile came forward a few feet, then stopped. The sailor was on his knees, covering his eyes with his hands.

"You and I will run at him yelling," Ramses told Setau. "Maybe they'll hear us back on ship. You go left and I'll take the right side."

Ramses' last thought was for Nefertari, so near and already so far away. Then he emptied his mind, gathered his energy, and looked straight at his huge opponent.

He was about to let go a scream when he noticed a rustling in the thorny brush along the shore. Next came a mighty trumpeting, so loud that even the crocodiles were terror-stricken.

The sound matched the proportions of a gigantic bull elephant rushing through the water toward the sandbank.

He snatched the crocodile by the tail with his trunk and flung him back in the water. The whole pack of reptiles scattered.

"So it's you, old friend!" exclaimed Ramses.

The elephant wrapped his trunk, flanked by mammoth tusks, around the King of Egypt's waist, depositing Ramses on his neck as his broad ears flapped.

"I saved your life once. Now you've saved mine."

The young male from whose trunk Ramses had long ago extracted an arrow was now a magnificent bull. His small eyes gleamed with intelligence.

When Ramses petted his forehead, the elephant once again trumpeted, this time with joy.

Nedjem, the secretary of agriculture, had just put the finishing touches on his report. Thanks to an optimum flood level, the Twin Kingdoms would have an abundant supply of grain. The Treasury scribes' careful management would bring tax relief. Returning to his capital, Ramses would note that each member of his cabinet had performed outstandingly, under Ahmeni's scrupulous supervision.

Nedjem hustled to the palace garden, expecting to find Kha and his sister, Meritamon. Only the girl was there, practicing on her lute.

"Has your brother been gone for long?"

"He hasn't been here."

"But this is where we were supposed to meet . . ."

Nedjem headed toward the library, where he had left Kha shortly after lunch. The boy had planned to copy passages from the books of wisdom dating from the time of the pyramids.

The prince was there, sitting cross-legged in the classic scribe's position. A fine brush flew over the papyrus spread on his lap.

"Aren't you tired by now?"

"No, Nedjem. These texts are so beautiful that copying them gives me energy."

"You may need to take a break."

"Oh, no, not now! I really wanted to study the engineering on the pyramid of Unas at Saqqara."

"But your dinner . . ."

"I'm not hungry, Nedjem. Please let me stay."

"All right, but only a little while."

The boy rose, kissed his guardian on both cheeks, then sat back down and immersed himself once again in reading, writing, and research.

On his way out of the library, Nedjem shook his head in wonderment. Once more he was amazed by Ramses' eldest son's exceptional gifts. The child prodigy was now an adolescent who confirmed his early promise. If Kha continued to grow in wisdom, the Pharaoh would be assured of having a worthy successor.

"How is agriculture faring, my dear Nedjem?"

The voice that broke into his meditation was that of an elegant, smiling Meba.

"Fine, just fine."

"It's been so long since we've had a chance to talk. Would you accept an invitation to dinner?"

"I'm afraid I have to refuse. Prior commitments, you know."

"Too bad. I wish you could join me."

"I do, too, but official duties come first, as I'm sure you'll agree."

"A faithful servant of Pharaoh could hardly do otherwise."

"Unfortunately, men are only men, and often forget their duty."

Meba hated this naive and pompous wet blanket, but to get the information he needed he was willing to put on a show of respect and consideration.

The old diplomat's situation was far from promising. Several fruitless attempts had convinced him he'd never break Ahsha's code and learn the content of his confidential messages. Ahmeni would remain on his guard.

"May I drive you home, then? I have a new chariot and two very steady horses."

"I'd just as soon walk," Nedjem said gruffly.

"May I ask how Prince Kha is doing?"

The agriculture secretary's face lit up. "Exceptionally well, thank you."

"What an amazing boy!"

"More than amazing. He has the makings of a king."

Meba grew serious. "Only a man like you, Nedjem, can shelter him from evil influences. A talent like his can't help inspiring jealousy and resentment."

"Don't worry. Setau has provided him with protection against the evil eye."

"Are you sure he's taken every precaution?"

"There's a papyrus-stem amulet to keep him growing strong, and a wristband with magical inscriptions. No matter what evil comes his way, he'll be safe."

"It does sound impressive."

"Not only that, every day Kha renews his knowledge of

secret inscriptions in the temple of Amon's laboratory. Believe, me the boy is well taken care of."

"You've reassured me. To show my thanks, may I invite you to dine some other time?"

"To be frank, I don't have much use for society."

"I know how you feel, my dear man. Unfortunately, in my position there's no way around it."

When the two men parted, Meba felt like jumping for joy. Ofir would be proud of him.

FORTY-ONE

When the flagship landed at Abu Simbel, the bull elephant, arriving overland, trumpeted a welcome. From atop the cliffs he would watch over Ramses, who now looked wonderingly on the creek with golden sand where the mountain parted and came back together. The king recalled how he had first discovered this enchanted place, how Lotus had come here in search of the goddess's magic stone.

The Nubian beauty could not resist plunging naked into the river and swimming smoothly toward the sunlit banks. Several sailors followed suit, glad to have reached their destination safely.

Everyone was in awe of the site's natural splendor. The cliff's rocky spur was a landmark for navigators. The Nile curved sinuously along the bluffs, divided into two promontories with a flow of tawny sand between them.

Her body shining with silver rivulets, Lotus scaled the cliff, laughing, followed by Setau in his antelope skin saturated with medicinal potions.

"What does this place say to you?" Ramses asked Nefertari.

"I feel the presence of the goddess Hathor. The stones are like stars with the gold of the sun on them."

"To the north, a steep slab of granite reaches almost to the high waters. To the south, the hills flatten out. The two rocky points are a couple; that's what matters most. Here I'll celebrate our love, building two temples intertwined for all time, like Pharaoh and the Great Royal Wife. Your image will be carved in stone, forever greeting the sun with each new day."

Although it was unseemly in public, Nefertari tenderly put her arms around Ramses' neck and kissed him.

When his boat was in sight of Abu Simbel, the Viceroy of Nubia rubbed his eyes, sure he was seeing a mirage.

On the shore, dozens of stonecutters had set up a full-scale quarrying operation. Some of them worked the cliffs with the aid of scaffolding, while others were extracting blocks of stone. Cargo ships had brought the necessary equipment, and to establish the indispensable discipline, gang leaders had divided the workmen into teams in charge of specific tasks.

The master builder was none other than Ramses himself. On the esplanade stood a scale model and plans. The king would make sure that his vision was perfectly translated, rectifying errors after conferring with the architect and head stonemason.

How could he make his presence known without disturbing the Pharaoh? The Viceroy of Nubia decided it was prudent to wait until Ramses noticed him. Didn't they say that the king was short-tempered and hated interruptions?

Something lightly touched his left foot, something smooth and cool . . . The viceroy looked down and froze.

A black and red snake, some three feet long. It had slithered through the sand and come to a halt at his feet. The slightest move and it would bite him. Even a cry for help would make the reptile strike.

A few feet away stood a bare-breasted young woman in a short kilt that flapped in the breeze, revealing more charms than it concealed.

"A snake," murmured the viceroy. Despite the heat, he had goosebumps.

Lotus saw no cause for alarm.

"What are you afraid of?"

"It's a snake!" he gasped.

"Speak up, I can't hear you."

The reptile slowly wound its way up his calf. The viceroy couldn't get a word out.

Lotus came closer. "Did you do something to upset it?"

He was close to fainting.

The pretty Nubian picked up the red and black snake, wrapping it around her left arm. Why was this flabby little man afraid of a snake whose venom she'd already milked?

The viceroy ran headlong into a rock and landed in a

heap not far from the king. Ramses considered this important personage sprawled in the sand with some curiosity.

"I expect you to bow to me, but aren't you overdoing it a bit?"

"Forgive me, Your Majesty, but a snake . . . I narrowly escaped with my life!"

The viceroy got to his feet.

"Have you arrested Shaanar?"

"I swear, Your Majesty, I've spared no effort. I've put all the wheels in motion."

"You haven't answered my question."

"We'll get him in the end. My soldiers have every bit of Nubia under control, both upper and lower. They'll find the scoundrel."

"Why haven't you come before?"

"The demands of local security . . ."

"In your eyes, is that more important than the security of your king and queen?"

The viceroy turned crimson. "Of course not, Your Majesty. That's not what I meant at all, and . . ."

"Follow me."

The provincial governor feared the wrath of Pharaoh, but Ramses remained calm.

The viceroy followed him inside one of the big tents set up at the edge of the work site. It served as Setau's infirmary. The snake charmer was treating a quarryman's leg abrasion.

"Do you like Nubia, Setau?" queried the king.

"Do you even need to ask?"

"Your wife seems happy here, too."

"She's wearing me out. She has twice her normal energy and can't seem to get enough of me."

The viceroy was aghast. How dare the man speak that way to the Lord of the Two Lands?

"You know this distinguished gentleman. He's finally done us the honor of paying a visit."

"I hate administrators," retorted Setau. "They end up smothering on a bed of roses."

"I'll be sorry to see that happen to you."

Setau looked at the king in astonishment.

"What do you mean?"

"Nubia is a vast territory, and governing it is a challenge. Don't you agree, Viceroy?"

"Yes, yes, Your Majesty!"

"The province of Kush alone demands a firm hand. Would you agree with that too?"

"Of course, Your Majesty."

"Since I have the greatest regard for your opinion, I've decided to name my friend Setau 'Royal Son of the Province of Kush' and allow him to run it."

As if unconcerned, Setau folded bandages. The viceroy looked like a lifeless statue.

"Your Majesty, think of the problems, my relations with Setau . . ."

"They'll be frank and cordial, I'm sure. Go back to the fortress of Buhen and work on arresting Shaanar."

Stunned, the viceroy withdrew.

Setau stood with his arms crossed. "I suppose this is your idea of a joke, Your Majesty."

"There's a wealth of snakes in the region. You'll harvest a great deal of venom. Lotus will be happy, and you'll be able to live on this incomparable site. I need you, my friend, to oversee the construction and see that the two temples of Abu Simbel go up as planned. They must immortalize the image of the royal couple, celebrating the central mystery of our civilization here in the heart of Nubia. But if my decision displeases you, you're free to refuse."

A sort of groan escaped from Setau. "You must have fixed this up with Lotus. And who can resist the will of Pharaoh?"

Through the magic of ritual, the king transferred his enemies' souls from south to north, west to east, and vice versa. Thanks to the reversal of cardinal directions, placing the site outside the manifest world, Abu Simbel would be sheltered from human torment. Where the temples would one day stand, the queen created a force field to protect them from outside attack.

In the small outer chapel in front of the facade, Ramses offered Ma'at the love that bound him to Nefertari, linking the royal couple's union to the light. Their marriage, perpetually celebrated at Abu Simbel, would serve as a beacon for divine energy, a spring to nourish the people of Egypt.

The twin temples came to life before the eyes of Ramses and Nefertari. The workmen dug the inner sanctum deep in the cliff. The stone would be cut a hundred feet high, a hundred twenty wide, almost two hundred deep.

When the names of Ramses and Nefertari were cut for the first time into the stone of Abu Simbel, the king would give the order to begin preparations to depart.

"Will you go back to Pi-Ramses?"

"Not yet. I'm going to look for a number of other sites in Nubia where temples can be built. The gods and goddesses will inhabit this fiery land, and you'll direct the construction. Abu Simbel will be the central flame, flanked by sanctuaries that will help consolidate the peace. The work will take years to finish, but in the end we'll conquer time."

Moved and thoughtful, Lotus watched the royal flagship sail into the distance. From atop the cliff she admired Ramses and Nefertari in the prow of their white-sailed vessel, gliding on the blue water in the image of Nubia's sky.

What before she had only sensed, Lotus today could formulate: loving Nefertari and winning her love were what had made Ramses a great pharaoh.

Nefertari, the Lady of Abu Simbel, blazed the paths of heaven and earth.

FORTY-TWO

Shaanar was angrier than ever.

Nothing was going according to his plans. After his failed attempts to eliminate Ramses, or at least sabotage his expedition, Shaanar had been forced to try to outrun him, fleeing deeper into the south.

He stole a boat in some village; unfortunately, the local fishermen complained to the authorities, and the viceroy's soldiers were in hot pursuit. Without the skill of his Nubian sailors, he would have been caught. Out of caution, he abandoned ship and made his way through the desert, hoping they'd lose his trail. Now Shaanar's right-hand man, a Cretan mercenary, was cursing the heat, the scorching air, the ever-present danger of snakes, lions, and other wild beasts.

But Shaanar was intent on reaching the land of Irem, where he could incite the tribesmen to rise up, attacking Abu Simbel and razing the construction site. Once uncertainty reigned in Nubia, Pharaoh's prestige would be damaged and his adversaries would regroup to finish him off.

Shaanar's little band approached the gold refineries, a restricted zone where skilled workers labored under supervision by the Egyptian army. This was the zone that the rebels would need to capture, interrupting shipments of gold to the homeland.

From the crest of a dune, Shaanar watched the Nubians washing the ore, separating the gold from the gravel that clung to it even after the preliminary crushing and sorting. The water, drawn from a well in the middle of the desert, filled a reservoir that sluiced down to a settling pool. The downhill flow shook the gravel loose. Nevertheless, to make sure the gold was completely pure, the process was repeated several times.

The Egyptian soldiers were numerous and well armed. A mere commando would have no chance of overcoming them. Shaanar saw that he would have to organize a full-scale revolt, gathering hundreds of warriors from various tribes.

On the advice of a Nubian guide, he met with a chieftain from the land of Irem, a tall man whose ebony skin was covered with scars. The chieftain admitted him to his spacious hut in the center of his village, eyeing him coldly.

"So you're Egyptian."

"Yes, but one who hates Ramses."

"I hate all the pharaohs who oppress my country. Who sent you here?"

"Powerful enemies of Ramses' from the north. If we help them, they'll oust Pharaoh and give you back your land."

"If we rebel, Pharaoh's soldiers will massacre us."

"It will take more than your clan alone, of course. We'll have to find allies."

"That will be difficult, very difficult. It will mean meeting and talking, moon after moon."

Patience was the virtue Shaanar lacked most. He checked his anger and swore he'd persevere, despite the inherent slowness of such negotiations.

"Are you prepared to help me?" he asked the chieftain.

"I need to stay here, in my village. To start the talks, we should go to the next village over. It's too far away."

The Cretan mercenary handed Shaanar a small bar of silver.

"With this," he told the tribal chief, "you can feed your clan for several months. Those who help me, I pay."

The Nubian's eyes bulged. "You're giving me that to start the talks?"

"And more, if you get results."

"It will still take a long, long time."

"Let's get started at sunrise."

Back in Pi-Ramses, Iset the Fair often thought of her trysts with Ramses in the reed hut, before he met Nefertari. At one time she'd hoped to marry the man she was still in love with, but who could rival the sublime woman who had deservedly become the Great Royal Wife?

At times, when frustration got the better of her, Iset the

Fair went without makeup, dressed carelessly, forgot her perfumed oils . . . But her affection for Kha and Merenptah, the two sons Ramses had given her, as well as Meritamon, the king's daughter with Nefertari, always roused her from her depression as she focused on the children's future. Merenptah was a sturdy, good-looking child, already showing signs of intelligence. Meritamon was a pretty and thoughtful girl, a gifted musician. Kha was a budding scholar. These three children were her hope; they would be her future.

Her chamberlain arrived bearing a necklace of four strands of amethyst and carnelian, silver earrings, a gold-embroidered multicolor dress. Behind him was Dolora, Ramses' sister.

"You look tired, Iset."

"It's not worth mentioning. But tell me, where are you taking these lovely things?"

"I was hoping you'd accept them. A little gift."

"I'm touched, Dolora. How can I thank you?"

The tall brunette, soothing and protective, decided to go on the offensive.

"Doesn't your existence weigh on you, my dear?"

"No, of course not, since I'm lucky enough to be raising Ramses' children."

"Why be content to stay in the background?"

"I love the king, I love his children. The gods have given me a charmed existence."

"The gods! They're only an illusion, Iset."

"What are you saying?"

"There is only one God, the one Akhenaton worshiped, the God of Moses and the Hebrews. It is to Him that we must turn."

"That's fine for you, Dolora, but leave me out of it."

Ramses' sister realized that she would never make a convert of Iset the Fair. She was too conventional. But there was one other tactic that might prove successful.

"I don't think it's fair that you've been relegated to the role of secondary wife."

"I disagree, Dolora. Nefertari is prettier and smarter than I am; there's no match for her."

"That's not true. Besides, she has one terrible flaw."

"Oh?"

"Nefertari doesn't love Ramses."

"How dare you imply . . ."

"I'm not implying. I'm stating facts. You know that I always keep up with court gossip. That's how I know that Nefertari is a fake and a schemer. What was she before she met Ramses? A provincial music student who would have ended up in some second-rate temple! Then Ramses laid eyes on her and overnight she changed from a shy young girl into a power-hungry woman."

"Pardon me, Dolora, but I find it hard to believe."

"Do you know what's behind this trip to Nubia? Nefertari has demanded a huge temple as a monument to her glory! Ramses gave in and has started a costly project that will take years to complete. Nefertari's true ambition is finally surfacing: she wants to take the king's place and rule the country. She has to be stopped, no matter how."

"You're not suggesting . . ."

"No matter how. Only one person can save Ramses: you, Iset."

The young woman was shaken. Of course she mistrusted Dolora, but there might be something to her allegations. Still, Nefertari seemed so sincere. Power could be a corrupting influence. Suddenly her image of a loving Nefertari, worshiping Ramses, grew cracks. For a true schemer, what could be better than seducing the Lord of the Two Lands?

"What do you advise me to do, Dolora?"

"Ramses has been fooled. You're the one he should have married. You're the mother of his eldest son, Kha, whom the court already accepts as the likely successor. If you love the king, Iset, if you love Egypt and want the best for it, there's only one thing to do: get rid of Nefertari."

Iset the Fair shut her eyes. "Dolora, that's impossible!"

"I'll help you."

"Murder is an abominable crime that destroys the spirit, the soul, the name . . . an attempt on the queen's life would mean eternal damnation."

"Who'd know it was you? When you decide to strike, you'll have to move stealthily and leave no trace."

"Is this the will of your god, Dolora?"

"Nefertari is a perverse woman who sullies Ramses' heart and leads him to commit grave errors. You and I must unite to combat her influence. That's how we'll prove our loyalty to the king."

"I need to think it over."

"What could be more natural? I have great esteem for you, Iset, and I know you'll make the right decision. No matter what you decide, you have my undying affection."

Iset the Fair smiled so wanly that before leaving Dolora kissed her on both cheeks.

Ramses' lesser wife could hardly breathe. She stumbled to the window looking out on one of the palace gardens and soaked up the strong sunlight without relief.

A rival! For the first time, Iset the Fair truly considered Nefertari as a rival. Their unspoken agreement was shattered and the latent conflict burst forth with years of repressed violence behind it. Iset was the mother of Ramses' two sons, his first love, the woman who ought to have reigned at his side. Dolora had revealed a truth she had been trying to ignore.

With Nefertari out of the way, Ramses would finally realize that she was only a passing fancy. The spell would be broken, and he would return to Iset the Fair, the love of his youth who had never stopped loving him.

FORTY-THREE

While harboring a deep mistrust of the Hebrews, the sinister Ofir had cynically concluded that the brick-makers' quarter was the ideal hideout. Even so, he moved every so often as an extra security measure. Skillfully planted misinformation had led Serramanna to believe that the sorcerer had fled the country. He had backed off on his investigation. Only the usual patrols roamed the neighborhood, keeping things quiet at night.

Yet the sorcerer was far from happy. For months now, he had been at a stalemate. Year Fifteen of Ramses' reign, the thirty-seventh year of his life, found Egypt healthier than ever, to Ofir's chagrin.

The news from the Hittite empire was disquieting. Uri-

Teshoop still favored all-out war with Egypt, but launched no offensive. Furthermore, seasoned Egyptian troops occupied the buffer zone formed by southern Syria and Canaan, ready to counter the most massive attack. Why was the impetuous Uri-Teshoop so reluctant? The sketchy messages relayed by the Bedouins offered no explanation.

Down in Nubia, Shaanar seemed unable to incite the tribal leaders to action. So far there had only been endless talks.

At court, Dolora was still making overtures to Iset the Fair, but the king's lesser wife seemed unable to commit. Meba was virtually useless, failing to crack Ahsha's coded messages. Yes, he'd been able to provide detailed information about the magic charms protecting Prince Kha, but the boy led a studious and blameless existence in which Ofir could find no opening.

After his long journey, during which he founded a number of temples, Ramses had returned to his capital. Nefertari seemed radiantly happy. Despite the threat of war, the royal pair enjoyed tremendous popularity. Everyone credited them with the country's lasting prosperity, convinced that Ramses would keep them safe from attack.

Ofir's reading of the situation was full of gloom. As the years went by, the hope of overthrowing Ramses dwindled. Even he, the master spy who had never questioned his mission's eventual success, was beginning to worry and feel discouraged.

He was sitting in back of the main room, in the shadows, when a man entered his dwelling.

"I'd like to speak with you."

"Moses . . ."

"Are you busy?"

"No, I was only thinking."

"Ramses is finally back, and I found the patience to wait for him, as you advised."

The firmness of Moses' tone lifted Ofir's spirits. Had the Hebrew finally decided to take the initiative?

"I called the tribal elders together," the prophet continued. "They chose me to represent them before the Pharaoh."

"The exodus is still in your plans, then."

"The Hebrew people will leave Egypt, because it's the will of Yahweh. Have you fulfilled your commitments?"

"Our Bedouin friends have delivered the weapons. They'll be stored in cellars."

"I won't advocate violence, but it would be preferable to have a means of defense in case we're persecuted."

"And of course you will be, Moses. Ramses will never permit an entire people to defy him."

"We have no desire to revolt, only to leave this country and make our way to the Promised Land."

Ofir felt an inner rejoicing. Finally something was going right! Moses would create a climate of insecurity, laying the groundwork for Uri-Teshoop's military intervention.

Facing the frieze of the twelve gods in the temple at Yazilikaya, the priestess Puduhepa, her long hair caught up in a bun and hidden beneath a cap, lay stretched out on a slab of stone, as if dead.

She had swallowed a dangerous potion that would plunge her into a deep sleep for three days and nights. There was no surer means of entering into contact with the forces of destiny and probing their intentions.

Consulting the usual oracles, still unfavorable to Uri-Teshoop, had not been an adequate basis for a decision on which Hattusili's life depended, as well as her own. She had therefore decided on this radical but dangerous method.

Yes, the entire merchant class and a solid percentage of the army (after considerable arm-twisting) would lend their support to Hattusili, but perhaps he and Puduhepa were overestimating their prospects. Ahsha's gold had convinced many superior officers that reinforcing the country's inner defenses and the frontier posts made more sense than Uri-Teshoop's plan to attack Egypt. Yet they might still be apt to change sides if Uri-Teshoop woke up and discovered the plot brewing against him.

Challenging Uri-Teshoop's takeover would sooner or later result in a civil war with an unsure outcome. Thus Hattusili, despite his growing support, was still hesitant to undertake a struggle that would end up costing thousands of Hittite lives.

That was why Puduhepa decided to summon a premonitory dream, which would come to her only during a long forced sleep.

Sometimes the subject never woke from the trance. Sometimes the mind never quite recovered. Hattusili had argued against the experiment, despite his wife's insistence. Puduhepa had to keep after him until he finally relented.

And here she lay, immobile, barely breathing, for three days and nights. According to the books of divination, she should now open her eyes and reveal what the forces of destiny had told her.

Hattusili drew his woolen mantle tighter around him. Time was running out.

"Puduhepa, wake up. Please wake up!"

She started. No, he was mistaken . . . she hadn't moved.

But here it was again! Puduhepa opened her eyes and stared at the rock carved with the images of the twelve gods.

Then out of her mouth came a voice, a deep, slow voice her husband didn't recognize.

"I saw the Storm God and the goddess Ishtar. Both of them told me: 'I support your husband and the whole country will rally behind him, while his rival will be left wallowing in the mud.'"

The hand was soft, so soft that it made him think of honey and spring rain. The caresses were so insistent that they aroused new sensations, a pleasure almost overwhelming in its intensity. Ahsha's fifth Hittite mistress was as charming as her four predecessors, yet he was beginning to miss Egyptian women, the banks of the Nile, the palm groves.

Lovemaking was his sole distraction from the Hittite capital's grim and boring atmosphere. There were also numerous talks with the merchants' principal representatives and secret meetings with military officers. Officially, Ahsha was pursuing long negotiations with Uri-Teshoop, the new ruler of Hatti, poised to succeed Muwattali when he finally lost his protracted struggle with death. The Egyptian emissary also had an unofficial mission: to flush Hattusili out of hiding and deliver him to Uri-Teshoop.

Three times now the prince's soldiers had nearly closed in on Hattusili, only to find that some insider had tipped him off at the last moment.

On this particular day Uri-Teshoop did not catch Ahsha and his mistress in the act. Entering the room, the warlord's expression was hard, almost stony.

"I have good news," said Ahsha, rubbing his hands with scented oil.

"So do I," declared Uri-Teshoop in a triumphant voice. "My father, Muwattali, died this morning. Hatti is finally mine!"

"Congratulations . . . But there's still Hattusili."

"He can't escape me much longer, no matter how vast my empire is. You said you had good news?"

"About Hattusili, as a matter of fact. A reliable informant has just told me his whereabouts. But . . ."

"But what, Ahsha?"

"Once your uncle is in custody, can you guarantee that we'll seal our pact?"

"You've made the right choice, my friend, don't worry. Egypt won't be disappointed. Where is the traitor?"

"In the temple at Yazilikaya."

Uri-Teshoop personally headed the detachment, kept small so as not to alarm potential lookouts. A full deployment would alert them, allowing Hattusili to take flight once more.

So it was Puduhepa's priests who had given shelter to Hattusili; Uri-Teshoop would punish them.

The late emperor's brother had unwisely taken refuge in an easily reached area close to the capital. This time he wouldn't escape. Uri-Teshoop was hesitating between execution on the spot and a trumped-up trial. Having little taste for things legal, even well arranged, he was leaning toward the first option. He regretted that in his new position, he'd have to refrain from personally slitting Hattusili's throat; he'd delegate the low deed to one of his men. Back in Hattusa, Uri-Teshoop would organize a grandiose funeral for Muwattali. He, the emperor's beloved son, would be his uncontested successor.

With a combat-ready army, he would invade southern Syria, join with the Bedouins as arranged, occupy Canaan, cross the border into Egypt, and confront Ramses, who had made the fatal error of believing in peace, as his ambassador kept insisting.

He, Uri-Teshoop, would rule the Hittite empire! He'd carry out his plan with no need of forming a costly coalition like Hattusili's. Uri-Teshoop felt strong enough to conquer Assyria, Egypt, Nubia, and all of Asia. His glory would outshine all his predecessors.

The small band of soldiers approached the sacred rock of Yazilikaya, where several shrines had been erected. According to legend, this was the home of the supreme divine couple, the Storm God and his wife. The new emperor bore the fearsome god's name, did he not? Yes, he was Techop, the heavenly Storm. His enemies would feel his thunder.

In the temple doorway stood a man, a woman, and a child: Hattusili, his wife, Puduhepa, and their eight-year-old daughter. The fools were surrendering, counting on Uri-Teshoop's mercy!

He halted his horsemen, savoring his triumph. Ahsha had delivered on his promise. Once the new emperor was rid of his ultimate enemy, however, the Egyptian ambassador would have outlived his usefulness. Uri-Teshoop would have him strangled. To think that Ahsha believed he would ever want peace! So many years of waiting, so many trials had led up to this moment. All power was his.

"Have at them," Uri-Teshoop ordered his soldiers.

As they stretched their bowstrings, Uri-Teshoop felt a

surge of intense pleasure. The perfidious Hattusili, the arrogant Puduhepa, their bodies riddled with arrows, their corpses burnt . . . what prospect could be more delicious?

But no arrow split the air.

"Have at them!" Uri-Teshoop shouted furiously.

The bows turned on him.

Betrayed . . . finally emperor, and he was being betrayed! That was why Hattusili, his wife and daughter, stood there so calmly.

Muwattali's brother came forward.

"You're our prisoner, Uri-Teshoop. Surrender, and you'll be allowed to stand trial."

With a cry of rage, Uri-Teshoop reared on his horse. The archers recoiled in surprise. With the dash of a seasoned fighter, the son of the newly dead emperor broke through the circle and shot off toward the capital.

Arrows whizzed past his ears, but not one hit him.

FORTY-FOUR

Uri-Teshoop rode through the Lion Gate and galloped toward the palace, forcing his horse until its heart gave out. It collapsed at the top of the citadel from which the Emperor of Hatti would contemplate his kingdom.

The head of the imperial bodyguard came running.

"What's going on, Your Majesty?"

"Where's the Egyptian?"

"In his rooms."

This time, Ahsha was not in the arms of some lovely young blonde, but draped in a heavy mantle, dagger at his side.

Uri-Teshoop unleashed his fury.

"A booby trap, that's what it was! My own soldiers turned against me!"

"You'd better get away," advised Ahsha.

The Egyptian's words stunned Uri-Teshoop.

"What do you mean, get away? My army will raze that damned temple and massacre the rebels."

"You have no more army."

"No army?" Uri-Teshoop repeated dumbly. "What does that mean?"

"Your generals respect the omens and the gods' revelations to Puduhepa. That's why they've sworn allegiance to Hattusili. You still have your private bodyguard and one or two regiments that won't be able to hold out long. Within hours, you'll be trapped inside your own palace, awaiting Hattusili's triumphant arrival."

"It can't be true, it's not possible."

"You have to face reality, Uri-Teshoop. Bit by bit, Hattusili has taken control of the empire."

"I'll fight to the finish!"

"That would be suicidal. There's a better way."

"Tell me!"

"You know all about the Hittite army, its fighting power, armament, organization, weak points . . ."

"Of course I do, but what—?"

"If you leave immediately, I think I can get you out of Hatti."

"Where would I go?"

"To Egypt."

Uri-Teshoop looked stricken. "You can't be serious, Ahsha."

"Where else would you be safe, beyond Hattusili's reach? Of course, the right to asylum is negotiable. In exchange for your life, you'll have to tell Ramses all you know about the Hittite army."

"You're asking me to become a traitor?"

"You be the judge."

Uri-Teshoop felt like killing Ahsha. The Egyptian had clearly outmaneuvered him. But he was also offering the only real possibility of survival—without honor, naturally, but survival all the same—not to mention the chance to harm Hattusili by revealing military secrets.

"I accept."

"It's the reasonable course."

"Will you be escorting me, Ahsha?"

"No, I'll stay in Hattusa."

"Isn't that risky?"

"My mission isn't finished. Have you forgotten about the peace agreement?"

As soon as the news of Uri-Teshoop's flight was made public, his last few supporters rallied to Hattusili. The king's brother was officially proclaimed the new emperor. His first duty as a ruler was to pay homage to Muwattali, whose corpse was burned on a gigantic pyre during a grandiose funeral ceremony, followed by a week of feasting.

At the banquet closing the rites of coronation, Ahsha occupied a place of honor at Emperor Hattusili's left.

"Permit me, Imperial Highness, to wish you a long and peaceful reign."

"No trace of Uri-Teshoop . . . you have eyes and ears everywhere, Ahsha. Don't you have some idea where he's gone?"

"None at all, Your Majesty. You've probably heard the last of him."

"I'd be surprised. Uri-Teshoop is a resentful and obstinate man who'll never stop seeking revenge."

"Provided he has the means to do so."

"A warrior of his mettle never gives up."

"I don't share your fears."

"It's curious, Ahsha . . . I have the feeling you know more than you're telling."

"It's only a feeling, Your Majesty."

"Couldn't you have helped Uri-Teshoop leave the country?"

"The future certainly holds surprises, but I'm not responsible for them. My only mission is persuding you to enter into peace negotiations with Ramses."

"You're playing a very dangerous game, Ahsha. Suppose I change my mind and decide to wage war against Egypt?"

"You're too aware of the international situation to deny the Assyrian threat and too concerned with your people's welfare to risk it in a useless conflict."

"Your analysis has merit, but why should I endorse your viewpoint? Truth is of little use in governing. War would have the advantage of stifling protest and uniting the country."

"You wouldn't care how many lives it cost?"

"That's unavoidable."

"Not if you concentrate on building peace."

"I admire your determination, Ahsha."

"I love life, Your Majesty. War destroys too many joys."

"You must not be happy with the world as it is."

"In Egypt we have our own unique goddess, Ma'at, who requires everyone, even Pharaoh, to respect the law of the universe and strive for justice on earth. It's a world I can live in."

"A pretty fable, Ahsha, but only a fable."

"Make no mistake, Your Majesty; if you decide to attack Egypt, you'll come up against Ma'at. And if you were to win, you'd be destroying a civilization with no equal."

"What would it matter, if Hatti rules the world?"

"Impossible, Your Majesty. It's already too late to stop Assyria from becoming a great power. Only an alliance with Egypt can safeguard your territory."

"Unless I'm mistaken, Ahsha, you're not my adviser, but a foreign ambassador. You're bound to protect your own interests."

"That's only how it looks. Hatti may lack my country's charms, but I've grown fond of it here. I have no wish to see your empire crumble."

"Do you mean it?"

"I admit that a diplomat's sincerity is always in question . . . but I beg you to believe me. Peace is our one true goal."

"Will you swear it in the name of Ramses?"

"In an instant. When I speak, you hear his voice."

"The two of you must be very close."

"We are, Your Majesty."

"Ramses is lucky, very lucky."

"So all his enemies claim."

Every day for the last five years Kha had spent at least an hour in the laboratory at the temple of Amon. He knew all the texts by heart now. Over the years, he had come to learn about astronomy, geometry, symbolism, and other sacred sciences, discovering realms of thought and traveling the pathways of knowledge.

Despite his young age, Kha would soon be initiated into the temple's first mysteries. When Ramses' court heard the news, there was general amazement. The king's eldest son was clearly destined for the highest religious calling.

Kha removed the amulet around his neck as well as his magic wristband. Naked, eyes closed, he was led into a temple crypt to meditate on the secrets of creation revealed on the walls. Four male frogs and four female snakes formed the primordial couples creating the world. Wavy lines represented the primordial waters in which the Principle had awakened to create the universe. A celestial cow gave birth to the stars.

Then the young man was led to the threshold of the hall of columns where two priests, wearing the masks of Thoth the ibis and Horus the falcon, poured cool water over his head and shoulders. The two gods dressed him in a white kilt and led him to worship the divinities present on the columns.

Ten priests with shaved heads surrounded Kha. The young man had to answer a thousand questions on the hidden nature of the god Amon, the elements of creation contained in the egg of the world, the meaning of the major hieroglyphs, the content of offering rituals, and many subjects that only a well-versed scribe could discuss without error.

His examiners made no remarks or comments. Kha awaited their verdict at length in a silent chapel.

In the middle of the night, an aged priest took him by the hand and led him to the roof of the temple, inviting him to sit in contemplation of the starry sky, the body of the goddess Nut, who alone could transform death into life.

Raised to the rank of bearer of the law, Kha thought only of the glorious days he would soon be passing in the temple, learning the rituals. Thus preoccupied, he left behind his magical wristband and amulet.

FORTY-FIVE

At Abu Simbel, Setau had grown passionate about the work in progress, pouring all his energy into building a peerless monument to the royal couple. In Thebes, Bakhen was keeping the construction of Ramses' Eternal Temple on track. As for Pi-Ramses, the Turquoise City, it seemed to increase in beauty day by day.

As soon as Pharaoh was back in Pi-Ramses, Ahmeni began camping in his office. Unable to rest at the thought that he might have committed some error, the king's private secretary and sandal-bearer worked night and day. Nearly bald and somewhat thinner (despite his hearty appetite), the man who ran Egypt behind the scenes slept little, knew everything that went on without ever taking part in court activities, and stubbornly refused all official titles. Although he complained about his bad back and aching bones, Ahmeni personally carried the confidential documents relating to matters he wished to discuss with Ramses, regardless of how heavy the stacks of papyrus and wooden tablets were.

Equipped with the gilded writing kit the king had long ago given him, the scribe felt a true devotion to Ramses, with whom he shared an invisible but unbreakable bond. Who could help but admire the Son of Light, whose deeds already marked his reign as one of the most remarkable in the long history of the pharaohs? Ahmeni gave thanks every day for being born in the age of Ramses.

"Have you run into any serious problems, Ahmeni?"

"Nothing insurmountable. Queen Mother Tuya helped a great deal. When certain members of your government balked, she intervened forcefully. Our Egypt is thriving, Your Majesty, but we must take care. A few days' delay in routine canal maintenance, a lack of vigilance in the livestock tallies, failure to discipline ineffective scribes, and the whole structure could easily come apart."

"What's the latest from Ahsha?"

Ahmeni's chest swelled. "I can state in all confidence that our old school friend is a true genius."

"When is he coming back from Hatti?"

"For the moment, he's staying in the Hittite capital."

Ramses was astonished. "His mission was supposed to end when Hattusili took the throne."

"He's been forced to extend it, but meanwhile he's pulled off something amazing."

Ahmeni's high spirits told Ramses that he was in for a

surprise. Ahsha must have executed their entire plan, despite insurmountable odds.

"Would Your Majesty allow me to introduce a distinguished guest?"

Ramses gestured toward the door in agreement. A triumph of Ahsha's would have to be spectacular.

Serramanna entered, pushing a tall, well-built man before him, a man with long hair and a reddish fleece on his chest. Offended by the Sard's brusqueness, Uri-Teshoop turned around and shook a fist at him.

"That's no way to treat the rightful Emperor of Hatti!"

"What about raising your voice to the Pharaoh?" inquired Ramses.

Uri-Teshoop tried to hold Ramses' gaze, but broke off after only a few seconds. The Hittite warrior was feeling the cruel weight of defeat. Appearing before Ramses this way, like a common fugitive . . . Ramses, whose strength both fascinated and subdued him.

"I request political asylum, Your Majesty, and I know the price. I'll answer all your questions about the strengths and weaknesses of the Hittite army."

"Then let's get started," said Ramses.

With the fire of humiliation coursing through his veins, Uri-Teshoop obeyed.

The palace orchard was flourishing with juniper, pomegranate, fig, and frankincense trees, each more beautiful than the next. Iset the Fair loved to stroll here with her son Merenptah. The nine-year-old's robust constitution surprised his teachers. Ramses' younger son liked playing with

Watcher, and the yellow-gold dog, despite his advancing years, indulged the child's whims. Together they chased butterflies, then Watcher slowly stretched out and settled down to a restorative nap. The dog's companion, the Nubian lion Fighter, let Merenptah pet him, diffidently at first, then with confidence.

Iset felt a pang of nostalgia for the already distant days when Kha, Meritamon, and Merenptah were all carefree children playing in this orchard and the adjoining gardens. Today Kha was a temple novice and the lovely Meritamon (who had already received proposals from several influential men) was studying sacred music. Iset the Fair recalled the serious little boy with his writing materials, the beautiful little girl dragging the harp that was too big for her. All that was yesterday, a happiness now beyond reach.

How many times had Iset met with Dolora, how many hours had they spent discussing Nefertari, her ambition, her hypocrisy? The thought made her head spin. Worn down by Dolora's insistence, she had finally resolved to act.

On a low sycamore table painted with blue lotuses, Iset had set two cups full of carob juice. The one she'd hand to Nefertari contained a slow-acting poison. In four or five weeks, when the Great Royal Wife finally died, no one would think of pointing a finger at Iset the Fair. Dolora had provided the invisible weapon, insisting that divine justice would be solely responsible for Nefertari's death.

Shortly before sunset, the queen appeared in the orchard. She removed her headdress, kissing Merenptah and Iset.

"An exhausting day," she confided.

"Have you seen the king, Your Majesty?"

"Unfortunately not. Ahmeni is keeping him tied up, and I have a thousand and one matters to attend to myself."

"Don't you get tired of public life and all your official duties?"

"More than you could imagine, Iset. How happy I was in Nubia! Ramses and I were together constantly, each second was a joy."

"I thought . . ."

Iset's voice wavered; Nefertari was intrigued. "Are you feeling all right?" she inquired.

"Fine, it's just that . . ."

Iset the Fair could no longer control herself. She asked the question that burned on her lips, in her heart.

"Your Majesty, do you really love Ramses?"

Consternation flickered momentarily on Nefertari's face. Then a radiant smile dispelled it.

"How could you doubt it?"

"At court they've been saying . . ."

"At court gossip is the only sport. No one knows who 'they' are, but 'they' never find anything good to say. I'm sure this isn't news to you, though."

"Of course not, but . . ."

"But I come from a modest background and I married Ramses the Great. That's bound to feed the rumor mill."

Nefertari looked Iset straight in the eye.

"I've loved Ramses from the first moment we met, though I didn't dare admit it to myself. My love for him only grew stronger until we married. It's kept growing ever since, and it will outlive us."

"But didn't you make him build a temple to you at Abu Simbel?"

"No, Iset. Pharaoh was the one who wanted to commemorate our union. Who but him would conceive of something so grandiose?"

Iset the Fair stood up and walked to the table where the two goblets waited.

"Loving Ramses is a great privilege," continued Nefertari. "I'm all for him, and he's everything to me."

Iset nudged the table with her knee, upsetting the two cups and spilling their contents onto the grass.

"Excuse me, Majesty. Your words are so moving. Please forget I ever said anything."

Emperor Hattusili had stripped the palace audience chamber of its war trophies. The cold gray stone, too stark for his taste, would be covered with gaily colored wall hangings in geometric patterns.

Draped in an ample length of striped fabric, a silver cuff at his left elbow and his hair tied back with a headband, Hattusili wore a woolen cap that had belonged to his late brother. Thrifty, little concerned with his appearance, he planned to manage the imperial finances with a rigor hitherto unknown in Hatti.

The principal representatives of the merchant class filed through the audience chamber, helping the emperor define the country's economic priorities. Empress Puduhepa, heading the religious contingent, also participated in the discussions and lobbied for a large reduction in credits for the army. Despite their newfound status, the merchants found this shocking. Hatti was, after all, at war with Egypt.

Using his tried and true method, Hattusili held one-on-one talks with traders as well as commanding officers, briefing them on the need for a prolonged truce, while never pronouncing the word *peace*. Puduhepa deployed the same strategy in religious circles. The Egyptian ambassador Ahsha was living proof of the improved relations between the two powerful adversaries. Since Egypt now refrained from attacking Hatti, shouldn't they take their own initiatives toward halting the conflict?

But then a thunderbolt struck, destroying this castle in the air. Hattusili at once summoned Ahsha.

"I must inform you of a recent decision I wish you to communicate to Ramses."

"A peace proposal, Your Majesty?"

"No, Ahsha. Confirmation of our intent to pursue the hostilities."

The ambassador slumped. "Why this sudden reversal?"

"I've just learned that Uri-Teshoop has requested and been granted political asylum in Egypt."

"Why should that affect our agreement?"

"Because it was you, Ahsha, who helped him get out of Hatti and seek refuge in your country."

"Be that as it may . . ."

"I want Uri-Teshoop's head. The traitor must be tried and executed. No peace negotiation can proceed until my brother's murderer is returned to Hatti."

"Since he's in exile in Pi-Ramses, what have you to fear from him?"

"I want to see his body burned at the stake, here, in my capital."

"It's quite unlikely that Ramses would go back on his word and extradite a man to whom he's granted his protection."

"Leave immediately for Pi-Ramses, convince your king, and bring me back Uri-Teshoop. Otherwise, my army will invade Egypt and I'll capture the traitor myself."

FORTY-SIX

The sweltering month of May was harvest time, after the standing crops were counted. The reapers cut the golden ears with their scythes, leaving the stubble. Staunch donkeys transported the wheat to the threshing floor. The work was hard, but there was no lack of bread, fruit, or cool water. And no foreman would have dared deny the reapers an afternoon rest.

It was at this time of year that Homer chose to stop writing. When Ramses went to visit the old poet, for once he did not find him smoking sage leaves in his snail-shell pipe. Clad in a woolen tunic despite the heat wave, he lay on a cot at the foot of his lemon tree, a pillow propped beneath his head.

"Your Majesty . . . I'd given up hope of seeing you."

"What's going on here, Homer?"

"Old age is all. I'm tired to the bone."

"Why haven't you called for the palace doctors?"

"I'm not ill, Your Majesty. Death is a natural part of life. Hector, my black and white cat, has left me. I haven't the heart to replace him."

"You still have tales to tell."

"I've given the best of myself in the *Iliad* and the *Odyssey*. Now that it's time for the final passage, why should I resist?"

"We're going to take care of you, Homer."

"How long have you been on the throne, Your Majesty?"

"Fifteen years."

"You aren't experienced enough to fool an old poet who's seen so many men leave this world. Death has crept inside me, chilling my blood, and no medicine can halt its progress. But we have more important matters to discuss. Your ancestors have built a unique country; you must take good care of it. What of the war with the Hittites?"

"Ahsha has fulfilled his mission. We hope to sign a treaty that will put an end to the hostilities."

"How sweet it is to leave this earth at peace, after writing so much about war . . . as I had one of my heroes say, '*The sunlight falls into the ocean, burrows into the fertile earth, and comes the dark night, the shadowy night that the vanquished crave.*' Today I'm the one who's vanquished and heading for darkness."

"I'll build you a magnificent house of eternity."

"No, Your Majesty . . . I've stayed a Greek, and for my people the afterlife brings only pain and oblivion. At my age, it's too late to change my beliefs. Grim as it may seem to you, it's what I'm prepared for."

"Our sages claim that the works of great writers will last longer than the pyramids."

Homer smiled.

"Would you grant me one last favor, Your Majesty? Take my right hand, the one I wrote with . . . your strength will help me to the other side."

And the poet peacefully breathed his last.

Homer lay beneath a small mound close to his lemon tree. In his shroud were copies of the *Iliad* and *Odyssey* and a papyrus with the tale of the battle of Kadesh. Only Ramses, Nefertari, and Ahmeni, deeply affected, had attended the burial.

When the monarch returned to his office, Serramanna presented him with a report.

"No trace of the sorcerer Ofir, Your Majesty. He's probably left the country."

"Could he be hiding among the Hebrews?"

"If he's changed his appearance and gained their confidence, why not?"

"What are your informers saying?"

"Since Moses has become the Hebrews' acknowledged leader, they've stopped talking."

"Then you don't know what the Hebrews are plotting?"

"Yes and no, Your Majesty."

"Explain yourself, Serramanna."

"It can only be a revolt led by Moses and the enemies of Egypt."

"Moses has requested a private audience with me."

"Don't grant him one, Your Majesty!"

"What are you afraid of?"

"That he may try something drastic."

"Surely you exaggerate."

"A revolutionary will stop at nothing."

"Moses is my childhood friend."

"Not any longer, Your Majesty."

The May sunlight streamed into Ramses' office, lit by three barred windows, one giving on the inner courtyard where several chariots stood. The decor was stark: white walls, a straight-backed armchair for the monarch and straw-seated chairs for his visitors, a papyrus cabinet, and one large table. Seti would have approved, and Ramses often glanced at the statue of his father that was the room's only ornament.

Enter Moses.

Tall, broad-shouldered, with flowing hair, a full beard, and a weathered face, the Hebrew was in the prime of his manhood.

"Sit down, Moses."

"I prefer to stand."

"What do you want from me?"

"I spent a long time in the desert. It allowed me to think."

"And did you find wisdom?"

"I was schooled in the wisdom of the Egyptians, but what is that in regard to the will of Yahweh?"

"Then you're still full of your wild notions."

"More than ever, and now the majority of my people agree with me. Soon they'll all follow me out of Egypt."

"I remember what my father, Seti, told me: Pharaoh must tolerate no rebel or instigator. It would mean the end of the law of Ma'at and the advent of disorder, bringing trouble to great and small alike."

"The law that Egypt observes no longer applies to the Hebrews."

"As long as they live in this land, they must obey it."

"Grant my people permission to make a three days' journey into the desert, where we can sacrifice to Yahweh."

"The security constraints I've already outlined force me to deny your request."

Moses gripped his gnarled walking stick more tightly.

"I cannot accept that as your final answer."

"In the name of friendship, I'll overlook your insolence."

"I know I'm addressing Pharaoh, the Lord of the Two

Lands, and I have no wish to show disrespect. However, Yahweh must still come first, and I will continue to serve as the mouthpiece for His demands."

"If you incite the Hebrews to revolt, I'll be forced to suppress it."

"I'm aware of that. That's why Yahweh will use other means. If you persist in denying the Hebrews' demands for freedom, God will visit dreadful plagues upon Egypt."

"Do you think you can frighten me?"

"I'll plead my cause before your notables and your people, and Yahweh's infinite power will persuade them."

"Egypt has nothing to fear from you, Moses."

How lovely Nefertari was! As she officiated at the consecration of a new chapel, Ramses admired her.

His queen, the "sweet of love" whose voice gave joy and said nothing superfluous, who filled the palace with her scent and her grace, who perceived good and evil clearly— this was the woman who had become the beloved Lady of the Two Lands. Wearing a six-strand necklace and a headdress topped with two tall plumes, she seemed to belong to the universe of goddesses where youth and beauty never faded.

On his mother Tuya's stern face Ramses discerned a certain satisfaction in the knowledge that her successor was worthy of Egypt. Tuya's discreet but skillful guidance had helped Nefertari find the inner harmony that was the hallmark of a great queen.

The ceremony was followed by a reception in Tuya's honor. She stood in the receiving line, half listening to the usual platitudes. The diplomat Meba finally reached Tuya and the Pharaoh. Smiling broadly, he launched into praises of Seti's widow.

"I'm dissatisfied with your work at the State Department," interrupted Ramses. "With Ahsha away, you should have been exchanging more messages with our allies."

"Your Majesty, the quantity and quality of the forthcoming tributes is exceptional! Rest assured that I've set a high price on Egypt's support. Any number of envoys are seeking to pay homage, for no pharaoh's prestige has ever been greater!"

"Have you no other news for me?"

"Yes, Your Majesty: Ahsha has just sent word of his imminent return to Pi-Ramses. I plan to hold a fine reception in his honor."

"Does his dispatch give the reasons for this return voyage?"

"No, Your Majesty."

The king and his mother turned to the next in line.

"Is peace still at hand, Ramses?" asked Tuya.

"If Meba is right and Ahsha has left Hatti without warning, it's probably not because he's bringing good news."

FORTY-SEVEN

After some ten long sessions with Uri-Teshoop, Ramses knew all about the Hittite army, its preferred strategies, its armaments, its strengths and weaknesses. The deposed commander, in his eagerness to harm Hattusili, had proved most cooperative. In exchange for the information he offered, Uri-Teshoop was kept under house arrest in a pleasant villa with two Syrian domestics and provided with an ample diet he took to immediately.

Ramses, for his part, came to appreciate the size and ferocity of the monster he had tackled with all the fire of his youth. Without Amon and Seti helping him, his rashness might have been Egypt's ruin. Even in its weakened state, Hatti remained a military power to be reckoned with. Any alliance between the two powers would translate into lasting peace for the region, for no warring people would dare take them on.

Ramses and Nefertari were discussing the possibility in the shade of a sycamore when a breathless Ahmeni announced Ahsha's arrival.

The secretary of state's long absence had done nothing to change him. His face was long and fine-boned, his mustache trim, his eyes bright and intelligent, his build slender. He could appear haughty and distant, and it would be easy to assume that his view of life was supremely ironic.

Ahsha bowed to the royal couple.

"I beg forgiveness, Your Royal Highnesses, but I haven't had time for a shower or massage . . . I apologize for my appearance, but the message I bring you is so urgent that it must take precedence over my personal comfort."

"Then we'll save our congratulations for later," Ramses said with a smile. "Although we're overjoyed to see you safely back."

"In my state, accepting your ceremonial embrace would amount to high treason. You don't know how beautiful Egypt seems, Ramses! The more I travel, the better it is to come home."

"Humph," said Ahmeni. "You'd be better off staying put. Watching the seasons change from your office window is the real way to appreciate the pleasures of life in Egypt."

"You two can argue later," Ramses broke in. "Tell me, Ahsha, were you expelled from Hatti?"

"No, but Emperor Hattusili wanted his demands transmitted directly."

"Are you announcing the establishment of peace talks?"

"That would have been my fondest wish. Unfortunately, I'm bringing you an ultimatum instead."

"Is Hattusili going to be as warlike as Uri-Teshoop?"

"Hattusili comprehends that peace with Egypt would keep Assyria in check. Uri-Teshoop is precisely the problem."

"Your move was inspired! Now I know everything about the Hittite army."

"Very useful in case of a conflict, I agree. But if we don't hand over Uri-Teshoop, Hattusili will wage war on us."

"Uri-Teshoop is our guest."

"Hattusili wants to see his corpse burned at the stake."

"I've granted Muwattali's son political asylum and I'll never go back on my word. That would mean the end of Ma'at, and Egypt would soon be mired in deceit and cowardice."

"That's what I told Hattusili, but his position is firm. Either we extradite Uri-Teshoop and peace becomes a possibility, or else the conflict continues."

"Mine is just as firm: Egypt won't trifle with the right to exile, and Uri-Teshoop won't be extradited."

Ahsha slumped in a low-backed armchair.

"All these wasted years, all this trouble for nothing . . . but Your Majesty is right: better war than dishonor. At least we have more accurate information to fight the Hittites."

"May I say something, if it pleases Pharaoh?" asked Nefertari.

The Great Royal Wife's soft, even voice enchanted the monarch, the ambassador, and the scribe.

"It was the women of Egypt who liberated the country from its occupiers in the past," Nefertari reminded them. "And women negotiated peace treaties with foreign powers. Hasn't Tuya herself continued this tradition, teaching me by her example?"

"What are you proposing?" queried Ramses.

"I'm going to write to the Empress Puduhepa. If I can persuade her to begin negotiations, won't she persuade her husband to modify his stance?"

"We mustn't discount the stumbling block Uri-Teshoop represents," objected Ahsha. "Still, Empress Puduhepa is a capable and intelligent woman, more concerned with Hatti's welfare than with her personal interest. She would hardly be indifferent to a personal appeal from the Queen of Egypt. And since her influence over Hattusili is considerable, the outcome might be favorable. The Great Royal Wife should be aware, however, that it is a most difficult undertaking."

"Forgive me for leaving you," said Nefertari, "but you'll understand that I need to begin at once."

Ahsha watched admiringly as the queen withdrew, airy and luminous.

"If Nefertari's overtures work," said Ramses to his chief of diplomatic affairs, "you'll go back to Hatti. I'll never extradite Uri-Teshoop, but you'll win the peace for us."

"You're asking the impossible. That's what I like about working for you."

The king turned to Ahmeni. "Have you asked Setau to return at once?"

"Yes, Your Majesty."

"What's going on?" Ahsha asked edgily.

"Moses now considers himself the mouthpiece of his One God, this Yahweh that's telling him to lead the Hebrews out of Egypt," explained Ahmeni.

"You mean *all* the Hebrews?"

"He sees them as a people with a right to independence."

"That's madness!"

"Not only is it impossible to reason with Moses, but he's beginning to make threats."

"And you're afraid of him?"

"I fear that our friend Moses may become a powerful enemy," declared Ramses, "and I've learned not to underestimate my adversaries. That's why I need Setau here with me."

"I can't believe it's come to this," Ahsha said gloomily. "Moses was always so strong and true."

"He still is, but now he's become a fanatic."

"You frighten me, Ramses. This conflict with Moses seems far more dangerous than war with the Hittites."

"We have to win it or perish."

Setau put his broad hands on Kha's frail shoulders.

"I swear by all the snakes on earth, you're almost a man!"

The contrast between the two was striking. Kha, Ramses' eldest son, was a pale, fragile-appearing young scribe. Setau, stocky, virile, swarthy, with bulging muscles, a square, stubbly jaw, dressed in a pocket-studded antelope tunic, looked like an old prospector.

At first glance, no one would have imagined the two could be close. Yet Kha considered Setau as the master who had introduced him to the invisible, and Setau saw Kha as an exceptional young man who could probe the deepest mysteries.

"I'm afraid you've done some stupid things while I've been gone," frowned Setau.

Kha smiled. "Well, I hope you won't be too disappointed in me."

"You've joined the priesthood!"

"I perform a few duties at the temple, yes . . . it's what was expected of me. And besides, I wanted to."

"Good for you, my boy. But tell me . . . what's happened to the amulet I gave you, the magic band I put around your wrist?"

"I took them off during my purification ceremony, when I entered the temple, and I haven't seen them since. Now that you're back, I'm no longer at risk, and the priesthood has given me new protection."

"You should still wear your amulets."

"Do you wear any?"

"My antelope skin protects me."

An arrow whizzed past them, making a bull's-eye in a nearby target. Ramses had told the two men to meet him at an army archery range.

"Your father is as good a shot as ever," Setau said coolly.

Kha watched his father set down the bow he alone had the strength to draw, the bow he had used at the battle of Kadesh. The monarch's stature seemed only to increase. His mere presence embodied supreme authority.

Kha bowed low to this being who was so much more than his father.

"Why did you have us meet here?" asked Setau.

"Because you and my son are going to help me wage a battle. We need to set our sights."

Kha responded forthrightly: "I'm afraid I'm not much of a fighter."

"Don't worry, son; I'm asking you to fight with your mind and your magic."

"I'm attached to the temple of Amon and . . ."

"And the priests have unanimously chosen you as the new superior of their community."

"But I'm not even twenty!"

"Age makes no difference. However, I rejected the nomination."

Kha was relieved.

"I've had bad news," revealed Ramses. "The high priest of Ptah has just passed away in Memphis. You're my choice to succeed him, Kha."

"The high priest of Ptah? But I'm . . ."

"It's my wish. In your new role, you'll be among the notables to whom Moses brings his appeal."

"What is he up to now?" asked Setau.

"Since I've refused to let the Hebrews go forth into the desert, Moses is threatening to have his god visit plagues on Egypt. I'm counting on the new high priest of Ptah and the best magician I know to deal with him."

FORTY-EIGHT

Accompanied by Aaron, Moses appeared at the door to the palace audience chamber in Pi-Ramses, under the surveillance of Serramanna and the royal bodyguard. The Sard cast an angry glance at the passing Hebrew. If he were king, he would have thrown this rebel into the deepest dungeon, or better yet exiled him to the desert. The old pirate trusted his instincts, and his instincts told him that Moses intended nothing but harm to Ramses.

Walking down the center of the room, between the two rows of columns, the leader and spokesman of the Hebrew people noted, not without pleasure, that the audience chamber was packed.

At the king's right was his son Kha, wearing a panther skin decked with gold stars. Despite his young age, Kha had just been elevated to a very high office. Given his intellect and achievements, no priest had protested the decision. Now it was up to Pharaoh's older son to prove himself, capturing godly messages in hieroglyphs. Everyone would be watching him closely, since he would be responsible for preserving traditions from the time of the pyramids, that golden age when the core values of Egyptian civilization had been formulated.

Kha's appointment had astonished Moses, but seeing the

prince up close, he could tell that the young man's maturity and determination were exceptional. There was no doubt that he would make a tough opponent.

And what of the character to Pharaoh's left? Setau, the snake charmer, the kingdom's de facto chief magician? Setau was his old classmate from the royal academy, just like Ramses and Ahmeni (who sat in the background prepared to take notes on the meeting).

Moses no longer wished to think of those days, when he had worked for the glory of Egypt. His past had died the day Yahweh had assigned him this mission, and he had no right to sigh over his lost youth.

Moses and Aaron stopped at the foot of the steps leading to the platform where Pharaoh and his dignitaries sat.

"What subject do you wish to debate before this assembly?" inquired Ahmeni.

"I do not intend to debate," replied Moses, "but rather to demand what is due me, in accordance with the will of Yahweh: Pharaoh's permission to lead my people out of Egypt."

"Permission denied, in the interests of national security."

"This refusal constitutes an offense to Yahweh."

"Yahweh does not rule Egypt, as far as I know."

"Yet His wrath will be terrible! God protects me, and He will accomplish wonders to show His power."

"I once knew you well, Moses; we were even friends. In your younger days you weren't so full of delusions."

"You're an Egyptian scribe, Ahmeni; I'm the leader of the Hebrew people. Yahweh spoke to me on the mountain, and I can prove it!"

Aaron threw his walking stick to the ground. Moses fixed his gaze on it intensely. The knots of wood began to move as the stick turned into a writhing snake.

Several courtiers recoiled in horror. The snake slithered toward Ramses, who showed no fear. Setau leapt up and grabbed the serpent by the tail.

Exclamations broke out as he reached for it, growing louder as the snake turned back into a stick in Setau's hand.

"It's an old trick," announced the magician. "I taught it to Moses myself, years ago at the harem of Merur. It would take more than this to impress our Pharaoh."

Moses and Setau locked eyes. All traces of friendship between the two men had vanished.

"Wait a week," said the prophet, "and you'll see something that will strike terror into your people's hearts."

Guarded by Watcher, who dozed in the shade of a tamarisk, Nefertari swam nude in the garden pool nearest the palace. It was always crystal clear, thanks to copper plates attached to the stones, bacteria-eating plants, and a system of canals that kept the water circulating, not to mention a copper sulfate powder the staff regularly sprinkled on the surface.

As the inundation approached, the heat grew stifling. Before beginning her day, the queen enjoyed this delightful interval when her body, relaxed and happy, gave free rein to her thought, light as an egret. As she swam, Nefertari thought of the words she would say, some comforting, some stern, as each petitioner approached her, more eager than the last.

In a dress with shoulder straps that left her breasts bare, her hair undone, Iset silently approached the garden pool. They called her "Fair," yet she felt almost plain as she admired Nefertari. Each gesture of the queen's was perfect, each pose seemed to come from some brilliant painter who captured ideal beauty in the body of a woman.

After much more thought and one last session with Dolora, insistent as ever, Iset had finally come to a decision.

This time she'd do it.

Emptying her mind of any fear that might hinder her, Iset went one step closer to the pool. She'd do what must be done.

Nefertari caught her eye. "Come in with me!"

"I'm not feeling well, Your Majesty."

The queen swam smoothly to the edge of the pool and climbed up the stone steps.

"What's wrong, Iset?"

"I'm not sure."

"Having problems with Merenptah?"

"No, he's fine. I can't believe how big he's getting."

"Stretch out here beside me. The stones are warm."

"I'm sorry, the sun is too hot for me."

Nefertari's body was an enchantment. She was like the goddess of the West, whose smile lit this world as well as the next. Lying on her back, her arms along her body, eyes closed, she was at once present and inaccessible.

"Why are you so upset?" she asked again.

Again, doubts assailed Iset. Should she stick with her decision or run, at the risk of seeming crazy? Fortunately, Nefertari had looked away from her. No, the chance was too good to miss. This time Iset must not let it pass.

"Your Majesty, I— I'd like . . ."

Iset the Fair knelt near Nefertari's face. The queen lay still, clothed in light.

"Your Majesty, I wanted to kill you."

"I don't believe you, Iset."

"Yes, I've needed to confess. It's been hard to keep it inside. Now you know."

The queen opened her eyes, sat up, and took Iset by the hand.

"Who tried to make a murderer of you?"

"I was convinced that you had no love for Ramses, only ambition. I was blind and stupid! How could I pay any mind to such slander?"

"Everyone has moments of weakness, Iset, moments when our hearts are prey to evil. You resisted it in the end, isn't that what's important?"

"I'm so ashamed of myself . . . when you bring charges against me, I won't contest my sentence."

"Who told you these lies about me?"

"I wanted to confess my own guilt, Your Majesty, not act as an informer."

"In any attempt on me, the real target is Ramses. You owe me the truth, Iset, if you love the king."

"You don't hate me?"

"You're not a schemer, and you're brave enough to admit your mistakes. Not only do I not hate you, I respect you."

Iset unleashed a flood of tears and told Nefertari everything.

On the banks of the Nile, Moses had gathered thousands of Hebrews, accompanied by a crowd of curious onlookers from all over the capital. According to the rumors, the Hebrew's angry god was about to do something spectacular, proving he was more powerful than all the gods of Egypt put together. Perhaps Pharaoh ought to meet the prophet's demands after all!

Against the advice of Ahmeni and Serramanna, Ramses had decided not to intervene. Sending the army and the police to break up the gathering would have been over-reacting. Moses and his people were hardly disturbing the peace, and the street vendors were delighted with the milling crowds.

From his palace balcony, Ramses looked out at the river and the expectant throng on the banks, but his mind was occupied with the frightful revelations he had just heard from Nefertari.

"Is there any room for doubt?"

"No, Ramses. Iset was telling the truth."

"I ought to punish her harshly."

"I beg your indulgence. It was love that led her to the brink of a horrible crime. She stopped herself in time, and now thanks to her we've learned your sister's true inten-tions."

"I hoped that Dolora had finally overcome the demons eating away at her all these years. But I was wrong. She'll never change."

"Will you put Dolora on trial?"

"She'll deny the charges and point her finger at Iset the Fair. It would probably be a farce."

"You'll let her crime go unpunished?"

"No, Nefertari. Dolora used Iset, so we'll use Dolora."

From the riverbank came the sounds of a commotion.

Moses threw his rod into the Nile, turning the water around it red. The prophet scooped up a cupful of water and poured it on the ground.

"Witness this miracle! Yahweh has changed the water of

the Nile into blood. Unless Yahweh's will is done, this blood will flow through the country. The fish will die. This is the first plague visited upon Egypt."

Now Kha scooped up some of the strange, bitter-smelling water.

"Nothing of the sort will happen, Moses. What we have here is only the red water that comes with the flood stage. For a few days hence no one must drink the water or eat any fish from the Nile. If this is a miracle, we owe it to nature, and hers is the law we must obey."

The frail young Kha was composed as he faced the towering Hebrew. Moses suppressed his anger.

"Fine words, young man, but how do you explain the fact that my rod brought forth the bloody water?"

"No one challenges your gifts as a prophet. You sensed the change in the water, the rise coming from the south, and the day the red tinge would appear. You know this country as well as I do. It holds no secrets for you."

"Until today," boomed Moses, "Yahweh has been content with warnings. Since Egypt refuses to listen, He will surely inflict other plagues, far more terrible."

FORTY-NINE

Ahsha personally delivered the letter to the Great Royal Wife as she conferred with Ramses about the state of the grain stores.

"Here's the reply you've been waiting for, Your Majesty, a personal letter from the Empress Puduhepa. I hope the contents won't disappoint you."

The tablet, wrapped in precious cloth, bore Puduhepa's seal.

"Would you open it, Ahsha? For one thing, you're better than we are at reading Hittite. For another, any information from Hattusa directly concerns you."

The head of Egyptian diplomacy obeyed.

> To my sister, Queen Nefertari, spouse of the Sun, Ramses the Great,
>
> I hope this finds my sister well, her family in good health, her horses strong. Good weather has finally come to Hatti. For Egypt I wish a favorable inundation.
>
> I received my sister Nefertari's long letter and read it with interest. Emperor Hattusili is very cross to have learned that the vile Uri-Teshoop resides in Pi-Ramses. Uri-Teshoop is an evil man, violent and craven. He should be extradited and returned to Hattusa for trial. Emperor

Hattusili will not give in on this point.

Yet since peace between our two countries is our highest goal, we must be prepared to make certain sacrifices. No compromise is possible regarding Uri-Teshoop; the king is within his rights to demand extradition. Yet I have helped him understand the moral grounds for Pharaoh's position; the emperor respects your husband for honoring his word. Indeed, we could never trust a sovereign who did not do so.

Therefore, while the issue of Uri-Teshoop is nonnego-tiable, why not move beyond it and work toward estab-lishing a pact of mutual nonaggression? Drawing up such a document will take a long time. It would thus be expe-dient to begin discussions at once.

Does the Queen of Egypt, my sister, share my thoughts? If such were the case, it would be wise to send us at once a trusted and high-ranking diplomat. I put forth the name of Ahsha.

I close with my friendship, dear queen and sister.

"We're forced to turn down her proposal," said Ramses dejectedly.

"But why?" objected Ahsha.

"Because it's a trap. The emperor can't forgive you for smuggling Uri-Teshoop out of Hatti. If you go back there, you won't come home again."

"I analyze this letter somewhat differently, Your Majesty. Queen Nefertari made some convincing arguments; Empress Puduhepa is affirming her desire for peace. Given the influence she exerts over the emperor, it's a step in the right direction."

"Ahsha is right," said Nefertari. "My sister Puduhepa clearly understood my message. Let's set aside the issue of Uri-Teshoop and begin negotiations in good faith."

"Uri-Teshoop is no illusion!" objected Ramses.

"Must I clarify the position I share with Puduhepa? Hattusili demands Uri-Teshoop's extradition; Ramses refuses. The issue remains at a stalemate while you pursue negotiations for a peace treaty. Isn't that what you call diplomacy?"

"I trust Puduhepa," added Ahsha.

"If you and the queen are in league against me, how can I resist? We'll send a diplomat, then, but not you."

"Impossible, Your Majesty. The empress's wish is clearly a command. And who knows Hatti and the Hittites better than I do?"

"Are you prepared to take such great risks, Ahsha?"

"Failing to jump at this chance for peace negotiations would be criminal. We must focus all our energies on the task. Accomplishing the impossible—isn't that what you're famous for?"

"I've rarely seen you show such enthusiasm."

"I love life. And love. War interferes with them."

"I won't sign just any treaty. Egypt must not be the loser on any score."

"I expect a few sticking points, but they come with the job. We're going to work several days straight to put together an acceptable proposal. I'll say my goodbyes to a few lady friends, then I'll leave for Hatti. And I'll come back with a treaty you'll be proud to sign."

First came a surprising jump. Then the creature stopped just an arm's length in front of Setau where he sat on the riverbank, studying the Nile with satisfaction as the waters cleared.

Now another jumped, and another, healthy and playful, in varying shades of green: magnificent frogs emerging from the river silt that overflowed the banks to fertilize the land and feed Pharaoh's people.

At the head of an imposing procession, Aaron raised his staff above the Nile and spoke in a strong voice.

"Since Pharaoh refuses to deliver the Hebrew people from bondage in Egypt, here is the next plague that Yahweh is visiting upon the oppressor: frogs, thousands of frogs, millions of frogs that will overrun the country, filling workshops, houses, rich men's bedchambers!"

Setau headed calmly back to his laboratory, where Lotus was mixing new remedies from the excellent cobra venom they had harvested around Abu Simbel. There was good news from that quarter: the temple was going up on schedule. The snake charmer and his wife looked forward to returning to Nubia as soon as Ramses permitted.

Setau smiled. Neither he nor Kha would have to take any measures against Aaron and his latest plague. Moses' lieutenant should have consulted with his chief before announcing a curse that no Egyptian would take seriously.

At this time of year, there was nothing unusual about an abundance of frogs. In fact, the people took it as a good sign. In hieroglyphic writing, the frog formed the figure 100,000, a nearly incalculable multiplicity in tune with their proliferation during the flood stage.

Observing the creature's metamorphosis, the priests of the earliest dynasties saw life's incessant mutations. The frog had come to symbolize both successful childbirth (after all the stages of growth inside the womb) and eternity (which continues through time and beyond time).

The following day, Kha arranged a giveaway of frog amulets. Thrilled with this unexpected present, the people of Pi-Ramses praised the name of Pharaoh and felt grateful toward Aaron and the Hebrews. Thanks to their so-called plague, many humble folk became the proud possessors of a precious object.

Ahsha put the finishing touches on the proposed treaty he had written in concert with the royal couple. It had required more than a month of intensive work to weigh each term, and Nefertari's editing had been most valuable. As the secretary of state had supposed, Pharaoh's demands would make the negotiations difficult. Still, Ramses was not treating Hatti as a conquered nation, but rather as a partner that would find the agreement to their advantage. If Puduhepa truly wanted peace, Ramses just might bring it off.

Ahmeni arrived with a magnificent amber-colored papyrus on which Ramses himself would inscribe his proposals.

"I've had a complaint from one of the neighborhood councils," the scribe announced. "It's about mosquitoes."

"They can get out of hand at this time of year unless sanitary measures are strictly enforced. Is there a pond that someone forgot to drain?"

"Aaron claims it's Yahweh's third plague, Your Majesty. He stirred up the dust to turn it into mosquitoes. Does that sound like the wrath of God to you?"

"Our friend Moses is nothing if not persistent," Ahsha observed.

"Send a squad of health inspectors into the neighborhood in question," Ramses told Ahmeni. "The people need relief."

The inundation promised a fruitful year. Ramses celebrated the rites of dawn at the temple of Amon, then
allowed himself a walk on the river landing with Fighter.
The rest of his morning would be spent inside the palace,
composing a letter to Hattusili.

Suddenly Moses' staff echoed on the flagstones. The
enormous lion stared at the Hebrew but made no sound.

"Let my people go, Ramses, that we may worship
Yahweh as He demands."

"Have we anything more to say to each other, Moses?"

"Wonders and plagues have shown you the will of
Yahweh."

"Is that my friend behind those strange words?"

"No friend, but the messenger of Yahweh! And you, my
Pharaoh, are an unbeliever!"

"How can I make you see the light?"

"You're the one who's blind."

"You go your way, Moses, and I'll stick to mine, no
matter what happens."

"Grant me one favor: come see my Hebrew brethren's
livestock."

"Is there something special about them?"

"Just come."

Fighter, Serramanna, and a squadron of mercenaries
went along to provide security. Moses had herded the
Hebrews' livestock together in a marshy area some two
leagues outside the capital. Thousands of horseflies buzzed
mercilessly around the bleating animals.

"This is the fourth plague sent by Yahweh," Moses

revealed. "If I drive these beasts apart, the horseflies will swarm over your capital."

"Nice try . . . but did you really need to leave this herd so filthy and make the animals suffer so?"

"Yahweh demands that we sacrifice rams, cows, and other animals sacred to the Egyptians. If we perform our rites within your country, the farmers will resent us. Let us go into the desert, Ramses, or else the horseflies will attack your subjects."

"Serramanna and an armed contingent will accompany you, your priests, and the diseased livestock to a place in the desert where you can make your sacrifices. The rest of the animals will be cleaned and sent back to their regular pastures. Once your rites are over, you'll return to Pi-Ramses."

"I'm not giving up, Ramses. One day you'll be forced to release us from Egypt."

FIFTY

It's time to hit harder," Ofir advised. "Much harder."

"We got them to let us sacrifice out in the desert, didn't we?" observed Moses. "Ramses gave in. He'll make more concessions."

"Don't you think he's running out of patience?"

"Yahweh is protecting us."

"I have another idea, Moses, an idea for a fifth plague that will hurt Pharaoh to the quick.

"It's not up to us, but to Yahweh."

"Shouldn't we lend him a hand? Ramses is a hardheaded tyrant who can only be daunted by signs from on high. Let me help you."

Moses acquiesced.

Ofir left the prophet's dwelling and met his accomplices, Amos and Keni. The two Bedouin chiefs had continued to stockpile weapons in the local Hebrews' cellars; just back from southern Syria, they brought messages from Hittite agents. The sorcerer was eager for fresh news, if not instructions.

Amos had oiled his bald pate.

"Emperor Hattusili is furious," he revealed. "With Ramses refusing to extradite Uri-Teshoop, he's ready to resume the fighting."

"Perfect! What does he expect of my network?"

"The orders are simple: keep agitating the Hebrews here in Egypt, make trouble all over the country to undermine Ramses, arrange for Uri-Teshoop's escape and bring him back to Hattusa. Or else kill him."

Crooked-Fingers was a peasant who loved his plot of land and his herd of some twenty cows, each one sweeter than the last; gentle beasts, although their leader did have her own ideas and wouldn't let just anyone approach her. Crooked-Fingers spent hours conversing with her.

The impish Redhead woke him each morning, licking

his forehead. The cowherd tried to grab her by the ear, but he always ended up getting to his feet.

But this morning the sun was already high in the sky when Crooked-Fingers rose.

"Redhead . . . Where have you gotten to, Redhead?"

He rubbed his eyes and advanced a few steps into his field, where he saw the cow lying on her side.

"What's the matter with you, Redhead?"

Glassy-eyed, gagging, her belly swollen, the pretty young cow was near death. A bit farther back in the field, two others were already gone.

The frantic peasant ran to the village square to get help from the local veterinarian. He found a dozen other similarly afflicted herdsmen already besieging the doctor.

"An epidemic!" cried Crooked-Fingers. "We'd better tell the palace right away."

When Ofir, watching from the balcony of his house, saw a cohort of worried and angry peasants, he knew his orders had been correctly executed. By poisoning a few head of cattle, the Bedouin chiefs Amos and Keni had sown panic.

In the middle of the avenue leading to the palace, Moses halted the procession.

"Here is the fifth plague that Yahweh has visited upon Egypt! His hand will spare no herd or flock, and only the livestock belonging to my people will be free of pestilence."

Serramanna and a large detail of soldiers were preparing to disperse the peasants when Lotus arrived, her black horse at a gallop, reining in at the edge of the gathering.

"Don't lose your heads," she said in a calm voice. "What we have here is no pestilence, but a poisoning. I've already saved two milk cows, and with the help of the animal doctors I think I can cure the rest of the victims."

The crowd's dismay gave way to a mood of hope. And

when the agriculture secretary announced that Pharaoh would replace the dead livestock at government expense, all was well once more.

Ofir had enough poison left to keep helping Moses, this time without letting him know. Using an old magic formula, on orders from Yahweh, the prophet had taken handfuls of soot from a furnace and scattered it in the air so that dust would fall on man and beast, causing them to break out in boils. This sixth plague would be so terrifying that Pharaoh would finally be forced to capitulate.

Ofir had another idea. How better to impress the monarch than by touching his inner circle? Bald-headed Amos, unrecognizable in a wig that covered half his forehead, had delivered tainted food to the cook who prepared the meals for Ahmeni and his staff.

When the sandal-bearer appeared for the king's daily briefing, Ramses noticed a reddish sore on his friend's cheek.

"Have you hurt yourself?"

"No, but this pimple keeps getting worse."

"I'll call for Dr. Pariamaku."

The palace doctor arrived out of breath, accompanied by an attractive young woman.

"Are you ill, Your Majesty?" inquired Pariamaku.

"As you know, Doctor, I'm never ill. I'd like you to examine my private secretary."

The physician circled Ahmeni, prodded his arms, took his pulse, and put his ear to his rib cage.

"Nothing abnormal at first glance . . . I'll have to think."

"If it's a skin ulceration resulting from gastric difficulties," the girl spoke up timidly, "shouldn't we have him try a mixture of sycamore, anise, honey, pine resin, and fennel, to be applied externally as well as drunk in a potion?"

Dr. Pariamaku assumed an important expression.

"Not a bad idea . . . we'll give it a try and see. Go to the laboratory, my child, and prepare the remedy."

The girl withdrew, after bowing tremulously to the monarch.

"What's your assistant's name?" asked Ramses.

"Neferet, Your Majesty. Pay no attention to her, she's only an intern."

"She seems quite competent."

"She was simply reciting a formula I taught her. Just a beginner, with no great talent."

Ofir was bemused.

Medicine had worked against the plague of boils, and Ramses remained as obstinate as ever. Moses and Aaron were restraining the Hebrews, since any untimely agitation would bring swift reprisals from Serramanna and the police.

An additional setback was the loss of contact with Dolora, the king's sister. There was no doubt that she had failed in her mission. Nefertari was alive and well, showing no signs of chronic illness. Sensing she was watched, Dolora no longer dared venture into the Hebrew quarter, even at night, which meant that Ofir was cut off from his most direct source of palace information.

This did not prevent the Hittite spy from fanning the flames of revolt among the Hebrews. A core faction, united

behind Moses and Aaron, was ready to spearhead the movement.

Arranging Uri-Teshoop's escape would be difficult.
Assigned to a villa guarded day and night by Serramanna's
men, Uri-Teshoop was a has-been and a liability. Rather
than taking undue risks, the better solution might be to
eliminate him, which would immediately win favor with
Hattusili. The new emperor was shrewd and merciless, a
worthy successor to his brother.

Ofir still had one undercover ally: the diplomat Meba.
The man was a weakling, but he was the one who would
help the sorcerer get rid of Uri-Teshoop.

Ahsha's escort was kept to a bare minimum, since the
head of Egyptian diplomacy thought he had no better than
one chance in a hundred (contrary to the queen's opinion)
of finding a warm welcome in the Hittite capital. In the
eyes of the new emperor, he was a suspect character who
had helped Uri-Teshoop go free. Hattusili was likely to let
his resentment get the better of his political savvy. If he did,
he would have every member of the Egyptian delegation
arrested, if not executed, starting with Ahsha, to force
Ramses' hand. A confrontation, Hattusili might think,
would allow him to even the score.

Puduhepa did seem to favor peace, but how far could she
diverge from her husband's wishes? The Empress of Hatti
was not one to back a hopeless cause. If negotiation proved
too difficult a route, she would fall in line with the war effort.

A buffeting wind, common on the plateaus of Anatolia,
accompanied Ahsha and his contingent to the gates of

Hattusa. Its fortress-like grimness struck him even more forcibly than on his earlier visits.

The secretary of state presented his credentials to the sentry post commander, waiting for more than an hour before he was granted entry through the Lion Gate. His hopes were dashed when he found he was being led not to the palace but to a dingy gray freestone building, where he was assigned a room. The single window was fitted with iron bars.

Even to an optimist, the place looked like a prison.

Playing the Hittites correctly demanded both skill and luck, a great deal of luck. Ahsha felt that his might be running out.

As evening fell, a helmeted officer in heavy armor came to fetch him. This time they headed up the incline to the citadel where the imperial palace stood.

Ahsha was approaching the moment of truth, if such existed in the world of diplomacy.

In the audience chamber, hung with tapestries, a fire blazed. Empress Puduhepa was basking in its warmth.

"I beg the Egyptian ambassador to sit before the hearth with me. The night may be cool."

Ahsha sat unceremoniously in a chair a respectful distance from her.

"I greatly appreciated Queen Nefertari's letters," declared the empress. "Her thinking is inspired, her arguments convincing, her intentions forthright."

"Am I to understand that the emperor agrees to open negotiations?"

"The emperor and I wish to see concrete proposals."

"I am the bearer of a document conceived by Ramses and Nefertari and drawn up by Pharaoh himself; it will serve as a basis for our discussions."

"Exactly the initiative I was hoping for. Hatti must, of course, impose certain conditions."

"I'm here to find out what they are, with the firm intention of reaching an agreement."

"Your words warm my heart as much as the fire does. I trust your initial welcome didn't trouble you?"

"I can't complain."

"Hattusili has caught cold and spent the last few days in bed. I've been so busy that I had to make you wait. But by tomorrow the emperor should be able to open the discussions."

FIFTY-ONE

Ramses was on his way to the temple of Amon well before daybreak when suddenly Moses stood in his way. The guard accompanying the king drew his sword, but Ramses checked it.

"I need to speak to you, Pharaoh!"

"Keep it short."

"Can't you see that Yahweh has been indulgent so far? If He'd so wished, you and your people would already be annihilated. He spared your life the better to show that He alone is almighty and powerful. Now let the Hebrews out of Egypt, or else . . ."

"Or else?"

"A seventh plague will visit intolerable suffering upon your country: a hailstorm so violent that it will take countless victims. When I raise my staff toward the sky, there will be thunderclaps and bolts of lightning."

"You must know that one of this capital's main temples honors Set, the Lord of the Storm. His is the wrath of the sky, and I know the rituals that tame it."

"This time they won't work. The hail will take its toll of beasts and men."

"Out of my way, Moses."

That very afternoon, the king consulted with the "priests of the hour" who observed the heavens, studied the movements of the planets, and predicted the weather. They were in fact anticipating heavy rains that might wipe out part of the flax harvest.

As soon as the dark clouds gathered, Ramses closeted himself in Set's inner sanctum, facing the angry god alone. The monumental statue's red eyes glowed like coals.

The king did not have the power to oppose Set's will and stop the storms he unleashed; he could only shorten them and diminish their strength by communing with the god's spirit. Seti had taught his son how to deal with Set and channel his destructive power without risking destruction himself. It took all his energy to hold his own against Set's invisible flames, but once again it was worth the effort.

Meba felt shaky. Though disguised in a short wig and a coarse, poorly cut cloak, he was afraid that he'd be spotted. But who would recognize him in this house of beer near the docks, where stevedores and sailors came to relax?

Amos, the bearded bald man, took a seat across from him.

"Who sent you?" Meba asked in a faltering voice.

"The sorcerer. And you're . . ."

"No names, please. Give him this tablet. It contains information that may well interest him."

"The sorcerer wants you to take care of Uri-Teshoop."

"But he's under house arrest!"

"Your orders are strict: kill Uri-Teshoop or we'll turn you in to Ramses."

Doubt was beginning to make inroads among the Hebrews. Seven plagues had already been inflicted on Egypt, and Pharaoh was obstinate as ever. When the council of elders met, however, Moses was still able to retain his hold.

"What will you do next?" the chairman asked him.

"Unleash an eighth plague, so terrible that the Egyptians will feel abandoned by their gods."

"What will it be?"

"Look to the east for your answer."

"Will we finally be released from Egypt?"

"Be as long-suffering as I was for years in the desert. Put your faith in Yahweh: He will lead us to the Promised Land."

In the middle of the night, Nefertari woke with a start.

At her side, Ramses was fast asleep. The queen crept out of the bedroom and stepped onto the balcony. The air was sweet, the city silent and peaceful, yet the Great Royal Wife grew increasingly anxious. The vision that had tormented her would not fade; she was still in the grip of a nightmare.

Ramses took her gently in his arms.

"A bad dream, Nefertari?"

"If only that were all . . ."

"What's the matter?"

"A peril coming from the east, on a frightful wind . . ."

Ramses looked hard in that direction, as if seeing into the darkness. The king's mind became night and sky, traveling to the ends of the earth, where the winds are born.

What Ramses saw there was so awful that he threw on his clothes, woke the palace staff, and sent for Ahmeni.

The cloud blowing in from the east was made up of locusts—millions, billions of them. A plague of insects was not unknown, but never on such a scale.

Thanks to Pharaoh's early warning, the Delta peasants had lit bonfires, smoking out the locusts with noxious smells. Certain crops were covered with coarse linen sheeting.

When Moses proclaimed that the insects would devour every tree in Egypt, leaving not a single piece of fruit, royal messengers had quickly spread advance warning through the countryside. Now everyone was glad that Ramses' precautionary measures had been so swiftly instituted.

The damage was minimal. The locust, people recalled, was one of the symbolic forms Pharaoh's soul took, reaching the heavens with one gigantic leap. In small numbers, the insect was considered beneficial; only the swarms were a problem.

The royal couple toured the area around the capital in their chariot, stopping in several villages that feared a new infestation. Ramses and Nefertari reassured them that the plague would soon abate.

As the Great Royal Wife had predicted, the east wind calmed, to be replaced by fresh gusts that blew the locusts away from the croplands toward the Sea of Reeds.

"There's nothing wrong with you," Dr. Pariamaku told the old diplomat Meba. "Though I'm sure you could stand a few days' rest."

"Then why don't I feel well?"

"Your heart is in excellent shape, your liver is fine. Don't worry, you'll probably live to be a hundred!"

Meba had feigned illness in the hope that Pariamaku would confine him to his room for several weeks, during which time Ofir and his accomplices might be arrested.

His childish plan had gotten him nowhere. And fingering the sorcerer was no alternative—he'd only be implicating himself.

His only choice was to carry out his mission. But how could he get to Uri-Teshoop without alerting Serramanna and his handpicked guards?

When all was said and done, diplomacy was his sole advantage. The next time he encountered the Sard in the palace corridors, Meba hailed him.

"I've just received a dispatch from Ahsha ordering me to interrogate Uri-Teshoop on certain aspects of the Hittite government," declared Meba. "Whatever he tells me must be kept strictly confidential, so it will need to be a one-on-one interview. I'll record his statement on papyrus, seal it, and submit it to the king."

Serramanna seemed vexed. "How long will it take?"

"I have no idea."

"Are you in a hurry?"

"The request is urgent."

"All right. Let's get going."

Uri-Teshoop gave the diplomat a cold reception, but Meba quickly won his way into the Hittite's good graces. Rather than pressing Uri-Teshoop with questions, he applauded the prince's cooperation and painted a rosy picture of his future.

Uri-Teshoop described his finest moments in battle and even ventured a jesting comment or two.

"Are you satisfied with how you're being treated?" inquired Meba.

"The food and lodging are fine, I get plenty of exercise . . . if only they let me have women."

"I may be able to help you."

"How?"

"Ask for a walk in the gardens; say you'd enjoy the cool of the evening. In the tamarisk grove, near the back gate, a girl will be waiting."

"I think we'll become good friends."

"That's my fondest wish, Your Highness."

The air was muggy, the clouds grew dark. The god Set was again displaying his powers. Uri-Teshoop's evening stroll would bring no relief from the stifling heat. Two guards walked with him, letting him wander among the flower beds. After all, there was no way the Hittite prince could escape. And besides, why would he want to leave this gilded retreat?

Hiding in the tamarisks, Meba trembled. A mandrake potion had put him in an altered state; he had scaled the garden wall and was ready to strike.

When Uri-Teshoop leaned his head into the bower, Meba would slit his throat with the dagger he'd stolen from an infantry officer. He'd leave the weapon behind to cast suspicion on the military. It was quite feasible that the Pharaoh's soldiers would plot to kill the enemy chief responsible for so many Egyptian deaths.

Meba had never killed before, and he knew that the act would lead to his damnation. When he arrived at the Judgment Hall of the Dead, he'd plead that he'd been forced into it. But for the moment he must think of nothing but the dagger and Uri-Teshoop's neck.

Footsteps.

Slow, cautious footsteps. His prey was coming closer, pausing, stooping. Meba raised his arm. Then a violent blow to the skull knocked him unconscious.

Serramanna hoisted the diplomat by the collar of his tunic.

"Wake up, you traitor. Wake up, fool!"

The old man remained limp.

"Don't play games with me!"

Meba's head lolled strangely sideways. Serramanna realized he'd once again hit too hard.

FIFTY-TWO

In the course of the inevitable inquest into Meba's violent death, Ahmeni subjected Serramanna to a close interrogation. The Sard was unsure whether he would face consequences.

"The evidence is clear," concluded the scribe. "You had ample grounds for suspecting the diplomat Meba of lying to you and intending to kill Uri-Teshoop. When you attempted to catch the perpetrator in the act, he struck out at you and succumbed in the ensuing struggle."

The former pirate breathed a sigh of relief. "An excellent account."

"Though deceased, Meba will be tried and convicted. His name will henceforth be struck from all official documents. Yet one question remains: who was he working for?"

"He claimed he was acting on Ahsha's orders."

Ahmeni bit the tip of his brush.

"Ahsha might want to eliminate a stumbling block in the peace negotiations . . . but he wouldn't have given the job to a bungling old bureaucrat! More than that, he'd never violate Ramses' principles, including respect for the right to asylum. Meba was lying, as usual. What if he belonged to the Hittite spy ring you were investigating?"

"But weren't they supporting Uri-Teshoop?"

"Yes, but now Uri-Teshoop is only a renegade. Hattusili is emperor, and they'd be doing him an important favor if they took care of his only serious rival."

The Sard toyed with his luxuriant mustache. "In other words, Ofir and Shaanar are not only alive and well, but still operating in Egypt."

"Shaanar disappeared in Nubia. No one's heard from Ofir in years."

Serramanna clenched his fists.

"That damned sorcerer may be right under our noses! The reports that put him in Libya could have been faked just to make us stop looking."

"Ofir has always managed to elude us."

"No one stays out of my way forever, Ahmeni."

"Just this once, would you consider bringing him in alive?"

For three interminable days, thick black clouds hung over Pi-Ramses, blocking the sun. The Egyptian people feared that the goddess Sekhmet was about to compound the perils that Set had threatened.

Only one person could keep the situation from degenerating: the Great Royal Wife, the earthly incarnation of the eternal law that Pharaoh maintained with his constant offerings. It was a time for every Egyptian to examine his or her conscience and make amends. Assuming the weight of her people's transgressions, Nefertari traveled to Thebes. At the temple of Mut, she would lay offerings at the feet of the terrible goddess Sekhmet's statues. The queen would turn the darkness into light.

In the capital, Ramses granted one more audience to Moses, who was proclaiming that the darkness over the capital was the ninth plague Yahweh had sent to Egypt.

"Convinced now, Pharaoh?"

"You're only interpreting natural phenomena and attributing them to your god. That's your vision of reality, and I respect it. But I will not accept your upsetting my people in the name of your dogma. It's against the guiding principle of Ma'at and can lead to nothing but trouble and civil disturbances."

"Yahweh's demands remain unchanged."

"Leave Egypt with your band of followers, Moses, and go worship your god wherever you like."

"That's not how Yahweh wants it. I have to take the entire Hebrew people with me."

"Your cattle and flocks must remain behind, since for the most part your people don't own them but only keep them. Those who turn their backs on Egypt must not share in her wealth."

"Our chattel goes with us. Not one head of livestock will be left in your country, for all will be used in sacrifice to Yahweh as we make our way to the Promised Land."

"I call that stealing."

"Only Yahweh can judge me."

"What faith can justify such an outrage?"

"Don't bother trying to understand it. You can only bow to its power."

"Pharaohs through the ages have dealt with the scourge of fanaticism and intolerance. Don't you shudder to think what can happen when men impose an absolute truth on their fellow men? I know that I do."

"Bow to the will of Yahweh, Ramses."

"Have you nothing to offer but threats and invective, Moses? What's become of our friendship, the friendship that once led us toward greater understanding?"

"Only the future interests me, and that future is my people's exodus."

"Get out of my palace, Moses. This is the last I'll see of you. If you challenge me again, I'll brand you a rebel and you'll be brought to trial."

Blazing with anger, Moses stormed through the palace gates, ignoring former acquaintances who might have sought a word with him. He headed straight back to his house in the Hebrew quarter of Pi-Ramses, where Ofir was waiting.

From his informants, the sorcerer had learned about Meba's sorry death. Yet the diplomat's last written report contained one interesting bit of information: during a visit to the temple of Ptah in Memphis, Meba had noted that Kha now went without the talismans that once had formed Setau's magic wall. As a high priest, young Kha was endowed with special magical powers, but why not put him to the test once more?

"Did Ramses give in this time?" inquired the sorcerer.

"He never will!" snapped Moses.

"Ramses is utterly fearless. The situation will be deadlocked unless we resort to violence."

"A revolt . . ."

"We have the arms for it."

"The Hebrews will be exterminated."

"Who said anything about an open rebellion? Death will be our ally, the tenth and last plague inflicted upon Egypt."

Moses was still blind with rage. In Ofir's menacing words, he seemed to hear the voice of Yahweh.

"You're right, Ofir. We must strike so hard that Ramses will have no choice but to free the Hebrews. At midnight on the appointed day, Yahweh will kill the firstborn of every household in Egypt."

It was the moment Ofir had been waiting for. Finally, he'd have his revenge on Ramses, the conquering pharaoh.

"The list of firstborn sons will begin with Kha, Ramses' son and probable successor. The magic protecting him has been too strong for me, but now I think I can find a way through it."

"The hand of Yahweh will not spare the son of Ramses."

"We can take advantage of the Egyptians' good nature," proposed Ofir. "The Hebrews should fraternize with them, asking for presents of gold and silver. You'll need it during the exodus."

Moses was silent for a time, then said, "We'll make sacrifices, dipping hyssop blossoms into the blood of the lamb and marking our houses with it. On the night the firstborns die, the Exterminator will pass over our doorsteps."

Ofir made haste to his workshop. He still possessed the brush stolen from Kha so long ago. It still might serve to paralyze Ramses' eldest son and send him toward an eternal sleep.

The play of light and shadow in the garden made Nefertari seem lovelier than ever. Mysterious and sublime, flitting as gracefully as a goddess among the shrubs and flowers, she was happiness itself. Yet the moment he kissed her hand, Ramses could sense that her mood was somber.

"Moses hasn't left off with his threats," she murmured.

"He was my friend. I can't believe that he truly wishes us harm."

"I share your respect for him, but a raging fire has taken hold of his heart. I'm afraid of what he'll do next."

A concerned-looking Setau approached the royal couple.

"Forgive me for being blunt as ever, but Kha has been taken ill."

"Is it serious?" queried Nefertari.

"I'm afraid so, Your Majesty. My remedies don't seem to help."

"Do you mean . . ."

"There's no use denying it. He's under a spell."

As the daughter of Isis, goddess of magic, the Great Royal Wife hurried to the prince's bedside.

Despite his pain, the young high priest of Ptah impressed everyone around him with his dignity. As he lay on a cot, wan and hollow-eyed, Kha's breathing was shallow.

"My arms are numb," he told Nefertari. "Can't even move my legs."

The queen laid her hands on the young man's temples.

"I'll give you all my energy," she promised. "Together we'll fight this creeping death. You'll feel the happiness that has been mine, and you'll never die."

In the Hittite capital, negotiations were advancing very slowly. Hattusili reviewed each article of the proposed treaty, suggested changes in wording, locked horns with Ahsha, and eventually reached a compromise, carefully weighing each term. Puduhepa added her own comments, leading to further discussion.

Ahsha's patience was seemingly inexhaustible. He was acutely aware that this process would forge a peace agreement influencing the future of the entire Near East and much of Asia.

"Don't forget," Hattusili frequently reminded him, "that I'm still demanding Uri-Teshoop's extradition."

"That will be the last item we resolve," replied Ahsha, "once we've formulated the agreement as a whole."

"You're remarkably optimistic. But are you sure the Emperor of Hatti trusts you completely?"

"If he were unwise enough to do so, would he be the Emperor of Hatti?"

"If you're second-guessing me, doesn't that compromise the outcome of the negotiations?"

"We have to second-guess each other. Each of us wants the best possible terms for his country. My job is to help us strike a balance."

"You think that can be done?"

"The future of the world . . . Ramses has entrusted it to me. That's what you hold in your hands, Imperial Highness."

"I'm patient, clearheaded, and stubborn, my dear Ahsha."

"Just as I am, Your Highness."

FIFTY-THREE

Serramanna stuck close to the guardhouse reserved for his mercenaries. At most, he allowed himself some fun with a bargirl from the most reputable house of beer. Not even sex could make him lower his guard. Sooner or later, the enemy would make a mistake, and he had to be ready when the moment came.

Kha's illness had profoundly upset the Sardinian giant. Everything touching on the king and his relatives affected him as if the royal family had become his own. He was furious with himself for not having Ramses' enemies under better control.

One of the mercenaries arrived to brief him.

"Something strange is going on with the Hebrews."

"Explain yourself."

"It looks like red paint on their doors. I don't know why, but I thought you might want to know."

"Good work. Now bring me the brickmaker Abner. Charge him with anything you can think of."

After testifying in favor of Moses, Abner had dropped out of sight, apparently no longer demanding kickbacks from younger workers.

Now, appearing before Serramanna, Abner was visibly nervous.

"What is this latest offense?" inquired the Sard crossly.

"I've done nothing, sir! My conscience is clean as a priest's white vestment."

"Then why are you shaking?"

"I'm only a humble brickmaker, and . . ."

"Enough, Abner. Tell me why you've smeared your doorway with red paint."

"An accident, sir."

"And the same accident happened to dozens of other houses in your neighborhood? Stop treating me like an imbecile, man."

The towering Sard cracked his knuckles, and the Hebrew jumped. "It's nothing . . . a neighborhood fad, that's all."

"Oh? And what if the latest police fad was to cut off your nose and ears?"

"You have no right. It's against the law."

"But there are extenuating circumstances. I'm investigating the spell cast on Ramses' eldest son, and it wouldn't surprise me to find out that you're mixed up in it."

Judges dealt harshly with charges of black magic; Abner could face a stiff sentence.

"I'm innocent!"

"With your record, that's hard to believe."

"Don't do this to me, I beg of you. I have a wife and children . . ."

"Talk or else I'll bring charges."

For Abner, it was no hard choice between his own skin and Moses' safety.

"Moses is putting a curse on the children of Egypt," he confessed. "One night soon every firstborn will die at the hands of Yahweh. A sign on the doorway will spare the Hebrews."

"By all the monsters of the deep, this Moses is a demon!"

"Will you let me go, sir?"

"You'll only warn them, vermin. You'll be safer in prison."

Abner nodded, looking somewhat relieved.

"When will I be released?"

"What date has been set for this slaughter?"

"I'm not sure, but it must be soon."

Serramanna rushed to the palace, where Ramses saw him as soon as he was finished with the agriculture secretary. As Kha clung to life, sustained only by Nefertari's magic, Nedjem was so distraught that he could barely function. Ramses had convinced him that public service and the greater good of all Egyptians must take precedence over everything else, even a personal tragedy.

The Sard outlined Abner's confession for the monarch.

"The man is lying," said Ramses. "Moses would never sanction such an abomination."

"Abner is a coward and scared to death of me. He was telling the truth."

"Serial killings, the cold-blooded and systematic elimination of every firstborn . . . only a sick mind could conceive of such horror. It can't come from Moses."

"I recommend immediate action to make sure the plan is never implemented."

"Yes. Put the provincial police on alert as well."

"Excuse me, Your Majesty, but isn't it time we arrested Moses?"

"He's committed no crime. A jury would acquit him. I need to think of another solution."

"I'd like to propose a strategy that should prove effective, though it may offend you."

"Since when are you so tactful? Spell it out, Serramanna."

"We could spread the rumor that Kha won't live more than three days."

The mere thought sent a chill up Ramses' spine.

"I knew it would shock you, Your Majesty. But the news will force the assassins' hand, and I think their haste will be to our advantage."

The king paused only momentarily.

"Make sure you get them, Serramanna."

Dolora, Ramses' sister, slapped her hairdresser for pulling too hard on a strand of her beautiful dark hair.

"Off with you, clumsy wench!"

The hairdresser exited sobbing. Since it was time for Dolora's pedicure, another servant replaced her at once.

"Trim the dead skin and touch up the red on my nails . . . and take care not to hurt me."

The pedicurist was glad she had years of experience.

"You do good work," said Dolora after a time. "You'll get a good tip and I'll tell my friends about you."

"Thank you, Your Highness. You've made me happy on this sad day."

"Oh? What's so sad about it?"

"My first client this morning, a great lady whose name you'd know, just told me the terrible news. The king's eldest son is about to die."

"Isn't that just a rumor?"

"I'm afraid not. The palace physician is saying that Prince Kha can't last more than two or three days."

"Hurry up now," said the princess. "I have things to do."

An emergency. For once, Dolora felt she must circumvent the normal security precautions. Forgoing makeup, she pulled on her simplest wig and threw a brown cape over her shoulders. No one would recognize her.

Dolora mingled with the crowd and cut across town to where the Hebrew brickmakers lived. Threading her way between a water bearer and a cheese seller, she jostled two girls playing with dolls in the middle of the street, nudged a doddering old man who got in her way, and finally came to a dark green door, where she knocked five times.

The door creaked open.

"Who are you?" asked a brickmaker.

"The sorcerer's lady friend."

"Come in."

The brickmaker led Dolora down a stairway to a cellar. The dim light of an oil lamp flickered on the sorcerer's sinister face—a hawk face, with the high cheekbones, hook nose, and mysterious angles that fascinated her.

Ofir was holding Kha's old paintbrush. It was scrawled with strange markings and partially burnt.

"What's the emergency, Dolora?"

"Kha isn't much longer for this world."

"Have the palace doctors given up on him?"

"Pariamaku thinks his death is imminent."

"Excellent news, though it may change our plans somewhat. You were right to come."

The fateful night would come sooner than expected. All over the land, firstborn children would die, beginning with Ramses' son. The people of Egypt would be stricken with despair. Terrified by the wrath and the might of Yahweh, they would turn against Ramses in a wild and spontaneous uprising.

Dolora threw herself at the sorcerer's feet.

"What's going to happen, Ofir?"

"Ramses will be swept aside. Moses and the True God will triumph."

"Our dream come true . . ."

"Only because we've made it a reality. Remember how hard we've worked, my dear Dolora."

"Isn't there any way to avoid . . . certain bloodshed?"

Ofir brought Dolora to her feet and laid his palms to the cheeks of this tall, dark, almost languid woman.

"Moses makes the decisions, and Moses is inspired by Yahweh. We mustn't dispute his orders, no matter what the consequences."

Then came the sound of a door flying open, a smothered cry, rapid footsteps down the stairs, and the towering Sard burst into the cellar.

Dolora, whom he had trailed to the sorcerer's den, was shoved aside as Serramanna reached for Ofir, felling him with a blow to the head. The master spy was still clutching Kha's old paintbrush when the onetime pirate stepped on his wrist, forcing his fingers open.

"Ofir . . . I've finally got you."

FIFTY-FOUR

Setau entered Kha's sickroom, threw the enchanted paint-brush on the floor, and stomped furiously until it was no more than tiny fragments.

Nefertari, who had been magnetizing Ramses' eldest son nonstop, watched him with gratitude.

"The spell is broken, Your Majesty. Kha will get better now."

Nefertari removed her hands from the young man's neck, then swooned in an exhausted heap.

After Dr. Pariamaku prescribed his harmless tonics, Setau administered a real remedy to the queen, one that would restore her flagging energy.

"The Great Royal Wife has gone beyond the limits of fatigue," he informed Ramses.

"I want the whole truth, Setau."

"In sharing her magic with Kha, Nefertari has taken years off her own life."

Ramses remained at the queen's bedside, trying to give her the strength that emanated from him, the strength that was the foundation of his reign. He was ready to sacrifice everything if only Nefertari could live to a ripe old age, letting her beauty shine over the Twin Kingdoms.

It took all Ahmeni's persuasion to redirect Ramses toward affairs of state. The king agreed to confer with his friend and secretary only after Nefertari's soothing voice assured him that she was feeling the darkness retreat from her.

"Serramanna gave me a long report," declared Ahmeni. "The sorcerer Ofir has been arrested and will stand trial for espionage, the illicit practice of black magic, attempts on the life of royalty, and murdering the unfortunate Lita and the servant girl. But he's not the only guilty party: Moses is just as dangerous as Ofir. The sorcerer implicated Moses in the plot to kill every firstborn child in Egypt. If Serramanna hadn't been so vigilant, how many victims would we be mourning?"

From oldest to youngest, richest to poorest, most blasé to most naive, every single Hebrew was amazed. No one expected to see Pharaoh appear in person, at the head of a detachment of soldiers commanded by Serramanna. The streets were deserted; curious eyes peeped at the monarch from behind half-closed shutters. Ramses went directly to Moses' dwelling.

The prophet, alerted by a follower, stood on his doorstep, staff in hand.

"I thought we were never supposed to meet again, Your Majesty."

"This will be our last conversation, Moses, you can be sure. Why attempt such slaughter?"

"Obedience to Yahweh is all that occupies me."

"Then your god is far too cruel. I respect your faith, my

friend, but I refuse to let it become a source of discord in the land of which my ancestors have left me in stewardship. Get out of Egypt, Moses. Take your people with you. Go live your truth somewhere else. It won't be an exodus at your demand, but an order from me to leave."

Dressed in a long red and black woolen cloak, Emperor Hattusili contemplated his capital from the hilltop citadel. His wife, Puduhepa, took him tenderly by the arm.

"Our country is harsh, but beautiful in its own way. Why sacrifice it because of a grudge?"

"Uri-Teshoop must be punished," the emperor said firmly.

"He already is, don't you think? Imagine a warrior like him under house arrest, at the mercy of his worst enemy! It must be a mortal blow to Uri-Teshoop's pride."

"I have no right to concede on the issue."

"Assyria won't care about the deadlock. Their army is growing restive; they'll soon attack if they learn that peace negotiations with Egypt have failed."

"The negotiations are secret."

"Do you really believe that? With messengers constantly traveling back and forth between Hatti and Egypt, they must know something is going on. Unless we sign a nonaggression pact in the very near future, the Assyrians will consider us easy prey, since Ramses won't make a move to stop them."

"We Hittites know how to defend ourselves."

"Since you've come to power, Hattusili, your people have changed a great deal. Even the soldiers are eager for peace. I know it's what you want, too."

"Nefertari has influenced you."

"My sister the Queen of Egypt shares my convictions. She's managed to persuade Ramses to suspend hostilities against our nation. Now shall we dash her hopes?"

"Uri-Teshoop . . ."

"Uri-Teshoop belongs to the past. Let him marry an Egyptian princess, assimilate with Pharaoh's people, and disappear from our future!"

"You're asking a lot of me."

"Isn't that my duty as your consort?"

"Ramses will take my backing down as a sign of weakness."

"Nefertari and I will interpret it differently for him."

"Are women directing the foreign policy of Hatti and Egypt?"

"Why not," replied Puduhepa, "if the outcome is peace?"

During his trial, the sorcerer Ofir had much to say. He boasted about his role as a Hittite spy and his crippling of Kha. When he described how he had murdered poor Lita and the servant girl Nani, the jurors were convinced that Ofir felt no remorse and would kill again in cold blood if he felt the need.

Dolora sobbed. Implicated by Ofir, she denied nothing, imploring Ramses' mercy and accusing their brother, Shaanar, of leading her astray.

After brief deliberations, the vizier delivered the verdict. Ofir was sentenced to death by self-administered poison. Dolora, whose name would be expunged from all official documents, would spend the rest of her life doing heavy labor in southern Syria. Shaanar received a death sentence in absentia; his name would also disappear from the public record.

Setau and Lotus left for Abu Simbel the same day Ahsha returned to Egypt. They barely had time to congratulate one another before going their separate ways.

Ahsha was immediately ushered in to see the royal couple. Despite her weakness, Nefertari had kept up her correspondence with Puduhepa. Fighter, the Nubian lion, and his partner Watcher (now old and grizzled), stayed close to the queen, as if aware that their presence lifted her spirits. Whenever his responsibilities allowed, Ramses spent time with his spouse. They strolled in the palace gardens; he read ancient texts to her; both grew increasingly conscious of the endless love that united them, the secret love no word could describe, ardent as a summer sky and sweet as the Nile sunset.

It was Nefertari who urged Ramses to return to his duties, to keep the ship of state heading in the right direction, responding to the innumerable demands of his administration. Thanks to Iset the Fair, Meritamon, and Kha (who was well on the road to recovery), the queen's convalescence was full of youth and joy. She enjoyed visits from Merenptah as well as Tuya, adept at hiding her own fatigue.

Now Ahsha bowed low to Nefertari.

"I've missed your wisdom and beauty, Your Majesty."

"Do you bring good news?"

"Yes, excellent news."

"Does Hattusili want to sign a treaty?" Ramses asked warily.

"Thanks to the Queen of Egypt and Empress Puduhepa, the extradition issue has been set aside. Uri-Teshoop is to remain in Egypt and marry into our society. Thus nothing stands in the way of an agreement."

A broad smile lit Nefertari's face.

"This could be the greatest of all victories."

"Our main support came from Empress Puduhepa. The tone of your letters touched her heart. Since Hattusili assumed the throne, the Hittites have been uneasy about the Assyrian army. They understand that their enemy of yesterday is now their best hope for tomorrow."

"Let's act quickly," advised Nefertari, "to capitalize on this rare opportunity."

"I've brought back the version of the nonaggression pact proposed by Hattusili. We'll go over it word for word. As soon as you and Pharaoh give your consent, I'll return to Hatti."

The three of them set to work. Not without surprise, Ramses saw that Hattusili had agreed to most of his conditions.

Ahsha had done an amazing job, faithfully interpreting the king's views. Tuya was also asked to give the document a close reading, and in the end she too approved.

"What's going on here?" the Viceroy of Nubia asked the driver who was expertly steering his two-horse chariot through the noisy and crowded streets of Pi-Ramses toward the palace.

"The Hebrew exodus," replied the driver. "Moses is leading them out of Egypt to their Promised Land."

"Why would Pharaoh allow such a thing?"

"Ramses expelled them for disturbing the peace."

In stunned silence, the Viceroy of Nubia, on an official visit to the capital, watched thousands of men, women, and children leaving the city, driving their livestock and pulling carts full of clothing and provisions. Some were singing, others looked sad. None looked overjoyed to be leaving the land where they'd lived so pleasantly, but they dared not contradict Moses.

Greeted by Ahmeni, the Viceroy of Nubia was shown into Ramses' office.

"What is the reason for this visit?" inquired the monarch.

"I wanted to inform you at once, Your Majesty. I took the fastest boat I could find to bring you my personal report on the tragic events that have recently swept through the province entrusted to me. It's all been so unexpected, so brutal. I could never imagine . . ."

"Get to the point," interrupted Ramses.

The Viceroy of Nubia gulped.

"A revolt, Your Majesty. A tribal coalition up in arms."

FIFTY-FIVE

Success at last.

Month after month, Shaanar had held round after round of talks, determined to win the tribal chiefs over one by one. When they all joined forces, they could take over Nubia's main gold mine. Even with all the silver he offered them, the black warriors were reluctant to defy Ramses the Great. Wouldn't it be madness to take on the Egyptian army, which had dealt them such a resounding defeat during Seti's reign?

Despite the frustration, Shaanar plodded on. His last chance to get Ramses was to draw him into this ambush. To do that, he needed seasoned fighters, hungry for riches and unafraid of the Pharaoh's soldiers.

Shaanar's perseverance finally paid off. A first chieftain signed on, then a second, a third, then several more. More talks ensued to choose who would head the rebel troops.

The discussion had degenerated into a fight in the course of which two chieftains and the Cretan mercenary were killed. At length Shaanar was selected as the leader. While not a Nubian, he was the most familiar with Ramses and his army.

The guards at the gold mine put up little resistance to the horde of warriors armed with spears and bows. Within a few hours, the rebels had taken control of the site; a few days later, they repelled the expeditionary force sent from the fortress of Buhen.

With a full-scale revolt on his hands, the Viceroy of Nubia would have no choice but to report to Ramses.

Shaanar knew that his brother would come in person to put down the rebellion. That would be his fatal mistake.

Parched hills, granite outcroppings, a narrow band of greenery resisting the desert's advance. A sheer blue sky dotted with pelicans, flamingos, crested cranes, jabirus. Palm trees with double trunks.

This was Nubia at its purest, a place that Ramses found endlessly enchanting despite the grave concerns that had sent him hurrying south with his army.

According to the viceroy's report, the rebel tribes had seized the province's main gold mine. Any halt in production of the precious metal had catastrophic consequences. First of all, goldsmiths were hard at work on Ramses' new temples, and furthermore he needed gold for presents to his vassals, the best method for maintaining excellent diplomatic relations.

While he hated leaving Nefertari, Ramses knew he must strike quickly and hard, propelled by the certainty that only Shaanar could be the instigator of this revolt, a certainty that Nefertari's psychic powers had confirmed.

His older brother had not disappeared into the desert reaches, as they had once believed. He had found a new way to make trouble. With mining operations under Shaanar's control, he could raise a horde of mercenaries, attack the

Egyptian fortresses, and attempt against all reason to take over the land of the pharaohs.

Between Shaanar and Ramses, all family ties had been severed. Not even Tuya protested when the Pharaoh confided his intentions. This fratricidal confrontation would be their last.

Several of the royal sons were at Ramses' side, eager to prove their valor. Wearing wigs with long panels, tucked shirts with billowing sleeves, and vented kilts, they proudly waved the insignia of the jackal god, "the trailblazer."

When a gigantic elephant blocked their progress, even the hardiest of them were ready to bolt. But Ramses advanced toward the hulking beast, let the elephant lift him with his trunk and deposit him between the two huge ears that flapped in delight. If anyone doubted that the Pharaoh enjoyed divine protection, those doubts now vanished.

Fighter, his magnificent mane bristling, marched toward the mine at the elephant's side. Archers and foot soldiers conjectured that Pharaoh was planning to rush the enemy ranks. Yet Ramses made camp a good distance from the mine site. The cooks set to work immediately, the men cleaned their weapons and sharpened blades, the donkeys and oxen were fed.

One royal son, a youth of twenty, ventured a protest.

"Why wait, Your Majesty? A few Nubian rebels are no match for our forces!"

"You don't know this country and its people. The Nubians are sharpshooters and ferocious fighters. If we're overconfident, it could cost us many lives."

"Aren't lives always lost in a war?"

"My aim is to lose as few men as possible."

"But the Nubians will never surrender."

"Not in a confrontation, no."

"Don't tell me we're going to negotiate with these savages, Your Majesty!"

"We have to stop them cold. What will work is might, not a mere show of arms. The Nubians customarily lay traps, attack from the rear, and take the enemy by surprise. We won't give them the chance. They'll be too stunned."

Yes, Shaanar knew Ramses all too well. The king would march straight ahead, taking the only track that led to the mine. On either side of the site were boulders that would shelter Nubian sharpshooters. They'd pick off the squadron leaders, sending the king's troops into disarray. Shaanar would finish off Ramses with his own hands as the king begged for mercy.

No Egyptian soldier would come out of it alive.

Then Shaanar would lash Ramses' corpse to the prow of his boat and make a triumphant entry into Elephantine, before taking Thebes, Memphis, Pi-Ramses, and all of Egypt. The people would rally to his cause, and Shaanar would at last ascend to the throne, taking revenge on everyone who had underestimated him.

The king's brother emerged from the stone hut once occupied by the foreman of the ore refinery and climbed to the top of the sorting area. Water trickled down the sluice, freeing the precious metal from the gravel until the heavier metal sank in the collecting pool. This purification process required both patience and concentration. Shaanar considered his own life, the long years spent trying to break through Ramses' magic. He could finally taste victory and revenge. It made him feel almost drunk.

A lookout waved frantically, cries broke the silence. With plumes stuck in their woolly hair, the Nubian warriors were running in every direction.

"What's going on? Get a grip on yourselves!"

Shaanar came down from his ledge and nabbed an agitated chieftain.

"Calm down. You're under orders! I'm in charge here."

The warrior chief pointed his spear toward the surrounding hills and boulder.

"Everywhere . . . they're everywhere!"

Shaanar advanced to the center of the esplanade, looked up, and saw them. Thousands of Egyptian soldiers encircled the mine.

On top of the highest hill, a handful of men set up a dais, upon which they placed a throne. In his blue crown, Ramses mounted it. His lion sat at his feet.

The Nubians' eyes were glued to the monarch. At forty-two, in the twentieth year of his reign, he was reaching the height of his powers. Brave as they were, the Nubian warriors understood that any attack on Ramses would be suicidal. Shaanar was caught in his own trap. Pharaoh's soldiers had killed off the sentinels, leaving the rebels no chance to escape.

"On to victory!" roared Shaanar. "Everyone follow me!"

The Nubian chieftains revived. Yes, they must fight.

One of them, leading twenty men shouting war cries and brandishing spears, scaled the hill where the Pharaoh sat.

A volley of arrows pinned them to the ground. One young warrior fought on, making a nimble zigzag to the foot of the throne. Fighter stretched out and sank his claws into the Nubian's head.

Scepter in hand, Ramses sat like a statue. Fighter scratched the sand, shook out his mane, and settled back at his master's feet.

Almost all the Nubians lay down their arms and fell to the ground in submission. Furious, Shaanar ran to kick the chieftains.

"Get up and fight! Ramses isn't invincible!"

When no one obeyed him, Shaanar rammed his sword through the back of an old tribal leader whose limbs jerked wildly, but not for long. His death rattle unnerved his peers. They rose to stare balefully at Ramses' brother.

"You betrayed us," one of the chieftains declared. "You betrayed us and lied to us. No one can win against Ramses. You've only made it worse for us."

"Fight, you cowards!"

"You lied," came the chorus.

"Follow me and we'll kill Ramses!"

Wild-eyed, stabbing the air, Shaanar climbed back to the ledge overlooking the reservoir and the sluice.

"I'm Lord of Egypt, Lord of Egypt and Nubia . . ."

Ten arrows from the chieftains' bows pierced his head, neck, and chest. Shaanar fell backward down the slope, his body slowly tumbling toward the pool at the bottom, sinking like gravel beneath the water that trickled down from the sluice.

FIFTY-SIX

The Hebrews' departure had gone without incident. Many Egyptians mourned the loss of friends and acquaintances to this wild adventure. For their part, a number of the Hebrews dreaded the danger-filled trek through the desert. How many enemies would they have to confront, how many peoples and tribes along the way would resist letting Yahweh's worshipers pass?

Serramanna fumed.

Before leaving for Nubia, Ramses had entrusted Ahmeni and the Sard with maintaining order in the capital. At the least sign of trouble from the Hebrews, security forces were to clamp down. Since the exodus was proceeding calmly, Serramanna had had no grounds for questioning Moses and Aaron.

The Sard was still convinced that the Pharaoh had made a mistake in sparing the Hebrew leader. There was no justification for such lenience, no matter how enduring their friendship. Even in exile, Moses was liable to cause a great deal of trouble.

To be on the safe side, Serramanna had asked a dozen mercenaries to follow the Hebrews and send back regular reports on their progress. Much to his surprise, the prophet did not take the Sileh road, studded with watering spots and policed by the Egyptian army. Instead he chose a difficult route that lead to the Sea of Reeds. In this way, Moses removed the temptation of turning back.

"Serramanna!" exclaimed Ahmeni. "I've been looking all over for you. Are you going to stay there forever studying routes to the north?"

"I hate seeing Moses get off scot-free," he muttered. "It isn't fair."

"Before he died, Ofir gave us one last interesting bit of information, as if he wanted to self-destruct like a scorpion. It seems that two Bedouin tribal chiefs, Amos and Keni, are part of the exodus. They've apparently furnished the Hebrews with arms to use in case of trouble on the march."

Serramanna slammed his right fist into his left palm.

"Illegal arms dealing . . . That means I can arrest them, along with Moses, for receiving the weapons."

"It's an airtight case."

"I'll leave at once with fifty chariots and bring the bunch of them back for a nice rest in prison."

Ramses held Nefertari tight. The "sweet of love," wearing almost no makeup, scented like a goddess, was lovelier than ever.

"Shaanar is dead," the king reassured her. "And the Nubian revolt is over."

"Will Nubia finally remain at peace?"

"The rebel chieftains were executed for high treason. The villages they were tyrannizing organized celebrations to mark their death. The stolen gold has been returned to me; I deposited part of it at Abu Simbel and the rest at Karnak."

"How is the work progressing at Abu Simbel?"

"Setau is keeping up a remarkable pace."

The queen decided not to keep the latest news to herself any longer.

"Serramanna has taken a chariot battalion to arrest Moses."

"What is he wanted for?"

"It seems that two Bedouin chiefs, both Hittite agents, are traveling with the Hebrews. Serramanna wants to bring them in, along with Moses. Ahmeni didn't try to stop him, since the law is on Serramanna's side."

Ramses imagined Moses at the head of his people, pounding the ground with his staff, leading the way, moving the stragglers along, and imploring Yahweh to appear by night as a column of fire, by day as a column of clouds. No obstacle could make him turn back, no enemy could frighten him off.

"I've just had a long letter from Puduhepa," added Nefertari. "She's sure that the treaty will be signed eventually."

"That's good news," Ramses said halfheartedly.

"You're afraid for Moses, aren't you?"

"I hope I never see him again."

"About the peace treaty, there's still one delicate issue."

"Uri-Teshoop again?"

"No, a problem with the wording. Hattusili doesn't want to assume sole responsibility for the prevailing climate of war. He complains that it makes him look like an inferior, obliged to submit to Pharaoh's will."

"Isn't that the truth?"

"The text of the treaty will be made public. Future generations will read it. Hattusili refuses to lose face."

"The Hittite must either submit or face annihilation."

"Are we going to let the peace agreement fall apart over a few strong words?"

"Each word has its weight."

"Still, I'd like to propose a new version, if I may."

"Taking Hattusili's demands into account, I suppose?"

"Taking the future of both our peoples into account—a future free of war and misfortune."

Ramses kissed Nefertari on the forehead. "I suppose there's no resisting the Great Royal Wife's peacemaking tactics."

"Quite right, Your Majesty," she replied, laying her head on Ramses' shoulder.

Moses was in a violent temper. Aaron had to use his stick on several slackers who insisted they wanted to return to Egypt, where they'd have enough to eat and a comfortable place to sleep. Most of the Hebrews hated the desert; it was hard for them to adapt to camping out. Many of them were beginning to grumble about the harsh existence their prophet had forced on them.

The prophet's voice boomed, urging the weak and cowardly to obey Yahweh and continue on their way to the Promised Land, no matter what trials and pitfalls awaited them. The long march resumed, beyond Sileh, through swamp country. The Hebrews got stuck in the mud, chariots overturned, leeches attacked both humans and animals.

Moses decided to stop for a time not far from the border, near Lake Sarbonis and the Mediterranean. The place was considered dangerous, for the desert wind deposited vast quantities of sand on unstable surfaces, creating what was known as the Sea of Reeds.

No one lived in this desolate countryside, prey to squalls and the whims of sea and sky. Even fishermen avoided it, frightened off by quicksand.

A wild-eyed woman threw herself at Moses' feet.

"We're all going to die in this godforsaken place!"

"You're wrong."

"Look around you. Is this any Promised Land?"

"Of course not."

"We won't go a step farther, Moses."

"Yes you will. In the next few days we'll cross the border and go where Yahweh is calling us."

"How can you be so sure of yourself?"

"Because I've seen His presence, woman, and He spoke to me. Go get some sleep now. We have a great deal more to accomplish."

Subdued, the woman obeyed him.

"This place is horrible," agreed Aaron. "I wish we could leave right away."

"A long rest is necessary. Tomorrow, at dawn, Yahweh will give us the strength to continue."

"Do you ever doubt we'll succeed, Moses?"

"Never, Aaron."

Serramanna's chariot battalion, commanded by one of Ramses' royal sons, had lost no time catching up with the Hebrews. When he smelled the sea air, the old pirate's nostrils flared. He signaled his men to stop.

"Anyone know about this place?"

A veteran charioteer spoke up. "These swamps are haunted. I don't advise you to disturb the demons."

"Still, this is the way the Hebrews headed," objected the Sard.

"They're free to act insane. We ought to have the sense to turn around."

In the distance smoke rose.

"The Hebrew camp isn't far from here," the royal son remarked. "Let's go arrest the men we want."

"Yahweh's followers are armed," Serramanna reminded him, "and they outnumber us."

"Our men are trained soldiers and our chariots give us the advantage. At a good distance, we'll fire a volley of arrows and demand that they hand over Moses and the two Bedouins. Otherwise we'll charge."

Not without foreboding, the chariots slogged on.

Aaron woke with a start. Moses was already awake, staff in hand.

"That rumbling . . ."

"Yes, it's Egyptian chariots."

"They're heading our way!"

"We still have time to escape."

The two Bedouins, Amos and Keni, refused to set foot in the Sea of Reeds, but the frantic Hebrews readily followed Moses. In the gathering darkness, it was hard to tell sand from water, but Moses made his way unfalteringly between sea and lake, guided by the fire that had burned in him since adolescence, the fire that had become his quest for the Promised Land.

The Egyptian chariots found the going much more difficult. Some sank in quicksand, others lost their way in the swamps. The royal son's chariot got stuck in a sinkhole, while Serramanna's ran smack into the two Bedouins in flight.

A wind blew in from the east, on top of the desert wind, drying a path across the Sea of Reeds for the Hebrews.

Hardly caring that the two Hittite agents had been crushed beneath his wheels, Serramanna cursed to find that his chariot would no longer budge. By the time they freed the vehicles and found the scattered troops, including a few injured men, the wind had changed. Moisture-laden gusts stirred up waves that closed the path through the reeds.

Seething with frustration, Serramanna watched Moses escape.

FIFTY-SEVEN

Despite the excellent care she received from Neferet, an exceptionally gifted young woman doctor, Queen Mother Tuya was preparing for the great journey. Soon she would be joining Seti, leaving Egypt's future happiness a virtual certainty. Only virtual because the peace treaty with the Hittites had not yet been finalized.

When Nefertari came to find her in the garden where she was meditating, Tuya could read the emotion in the Great Royal Wife's face.

"Your Majesty, I've just received this letter from Empress Puduhepa."

"My eyes are bad, Nefertari. Please read it to me."

The queen's spellbinding voice gladdened Tuya's heart.

> *To my sister, spouse of the Son of Light, Nefertari,*
> *All is well with our two countries. I hope this letter finds you and your family in the best of health. My daughter is becoming a fine big girl and my horses are magnificent. May it be the same for you and your family, your horses, and Ramses the Great's pet lion. Your servant Hattusili bows at the feet of Pharaoh.*
> *Peace and brotherhood: these are the terms in order, since the Sun God of Egypt and the Storm God of Hatti wish to fraternize.*
> *Bearing the text of the treaty, the ambassadors of Egypt and Hatti are on their way to Pi-Ramses so that Pharaoh may set the final seal upon our joint decision.*
> *May my sister Nefertari enjoy the protection of all the gods and goddesses.*

Falling into each other's arms, Nefertari and Tuya wept with joy.

Serramanna felt like an insect about to be crushed under Ramses' sandal. The downcast Sard was sure he would be banished from the palace. The thought of rejection hurt.

The old pirate had grown used to his role as a peacekeeper and righter of wrongs. His absolute devotion to Ramses had given his life meaning and put an end to his wandering. The country he had come to plunder was now his homeland. The old sailor had come ashore. He wanted to stay.

Serramanna was grateful to Ramses for not calling him to task in front of the court and his subordinates. The monarch would see him in his office, man to man.

"Your Majesty, I made a gross miscalculation. No one knew the area, it was . . ."

"The two Bedouin spies?"

"I ran over them with my chariot."

"Are you certain that Moses made it through the swamp?"

"He and his followers crossed the Sea of Reeds."

"Let's forget about them, since they've crossed the border."

"But Moses betrayed you!"

"He's following his god, Serramanna. Since he'll no longer trouble the harmony of the Two Lands, we may as well let him go. I have an important mission for you to handle."

The Sard could hardly believe his ears. Would the king overlook his fiasco?

"You're to head for the border with two chariot detachments to meet the Hittite delegation and escort them to the capital."

"I'd be, well, I'd be . . ."

"You'll have the peace of the world in your hands, Serramanna."

Hattusili had given in.

Trusting his instincts as a statesman, the advice of his wife, Puduhepa, and the recommendations of the Egyptian ambassador Ahsha, he had reworded the nonaggression pact, without opposing the conditions set by Ramses. Two messengers were appointed to deliver the silver tablets covered with cuneiform writing to the Pharaoh.

Hattusili promised Ramses to exhibit the treaty in the temple of the sun goddess in Hattusa, providing that his Egyptian counterpart promised to do the same in one of his great sanctuaries. But would Ramses ratify the treaty without adding further clauses?

From the Hittite capital to the Egyptian border, the atmosphere was tense. Ahsha knew he had pushed Hattusili to the limit. If Ramses rejected any part of the agreement, the treaty would remain invalid. As for the Hittite soldiers, they were clearly nervous. Groups of dissidents were liable to attack them to keep the peace delegation from reaching its destination. Traps seemed to lurk in every mountain pass, every forest. Yet the journey proved uneventful.

When he spied Serramanna and the Egyptian chariots, Ahsha breathed a long sigh of relief. It would be clear sailing from now on.

The Sard and the lead Hittite chariot officer saluted each other coolly. The onetime pirate would gladly have exterminated the barbarians, but he bowed to his duty to Ramses and concentrated on the mission at hand.

For the first time, Hittite chariots entered the Delta and traveled down the road to Pi-Ramses.

"What happened with the revolt in Nubia?"

"You heard about that in Hattusa?" the Sard asked edgily.

"Don't worry, the information remained confidential."

"Ramses took matters in hand. Shaanar's confederates turned on him and killed him."

"We may achieve peace in the north as well as the south, then! If Ramses accepts the treaty that the Hittite delegation is delivering, it will bring an era of prosperity that future generations will envy."

"Why would he refuse?"

"Because of a detail that's more than a detail. But let's be optimistic, Serramanna."

On the twenty-first day of the winter season in the twenty-first year of Ramses' reign, Ahmeni escorted Ahsha and the two awestruck Hittite diplomats into the audience chamber in the palace at Pi-Ramses. The grimness of their warlike nation was in stark contrast to this colorful universe, a combination of splendor and refinement.

The messengers presented the Pharaoh with the silver tablets. Ahsha read the preliminary declaration.

> *May a thousand divinities, among the gods and goddesses of Hatti and Egypt, witness this treaty drawn up by that the Emperor of Hatti and the Pharaoh of Egypt. As witnesses we call the sun, the moon, the gods and goddesses of heaven and earth, the mountains and rivers, the sea, the winds, and the clouds.*
>
> *These thousands of divinities would destroy the house, country, and subjects of any party not observing the treaty. As for those who do observe it, these thousands of divinities will act to make them prosper and live happily with their households, children, and subjects.*

In the presence of the Great Royal Wife Nefertari and Queen Mother Tuya, Ramses approved the declaration, which Ahmeni transcribed on papyrus.

"Does Emperor Hattusili acknowledge the Hittites' responsibility for the acts of war committed over the past few years?"

"Yes, Your Majesty," replied one of the envoys.

"Does he allow that this treaty involves our successors?"

"It is his wish that this agreement engender peace and brotherhood. It therefore applies to our children and our children's children."

"What borders will we respect?"

"The Orontes; a line of fortifications in southern Syria; the route separating Egyptian Byblos from the province of Amurru, considered a Hittite protectorate; the route passing south of Hittite Kadesh, marking the northern end of the Bekka desert, which will be in the Egyptian sphere of influence. The Phoenician ports will remain under Pharaoh's control; Egyptian diplomats and merchants will have free access to the route leading to Hatti."

Ahsha held his breath. Would Ramses permanently relinquish the fortress of Kadesh, and especially the province of Amurru? Neither Seti nor his son had been able to take the famous fortress, the site of Ramses' greatest victory, and it seemed logical that Kadesh would remain in the Hittite fold.

But Amurru . . . Egypt had fought hard to keep the province. Lives had been lost in the process. Ahsha was afraid that Pharaoh would never concede it.

The monarch glanced at Nefertari, reading the answer in her eyes.

"We accept," declared Ramses the Great.

Ahmeni continued to write. Ahsha felt an immense joy surge through him.

"What more does my brother Hattusili desire?" inquired Ramses.

"A definitive nonaggression pact, Your Majesty, and a defensive alliance against any parties that might attack Egypt or Hatti."

"We, too, desire this pact and this alliance, which will ensure prosperity and happiness."

Ahmeni unfalteringly continued his notation.

"Your Majesty, Emperor Hattusili also wishes to see the royal succession in our two countries respected and safeguarded according to rites and traditions."

"We would not expect otherwise."

"Our sovereign hopes to resolve the problem of mutual extradition of fugitives."

Ahsha was afraid to hear what came next. A single disputed clause could invalidate the entire treaty.

"I demand humane treatment for extradited persons," declared Ramses. "When returned to their own country, be it Egypt or Hatti, they should suffer no punishment nor insult, and their homes should be returned to them intact. Furthermore, Uri-Teshoop, having become Egyptian, will be free to determine his own fate."

The two envoys, empowered by Hattusili to accept these conditions, readily agreed.

The treaty could take effect.

Ahmeni entrusted the final version to royal scribes, who would inscribe it on the finest papyrus.

"This text will be written in stone at several of our major temples," announced Ramses, "particularly the shrine to Ra in Heliopolis, the south side of the east wing of the ninth pylon at Karnak, and the southern facade of my great new temple of Abu Simbel. From north to south, from the Delta to Nubia, Egyptians will know they are to live forever at peace with the Hittites, as the gods are their witness."

FIFTY-EIGHT

The Hittite ambassadors, given accommodation at a palace reserved for foreign guests, were swept up in the capital's mood of celebration. They noted Ramses' overwhelming popularity. Everyone seemed to be singing his praises: "He dazzles us like the sun, refreshes us like water and wind. We love him like bread and fine linen, for he is father and mother to the entire country, the light of both banks of the Nile," went the refrain.

Nefertari invited the Hittites to attend a service in the temple of Hathor. They listened to her invocation of the unique power that spontaneously created itself each day, giving rise to all forms of life, illuminating human faces, making the trees and flowers quake with joy. When all eyes turned to the Principle concealed in the gold of the sky, the birds soared heavenward and humankind was headed toward peace.

Moving from amazement to delight, the Hittites were

invited to a banquet featuring pigeon pie, marinated kid-
neys, roast beef, Nile perch, grilled goose, lentils, mild garlic
and onions, zucchini, lettuce, cucumbers, peas, beans,
stewed figs, apples, dates, watermelon, goat cheese, yogurt,
round honey cakes, fresh bread, sweet beer, red and white
wine. On this special occasion, the palace broke out jars
sealed on the sixth day of Year Four of Seti's reign, marked
with the sign of Anubis, the master of the desert. The
abundance and quality of the food was astounding, the
stone dishware remarkable. In the end, they surrendered to
the moment, singing in Egyptian, verse after verse in praise
of Ramses.

Yes, this was peace.

The capital had finally gone to sleep.

Despite the late hour, Nefertari was writing a letter to
her sister Puduhepa in her own hand, thanking her for all
her efforts and telling her of the wonderful outcome for
Hatti and Egypt. When the queen put her seal to it, Ramses
gently placed his hands on her shoulders.

"Isn't it late to be working?"

"There aren't enough hours in the day, which is as it
should be. Isn't that what you tell your cabinet? The Great
Royal Wife must not shirk the law."

Nefertari's fragrance enchanted Ramses. The temple's
master scentmaker had used no fewer than sixteen ingredients, including fragrant reeds, juniper, broomflower, pine
resin, myrrh, and aromatic herbs. Green eyeliner rimmed
her elegant lids, a wig anointed with oils from Libya set off
the sublime loveliness of her face.

Ramses lifted the wig and uncoiled Nefertari's long, wavy hair.

"I'm happy," she said dreamily. "We've done well by our people, haven't we?"

"Your name will always be associated with this treaty. You're the one who paved the way for peace."

"Our personal glory is nothing in the proper sequence of days and rituals."

The king slipped the strap of Nefertari's gown off her shoulder, kissing her on the neck.

"How can I say how much I love you?"

She turned and pressed her lips to his. "Enough speeches for one night," she said.

The first official letter originating from Hatti following the peace treaty's acceptance piqued curiosity at the palace in Pi-Ramses. Did Hattusili want to revisit some essential point?

The king broke the seal affixed to the cloth wrappings, uncovered the rare wood tablet, and skimmed the cuneiform text of the message.

He immediately went to find the queen. Nefertari had just finished reading through the liturgy to mark the return of spring.

"A strange message, in truth!"

"A serious incident?" frowned the queen.

"No, a sort of cry for help. Some Hittite princess, with an unpronounceable name, has taken ill. According to Hattusili, she appears possessed by a demon that Hatti's best doctors have failed to exorcise. Since Egyptian medicine is world famous, our new ally is begging me to send him a healer from the House of Life to help the princess recover her health and bear the child she desperately wants."

"This is excellent news. It can only strengthen the ties between our two countries."

The king sent for Ahsha and outlined the contents of Hattusili's communiqué.

The head of Egyptian diplomacy burst out laughing.

"Does this request seem so outlandish?" the queen asked, nonplussed.

"The Hittite emperor has limitless faith in our medicine! He's asking for nothing short of a miracle."

"Do you think our doctors are so incompetent?"

"Of course not, but how can a woman over sixty have a baby, even if she is a Hittite princess?"

They had a good laugh. Then Ramses dictated a reply to his brother Hattusili as Ahmeni took it down.

> *As for the princess who has been incapacitated—mainly by her age—we know her identity. There are no medicines that will lead to her pregnancy. But if the Storm God and the Sun God so decide . . . I will therefore send you an excellent magician and a competent doctor.*

Ramses immediately dispatched a magical statue of the healing god Khonsu, the space traveler, whose symbol was the crescent moon. Who else but a divinity could amend the laws of nature?

When word from Nebu, the high priest of Karnak, arrived in Pi-Ramses, the king decided to move the court to

Thebes. With his usual efficiency, Ahmeni handled the arrangements.

The royal flagship housed everyone that Ramses held dear: his wife, Nefertari, in all her glory; his mother, Tuya, content that she had lived to see peace between Egypt and Hatti at last; Iset the Fair, thrilled to take part in the great occasion at hand; his children, Kha, the high priest of Memphis, the musical Meritamon, sturdy young Merenptah; his faithful friends Ahmeni and Ahsha, with whose help he had achieved so much for Egypt; and Nedjem and Serramanna, his loyal servants. Only Setau and Lotus were missing; on their way north from Abu Simbel, they would be meeting the royal party at Thebes. No one but those two . . . and Moses, who had forsaken Egypt.

At the landing, the high priest of Karnak came out to greet the royal couple in person. Now Nebu really did look old. Hunched, shuffling, clutching his cane, weak-voiced, he suffered from crippling arthritis. Yet his eyes remained lively and his sense of authority had not diminished.

The king and the high priest embraced in ceremonial style.

"I've kept my promise, Your Majesty. Thanks to Bakhen and his workmen, your Eternal Temple is finished. The gods have granted me the grace of seeing their dwelling place completed—and it's a masterpiece."

"I'll keep my promise, too, Nebu. We'll climb to the temple roof together and look over the shrine, its outbuildings, and the palace."

There was the enormous pylon, or monumental gateway, whose inner wall was decorated with scenes of the victory at Kadesh; the vast forecourt with pillars representing the king as Osiris; the colossal statue of the seated king; a second pylon unveiling the harvest ritual; the huge hall of columns; the sanctuary with reliefs relating the mysteries of daily worship; the tall sculpted tree symbolizing the everlasting nature of pharaonic rule. There were so many marvels to admire that the king and queen were beside themselves with joy.

Events surrounding the dedication of the Eternal Temple lasted several weeks. For Ramses, the height of the celebration would be the ritual birth of the chapel in memory of his parents. He and Nefertari recited the prayers that brought it to life, the words of which were carved forever on the chapel's columns.

As Pharaoh finished donning the vestments for the "House of Morning," Ahmeni appeared, his face ashen.

"Your mother . . . your mother is asking for you."

Ramses ran to Tuya's bedchamber.

Seti's widow was lying on her back, arms at her sides, eyes half closed. The king knelt and kissed her hands.

"Are you too tired to attend the dedication?"

"It's not just fatigue, my son. I feel my death approaching."

"Let's send it away. We can do it together."

"I no longer have the strength. And why should I fight it? The time has come for me to join Seti. It's nothing to be sad about."

"You'll be abandoning Egypt."

"You and your queen have the country on the right track. I know that the next inundation will be a good one. I know that justice will be respected. I can leave contented, my son, thanks to the peace that you and Nefertari have crafted. You'll make it last. There's nothing finer than a country at peace, where children play, cattle come back from pasture with their herdsmen piping a tune, and people respect one another, knowing that Pharaoh protects them . . . Keep Egypt happy, Ramses, and pass this harmony on to your successor."

Facing the ultimate test, Tuya was steadfast. She remained serene and regal, her unwavering gaze fixed on eternity.

"Love Egypt with all that is in you, Ramses. Let nothing interfere with you duties as Pharaoh—no human attachment, no personal tragedy, however painful it may be."

Tuya's hand gripped her son's tightly.

"Wish me well, King of Egypt. I'm off to a happier place, to dwell in the land of light and water, with Seti and all our ancestors . . ."

Tuya's voice faded in one last breath as deep as the great beyond.

FIFTY-NINE

In the Valley of the Queens, a place of beauty and perfection, Tuya's eternal dwelling was close by the one reserved for Nefertari. The Great Royal Wife and Pharaoh conducted the funeral rites for Seti's widow, whose mummy would henceforth repose in a golden chamber. Transformed into Osiris and Hathor, Tuya would survive in the body of light renewed each day by the invisible energy that came from deep in the heavens. Her tomb was filled with the ritual furnishings, canopic jars containing her vital organs, precious fabrics, wine jars, flasks of oil and unguents, food-stuffs, vestments, scepters, adornments, jewelry, golden and silver sandals, and other treasures that would equip Tuya for her journey through the West and the realms of the next world.

Ramses tried to deal evenhandedly with joy and sorrow. First there was the hard-won peace with the Hittites to cel-ebrate, along with the completion of his Eternal Temple; then there was his mother's death to mourn. The son and man in him mourned for her, yet as Pharaoh he could not allow himself to betray her spirit. The Queen Mother had been so unshakable that even death did not seem to faze her. He must abide by the message she had left him: Egypt must come before his feelings, before his own happiness or pain.

So Ramses bowed to necessity, assisted, as always, by Nefertari. He continued to steer the ship of state as if Tuya were still with them. He must learn to do without her advice and initiatives. Now Nefertari must assume the tasks that had fallen to Tuya. Despite his helpmate's valiant spirit, Ramses sensed that the burden might prove too great for her.

Every morning, after the rites of dawn, the two of them prayed together in the chapel at the Ramesseum dedicated to Tuya and Seti. The king needed to steep in the invisible reality created by the living stone and the hieroglyphs bearing witness to the Word. Communing with the souls of their ancestors, Ramses and Nefertari drew on the secret light that fed the spirit.

Once the seventy-day mourning period was over, Ahmeni approached Ramses with a number of urgent matters. Working from the Ramesseum offices with a reduced but efficient staff, Pharaoh's private secretary was in permanent contact with Pi-Ramses and used every moment wisely.

"The flood level is excellent," he told Ramses. "The Royal Treasury is healthier than ever, food storage is operating smoothly, the craftsmen's guilds are hard at work. Furthermore, prices are stable with no foreseeable threat of inflation."

"What about gold from Nubia?"

"Production continues at a satisfactory pace."

"It sounds like paradise."

"Hardly. But we're doing our best to follow in Tuya and Seti's footsteps."

"Then why don't you sound happier?"

"Well . . . Ahsha wants to talk to you, but he's not sure whether the time . . ."

"Sounds like his diplomacy is rubbing off on you. Have him meet me in the library."

The Ramesseum's library rivaled the famous one at the House of Life in Heliopolis. Day after day, scrolls and tablets arrived and were catalogued according to Ramses' explicit directions. A personal knowledge of the primary sources was essential if he were to govern Egypt correctly.

Ahsha was elegant in a well-cut linen robe trimmed with colored fringe. He went into raptures over the library.

"Working here would be a gift from the gods, Your Majesty."

"The Ramesseum will be one of the kingdom's vital centers. Are you here to consult some learned work?"

"I wanted to see you, quite simply."

"I'm fine, Ahsha. I grieve for Tuya; I still miss my father. Yet they left me a shining example. Now tell me, are the Hittites causing us problems?"

"Not at all, Your Majesty. In fact, Hattusili is delighted because the news of our treaty has made Assyria draw in its horns. The Assyrian generals seem to understand that any attack would bring an immediate and massive response. Trade with Hatti is on the increase, and I'm certain the peace will hold for years to come. A king's word is solid as granite, after all."

"What seems to be bothering you?"

"Well, it's Moses. Do you mind discussing him?"

"Go ahead."

"My operatives haven't lost sight of the Hebrews."

"Where are they?"

"Still wandering in the desert, though most of them are unhappy about it. Moses rules his people with an iron fist. 'Yahweh is an all-consuming fire and a jealous god,' he's fond of saying."

"Do you know where they're headed?"

"It's probable that their Promised Land is Canaan, but taking it over will be difficult. The Hebrews have already clashed with the Midianites and the Amorites. They now occupy the land of Moab. The local tribes are afraid of these new wanderers. They see them as pillagers."

"Moses won't give up. If he has to wage a hundred battles, he will. I'm sure he studied Canaan from the top of Mount Negeb and that it looked like a land of milk and honey."

"The Hebrews are stirring up trouble, Your Majesty."

"What do you suggest, Ahsha?"

"Let's eliminate Moses. Without their leader, the people will return to Egypt, provided you grant them amnesty."

"Rid yourself of that notion. Moses will follow his destiny."

"As his friend, I applaud your decision, but as a diplomat I deplore it. Like me, you're convinced that Moses will achieve his ends and his arrival in the Promised Land will upset the balance of power in the region."

"As long as Moses doesn't export his doctrine, can't we come to terms with him? Good relations between our two peoples could have a stabilizing influence."

"Are you giving me a lesson in foreign relations?"

"No, Ahsha. I'm only trying to keep some hope alive."

In Iset the Fair's heart, tenderness had taken the place of passion. As the mother of Ramses' two sons, she still felt the same admiration for the king, yet had given up trying to win him. Who could rival Nefertari, who grew more beautiful and radiant with each passing year? As she matured, Iset the Fair had grown more content with what life had to offer her. She was happy talking with Kha about the mysteries of creation, listening to Merenptah tell her about the workings of Egyptian society (which he studied with the earnestness of a future leader), chatting with Nefertari in the palace gardens, basking in Ramses' presence as often as possible . . . in truth, Iset considered, she was a fortunate woman.

"Come," the Great Royal Wife proposed, "let's take a boat ride on the river."

It was summer. The inundation had transformed Egypt into one immense lake. People rowed from village to village. The hot sun made the life-giving waters sparkle. In the sky, hundreds of birds danced.

The two women, seated on a white dais, had rubbed their skin with scented oil. Earthenware jugs held water at their disposal.

"Kha has gone back to Memphis," said Iset the Fair.

"Are you very sorry?"

"The king's eldest son is interested only in ancient monuments, symbols, rituals. When his father calls on him to help in affairs of state, how will he react?"

"He's so intelligent that he'll adapt."

"What do you think of Merenptah?"

"He's very different from his brother, but it's already clear that he'll be someone exceptional."

"Your daughter, Meritamon, is a wonderful young woman."

"She's fulfilling my childhood dream, living in a temple and playing music for the gods."

"The people of Egypt worship you, Nefertari. Their love is the measure of all you give them."

"How you've changed, Iset!"

"I let go, and my soul was freed from the demons of envy. If you knew how much I admire you for who you are, for the good you do . . ."

"With your help, Tuya's absence will be easier to bear. Since you no longer have the children to supervise, would you agree to work alongside me?"

"I don't deserve to."

"Let me be the judge of that."

"Your Majesty . . ."

Nefertari kissed Iset the Fair on the forehead. It was summer, and Egypt was a happy land.

The palace at the Ramesseum was already as lively as the one in Pi-Ramses. As the king had wished, his Eternal Temple was fast becoming a major economic force in upper Egypt, working in concert with the great estates of Karnak. On the West Bank at Thebes, the Ramesseum proclaimed forever the magnificence of Ramses. The greatness of his reign was already apparent.

Ahmeni was the one who received the message signed by Setau. Dropping everything, choked with emotion, the scribe went to look for Ramses, finding him in the pool adjoining the palace. Every day during the summer months the king swam for half an hour at least.

"Your Majesty, a letter from Nubia!"

The king quickly reached the side of the pool. Stooping, Ahmeni handed him the papyrus.

It contained only a few words, but they were the words that Ramses had been hoping for.

SIXTY

In the prow of the royal couple's boat stood a gilded bust of the goddess Hathor, holding the solar disk between her cow horns. The queen of the stars was also the patroness of navigation; her watchful presence would guarantee a peaceful journey toward Abu Simbel.

Abu Simbel, its two temples celebrating Ramses and Nefertari's eternal union, was finished. Setau's message was unambiguous, and the snake charmer was never one to boast.

Amidships was a cabin with a domed roof atop two small columns, their capitals carved with papyrus tufts in back, lotus blossoms in front. Openings allowed the air to circulate. For the queen, this long, leisurely voyage was a treat.

Nefertari was concealing her fatigue so as not to worry the king. She rose and went to him on deck, standing beneath the white awning set on four stakes. Lying on his side, Fighter dozed in the heat, back to back with the old yellow dog. Watcher knew that his friend would protect him as he napped, regaining his strength.

"Abu Simbel . . . Has ever a king given such a gift to his queen?"

"Has ever a king been blessed with Nefertari?"

"So much happiness, Ramses. Sometimes it makes me afraid."

"Our happiness is a gift we must share with our people, with all of Egypt and the generations to come. That's why I want our presence to live forever in stone at Abu Simbel. Not you and I, Nefertari, but Pharaoh and the Great Royal Wife, whose roles we fulfill on this earth for so short a time."

Nefertari snuggled against Ramses and contemplated Nubia in all its wildness and splendor.

And here were the sandstone bluffs, domain of the goddess Hathor, framing a curve of the Nile on the east. Not long before, a stretch of tawny sand separated the two cliffs that appealed for an architect or sculptor's touch—and that hand had acted, carving twin temples from the heart of the sun-kissed rock face. The facades were of a power and grace that stunned the queen. In front of the southernmost shrine sat four colossal statues of Ramses; the northern temple boasted statues of the Pharaoh standing and walking, flanking smaller statues of Nefertari.

Abu Simbel would no longer be a simple landmark for sailors, but a transfigured site where a spiritual fire would blaze, immobile and immutable, in the golden sands of Nubia.

On the riverbank, Setau and Lotus waved in welcome, with all the workmen following suit. Some shrank back as Fighter strolled down the gangway, but the king's commanding stature allayed their fears. The lion walked on his right, the old yellow dog on his left.

Ramses had never seen an expression of such contentment on Setau's face.

"You should be proud of yourself," said the king, embracing his friend.

"The designers and stoneworkers deserve your praise more than I do. I only encouraged them to build something worthy of you."

"Worthy of the mysterious powers residing within this temple, Setau."

At the end of the gangway, Nefertari faltered. Lotus, giving her a hand, realized that the queen was feeling faint.

"Keep going," Nefertari said firmly. "I'm fine, just fine."

"But Your Majesty . . ."

"Let's not spoil the dedication, Lotus."

"I have a remedy that may help."

The rugged Setau never knew quite how to act around Nefertari, whose beauty fascinated him. He bowed and stammered, "Your Majesty . . . I mean to say . . ."

"Let's celebrate the birth of Abu Simbel, Setau. I want it to be unforgettable."

Every tribal chief in Nubia had been summoned to Abu Simbel for the dedication. Wearing their finest necklaces and fresh kilts, they kissed the feet of Ramses and Nefertari, then boomed a victory chant that mounted to the starry skies.

That night, there was more delicious food than grains of sand on the riverbanks, more slices of roast meat than flowers in the royal gardens, and a wealth of bread and pastries. The wine flowed like a stream at flood stage, incense burned on the outdoor altars. Just as peace had been reached with the Hittites to the north, here in the Deep South it was also back for the foreseeable future.

"Abu Simbel is henceforth the spiritual center of Nubia and the symbolic expression of the love uniting Pharaoh and the Great Royal Wife," Ramses confided to Setau. "I want you, my friend, to call the tribal chiefs together here at regular intervals, involving them in the rites that make this place holy."

"In other words, you're letting me stay in Nubia. Good. Lotus will stay in love with me."

The mild September night was followed by a week of feasting and ritual during which the awestruck participants were introduced to the great temple's interior. In the hall of three naves and eight tall pillars backed by statues of the king as Osiris, they admired the scenes of the battle of Kadesh and the monarch's encounter with the gods, their arms around him to infuse him with their energy.

On the day of the autumnal equinox, Ramses and Nefertari alone entered the holy of holies. When the sun rose, its rays followed the axis of the temple to light the back of the sanctuary. On their stone bench sat the four gods: Ra-Horus from the land of light; Ramses' *ka;* Amon the hidden god; and Ptah the builder. The latter remained in the shadows except at the two equinoxes. On those two mornings, the dawning light grazed it, and Ramses heard Ptah's voice from deep within the rock: *I am your brother, giving you stability and staying power. We are united in a joyful heart. I make it so that your thoughts are in tune with the gods'. I have chosen you; I give life to your words, I fill you full of life so that you may make others live.*

When the royal couple emerged from the great temple, Egyptians and Nubians alike gave shouts of glee. The time had come to dedicate the second temple, built for the queen and bearing the name "Nefertari for Whom the Sun Rises."

The Great Royal Wife made an offering of flowers to the goddess Hathor, to brighten the face of the mistress of the stars. Speaking as Sechat, the patroness of the House of Life, Nefertari addressed her husband:

"You have restored vigor and courage to Egypt, you are her master. As the heavenly falcon, you have spread your wings above your people, to whom you appear as a wall of celestial metal that no hostile force can penetrate."

"For Nefertari," came the king's response, "I have built a temple, cut in the pure sandstone cliffs of Nubia, to stand forever."

The queen wore a long yellow dress, a turquoise necklace, and golden sandals. On her blue wig perched a crown of two long, thin horns enclosing a solar disk adorned with two tall plumes. In her right hand she held the key of life, in her left a flexible scepter representing the lotus rising from the waters on the world's first morning.

Topping the pillars in the queen's temple were smiling faces of the goddess Hathor, and on the walls ritual scenes uniting Ramses, Nefertari, and the divinities.

The queen leaned on her husband's arm.

"What's happening, Nefertari?"

"It will pass . . ."

"Do you want us to stop the ceremony?"

"No, I want to view each scene on the temple walls with you, read each of the inscriptions, take part in every offering . . . Isn't this the dwelling place you've built for me?"

His wife's smile reassured the king. Following her wishes, they brought life to each iota of the temple, finally entering the *naos* where Hathor was carved from the rock in her guise as the celestial bovine.

Nefertari lingered in the dimly lit sanctuary, as if the nourishing goddess could dispel the cold creeping through her veins.

"I'd like to visit the coronation scene again," she requested.

Flanking the queen, whose delicate silhouette looked almost unreal in relief, were Isis and Hathor, magnetizing her crown. The stone carver had captured the moment at which an earthly woman became one with the world of the gods, testifying to its reality.

"Take me in your arms, Ramses."

Nefertari was freezing.

"I'm dying, Ramses, dying of exhaustion, but here in my

temple, with you, so close to you that we form a single being, for all time."

The king held her tight, believing that he could help her cling to life, the life she had given so unstintingly to her loved ones and to her country, keeping them safe from evil.

Ramses saw the queen's calm, pure face grow still and her head slowly droop forward. Without struggle or fear, Nefertari had breathed her last.

Ramses carried the Great Royal Wife in his arms, like a bridegroom carrying his bride over the threshold. He knew that Nefertari would become an imperishable star, born again in the sky, her true mother. He knew she would step into the boat that travels the heavens. But how could that knowledge ease the unbearable pain that tore at his heart?

Ramses walked toward the temple entrance. Looking like a lost soul, he went out the door.

Watcher, the old yellow dog, lay freshly dead between the paws of the lion that slowly licked his head, as if to make him better.

Ramses was in too much pain to cry. All his power and might were of no help at all to him now.

The Pharaoh lifted toward the sun the sublime body of the woman he would love for eternity, the Lady of Abu Simbel, Nefertari, for whom shone the light.